Free Men

Also by Katy Simpson Smith

———————

Fiction

THE STORY OF LAND AND SEA

Nonfiction

WE HAVE RAISED ALL OF YOU:
MOTHERHOOD IN THE SOUTH, 1750–1835

Free Men

A Novel

Katy Simpson Smith

HARPER

An Imprint of HarperCollins*Publishers*

HarperCollins books may be purchased for educational, business, or sales promotional use. For information, please e-mail the Special Markets Department at SPsales@harpercollins.com.

FIRST EDITION

Designed by William Ruoto
Palmetto trees: Copyright: bestofgreenscreen / Shutterstock, Inc.
Painting of palmetto leaf: Copyright: olies / Shutterstock, Inc.

Library of Congress Cataloging-in-Publication Data has been applied for.

ISBN: 978-0-06-240759-7

16 17 18 19 20   OV/RRD   10 9 8 7 6 5 4 3 2 1

For my own brother

About this time, a bloody transaction occurred in the territory of the present county of Conecuh. . . . The party consisted of a Hillabee Indian, who had murdered so many men, that he was called Istillicha, the Man-slayer—a desperate white man, who had fled from the States for the crime of murder, and whom, on account of his activity and ferocity, the Indians called the Cat— and a blood-thirsty negro, named Bob.

ALBERT JAMES PICKETT, *History of Alabama, and Incidentally of Georgia and Mississippi, from the Earliest Period* (1851)

Contents

Free Men

March 9, 1788

Le Clerc

THE FIRST SIGN that order had slipped its axis was that the slave who came to tell us of the murders was riding a horse.

I was reclining on a mat this morning next to a chief of the Creeks, cleaning my pipe while his wife tended to his hair, and I was in the midst of reminding myself to make a note of this habit, the way she greased her fingers before the ritual untangling, when he snapped his head away from her and shouted at one of his lieutenants to get that man off the good horse. The Indians let their slaves ride mules and are generally rather lax with regard to discipline, but this steed was evidently of superior breeding, which detail briefly obscured the greater fact that the slave was alone and was clearly distraught.

I traveled down to the southern hunting grounds yesterday with my chief and his attendants and various wives, including my own, and I was expecting a reprieve from the recent flurry of negotiations and skirmishes that now color the postrevolutionary landscape of the inner American wilds. I am grateful for the role that I, an outsider and a Frenchman, have been given in such proceedings, but I have long preferred to take an observational seat. Though I can see how my intellect and experience are useful to these Creeks—or Muskogee, as they call themselves—I pursued this circuitous path to America in order to catalog the divergences of man. I left friends behind in Paris who dissect amphibians and sketch leaves, but I hope to earn my place in the burgeoning science by classifying human action, to construct not a hierarchy but rather a forecast for future generations. While history may be used to explain the present, I believe that the present may also offer prophecies.

So when he dismounted and brought us his story—that the trading party consisting of four American loyalists en route to Pensacola, who traveled south with our protection and with Creek slaves as guides, were brutally attacked and slaughtered in the dark of night by a band of ruthless highway robbers who stole their bags of silver and slit their throats, and that this band comprised a white man, a negro, and an Indian who appeared in the dark to be a member of the Creek nation—well, I saw this to be a rare encapsulation of the types of man, a scale model of American brutality and independence, and I volunteered to hunt them down.

Because I have yet to fail him, my chief Seloatka agreed, and I retired to my tent to prepare my belongings and inform my wife. She is a decent woman, and did not protest when she was matched to me in one of the early ceremonies of my attendance in this nation. I came from France via the Arctic and the northern American cities, but I have not been more pleasantly welcomed than in the towns of the Upper Creek. A marriage is seen as an act of trust and an invitation into their elaborate kinships, which remind me of the royal houses of Europe with their dueling clans and irrepressible gossip. The Indians, however, are far less savage and their hospitality unparalleled. I informed my wife that her paramount duty, besides the daily labor in the field that occupies these women, is to provide me with a steady supply of paper and ink. These commodities here are rare, but she must have a well-developed relationship with traders, for whenever I run out, there she is with a new sheaf bound and tied with twine. If my researches earn any audience among the European journals, I will credit her as my assistant.

Seloatka afforded me three Creeks and the original slave to guide me to the site of the outrage, which fortunately lies closer to these hunting grounds than our town of Hillaubee, so that my pursuit will be abbreviated. I am accustomed to such missions; when I first arrived in this riverine country in what are known as the Yazoo lands of West Georgia, I began earning my keep as a tracker and a deputy of justice. My singular obsession with the anthropology of men, my ability to predict their movements with ease, led me to the enemy, the errant wife, the fugitive slave. The tracking itself was simple; men left all manner of signs behind, and I had merely to trail in their path with my eyes attentive and lo, I'd find a broken branch at five feet high, or a print in the mud longer than a paw, or a spray of urine that had no musk to it, or ashes. Even rivers did a poor job of masking, for there was no invisible way to emerge from one. When I found the culprits, I'd rope them up and bring them back to my employer, or just their scalps, whichever he preferred. This put my interests to use, but there was little challenge: all the subjects I encountered were guilty, and each proclaimed his innocence. Only in later years have I taken on the heavier duties of war chief, but I am not sorry to return to this early occupation, testing as it does the strength of my scrutiny.

"I'll come with you?" my wife asked. It is true that she's accompanied me on similar excursions, but mostly because Indian women are difficult to dissuade, and she is certainly more help than hindrance. It was she, in fact, who found the Spanish drunkard last spring who set a Creek barn on fire.

"No, this needs somewhat more focus," I said, "and your charms, I fear, would distract me." She does have charms, though she tends to use them for her own amusement. It is curious that she has never attempted to grease my hair. She can seem more like a hired companion, albeit playful and generally attentive, than a wife, but I am aware that my expectations regarding female behavior are colored by my French upbringing; I cannot expect her to order my household in silence, for no other women here do.

She was not the least put out. She gathered up our pile of skins from the tent and carried them to a nearby dwelling, which I assume belonged to her sister. I never ask what she gets up to when I am traveling, but I believe in the visible thumbprint of guilt, and after years of leaving, returning, and scanning her face for signs of mischief, I have determined that, as far as I can tell, my wife has never felt the smallest breeze across her conscience. This, of course, is foreign to me, and not a little bewitching.

"Will you miss me?" I asked, per usual.

"Not until you return," she said with a smile.

We set out before the midday meal, packs filled with the stiff bread and dried meats customary on journeys, and now that we are an hour south of our camp, I begin to think not of my wife and her oddities or my compact with the chief, but of the green trail before us: the first warm gusts of March, the energy of the horses, the common exchanges between men of the same clan, and the prospect of something unusual on the horizon. Once my busy mind's been freed from thoughts of the future—where I plan to go after the Creeks lose their particularity, and what the Royal Society might think of my scribblings—I can more thoroughly consider the fruits of this expedition.

At thirty-six years of age, having ended the lives of many men and adventured from my native France to these lands where they say only savages reside, I believe I have some grasp on the enthusiasms of men, what spurs them to love, to kill, to congregate. This understanding brings me serenity, and I consider myself a man of pristine health and placid heart.

But I yearn to be surprised. It is perhaps the sole reason I'm pursuing these uncommon bandits, for I cannot make sense of their acting in concert. My notebooks are swollen with sketches of Indian life, descriptions of council meetings, meetings with foreign emissaries, meetings between lovers, but this country, like the countries I've known before, has its patterns; after a while, they can be summarized with some ease. What has been reinforced to me is that human existence is both practical and predictable. There are those who find themselves sunk in the little vicissitudes of life, who feel brought low by fortune, but I am skeptical of Fate, of anything imperceptible. What happens to us can be easily mapped by what has come before, this being a decidedly functional world, one of cause and effect. Men pursue their own interests and stick to their kind, simply. We grow walls and hide behind them. I knew this even as a boy.

AS A CHILD, if my mother were at her sewing or scolding the maids, I would creep out to her garden, kneel before a bud, and wait through the slow hours until it began to split. The flowers in that hedged garden in Thin-le-Moutier were each a promise of some other world, God-wrought and composite, which I dreamed about as one might dream of women one hasn't met. A single bursting stamen could remind me that there was life independent of my mother, that intricacy existed equally in man, and that I was merely observing the palest version of both in those tended beds. The more my mother complained of my dirtied knees, the more I saw the space beyond our house as splendidly transgressive. Disorder was intoxicating.

On the lowest shelf in the library, we had a few volumes of philosophy and a Dutch atlas, and though I couldn't make sense of Cicero, I found a match for my flowers in the maps of distant lands. The Orient, the New World, *Nouvelle Hollande* floating half drawn above the white blank of *Terres Australes*. I knew boys lived there; I knew there were mothers and perhaps fathers and certainly rivers winding through woods. What a glory to travel the world, cataloging every variance. I tore out the broad page with the Antilles, rough crumbs of islands, and folded it beneath my pillow so that I might sleep on its expanse.

It was a serving girl who found it and reported my crime. I only regret that I don't know her name to curse it; I was never taught their names. My mother did not believe in beating me, as a father might have done, but understood discipline to be a foundation for a righteous life, and so at every misdeed she locked me in an empty room at the end of a hallway on the third floor. She wore her wedding rings on a chain around her neck, and they chimed as she shut the door behind her. Boards had been nailed where the window once was, so that there was nothing for a child to gaze upon: none of the rich accoutrements of the other rooms, the gilt mirrors or glowering portraits, but also nothing of the world beyond. No sky, no distant green. I came to despise the bare floors and bare walls, for the emptiness forced my gaze within, where there was nothing I wished to consider. I did not admire myself then. She took her time; two or three hours always brought me to tears and back again, so that when she came to fetch me I seemed calm and penitent. I thought my mother must have hated me, and I could not discover why.

My father, who might have been a different breed of parent, was a soldier, and I was told by a sympathetic cook that one day when I was a baby he marched away from the house as if a battle were calling him, and he never marched back. If there was a pattern of men leaving my mother, I took pleasure in the thought of joining them.

The only joy was in my mother's garden. I don't know why I call it hers; I rarely saw her there, and certainly she never dug holes or hoisted around a watering can, though when young men would visit she sometimes took it upon herself to wear an apron and hold a trowel daintily. She did enjoy the sight of cut flowers inside. The garden was larger than the house and more elaborate, with rooms and knotted hedges and a canal that ran through the roses, the earth between each plant covered in a cold snow of stones. Beyond the regimented grounds was an actual river, which a boy could hear gurgling if he put his ear to the yew wall, and near it was a spread of lawn where she experimented with a *paysager* that eventually grew too wild, the sloping grasses and artfully scattered rocks returned, by a patient servant, to herb beds. My mother was not quite romantic enough to abide a winding path. But these flashes of the undomesticated soothed me, almost made up for the hours in the bare room, the lack of any friend.

When I felt lonely, which was certainly not all the time, I was imaginative enough to find my own company. We had a kitten once who was afraid of its tail, who would skulk among the vegetable rows and try to burrow in the dirt whenever a sparrow twittered by. I adored this cat, I wanted it to sleep in my bed with me and learn tricks, like shaking hands. Mother said it was no use, the creature was feral and should be left in peace, but I saw it wasn't wild at all, only deathly afraid of the natural world. It needed rescue. So for a summer I stalked the gardens. Between the box hedges there were countless places to hide; I walked slowly, and later crawled, along the borders of yew, through the delphiniums and love-in-a-mist, behind the stone pools where the lilies grew. Sometimes all I'd gain for my troubles was the end of a tail, slippering through a hedge, or the sound of its paws on the gravel path behind me. It could move beyond the borders of the garden, as I could not. But as the summer waned, I think it grew more accustomed, or I less obvious, and we would sit in the same leafy room for an afternoon, it dozing at the base of a rose while I chased away the lizards. When it first offered its back to be touched, I did so with one finger only, and watched with joy as it ran away bewildered and then returned a few moments later, standoffish and intrigued. I have had to work for few things in life, and nothing has been sweeter than this first struggle. I never touched its belly, or rubbed its ear between my fingers, or twirled its tail with affection, and I certainly never coaxed it into my bedchamber, but my stealth improved so that I could always find it, wherever in the garden it was cowering, and I suppose my temperament was quiet enough that it allowed me to coexist. I had told no one about my pursuits by the time I was sent to school at the end of the summer, and when I returned home that winter for a holiday, the kitten was gone, and there was no one to whom I could have conveyed my grief. My mother died a few years later, and so I began my acquaintance with the world. I have grown past this artlessness because men always move beyond such gardens.

THE THREE CREEKS behind me chatter, knowing that I will stop them when I spot the first sign of our fugitives. They are secondaries, not cousins to our chief but at one remove, men trusted with the smaller tasks of running a town's politics. For my purpose, they are merely extra arms to use for apprehending, but I enjoy listening to their little scandals. One of them seems to have met a woman on a recent trip to the Iroquois and is plotting their reunion.

"Next summer we'll go again, the *mico* said."

"Not that way, our treaties there are done. We'll go west if we go any way at all. The Caddo are bumping against the French."

"They're an ugly lot!" says the third.

"He means you'll find no woman there."

"It's not any bit I want, it's the one I already found. You're not listening."

"Whoever she was, a year goes by and she'll have found a dozen men instead, and taller too."

"Only Iroquois I saw was very short," says the third.

"Was he a child? Listen, brother, don't be a fool. There are plenty of girls within throwing distance who would take you into their beds. What about Sehoy?"

"But you didn't see the Iroquois girl. They look very different up there. I think she'd even refused an Englishman."

"So she has sense; doesn't mean she'll wait for a gawky Muskogee."

"I heard there's a spell to put muscle on your arms," says the third.

The slave, through all of this, is silent.

"Listen, give her up. Be sensible. Did you even——"

"Yes! I'm not entirely without talent. I tell you, she loves me."

"She said so?"

"Her eyes, that's where it was. But very clear. She wants me to come again."

"For another tumble in the longhouse, I'm sure, between tumbles with proper warriors."

"I've fought too."

"One summer."

"And with a scar! This one."

"From a falling walnut."

"She'll wait. She'll want me again."

"And you'll learn the language? Bundle up on those winter nights next to a nasty fire smelling of fat, with all her cousins crammed around you lovers, so you couldn't grab her bottom without pulling her sister's hair?"

The third laughed out loud.

"That's it, you have no sympathy."

And they didn't speak for ten minutes, during which I reminded myself to add this exchange to my section on inter-Indian relations.

Do I wish they included me in their banter? Perhaps for the same reason I don't engage the silent slave bringing up the rear, the Creeks keep me well out of their conversation. Though Donne may have claimed that every man is a piece of the continent, I'd wager he never visited this one.

The afternoon is a pleasant one for riding; the sun comes in

warm through the beeches and oaks, still mostly defoliated from
the winter, and the new jacket my wife made me keeps the wind
off, so that I exist in that perfect state of intermediacy wherein I
neither sweat nor shiver. If I stopped my horse, I believe the air
would feel like nothing on my face, as if there were no elements
at all.

Some ground bird, a robin or towhee, hops before us through
patches of light, flitting through the fingers of a low palmetto. I
give my whip a light crack and it startles off, and I promptly regret this. Wherever I am, I can hear the calls of birds too afraid
to show their feathers. Some of the men we pass on the trail know
who I am and keep a generous berth or else nod extravagantly.
Each one of them has some sin in his heart he wouldn't wish me
finding. But my primary role is not that of embodied justice but
exploration. If they knew me better—if anyone did, from my
mother to my wives to these half strangers—it would be evident
that I merely wanted to understand them. Give me your actions
for a day, and I can find the thoughts to match them.

I already picture the treatise this will make: three men of
diverse but foul character have forged a union out of mutual
greed—the Indian providing stealth and forest knowledge, the
white man serving as both intelligence and firepower, and the
negro with his black heart spurring them on—and have thereby
revealed the various motives that make the American back-
country a landscape of merciless individual pursuit. My readers will blush to learn of this breed of criminal, of the tenor of
this young nation, bumping along as it does without the comfort
or cohesion of monarchy and of each man residing within his
sphere: the poor thieving from the poor, and the rich impris-
oned in their ancestral gardens. Readers will wonder what sort

of future such a nation can anticipate; there will be a clamor for more *rapportage*. Will the Royal Society be taken aback when they learn that the author who holds this fresh mirror up to the machinations of humanity is not a pale pedant but the gentleman adventurer Louis Le Clerc Milfort?

That these three men will die at my hand at the end of this journey needn't be included in my account. No matter how lawless the country, freedom must be contingent on innocence.

March 9, 1788

Bob

MY SHOULDER FEELS like an angry rat has burrowed in and is nibbling on the nerves. Cat got the bullet out, bless him, but something alive's still in there, feeding itself. The others are walking faster than me now, for the rat in my arm doesn't care for the silver on my back. Think of all the shit I've borne for twenty-eight years, the pounds and pounds of cane I've cut and lifted and boiled down, think of the scars on my skin that have grown on top of scars like a new language building itself, all put there by men who never cared to hear my own tongue, and you'd think the way those wounds burned into my innards would've prepared me for one gunshot to the shoulder, one heavy bag of coins. But since taking my own body out of Master's reach, this is the one thing I've done. Those murders the one action on my new-freed soul. I twist my arm across my chest, stretch it back, roll my wrist a couple times. The day's waking up, and all the little birds are coming out to scold us.

Though the new man of me is already damned, I am used

enough to finding the good of things to be glad those two men are walking with me. We could've split after the creek, but that would've been a further ruin, and somehow they knew this too. I never learned how to be easy alone. My voice needs ears to hear it, even past when there's nothing to say. Like now.

Cat's carrying our knapsacks, since me and the Indian, being bigger, offered to take the silver. But he looks back once and sees a hiccup in my step—under the weight, he thinks, but really it's the damn rat eating my flesh—and calls out in his soft sad voice, "You all right?"

Istillicha glances back, but I say, "Mm-hm, mm-hm, just got to get where we're going," and we keep on moving, and the only thing keeps me from setting down the bag is the sight of their shoes ahead. The Indian in his quiet moccasins, the white man looking like he wrapped a bunch of random leather around his feet.

We didn't eat breakfast, being still fuddled from having taken men's lives—lives that if we had the chance we'd patch back together with our own muscle and bone, or maybe that's only me—and my stomach is doing somersaults, trying to figure out if it wants some food or wants to puke up all the food it's ever in its whole life had. *I'm just a man*, I keep telling myself, which is to say, *It's all right to be hungry* and *It's all right that I'm still walking while some men aren't*. What I love about the Indian is how good he is at catching meat. And he knows which parts of the pigeon taste better than you think they would. See, I'm already making a future for myself where I sit down for dinner, move my fingers to my mouth to fill my belly on purpose to keep living.

The red dust from the road has stuck to my wet legs, like I dragged blood out of that creek, and the grit is rubbing at my ankles. I set down the bag to scratch the muck off, and the others stop and wait. Cat comes and drops the sacks at my feet and lifts the bag of silver that's about as big as he is, hoisting it on his back with a grunt. I make a half-hearted grab at it.

"I got it," I say, and I think it's a sign of something that after just three days no one's suspecting that one of us'll run off with the coins while the others aren't looking.

Cat walks on with it, and I pick up our own small bags, filled with blankets and biscuits and a knife and whatever soil accompanied us from our various homes, soil that maybe our wives once walked on, though one of the many things I don't know about these men is whether they left behind any ladies. I shake my head a couple times so I won't start remembering mine.

Who I should be thinking about is the men who'll be following us. Not just the one Istillicha named—the Clerk, who gets paid by the chief and is some kind of slow bloodhound, too fancified to tramp after us, provided we tramp far enough—but also the men whose only job is to find slaves who think they're better than slaves. I'm still walking on my master's pass, good for a week, and I'm out of West Florida now, where patrols only look for their own lost negroes, but I am surely leaving a blazing trail behind me: first the horse that went missing, which probably trotted back home to sound the alarm, and then all those bodies stacked in the sand by the creek, with black witnesses in the trees beyond. We talked for half a minute about whether to kill them too, but I said I'd been put where I didn't want to be often enough to know it wasn't their fault they were forced to watch a murder, so we tied them up, strung rope around wrists that—I know—are so familiar with rope it starts to feel like skin. I gave them a wink, but they didn't wink back.

When they come for me, they'll want the story. They'll want to know whether I was stolen by traders, in which case maybe only an ear needs to get lopped off, or whether I ran off with intention, leaving behind a whole family of women whose rights of running are far greater than mine. In which case the body deserves the worst, from skin peeled off to tongue cut out to feet set on fire, all of which my daughters will be asked to watch like a bloody pageant. So no, it's not the Clerk I'm worried about; he's a white man from somewhere else, he doesn't know what all a black man who steals himself deserves. I'm just trying to figure what kind of a story I can tell that will make my hunters see me as a man.

Istillicha, who knows nothing of me beyond my four limbs, is taking us to see a doctor who will fix the hole in my arm; he drew a line between bodies that needed saving and bodies that didn't, and for some reason my black self wound up on the right side of the line. This is part of what I'd tell.

A quick rain shower comes in the early morning, not hard enough to shoo off the birds that still twitter at us, but just enough water so we start rubbing our hands together, smearing the dirt and the blood off whatever parts of us we can reach.

"Hold still," I say to Cat, and wipe my sleeve across the back of his neck so that a little of his white skin shines through.

Istillicha runs his fingers through his hair and ties it back again in a knot. The rainwater is replacing the creek water.

We hear a rumble from far off, not a scary kind, just like the sky was starting to get peckish, but Cat looks quick over at the Indian.

"You scared of storms?" I ask. He's like a child that way. Though he may have been a murderer long before we were, we're the ones who look after him: wipe his neck, give him food, let him sleep close by so he doesn't get lonely. If I could crack him open and get whatever secret's lying curled up inside, we'd probably spend less time fussing over those sad eyes.

"There was once a boy on a hunting party," Istillicha says, "who heard the same kind of noise and didn't know what it was."

The rain catches in my eyelashes, making little bubbles of the road, the pines, the palmetto spikes. I don't brush them off right away but let them play around with my sight, ballooning some things, washing others away.

"He went to find the sound, leaving behind his uncles and his brothers, and came upon a creature by a riverbank struggling to breathe. It was Thunder, and he had a snake wrapped around his neck."

That's the way you take the teeth out of something scary: make it pitiful. Sure enough, Cat's face shrinks, goes from fear to worry.

"Thunder begged the boy to save him, and the snake begged the boy to help him kill the creature."

"Couldn't save both," Cat says, but I can't tell if it's a question. The Indian keeps on.

"He pulled out an arrow and shot the snake clean through, which dropped to the ground and left Thunder to breathe again." Istillicha pauses, listens for something, which he does often enough that I sometimes think he's just trying to make us jumpy. "Thunder promised to help him, sending lightning to strike his enemies whenever he wished."

"What would the snake have given the boy?" I ask.

"We don't know," he says.

The rain's drifting east now, and Cat lifts his open mouth

for the last few drops. "He made a choice," Cat says. "Saved someone."

Another rumble comes at us, but it's quieter now, rolling around in some faraway hills, and Cat doesn't even notice, his face twisted around some new thought.

We hear cart wheels coming down the trail, but they're close enough that we can't crawl up the bank without getting caught, so we keep walking forward as innocently as our wet red shoes allow. The man pulling the cart, woolly-haired and beard-tangled, is no cleaner than us, and his wagon is filled with stacks of papers smudged by the drizzle. As he tugs one of the papers free and waves it in front of his face, saying something about *the news from the stars, heaven's own report, listen for your fate*, I feel the rat in my arm clamp down on a new nerve, and all I wish is for my body to be pulled safely out of this.

Bob

MY MOTHER ALWAYS said my mouth was too loud for what little I had to say, but she was the one who sat us down under the shake roof under the black night and gave us stories like they were rare sugar. What she talked of was all gone past, for that was all that was worth telling. Nothing happened day to day that we cared to stick in our memories for later, and the things that stuck we wished wouldn't've. It was Virginia, south of Petersburg, and a hungry belly was at least a sign you were alive. The stories filled up the holes, made our sorrow step back for a spell, though sorrow's maybe too grand a word, us being children then and feeling more boredom than grief at our endless captivity. Like a winter without any thaw, on and on. My own chatter I can't explain, but I did talk too much, my mother was right. I was a boy, I liked the sound of my voice.

She was a light-skinned woman who wore her hair in stripped rags, two teeth missing, and she had a pocket in her apron where she slid crusts and old biscuits for me to find. There were hills humpbacked on hills and trees so green they looked like moss underwater, like both sides of the earth were the same. But I didn't think it was beautiful then, and she didn't raise me. The granny was a soot-black woman who hunched on an old churn in the yard near all the women's children and hollered so loud every time we neared the fences that the crows would shoot out of those wet-green trees. I'd watch my mother in the fields out of one eye, her hair dancing like colored finches in the big yellow leaves, and the brick house out of the other, where buggies rode up every hour carrying men and ladies, white as sunlight, and my ears perked back the whole time to hear Granny jabbering about the dark country, from where she was nabbed ninety-six years ago, naked as the day she was born. I saw how those with the good tales got listened to, and so early on I started practicing my talking, empty though it was.

When Granny was tired of watching our games, she sent us into the near woods to fetch kindling, the oldest of us carrying the babies on our backs, the toddlers stopping to pee on sycamore leaves to hear them crackle. I didn't dig for worms or play hide-the-switch or even wander farther than I should, but I did tell the others the littlest things I saw and felt, thinking they'd enjoy the words. They were friendly enough about it, maybe because I always carried the fattest baby, but other than Primus none of them thought much of me. If it sounds like we children in the woods made for a charming scene, then you were never a child.

MY BROTHER PRIMUS was dark and shiny, like someone had wrapped an old brown sheet around a boy of gold. He would move to the fields that summer, but then he was the oldest in the pen and told us what was up and down with the world and we all believed him, every word. On one of those kindling nights when we did chores for Granny, the children one by one turned home, tipping on their legs with sleepiness, each with a clutch of sticks and some with the babies on their backs, all dreaming of their mothers' arms. But Primus pulled me back and we waited until the woods were empty and then he shared with me what he knew. He must have been eight or nine.

"Master's land stretches all the way out."

"How far?" I asked, following the sweep of his stubby arm.

"That far."

We were in the middle of a crowd of oaks and the stars didn't shine too deep there. I looked around and nodded, unimpressed.

"Where do you think our land is?" he asked.

"Don't have any," I said.

"Who told you that?"

I wasn't so much interested in looking at the trees, which seemed scrubby and no-count to me, or the way the dirt buckled up and crawled over roots and dipped thirsty under creeks. So what if this was Master's land? I didn't know what to call the birds, or which flowers smelled like sugar and which like rotten cheese. What I was watching was Primus, who shone there in the night and who was the same flesh as me but bolder. He had just lost the little rounded belly of being young and was now straight and strong, already with angry eyes that I tried to mimic, practicing on our sisters, who said I looked sick to my stomach. I admired every inch of him, most of all what I didn't understand, the secrets of him. I supposed he felt the same about what was past the far fences of the tobacco fields, the blank spaces being always the spaces that can be filled by whatever's overflowing in ourselves.

We walked out to the edge of the forest where a fence poked around the farthest trunks, cutting off the master's farm from the clear hills that loped down to the river that fed into the Nottoway, or maybe that glint of silver *was* the Nottoway—no one ever told us names. You could see a long way here, and though I didn't mind one way or another how far I could see, Primus's eyes grew slow and wide at all the land before him. It was thick night by now, but we were lit by the water and the speckling stars and the little campfires that showed in dots where humans were.

Primus kicked at one of the fence posts, which were linked together with half-rotten split rails, and when it leaned away from him, he looked at me with a boyishness that didn't much show in his face those days. He began kicking again, and I knew, so I started pulling from the top, and between the two of us we levered the post onto its side, the rails collapsing. I would do anything with him, would never need an explanation. We went along, post by post, and wobbled each one out of its hole, pushing and pulling until we were sweaty with laughing, until a whole stretch of them, maybe a quarter-mile long, were lying belly-up on the ground. Now we could run from the master's land to the open land and back, hopping over a tangle of wood, whooping like we had caught a buffalo, or something larger. When we were winded and collapsed, him on the far side, me on the near, he laughed and said, "*This* is our land."

He drew a kind of vision then, and it was so filled with real things that I knew he'd been dreaming it for years. He was the oldest and didn't have anything to look up to, the way I did. His farm was spread out, he said, far to the west, empty of trees or fields or crops, and in place of tobacco or cotton there'd be cows, calm lowing things that would grow fat with him taking such good care of them. To get around, he'd have a donkey, not a horse, and he'd train it to know its own name so he could call it from the porch and it'd come trotting up and he'd hop on without ever getting his feet in the mud. (There was mud there, just as there was mud everywhere.)

"A donkey?" I asked, thinking he'd gone too far. "They can't run like horses."

"Those belong to white folk," he said. "Master rides a horse. Farlan rides a horse. You ever seen a black man on a horse?"

I hadn't.

"A donkey'll listen to you. They know."

"Know what?"

"When it's you and your donkey and that wide-open land, can't nobody stop you and say, 'This is mine' or 'This ain't yourn.' " His stubby arms went up again to sweep the country for me, and I waited to see what he saw, but all I got was the little silver glints of the Nottoway, or the river that led to the Nottoway, whichever it was.

I asked if he would have a family, because I was just six years old and the best thing about life still was that I had a mother.

"That's *your* land, Bob, not nobody else's. What'd you want a family for?"

"A wife?" I said.

He shook his head. "Nobody wants one of those."

And I thought he was right, because he was always right.

We lay there dreaming for much of the night, our bodies just outside the fallen lines of fence, the hoot-owls circling us, wondering if we were overlarge mice. He dozed, and I got up to count each push-and-pulled post; there were a hundred and nineteen down on the ground, and all by myself I wiggled down one more to make it even. The splinters in my hands seemed to me proof that I was a big man.

Primus snorted himself awake just long enough to say, "We better put them back before sunup," and then we were both asleep, looking to the hoot-owls like rabbits curled for the night.

MY MOTHER USED to whisper to us in the frog-tickled night-time that we were cut of finer stuff than the folks around us, that we were sons and daughters of an African prince, and I believed her because her skin looked like bright gold and I sure thought myself smarter than everybody else, never thinking what it took to make skin so gold, what kind of stirring of brown and white, what unwilling love. When we talked about where we came from, we had to skip back to Africa to find the stories that made sense.

Primus got big eyes every time my mother started in on the princes of Africa. He'd nod and nod as if to say, *Yes ma'am, that's me*, and the older he got the more his eyes narrowed until he knew for sure he was one step next to the son of God, and when Farlan told him to move faster in the rows, he'd turn that shaven head of his most of the way round like a cat in the wild and give such a glare that Farlan would have to clear his throat to get free from the sight of him, and Primus by then all of twelve years. While he was living I thought maybe Mother was right and we were meant for something else.

The tale that always rang in my mind the loudest was of my great-grandfather Abraham, who was eight years old or nine, or—come to think of it—always as old as I was, and had tumbled down to the river with his friends, all brown, all naked, with sticks for spears and string for nets, their goal being to hunt lions, and in the reeds, hidden and laughing like river ghosts, they were leapt upon by a herd of men who wrapped them in real ropes and bound their open mouths and carried them in silent bundles back down the river. My mother said, although she couldn't have known, that his mother wept for five days to find her boy missing and cut her arms in stripes and burned her foot bottoms nightly until they built her a house beyond the village to hold her madness. I always wanted to hear more about the boys and if there were really lions or only pretend ones, but she would go on about the mother until we started to shift around and grab each other's bellies. When she got back to Abraham, he was stacked in a boat on an ocean, like a sailor lying down, and then was stood up on a piece of wood in a port town where a field of white men clamored. When he was very old, he told my mother, who was very young, that he had thought there weren't any women in the country of Virginia and he had come to hell indeed. "Take me back!" he said that he said to the men smoothing his chained small body with palm oil. "I aim to get married!" Even as a young boy, though, I knew my great-grandfather said no such thing, that he wouldn't have cared if there was a girl in that world unless it was his mother. Because this is how I felt. But my mother always told the story the same way, just as he told it to her, as if in the telling there would survive some frail thread between her soul and his, between all of us little souls and the great lost soul of Africa.

Sometimes that story ended with the truth, which was that my great-grandfather was eventually snatched from the fields and led gibbering in an African tongue and limping with age into a tobacco barn, where a white man cleared away the dry litter before painting him with pitch oil and setting him alight. This is not a story to tell to children unless they need to be taught to hate, a lesson that, of all of us, Primus learned best.

THE NIGHT WE knocked down the posts was a treasure to me, and I held on to it like truth, so when someone asked me about my brother I told them that, about our victory over our master's fence and Primus mapping all kinds of worlds for us, and I didn't tell them the end of the story, which is that we didn't wake up in time, and when the sun rose and we were scurrying along the line propping up the posts and stacking the rails as fast as our hands would let us, Farlan came picking through the woods on his big black horse. Our mother hadn't wanted to say about our not coming home, because better us dead somewhere from snakebite than dragged in by white hands, but Granny in the pen had a job to do and couldn't be losing little ones, so she told on us, and there Farlan was, reins in one hand, whip in the other.

He didn't want a story, so we saved it for Master. The cows had gotten to the fence, we said, and in all their lusting for each other had toppled a whole stretch of it, which we found when we were picking sticks for kindling. We'd shooed them away and were working hard to put the posts back up so none of the cows would come trampling into the tobacco fields, which we knew Master wouldn't like. "Did we do a good thing?" we said, our little hands pressed together like prayer.

I was too young to get anything more than ten smacks on the bottom. Only later did I hear from Primus about Master's small knotted whip, and how he made my brother stand in the broad hall away from the fine things, and how he whipped him hard, but not hard enough so blood would get on the new-varnished floor, polished the day before by black hands and too fine now for black blood.

That's when the big house stopped seeming like a grand place, one I'd like to live in, and turned into someplace haunted. It swallowed up screams and breathed them out in little whispers through the day, so that walking past made your ears hurt, though you couldn't tell why. I didn't tell the end of the story to people who asked, because the best part of my brother was the bit that lay dozing on the far side of the fallen fence, his land still whole and perfect in his head.

THE STORIES WERE what reminded us that what seemed real was just a passing fancy; this bound land, our broken cabins, the way we couldn't see our mother but at night, these were not all of what could happen. The best of life was not what we were living, but something already past, or up ahead. When Primus snuck out to the far creek Sunday evenings, I followed him, chattering away, carrying my shoes by their worn heels and sometimes a stick to fight off the panthers I knew were hiding and which my brother would be too creek-minded to notice till they were pouncing. My limbs turned into antelope legs; I bounded the way our mother told us Antelope bounded when he was climbing up toward heaven. He was a grandfather to us, same as Abraham but even further back, a thousand generations. Antelope was small, like us, and all the other animals wanted to eat him so that he was always running, never resting. He even ran at night, through the dark, dark forests and fields, and we all put our hands over our faces at this part, because Panther was right behind. She showed us how close with her hands: her right was Antelope, with four finger legs galloping hard, and her left was Panther, slinking as fast as the other could bound. She ran her hands all around the cabin floor and we followed with anguish until the left hand toppled the right and the baby started wailing. But just as Antelope stopped his spasming and Panther loosened his tight grip, lo! the right hand slinked up fast from the hold of the left, and Antelope scampered up the side of the baby, tickling her shoulder and onto her head, and when the baby laughed, the rest of us started to breathe again. Sure enough, Panther couldn't climb up where Antelope was, so he plopped down and waited and waited, and since there was no purpose to coming down, Antelope just kept on climbing, up off our baby sister's head and right up to heaven, where our mother's right hand balled up and drifted away, like a star.

I think this was once a longer story, with more tricks and turns, but it had settled down into the kernel of itself, which was no more than good and bad, and the triumph of the weak. We were the weak, and weakness to us just meant that we couldn't admit to our muscle. I adored playing Antelope by the creek and would not have wanted to be Panther, who for all his speed and strength and clawed paws never climbed up the baby's shoulder to heaven.

WHEN WE WERE a few years older and Primus was already in the fields, stripping the yellow leaves with the others, collecting his hate, we'd play at building houses in the evening—maybe because our own was so crowded and damp—him lying in the scrabble outside our cabin, his arms worn out but not his mind, directing me from the blueprints in his head. I made rooms for him out of bark and corn husks, two and three stories high, far grander even than the big house. I wallpapered them with our mother's hair rags, stuffed inside for color. When I was finished, he'd idle his eyes over and tell me what was missing, and then he'd be the one to find the donkey. It was usually a scrap of our dinner, or the dried-out canoe of a pecan hull, and Primus'd set it up alongside the twigged front porch so it was just right for whenever the owner decided to swagger out the door. We never really put a man inside, for we were the men, and it was our house.

I'd recite little stories about the owner, about how he'd had a long day building houses (my imagination was small) and what kind of dinner he'd eat, with plenty of beef and gravy, and sometimes he'd nap because the houses would be so easy, but he most looked forward to his evening donkey ride, when he'd roam around the land he owned, too big for fences, and if he was feeling handsome would go visit the lady who lived down the road. ("What lady?" Primus asked.) She was very fair, almost white, and had long, long hair that never broke off in the brush or had to be wrapped up in cloth, and her fingernails were little pearls, not a trace of dirt. Our man would lift her up on that donkey and when they went galloping off across the dry plain, no trees in sight, her hair flew out behind her like the donkey had two tails. I could go on and on.

He kicked the house down and scattered it before we went in for the night so that no one would find it, least of all our mother, who might think that we wanted something better than what we had. Sometimes I'd save the donkeys, would sneak the sponge of lichen that had been our steed into my pocket and then underneath my pillow, where I'd feel it all night between my finger and thumb.

I told him he should be a builder, for he had fine ideas of space

and how to use all the corners of a structure handily, and some
nights he'd smile at this and agree, and we'd picture how he'd
make mansions for white folk from Boston to Charles Town,
marking his name above the lintel in half-sized letters that only
we could make out. But other nights he'd tell me to hush up.

"But your name—"

"My name's in the back cover of Master's Bible, same as
yours."

"Master isn't giving you a donkey."

He'd tap his head. "That's in here, little brother. That's all."

I thought he was getting used to being who he was, but all the
talks we had were just him fighting around his own captivity.
The whole time I was making houses for him, he was feeding
all the little insults to his anger, soaking up the cuts and bruises
and spit until the bark house wasn't just what he wanted, but was
what he couldn't have, what some men owned but not him, not
Primus, because he didn't even belong to himself. I didn't know
this, like most things, until the time for knowing it had already
passed.

ON THE DAY before his fourteenth birthday, Primus crawled
out of our cabin shoeless before dawn, which I know because
I watched, and moved skink-like across the near fields up the
slope to the big house, which I know because I followed, and
from the base of a cherry tree I saw his shadow slip inside that
wide hall with a flint and a fist of straw, his aim I suppose to burn
the master down, and when I saw him come out again and run
toward the creek, tall on his toes, I slunk back to bed. When the
first bell rang, my mother sent me to fetch him, she thinking he
was in the bushes with his stomach trouble, and when he wasn't

in the bushes, I followed his prints down to the creek, his bare foot-marks the only ones in the dawn dust. I wanted to be curled back in my straw, is the only thing I was thinking when I came to the bank and saw his toes dipped in the water and followed them up to his bony knees and on up to his nightshirt that the wind was wrapping around him in a pretty kind of way and up to his face, which was a foreign purple swell, and I stopped look-ing and started screaming and so never even saw the rope that bound him to the willow, the rope of his own twisting, the knots of his own design. An old woman found me and brought me back to my mother, leaving Primus swinging on the low branch, his toes skating in the creek, making eddies where there were none.

The cook who we called Auntie had found the feeble brush-fire in the hallway as she was taking the master up his washing water; she had stamped it out with one foot and walked on.

FEELING IS TOO small a word. Words are too small. We worked in the fields and took our beatings for the extra time we had to stop to hold on to ourselves and at night we gathered again, my mother and all of us, and ate our collards and corn and went to sleep. The next day we'd work and eat our collards and sleep. We could never say it was the worst thing ever hap-pened to us, because who knew what was coming next.

A few months after Primus stole his own body from the men who stole his great-grandfather's, and before my mother was speaking again, Farlan came to me in the rows and said I was wanted in the big house, that they needed extra hands for bring-ing noon dinner to some folks stopping from out of town, so I went, happy enough to rest my hoe and not yet too bitter to serve the men who built my sorrow. I was only eleven, and just a mimic of a man.

Turns out there weren't any guests, no men from up the road or ladies out for an airing, so I scrubbed down the slick cedar-board halls after someone handed me a bucket of sand and a rag. When I was at the window with a jar of vinegar is when I heard her screaming, and I tried the door but it was locked and the key taken, so I stared with my hands spread on the window and my open mouth against the glass and my eyes nearly shut with tears, the shape of her blurred out, and still when I think of my mother I can taste vinegar and salt.

They had her hands bound but her feet were kicking out in a wild dance and though I'd seen my mother proud and worn down and silent with sadness, I had never seen her rage, and after not hearing her words to me for weeks, the sound of her screaming my name made me hope to crawl back in her belly. The trader had come for her and two other women and a man, and knowing her love—and *knowing* her love—they had locked me in the house to sell her barefaced, as a chair is sold, as a piece of land. The other children were in the pen with Granny and never knew. White men lashed her to the left side of the wagon, which I remember because that was the side shaded by the front drive's walnut, planted by Master's long-ago kin, so that though I could hear her, can hear her, screaming still, her face was blacked out in shadow, vanished.

Was that too much for a boy to bear? The next week, the younger ones were split into parcels and sold in town, and when the winter came, they handed me to a young man with black hair standing straight up and a round face red with pimples who said his name was Treehorn and that he had come to take me for his master a million miles away, and laughed like a wild dog, and I willing went, for I had lost all sense of who I belonged to.

A MILLION TURNED out to be a little less than a thousand, and we were two weeks on the road to Pensacola, all crammed in a wagon and some trailing behind. Treehorn didn't talk much, and the other white man said so little I never heard his name, and of the others they gathered like black flowers along the way, most were boat-fresh and spoke a dozen tongues, none of which sounded like words to me. In all this strange noise and silence, and with the vision of my mother like a heavy brick in my mind to be avoided, I started talking more and more until I was damn near narrating that expedition. I named the trees and the birds and the road animals, even when I didn't know their names, which was mostly. I asked where we were going and what kind of work we'd be doing and for what kind of man we'd be laboring, and when I got no answers, I described the future to myself and anyone who'd listen, and in this way I built a little room in my head where there wasn't any sorrow. I had never been much of an unhappy child, and now I was teaching myself not to be an unhappy man, a man being what I thought of myself on the road at eleven years old, approaching twelve, the past being what it was. When you lose what you love and still find yourself alive, what else do you do?

On the trail spiraling down from Virginia to Florida, us hobbled to the wagon and the whites on horses, I saw things I'd never seen before: low mountain passes and flat dry land and earth that looked solid till you put your foot in and water came seeping up or the sand dropped out from under you or you found your leg in a fox den, and anything that didn't look like the three hundred acres of forest and tobacco fields where I'd spent all my years now took me by surprise. I saw Indians for the first time, and they too struck me strange, for I never knew there were such things as Indian women, but there they were in the uplands, riding horses by themselves with baskets of baskets behind them. Treehorn and the other man bought their liquor from a Catawba near Columbia, and the three of them drank together round a fire while the rest of us were chained to trees outside the circle of light. I had thought Indians were just like us, but they're not at all. Their place is by the fire, but it's a fire they have to build themselves, so I don't know what they are.

When it rained we got wet, and when the sun baked, our skin started peeling in sheets, and when the horses were tired from pulling the wagon, we walked until our feet had burred soles. When the men with branded cheeks tried to escape before dawn, they were beaten until their backs matched their faces, and when the women dragged slow behind, the chains were tightened round their necks. And still I talked, and still I mumbled out all I saw for people who didn't care to understand a word I was saying, leaving out the sorrow, leaving in every bright thought I ever had. They could've whipped me for never shutting my mouth, and I sometimes looking back on it wonder why they didn't, and I figure they must could have used the sound.

We got to the farm in the warmest part of the late afternoon, when all the January sun seemed to have puddled in that one place, and it looked like a dream with trees I'd never seen, some with spiky leaves and some with branches longer than the trunk was tall, and moss hanging over everything so that things sounded softer, but there was a white wood house big in a clearing and shacks far behind it and behind them crops in the same

rows and rows I'd seen before, and nothing was really so different after all. Only the air hung heavier here and was saltier and
the cabin they put me in with some other slaves smelled sweet.

I got there in time to start planting, and though I didn't recognize the thick stems I was shuffling into the ground, I kept
my eyes down and moved my hands the way the men in front
of me moved theirs, and by the end of the first week, my back
felt the same as it ever had. Treehorn and his bullwhip stayed
with us in the fields and he was just as quiet as he had been driving the wagon, though his dog laugh came out sometimes. I
learned he liked jokes and dirty songs and whipping folks. We
nursed the big pole plants all through the summer and at some
point I learned to call them *caña* or sugarcane and to lie down
flat between the rows when Treehorn had left and suck the cut
stems until the sweetness hurt my teeth. In the fall, we toppled
the shoots, giants now that knocked and whispered when you
smoothed the ground beneath them, and we fed them into great
grinders, where the pulp of a man's arm now and again was
stirred into the syrup. The liquid we caught we kept in kettles
and boiled and skimmed and reboiled and mixed and waited and
with tired arms moved iron ladles from pot to pot and boiled
some more and always, always threw wood to the fire, which
burned for weeks and never slacked until the land around the
fields was bare of timber. From the sugar my master sold in barrels came the drippings he turned to rum; the barrels he rolled
downhill to boats in the Escambia, the liquor he distilled and
packed in stone jugs for paths north. After living there a year, I
could not stand the smell of sweet.

My master I only saw a few times a year when I was run up
to the house on some errand or other and on Christmas when

he came to the cabins to give us our gifts. He was a small man with a fat Spanish wife, and when they shouted at each other, they moved between their languages like they were searching for high ground. This used to be her farm, or was her father's, and when the English traded for West Florida a dozen years before, she held on to it by marrying this half-man, and no wonder they didn't much get along. Her family had kept cattle—we'd sometimes find pancakes of old dung in the turned-up earth— and she didn't understand why he'd switched to cane in this wilderness. They didn't have any children. His only friend was Treehorn, who he must have trusted like a brother for all he let him do, and him slipping his own bottles in to soak up some of Master's juice, which all saw and none spoke on.

Only when I turned sixteen did I learn Master's first name. The man he used to send to the Creeks with his rum had been shot dead through the gullet by the Choctaws and he needed a new one to ride his horse and carry his burdens—I'd caught his eye for seeming cheerful, there being nothing left to grieve over—and while I was standing in his front hall with my hat in my hands, being told of my new duty, his wife heaved onto the upstairs landing and said, "Josiah!" except it sounded to me like "Hosea." I was given a fast horse and a pass scrawled in two languages and was told which paths to follow to the Indian towns and I was never once told not to be afraid, so I went ahead and was. I'd been in Florida six years, and still didn't know where I stood.

My first trip, he launched me off at night. The crowding black trees on the trail looked so heavy I ducked my head for a mile, thinking they'd topple down, press me to death, at a single wind. I wasn't used to being sent out on my own, responsible for my own body but on behalf of another man. I had borrowed myself. The farther I got, of course, the straighter my head sat and the more I looked around at the wildness that swallowed the air, that choked it with musk and weeds. It didn't escape me that I was a black man on a horse. Would Primus be proud of me, or would he know something I didn't, about how the horse knew not to take me anywhere free, or about how I myself wasn't yet brave enough to run? I whistled so the owls wouldn't dive for me in the dark. Master had given me a note for a tavern that stood partway along the route, but I didn't trust this, so I took my horse two inches off the trail and burrowed behind a palmetto stand so that anyone who tried to get me would first send up a holy clatter. It was cold, and I was frightened of all the things I didn't know, and I thought of how my brother, long dead, would be halfway to freedom by now, how any red-blooded dark-skinned man would be leaping through swamp and bramble, scotch-hopping over alligator heads to get away from the scent of slavery. The bottom of a bog would be better land to stand on than this path that un-rolled like a limb from a sugar plantation. But there I was, arm's-length from the trading road, nervous to stray farther. I couldn't sleep that night, not knowing what my body should be doing.

But the morning brought other things to fuss over and fear, like the Indians that were waiting at the end of the path to take my master's rum and hand me money, and I didn't have high hopes for how that transaction would go. Master, who I now sometimes called Josiah in my head to bring him down to the size of other men, had told me not to mind about the language, that they would know what I was there for and as long as I didn't make a fool of myself I'd get out scratch-free. Don't move quickly, he'd said, and don't smile overmuch, for those teeth of yours are liable to fright them. I did in general smile more than I should, for it was easier than sorrow, of which there was enough to drown us if we opened our mouths to it. So all I knew was to stand still and frown and if they raised their bows at me I'd drop to the ground and cover my head so the arrows at that angle would have a difficult time finding purchase. This last I had thought about plenty.

As it turned out, the Indians were not wild animals, and they didn't have fangs or bared bottoms, and I saw no children boiled for supper. The men were mostly the same height as me and some smiled and some didn't, and one even shook my hand like an Englishman. I stayed with them for two days and though I only heard my language spoken a few times, we understood each other—they pointed where the river was for washing and showed me how to eat the acorn bread and in the evenings I played a game with the young ones where I threw a spear at a rolling stone, and every time it went sailing far past, they all laughed so hard that I thought I'd won. I even got to sample Josiah's liquor, which no white man would've ever let me do, so by the time I saddled up for home I had come to think of these men—not red at all but copper and brown, like the rest of us—as something more akin to me. They had slaves, but who didn't have slaves?

Those trips became dreams, where I like a witnessing bird could fly over strangeness, but it wasn't home, and it wasn't real. I was still mostly a boy, my heart still empty from my mother, and I thought finding family again was anyone's only intent. As far as I knew, life was just a rotten thing, and finding another person to take care of you—to cook your grits and comb out your hair and patch up the knees of your pants and maybe, if there was time, to sneak you a soft kiss—this was the only thing that made it bearable, for white and black men both. What was liberty without that? As I've said, I was very young and hadn't thought much through.

HER NAME WAS Beck, and she was more a woman than a girl, for she was older than me and had already had a husband, wed and buried. I would be gone to the Indians for a week once a month or so, and when I was home, in the time between stripping cane and sleeping, it wasn't hard to fall in love. She wore her hair in a purple wrap that came from I don't know where but it made her look like a queen, and she walked as tall and straight as one, no matter the curling lash marks round her calves. She took an interest in me in a motherly sort of way, but not at first seeing the mother in her sweetness, I took her gifts in the evening, biscuits and blue flowers and the fallen palm spines that looked like daggers.

She was the only one in the fields who wouldn't sing, and I figured she was saving her voice for something else, for someone, and I thought this very dignified. Maybe it was her being older that I found most lovable. I trailed her when she walked back to the cabins at night, I stood small behind a tree outside her window, hoping to catch the shadow of her undressing, I wrote a song for her that I never shared, believing she didn't like singing altogether. I wanted to hear another person's dreams again, for I had none of my own.

One night she came out with a cloth bundled up in her hand and warm. "For your vigil," she said, and walked back inside. I was hollowed out with shame; I unwrapped the cloth and found fried plantains, fresh from her skillet. She always knew I was there, since being a woman she had eyes in a ring around her head and could smell a man at fifty paces, but she didn't ask me to leave. I knocked on her door and she let me in and we ate plantains because I was too shy to feed them to her. She had skin that looked like she was always sitting near a fire, and I wanted so badly to put both my hands on her cheeks, just to feel them. She let me lie down on her pallet while she cleaned her dishes and tidied the two or three things she owned. It was dark, and the only home I had to return to was full of men, dank bodies stretched out, none of them knowing any piece of my past, despite having heard the whole story a hundred times. Here at least there was a woman, and didn't women hold the histories of all of us? I told her all sorts of things, stories about catching lizards by their tails, pretending to lose two of my fingers to scare my mother, about being six years old, and seven, and she puttered around, humming a little under her breath, like she knew I just needed to flush it all out of me and once I was done I'd be harmless again. I didn't even really notice that she was humming, which if I had thought about it was a kind of song. A while later she kicked me awake and told me to get on with myself, to scoot back to where I came from. I leaned in to kiss her, and she pushed me back and herded me right out of her cabin. I wonder what it is about these women that they put up with us for so long, don't ask for anything, just abide our selfishness. Maybe it's not so different from having a pet, an old hound dog that just licks itself and barks at snow.

I came back as often as I remembered something I had forgotten to tell her (I kept a list), and she'd listen and scrub her clothes in a pot of water and then hurry me along, and after a few weeks of this I had determined to marry her. She was already family, having all the knowledge now that any of my siblings did, and she was never unkind. This is all a man wants: familiarity and peace.

The first time I asked her I brought a fistful of yellow flowers and sat us down on the stoop of her cabin.

"What is this?" she said, pinning the purple cloth around her hair.

I made swampy eyes at her and handed over the sweat-heavy bouquet. I made more swampy eyes.

"Come on, now," she said. "Spit it or move along."

Did I say how kindly she was? Like Mother Mary herself, only firmer. I made my eyes get brimful of intention, I was so intentioned that all she'd have to do was say yes. But she kept looking at me like I was being peculiar, and I figured that maybe we didn't speak the same eye language after all, which wasn't a mark against her, it only made her more exotic. So I had to come right out and say it, with a lot of hacking and a hot face, not from being nervous but from being so certain.

"Marry you?" she said. "Marry you?" I repeated it to myself a hundred more times. She smiled and shook her head—not in a *no* kind of way, but because she was charmed—and I decided that we had reached an agreement.

"I'll call on you tomorrow," I said, to be formal.

"You can call whenever you like, little pup, it won't get you very far."

"We don't have to marry right away," I said, "but I'd better go ahead and tell Master, and then we can think about where our house should be." In other words, should our house be at my house, which was wall to wall with men, or her house, where there was a pallet and a pan for the fireplace and a good broom she already knew how to use. But I believed it was important to be polite in these matters.

She shook her head again, like a horse at the fence, like a mother over a cradle, and I knew better than to try again for a kiss, seeing as our love was holier than that, so I just squeezed her hand and stood and said, "We'll be happier than any man and wife has rights to be," and I marched off into the night again, proud, with only a hint left of loneliness.

I don't know how long she would have let me believe we were going to be married. When Treehorn found me in the fields and mentioned offhand that Master was going to wed me to one of Mr. Cunningham's negroes, I said that was all right, I had already picked a woman out for myself. I didn't know, for no one had ever told me, and my back took the brunt of it. When I slipped into Beck's cabin to have her hands soothe my wounds, she laughed and looked sad and said she wouldn't have me on no count and I should've made certain before making such a fool of myself. I told her she knew I loved her and she said she knew no such thing and that I better go find myself someone who would suit, for she had given up, at least in this world, on having any feeling again that even tasted like love.

I said I had feeling enough for both of us. And wasn't it my right, in the end, to love her? What did I know of rights?

On one of our last nights I asked her why she wouldn't have had me when there was a chance, and she took my chin in her hand and gave me her full direct stare, not swampy at all, but as kind as the best sort of lover. "Bob," she said, "little Bob. I've had my joy."

"You don't want any more than that?" I said, having never asked about the man who was her husband, never asked the widow any questions at all, really. (Months later, I'd learn from a gossipy old woman that Beck had had a baby, that the baby had lasted a year, and then one morning coddled in the quilt the baby just didn't open its eyes and its little chest stopped going up and down and though Beck and her still-alive husband shook it and shook it, it didn't wake up again. Oh, what did I know of children?)

"You'll see," she said. "Soon you'll be old enough to know what you want, and it'll take all of you to get it and hold it. It'll take all of you to keep on holding it, even after nothing's left. That's what all this is, just finding and then holding."

I thought her very stupid, because being young, I knew that the heart could hold a thousand things, that desire was endless, endless.

A MAN WANTS to communicate. There's no such things as stories told to no one. For a week or so after Beck said she wouldn't have me, I thought my heart would burn out of me, leaving an ashy hole in my chest. I laid down my cane knife so many times in the fields that my back bled each night from Treehorn's whip. I was in love with her, I told myself, full in love, and this is any man's broken heart. But that was only half true, because Beck was just a fancy in the end, just a marker I had used to measure how much I belonged, and when she didn't claim me I was cut loose, my lungs filling with water.

I lay in my cabin at night, cloths pressed to my back to soak up the splits in me, and it came to me that this world was a broken one, that all the humans I had ever loved were scarecrows, that all that was real was your own self. Beck was not a woman but just another test of myself, and I had failed. I didn't need a lover, or a mother, or a brother, because I had none and wasn't I still alive? Didn't the blood on my back prove it? This was what I learned those nights, that I am the only thing I can ever know. And this life, the way it was set up with its cabins and fields, its rounded women and its whips, this was all meant to put you in a kind of order, to connect you to a bunch of other things with little strings that called themselves fondness and fear. Those strings weren't real at all, because someone else strung them up. *I* wouldn't've chosen to hack all day at cane stalks with a dull knife. Wasn't *my* rum or money that went back and forth between white hands and Indian hands. Come to think of it, I thought, bent in a crook of pain between two snoring men, this wasn't my life at all.

Primus had it right. Get yourself a new life, a free one, make things that no one else can claim. Don't give your hands to any man; don't give your heart, which is worse. What was he doing, wherever he was, now that he was dead? It wasn't what I was doing: giving, giving, and hurting. No, he had it right. Not the rope around the neck, but the farm out west. So what if you were alone? You're always alone. Out there, won't be any scarecrows to fuddle you. I had to stop letting these worms in my heart.

I wiped my nose on my wrist, leaving a little slug trail, and started tracing my house in the dust on the floorboards. The men kept snoring. It would be this wide, and this long, with a porch along the south edge and a pen for the mule. Here was the blueberry field, and here the lake for swimming. Here were the miles and miles of emptiness all around it, not a white man or Indian in sight. Did I really believe it, even then? Remember that I was a cheerful boy.

. . .

SO A WOMAN was brought from Mr. Cunningham's like a mare
on a rope, and we were given our own cabin and the master's
blessing and left alone to carry on our fine bonded race. Her
name was Winna and she was about my age and I couldn't love
her quite the same, though I don't think she knew, or maybe
minded.

Turns out a body can't get settled into aloneness at the tip of
a hat. I hated Master for pairing me up with a woman I'd never
seen in my life, but damn me if I didn't try to cling to her those
first few weeks. Poor child, I'd hug on her and tell her stories
and then next thing, I'd be kicking her and telling her no, get
out, she wasn't real and didn't hardly matter. She had a worse
temper than Beck, and didn't just hum along when I got in a
mood. Those early months we picked at each other and fussed
and did our own chores not speaking, and sometimes talked
about general things, and once she let me try to braid her hair,
which was a challenge but I never balked at learning something
new.

I had just gotten back from another trip to the Indians when
she told me she was pregnant. This was an ordinary thing, it
was no mystery what had brought it about, but we both looked
at each other like we had found something dead in the room and
we didn't know which of us had killed it.

"When's it coming?" I said.

"In a bit."

I put my satchel on the chair and pulled out my road-soiled
clothes and the husk doll some Creek child gave me and then
shook out the crumbs of biscuit from the bottom of the bag.

"You better sweep that up," she said.

"Is it jumping around yet?" I pointed at her belly.

She looked down, surprised.

Did my father, whoever he was, have this conversation with my mother? Were children always such dreaded things, like the other side of ghosts? I didn't ask how Winna felt, or if she'd had a father.

Going to sleep that night, or trying to go to sleep—shutting my eyes tight against the sounds outside, the katydids and the man who wandered sleepless, muttering in a Spanish that was part African—in the trying to sleep I often found half truths, or quarter truths, like colored beads in my head. Wasn't this seed of a baby a sign that I was grown now, that I had no more need to be lonely of my mother or my lost siblings, but could find company in the family I built my own self? Isn't this what happened to people who lived long enough to get older? The man outside was chanting now. I understood when he said *Dios* and *caña*, but otherwise nothing.

When I thought about a little person coming into this world who would see things as I saw them, who would crouch in a pen looking at the far fields for a glint of his mother, it grew in my head that this life was not just a single thing, mine alone, but was a big circle that rolled over on itself again and again, that what struck me with pain would strike my child too, that this was not a life but a system, and for the first time my boyish grief took on the color of rage. I didn't just want my people back; I wanted out.

This was what Primus meant by the farm. How to get free of everything that made you not yourself but something else: a slave, a husband, an orphan, unloved. Primus's dream, then, wasn't only his. He wouldn't mind if I stole it.

I was still young, nineteen maybe, and so these thoughts were just quarter thoughts there in the smoke-smelling night, they'd take years still to grow, but that's where they came from: those women and that first whisper that I had made a whole other life again out of nothing. Damn me and every other slave that had done it, but there it was. The wheel rolling over on itself again.

IT WAS WHEN she was full with the second baby, and I was maybe twenty-one, that the unsettlings of the white men boiled over. And the Indians, I should say. I had picked up a few words by then, but while I was saying *hesci* and *estonko*, the Creeks were raising the conversation to something I couldn't make sense of, other than that war was involved, which all the musket-cleaning made clear. I still couldn't have told you their names, but being in their town with no fences, with folks who didn't want anything from me other than my master's drink, this let me step back a little and breathe something close to free air. They started sending me home with messages along with the skins, and if I knew anything about reading, I would've learned that the fighting that had been surging around to the north of us was headed south, and that the Spanish wanted their land back.

Standing in the hall of the big house, waiting to be sent home to wash the road off my clothes, I could hear Master and his lady squabbling upstairs, fast-talking over each other about who owned what and whether they still had friends in the West Indies.

The Spanish came, spring of 1781, just when the baby was ready to pop out. We were north enough of Pensacola to escape the siege, though Master had to stop carting things to the port for a few months. We waited and got news from folks who'd fled, black and white alike, war being the time when what you were supposed to do melted into what you *could* do. A woman snuck into the quarters one night and was queen for the evening as she told us all she'd seen. Cannon aimed both north and south, ships in the bay shooting at the forts (which we heard all the way from here), storms lashing about (which wetted us too), Indians running supplies both ways, not having decided who would be best for neighbors. "I even saw black men," she said, "in *uniforms*," and she stood up with her arm across her chest, formally, to show us she knew what a uniform was. "All six feet tall, and *handsome*." They were fighting for the Spanish, so we cheered for the Spanish, not knowing the difference but what we saw in our owners: our British master pale and simmering, his wife a round ball of fire.

Soon the sky to the south quieted down and the low booms stopped keeping us up at night, and then the barrels of sugar that came out of our farm were stamped with different words. All our neighbors moved to islands in the Gulf or back to England, while we pretended we were always Spanish, our mistress suddenly the figurehead again on her own farm. We lived because we pretended to have always been what we were not; we were spared because we spoke their language and were content. And so the lesson of the slave became the lesson of his master.

THE SECOND BABY came as soon as the British left, like she was waiting for quiet, though she died before the day was out, and a year or two later there was another baby, and still I bent every day in the fields with my cane knife, still I carried the hot ladle of syrup from kettle to kettle, still I waited for Master to send me to the Creeks with a wagon of rum, and still I stuck to that northward path, only pulling off to sleep in peace. Winna and I settled into ourselves and became friendly, for of all the things we were fighting in our lives, it wasn't worth fighting each other. I came to have a great affection for her, which some days is better than love.

By the time Beck was sold, no one knows where, I had settled my heart enough to say goodbye without any scene, because this was familiar after all, this was just the wheel turning. I saw her most days in the field and we said hello and asked the simple questions but that was all. You know how you can love someone for years without any hope, and this is all right, a little pain but mostly pleasure, and how you just wait for it to grow old like a dog and pass on? And it does, it weakens and turns to normal, and you and the woman you love are old friends after all, though sometimes when you see her breasts exposed to the whip for rudeness, your sorrow is struck through with a rare tenderness that goes past friendship. So maybe love never passes on, maybe it just covers itself over, curls into a seed, waits.

With her gone, all the strong feelings in me were sleeping.

WHEN OUR YOUNGEST baby was just a few months old, she got a coughing sickness that scared the granny enough to tell Treehorn, which I don't know that Winna would have done. Treehorn was fickle, but he had a fondness for babies. Master being in a good mood, he sent the white doctor to our cabin, a man who showed up not when the dysentery came or when a field hand got caught in a bear trap, but when Master had woken up in a sunny patch and was feeling kindly.

Me and Winna stood in the corner, arms crossed, as the doctor turned our baby over and patted her back, looked in her mouth, felt for lumps along her side. The baby cried the whole time, and I knew without looking that Winna was crying too. The sight of those white hands, clammy as skinned fishes, on the cool dry brown of our baby—it seemed like he'd leave a stain on her. He wasn't there for long, and after he named the sickness and dropped our baby back on the mattress like a corn sack, he gave us a rub to put on her chest and left the way he came, without looking at any of our eyes.

We sat down, and Winna was small and hunched, so I put my arm around her and then scooted over so my shoulder would warm up her shoulder. She was still crying, so I patted her back and then squeezed her neck, and when I bent my head to kiss her cheek, she just snuffled, so I kissed her face all over until she was crying harder, and for some reason this was a good thing. The baby was quiet now and we were the noisy ones. Her face all wet in my hands was like a body fresh from swimming, pure and good, and it made me think how right it was for Primus to do what he did over a creek, so that his shape would be reflected in the water and would be made innocent again. And I felt a wash of love for him that carried over to the woman beside me, the way you can see a rabbit in the cane and it's so rounded and sweet that when you turn back to see the broken-in face of the man next to you, it doesn't seem as cruel. All our bodies are curved by God the same way he curves everything else good in the world.

Her body was round and fit in my rounded hands, and I tried to promise myself that I'd always treat her like she was my only true love. She wasn't like Beck, she didn't humor me, she didn't listen when I talked, but so be it, maybe I talked too much.

The baby was asleep, and we were down beside her, our arms tangled up and Winna's face smooth now, shiny with old tears.

"I'm sorry," she said, quiet.

"You didn't do anything."

"For putting you in this place. For being a woman that a man had to marry."

I hushed her and pulled her close, but I didn't say, "Not your fault," or even "I accept your apology," because a little pinch of me still felt that maybe she was right to say she was sorry, so I wasn't going to stand in her way.

The baby wouldn't live through the week, but we didn't know that then, thinking we were lucky to have had the white doctor, loathsome as he was. Lucky for the scrap thrown our way.

That night when the man outside wandered by with his Spanish song, I mumbled some of the words along with him, keeping my voice low so as not to wake all the women in my house.

I HAD HEARD of slaves who lost their limbs one at a time for missing tobacco leaves in the field, men who were bred with women like bulls, women who were bent over by white men and taken like whores, children whose knuckles were broken by white women with canes and irons and rocking chairs. I had heard of slaves who were brought into the great house and given new clothes and fresh meat three times weekly and passes on Saturdays to see kin and were trained to make a living, the coins for horse-shodding and gun-fixing and egg-selling being their own. I was not the one or the other. I would not make a tale for the ladies to weep over, nor could I buy my freedom after three years and build a house next to my master's and share carriages to town. I had heard just enough through field tales and night meetings to know that I was not so good or bad off, which should have been something to find comfort in except it meant I had nothing much to complain about and nothing much to hope for. I was the ordinariest of slaves. (If white men were ever so ordinary, they'd die in a day.)

Four more years passed, and two more children, one that stayed alive and one that grew in Winna's belly and then shrunk again and let herself out of the womb in a little sweep of blood. You learned where to step and what to say, and when the whippings came, you took them because that's just what white men did. They couldn't tell what you were thinking of when your back was being split: what color welts a brand might raise on their own grub-pale skin. You treated your wife good, you chased the little ones in the yard at night so they'd get worn out before bed, you ate as much meat as you could get on Sundays but not enough to hurt your belly. Some did it as a way to get to heaven, since God seemed particular about those things; the way I acted, you'd think I listened hard at church. I was old enough now to see both the wrongness in a life and the comfort that comes from staying in it. "You want to make it alive each day," Winna would say, "that's it." But I knew that wasn't all anyone ever wanted, because my brother'd had a burning wish, and it had nothing to do with being alive, because he'd scratched that off quick.

Sometimes I thought back to those black men in uniforms, those handsome men who had held guns during the siege and won. They were a piece of something beyond this broken wheel. The way they carried their guns in my head, I could tell they were on their way to farms out west, land they owned because they owned themselves. Whether they died at Pensacola or not, they had those guns, had themselves.

I wouldn't know my heart from my hands till I was gone from

this. *Free*, I started muttering quiet in the rows. *Free*, though I didn't know how to get it.

It was a small step from thinking about it to talking about it, my mouth being what it was, so I started sharing little bits with Winna, trying to figure out where she stood. Well, she stood firmly in that cabin with those children, that's where. She took to knocking me on the head whenever I started out with "But what if——," and told our two girls not to pay any heed. The more she said no, we'd be dead before we were free, the more I thought about Primus and knew that being dead and being free were just about equal, and both better than what we had. I was like a man with a pick, just whiling away the time on a block of stone.

"If the moon were——," I'd say, and "Master'll be traveling next——"

I started talking to other folks: a man named Mingo who knew the roads, and a woman who'd seen her son slip beneath a wagon blanket and get trotted off who-knows-where.

"But he hasn't sent word?" I'd say.

"He hasn't wound up back here, has he?" she'd say. "That's all the word I need."

ON THE FIRST night of March, I slid from under Winna's arm, grabbed my pants and the shirt that used to be a flour sack until it wasn't even good enough for that, carried my shoes with their tongues flapping, stepped over two sprawled children breathing heavy as pull mules, and made a whistle as I slipped through the door so it sounded like the trees breathing out. I sat on the top stoop with the pipe I'd filched from Master's nephew, who left his things around when he visited and never seemed to wonder where they went. The night was warm and jangled with stars, like the Lord was shining a spotlight on me and saying, "Bob, you settle now. You couldn't move an inch without the whole world seeing." So I smoked instead, my shoes empty next to my feet.

Just as my eyes were closing, which is easy to do in spring when the air smells soft and bloomy, I heard Winna sneaking out, stepping past those sleeping bodies, slipping through the door with the same little whistle. She squatted down next to me and rocked on her heels a couple times to stretch them out. I smelled the char on her skin from cooking and it smelled like the stars being snuffed out one by one, a silent hand turning the night smoky.

"Boy, you're a damn fool," she said. "Where'd you get that pipe?"

"Ain't no pipe." I tossed it in the dirt under the porch. Night was the only time we could talk, and it made everything we said sound like the last time we'd say it.

"And where are you going with those shoes?"

I reached my arm out for her arm, but she shied away and stood up.

"Uh-uh, no sir. I'm just about done."

I rubbed my hands on my face and asked for maybe the tenth time if she'd run with me some day, knowing all the words but needing to hear them to keep my insides from running off without me.

She kneeled in front of me, her dust-blue shift in the brown dirt. "We got two children, Bob, if you don't recall, and Polly can't go more than a few steps without whining, and damned if I'm carrying her on my back for a hundred miles."

"Oh, it'd be longer than a hundred——"

"Hush up. If they go, we'll all get caught and strung up some-where, and if they stay— Well, I'm not leaving them here."

I looked at her hands on my knees and tried to remember why it was bodies like us got married at all, if marriage is what it's called. Why we let ourselves be taught that this is life, that this is what loving feels like.

She stood up and circled around herself a few times, her hands on that thin waist, her skirt scuffling around her legs. She did this when she was thinking, and sometimes when she was mad and she wouldn't tell me about what. "Honey," she said and stopped, and I sat up on my heels to hear her. "I want them to be safe."

"Not free?" I said.

"Safe," and she looked at me sad.

I heard her, I did, but we looked at things from opposite sides of the river. I thought I loved my children as much as anyone else, and I wanted them to live on their own land earning their own wage, same as me. If I'd risk my limbs cutting over night fields to earn that other kind of life, I figured the same went for them, and if they were caught and killed God knows I'd weep along with the rest, but wasn't that the entirety of the point, that we were putting up all we got against the chance of something better? I wanted for them what I wanted for me, but she wanted something else.

In the end they were not mine, they were hers. Being a mother meant that she'd always be a half-step closer to them, and what-ever I said on the matter would eventually sink to the bottom of that river we were talking through. I can't say I understood it. I knew women who had cut for it some night or other with their babies on their backs, and others who had left theirs behind, and one who stole a white baby to take with her, don't know if out of love or mischief or both, but I surely knew that mothers were nothing alike.

"Come on back to bed," she said, and she had stopped circling but her skirts still swayed. "Better go on and enjoy what you got while it lasts."

I took her meaning and grabbed her ankle and let her drag me inside again.

IN THE MORNING, windy warm, we rose up like children still sleeping, our actual children out cold on the dirt floor, and with our pudding arms we dressed and fried quick cakes. On those mornings I could never quite tell when it was that my eyes first opened. I thought it was just in time to see Winna stir the hominy with her snake-brown arm, her eyes still closed, and then the first bell rang and I kicked the little ones awake with a soft foot and I thought, *Today is the last day*, which is what I now thought every morning that rose with a sun. We were sowing in the fields today, and the women weeding, and my arms went out and down into the dirt and my legs stretched to hold me and sometimes bent and my head was heavy and flicked around to keep the flies from settling and my hands flinched in cramps every now and then so I had to stop and squeeze them, which was what we all did, in stages, so the whole long line of us was like a caterpillar heaving.

When the sun crawled a foot farther above the low stepped hills leading down to our flatness, the women broke for feeding and I saw Winna walk back as straight as a paling to the yard where the little ones were lined up at the fence beneath the shaking palms, staring out like they expected to see a shower of squirrels fall from the sky, and they reminded me of something, all in a line like that, their hands wrapped around the rails, their bare toes fiddling around in the sand. Our youngest was on her bottom, arms stretched up like two sunflower heads turning in the midmorning, searching out her mother. I stopped long enough to see Winna cradle her up fast, like business, if there was a business that lasted your whole life long, and I thought, *God damn it, that woman is no longer mine.* And then Treehorn stood between me and the vision of her and spoke through a pink mouth and my mouth replied—words used so often they didn't even make sounds in my head anymore—and I moved on down the row without looking at her again, the bent back in front of me filling my sight, turning the yellow day cotton-colored.

At the noon bell we laid our tools down, all whole and new since the last breakage half a year ago for which Cuffee took all the blame and the whipping, and I took my bowl of ladled greens and sat next to my wife and looked at her straight, my two eyes in her two eyes, and I said, "What keeps me here?"

She shook her head. I waited for her to speak, but she just looked at me with sad eyes that were masking as sure-of-themselves and I nodded and touched her knee and let it go and lifted my spoon to my mouth. "I'm not going to give you speeches," she said, and I knew.

THAT NIGHT I left Winna with the children, she stitching shirt-holes shut by candlelight and them wrestling and tugging at each other's pigtails, and I moved like Panther chasing Antelope, creeping on paws to Mingo's cabin. We shared a cup of parched-corn coffee and talked in whispers about the long roads north and west and even the boats he'd heard about that would take a man wrapped up in the hold over water. I said it sounded too risky, putting your black body in white hands on a white boat, and he said he knew plenty who had done it and one who forged his papers and now tailored in Baltimore. I voted for west; I didn't walk around calling myself a clever man, but what little I knew about this world was that east was just ocean and then the darkness again, where boys got snatched riverside and brought right back over.

But Mingo had a cousin in Boston. He was firm bound to get up there and had gotten hints where to stop along the way, like "this barn" and "that creek hollow," though it seemed to me if enough people knew about it then they all probably did, slave-snatchers included. I was listening, though, for I wouldn't know enough to get myself out of gunshot range, north or south, but would probably follow a possum instead, let her lead me in circles till we were all perched in a pine, me nursing her young. He said his cousin ran a shop where colored folk bought shoes and sometimes got their hair cut all at the same time. Said he had a sign out front that hung by a gold chain, "T. Brown, Cordwainer, Tonsor," and that when you moved to Boston, you could claim a surname, could draw one up out of thin air and even call your own self "mister."

"But I don't know how to make shoes," I said, and he leaned back in the one straw chair and fiddled along his legs for ticks.

"They probably teach you. Or you do something else, something you're good at."

"I'm fair at planting cane," I said.

He shook his head and said, "You'll learn something. They've got plenty of boats up there that need loaders, if nothing else."

But I couldn't stop thinking about the everything else out west that sounded better than the nothing else up north, and hauling cotton bales from shore to ship didn't ring the same as tilling my own land and resting in the evening in a house I built myself and owned and the wages of it all coming to me and no one else. I had inherited that want. He told me about the houses in Boston, which were back-to-back brick, and the harbor that was always moving and the white men that spent all day in thought and the black women that walked about free and fancy. By then the candle stub was worn out.

I snuck out the same way I came in, on paws, and they were asleep then except the littlest, who was sitting up in a pile of blankets and sucking on the end of her shirt, eyes looking like it was morning. I kissed her nose and nudged her with my foot into lying down and crawled in beside my wife, who was new-asleep and still breathing shallow and her body was so warm I wrapped around it like moss, wishing never to leave, and outside the man who'd lost his mind went by singing songs no one understood.

In the morning I said we needed to talk once and for all and if it was the last time, that's the way it was, and that night we asked Granny to sit with the children and I held Winna's hand and walked her to the near woods, where, under the pines, the new March leaves of the turkey oaks shone like falling stars: yellow-green, with catkins for tails.

SHE LET ME go. She said in the woods that she loved me fine but she already made a life and it was here and it was in those two children and her duty to them was holier than any desire of her own. I understood, because it was those children who had shown me what a rotten wheel this all was, and if my needs were precious, so too were theirs. I said I'd come back for her some day and she smiled and said not to bother, that she'd probably have a new man by then, and she tucked her head into my chest and kissed my chin under the last longleaf pines not cut for timber, just a stand of them and our love underneath, and I knew it was love after all.

Winna had these eyes that looked like someone dropped honey in molasses—they had shots of golden all in them. Primus had the same eyes, striped eyes, and I didn't know where they got them, except that maybe they were just shards of white folks creeping in, but those eye sparks always made me think that they knew something I didn't, that they'd come to a purpose that I hadn't. And for all Winna and Primus weren't anything alike—one just a woman after all and the other the best man I knew—they sure did know what they were after, and knowing was most of the way to having.

Though my eyes were as muddy as the rest of me, still I was moving myself, picking my body up out of the days of kneeling and cutting and stirring and not feeling much one way or the other, and taking it to an elsewhere that was unknown. I was making a choice, and if I never saw Winna or Primus's ghost in my dreams again, I'd find them in the place where people go who move their life with their own hands.

I DIDN'T WAIT for Mingo. The night after I talked with my wife and held her head under my head, Master sent me to the Indians with only one stone jug and a sheaf of letters that he called important. I stuffed my sack with boiled eggs and lace cookies I'd snatched from the kitchen and a stolen knife, and

I rode that horse slow up the trail that led from Master's sugar fields through the cotton of his neighbors who weren't so foolish and money-hungry as to plant cane on these sandy flats, and our steps fell into the dust prints of all the other steps I'd taken this way, and to the horned owls watching, it looked like this journey was no different from the others, that my horse and I would come back in a few days the same as ever. But I went slower. Maybe so as to look less like a runaway, but maybe so now I could watch everything that went past.

I didn't have much of a plan, for I thought that my mission being as righteous as it was, fate or something similar would point me where I needed to go, would guide me past the traps and men waiting with nets, right up the shoulder of a child to safety. In my mother's telling, Antelope made it to heaven every time.

I figured I had a week before they came after me. The slower I rode along this road, the more I thought to myself how I looked like a justified man, a man with rights of riding, and beyond the fact that this perhaps drew no suspicion, it made me feel like I had chosen justly. I was a just man riding a right path, and the burning of my blood kept me from falling weary. When the dawn reared up, I was halfway through the now-Spanish lands, trailing the Escambia and unperturbed. Once a burned-looking man passed on horseback and we nodded and I kept on walking that horse slow and I was beginning to be almost certain that I was the owner of this road, that river.

I never noticed how many kinds of trees there were along that path—not just the trembly palmettos, but taller palms, and low, bendy oaks, and trees with smooth bark and toothy leaves. I still didn't know most of their names, after living among them for how many years. They could've been my children, clearly different one from the other but only if you looked close, and still in all their beauty they didn't mean anything to me, didn't do anything but shade me on the path, and me not even grateful for the shade. I would make a point to write her and say I was sorry, once I made it someplace where they could teach me to write.

When the sun was straight up, I fell back from the trail into a patch of scrub to eat the hoecakes Winna made for me, and I wondered why she didn't cry and I wondered if I wished she would've. It was a warm day with clouds, which I noticed when I was thinking of things to be grateful for. When the sun sank again, I was back in an English world. Turns out all you needed was a knife and an open road and a choice. I passed a group of boys, six or seven of them, who were laughing and leaping on each other and tripping along the sides of the trail and I wasn't sure whether they were white or Indian, but they were headed south and unconcerned, and even when their small bodies were gone I heard their voices like they were caught in the brambles, slowly unraveling.

That night, I tied my horse to a branch before I lay down in the lap of a live oak and burrowed my legs in wet leaves, for in March the night still had wind in it. I slept for a little while, then woke to rustling, then slept longer and dreamed of treeless land stretched out like a green quilt forever, past the edge of any land, so there wasn't even a horizon, just land and land.

I woke into full sun and I opened my still-tired eyes into the blue eyes of another man who had my arms clamped to my chest between his knees and was crouched over me like a lover, holding my knife to my throat.

March 6–8, 1788

Bob

HIS EYES ARE blue as beads and his wrist bone so small I think of biting to snap it but his chest is going fast and I reckon he might have the dog madness so I stay rock still and let his short breaths puff in my face, the knife dizzy in his hands. He doesn't speak and I don't speak and we sit there for a while, each figuring, and when his face goes in shade from the sun passing behind a cloud, his knees droop and he drops his hand down and with his un-knifed hand he wipes beneath his nose like a boy. I breathe in big to watch his thin self rise on my chest and he looks such a sight perched like a bird with one claw that I try not to laugh, though having a white man this close has dried up all the shit in me. I roll him over and we stand up and brush our dust off and his hand is loose enough that it doesn't seem to mind me easing the knife back into my own.

I pull out my pass to show him, my hand still shaking, but his hand still shaking won't take it, and I reckon neither of us can read anyway. I don't know which of us should be most scared, a slave or a robber.

"You ain't patrol?" I ask.

He opens his mouth, but a rumble from his stomach rolls out of it and he claps his hand to cover it like he still has shame.

"Doesn't take a knife to get some food," I say. I break out some bread and hand it over and he eats head down.

When I look around to pour some water for the horse is when I notice there isn't a horse left or right. "What the hell? You take my horse?"

He shakes his head. "Tried to," he says. "Ran away."

"You tried to crawl up on it with your skinny arse and it bolted? That it? Good *lord*." I walk out into the road and try a few whistles and a *hey-up* to see if it's near, but even when I'm quiet I can't hear the sound of a leaf break anywhere. "How long ago'd you pull this?"

"Still night when I did."

"Damn it. And you just been sitting on me since?"

"Thinking, one way or the other."

I'm two days into running away and lost my horse. If I believed in God very much or anything like signs, I'd take this as a bad one. Nothing to do but walk now.

He follows me quiet when I move back onto the path with my road-hungry feet.

"Where you going?" I ask, but he has a finger in his mouth, poking around at the food that's left, not wanting to miss a bite. "Scoot!"

I don't look back for a quarter of an hour, and I try to whistle a little to show how unconcerned I am about white men. But soon someone passes us on a horse—not mine, I check—and gives us such a peculiar twice-over look that I worry I'm standing out worse than ever this way, with no better than a hound dog trailing after me. I turn around, and he stops so sudden I think he might tilt over.

What cause does a white man have to be hungry?

"I'm going up this way," I said, pointing ahead, "and then that way," my finger crooking off to the left.

He nods.

If I tell him to go away, or if he doesn't and I knock him on the head, he'll wake up and tell someone there's a nasty slave on the loose, pass or no pass. And if I let him drag on behind me without paying any mind, he'll try to kill me again as soon as I sleep. Maybe he's hungry or maybe he's crazy, or might be he's just looking for a way to get close to a soul, and I know what that's like after you walk a road for days without speaking. It's a relief I'm half again as big as he, and that my knife's back in my own pocket.

"You got a family?"

He nods his head, then shakes it.

"No? You own any slaves?"

Shakes it.

"Not one? Okay. Me neither. You going to try to kill me again?"

Nope.

"What do they call you?"

He looks up in the trees like he heard an uncommon rustling, eyebrows pinched, and then says, still looking, "Cat."

I never knew if that's what he saw or that's who he was.

So I call him Cat, and it feels a comfort to have another body on my side, as if someone said my journey was all right, no harm in it, no folks abandoned. Lonely, one can feel a guilt, can even forget where the road ends, but this little white man keeps me thinking of each hour as it comes, wondering if he'll turn me in or say he's a murderer or do a shuffle dance with a smile on his face, for all are as likely as the others.

He walks always a couple feet to the side and back, making me look like the master, which suits me fine. If you put a confidence on your face, people stop looking at you. There are enough funny-colored men on this path that I'm not so clear a runaway, and having a white man along never hurts. I've seen Indians dark as me trading slaves who looked like they had two white parents. Down here, color all depends on who you know, what people you can call your kin. But my plan is to walk until kin doesn't matter either, way out where the only colors are blue sky and brown ground and us humans are so little on the land, gnats, that you can hardly tell whether we're dark or light. When I find the westward road, it won't be any problem just shooing Cat on his way, and if he begs to come, I'll rope him to a tree and leave him with a solid meal and maybe a whistle so he can call for help when I'm well enough away. For now, he'll suit.

I set us up under an old oak for lunch, its roots billowing out like a dress mid-swing, and I give him a side of bread though not half, me being the leader of this all. He's gnawing away quiet, teeth not even meeting teeth, when a man looking more properly white drags a mule past us and then stops and turns on his heel right around, the mule backing up startled on its legs. He looks at Cat and me with pointy eyes and says, or more like growls, that he's looking for a man run away from murder, small and blue-eyed, who's known to have blood on his breeches and comes from up north, maybe Carolina, or else Delaware.

He's talking to Cat, who's still chomping on his bread and doesn't say anything. I won't lie and say my heart didn't go cold a little. But it only takes me a minute to look at one white man, dirt-thin and quiet, and then the other, who looks like he'd arrest any man who was cross-eyed, and figure out which one I'll line up with. I give a big spit like I don't care and say, "Haven't seen no man with such breeches. This here's my master, deaf and dumb. Been his slave for twenty-odd year and never left West Florida, him or me."

"You in West Georgia now, boy."

"Never left West Georgia neither."

"What's your farm called?"

I say a few words in Spanish that translate to something like "Sugar Whip God," and that sounds enough like a plantation to make him ask next where we're headed.

"Horse market," I say. "Couple mares died on us. Run 'em rough down there." I don't know where you get horses, but I suppose at a market like anything else. "That's a nice one," I say, pointing at his patchy old mule. "You selling?"

He squints at me and his bottom lip is tucking in and out of his teeth like he's thinking on it and he turns to Cat and asks, "You deaf?"

I hold my breath, but Cat doesn't even glance at him. I don't know whether he's protecting me or himself, or if he's as much an idiot as I'm pretending.

"*You deaf?*" he asks again louder, and Cat just sitting there chewing that damn piece of bread a hundred times.

"He was fine for many years, sir, but afore he was out of short pants he stood too close to a church bell and the ringing busted his ears all up. Hasn't said a word since." I'm real polite, not knowing at that point how high up church bells are, but the man must not know either because he says, "That right," like it isn't every day he sees such a thing, and he spits and turns again and drags that mule right on down the road, the two of them kicking up shoots of dust behind.

I send up a praise to Jesus and study Cat, whose white arms are hatched now with the branch shadows from above, this place we've stopped looking more, in fact, like church than trail. His brows don't even bend, his eyes still as stones under clear water.

"You kill a man?" I ask, and he doesn't look at me but shakes his head slow, back and forth.

"Not a man," he says, and his voice is hoarse.

"Well, that's a relief," I say and decide not to bully the point, though he is small and blue-eyed and I did first meet him when he was trying to cut my throat. That'll teach a man to fall asleep on the road. "You from Carolina?" I ask, but this is bullying, which I said I wouldn't do, and sure enough he doesn't make a peep to answer. I'll figure it out in time. If he had a reason to kill some old man up in Carolina, doesn't mean he'll go around shooting people willy-nilly. Just because I ran away from one place doesn't mean I'll run from another.

I'm all done eating before he's finished with those slow chews so I clean up our little patch, brushing crumbs from the root hollows like it was a table with linen to keep clean. I told myself I wouldn't get too wild, wouldn't lose those things that made me a man, like talking civil and cleaning myself and watching out for the weaker ones. Winna claimed I'd turn back to animal, hunched over creeks like a dog for water and tearing at raw bones, but she never saw I was climbing up from slave, not down from man. I won't say she was happy being bound on that land, which maybe wouldn't be fair, but she did see herself as living a life, like anyone else would, which I couldn't see for trying. Wasn't a life at all, just a way of dying.

The leaves of the live oaks, fallen last, start rustling up in the afternoon, it still being March and tending toward cool when the sun dips out. In the walking, I'm working my way toward a direction. It's not as straight as you'd first figure, for though the farm in my head lies between here and where the sun dies, the trail runs north, and my story of still being my master's man will fade out not many miles farther, and then what face will I put on, what food on my tongue? So I reckon as I walk, and I'm just as glad for the cover of a white man, however stickish and shifty.

Only when we collapse into the evening, color of a mourning dove, and shuffle our leaf piles for pillows a tossed rock's distance from the road do I think more carefully of the man looking for the murderer, the white man with his mule and his eyes searching. He could've been a man looking for me, there'd surely soon be men looking for me, and I hadn't even been sharp enough to know to be afraid. Of Cat, yes, but not of him. Mingo could've said something easy, or maybe Winna gave me up to get better bread for the girls. I'm not a brave man, though I've done what brave men do, and if I spoke to myself and was honest, I'd say I haven't thought things through. I think I can scamper off some-hundred miles and no one'll mind? No one will come hunting to fetch back their property, what they paid plenty dollars for? I'll be found and dragged, sure enough, straight back to the cane fields, and when I'm there, all worn out from the dragging, they'll make Winna watch my whipping and give her whatever bits of me they slice off. I lie down fidgety and in three seconds Cat is snoring and the sky has dressed itself in fast black and a rabbit is thumbing its nose through the scramble of brush between my feet, and I am now fully afraid. I can't shake the picture of my fingers, one by one, getting lopped off and passed on to my wife, who's long since disowned me. And it's not a guess or a what-if, but a firm truth, that I will die if here and now I don't prevail. And even short of death, what chance do I have without a single coin to pay my way? Am I just going to take that farm for free? My dream grew like a straight tall weed in the dirt around the slave cabins, bloomed as yellow as a hope, and I plucked it and stuck it in my breast patch and carried it gleaming down the road of my deliverance, and now, two days' hard walk from home, or the opposite of home, my weed is slumped and wilting and through its browning petals asks me what the hell I expect.

A night bird lets out a whistle above my head, its call stretched thin at the end, like someone was squeezing it through his hands. I tuck up my legs tight to my chest, scaring off the rabbit, and know my flower's dead; only God and his miracles will see me through alive.

The people I have loved aren't taking this walk—my mother, stolen from me; my brother, who stole himself; my children, who don't know what it means to steal. My outside eyelids are closed tight, because it's nighttime and I should be sleeping, knowing what a long walk I have tomorrow and every day after that, but there are some kind of inside eyelids that keep fluttering up and won't close, no matter how hard I try to squeeze them. Winna's in my head now, the woman I never loved more than myself, and she's pointing straight on, away from her belly, away from white sugar, from black bodies, westward, and I am going, if the Lord doesn't take me first, and I'm starting to think he will.

I WALK MORE timid in the morning. I am almost resolved that Cat will kill me after all, and then I turn my head quick and he's wiping a tear from his eye or gnawing on the side of his thumb, and if he's not an idiot then I'm the one fooled. I tell him what the plan is, which is that even though we're both free and honorable men, with a wink, best that we hide ourselves if ever there's likely to be trouble. No telling how many bounty hunters are maundering around, or who they're keeping eyes out for. So instead of pretending to be mighty today, we step a little more quiet and over to one side, in the dip that runs along the trail, so that we can scoot up the bank into the bushes if we hear a horse train coming. The plan is really that I'll just keep putting feet in a long straight row toward north, hoping I'll know when the left turn'll be. I ask Cat if he's ever been in this part of the world before, and he shakes his head.

"Your home look anything like this?" I try to picture where he comes from, what rocky hills or barren plain gave rise to such a flint of a man, because he's sure been traveling days. "You ever see a big old stretch of meadow, no trees or anything, with no white folks anywhere near? Maybe west of here? You been west of here?"

He shakes his head.

I don't push him. Sometimes it looks like he's been crying for a week and just left off. I keep talking to him, because talking is how to cross over all the big holes in the world.

A shuffling up ahead sends us over the bank, and while we're waiting there I think, *Good thing we lost the horse*, which is of course foolishness because if we had the horse we'd maybe already be where we're headed, and once again Cat strikes me as a useless sort. This close, his smell scratches at my nose, all sweaty and sad.

"You need a good washing." He doesn't answer. "Why don't

you stay in these parts and get a bed somewhere? Some place near a river you can splash in? Ain't you got any money?"

"Not enough to last."

"So you want to start over, be a frontier man, like me." I put my finger to my lips, but it's just a woodpecker flailing away somewhere up high. Always wondered where all the bits go when he pecks that hole. Guess they're so little they land on leaves and sit there till it's windy.

"I'm just waiting," he says.

The traders have passed now, and we're holding our breath a few minutes before we get back on the trail again. This is part of being cautious. "On what? A letter? News from home? Your daddy's sick, and you waiting on his fortune?"

He shakes his head. "On God. I suppose."

I don't even know what question you ask after that. If he killed a man, maybe he's worrying about judgment, but then if he's got God on his mind, doesn't seem like he'd have killed a man. I stare at him out the corners of my eyes, not turning my head, hoping he won't notice I'm staring. A handsome face, if you look at it sideways, though it could sure use some cleaning.

"He's going to send you a message?"

"Kill me. Or save me."

That right there is why I won't have no part of Christian non-sense. I do a quick prayer in case there is a God, of black men and not just white, and then I slide down the bank again and promise myself I won't ask anything else for at least an hour.

I'm telling some story about the time Old Joe taught me and Primus how to pull a thread out of a shirt so we could tie it around a fishhook without the whole shirt coming undone when Cat stops and I see the white man coming south on foot, which is why we didn't hear him. I'm trying to think whether we should play deaf-master again, but Cat puts a hand on my arm and says that he would like to try.

"Hold up," I say.

He raises his hand in a salute, and the man up the road waves back.

"No, no, no," I say, but can't spit out the rest: *You a white man, and cannot be trusted.* This is all a fine journey until the white man gets chatty, and white men together will always vote two against me, no matter how different their mothers were. But now the other fellow's too close for me to say more, or to slap Cat once across the face, so I think about just running. Just starting to run, and seeing what happens.

The other man's got a heavy beard and smells like he hasn't put down the bottle in a while. "If you ain't got a horse, why don't you ride your boy?" He grins, and one tooth is purple-black.

"Safe travels to you," Cat says. By his stiffness I reckon he's pretending to be a master. I'm holding my breath, waiting for what else he's going to say.

"You all don't look much better off than me. Got any money to you?"

Now's the time when we both should run, but I doubt Cat knows that, and if I hie off alone, there may be a musket ball waiting for me somewhere in that man's coat. Or maybe the road's just full of kindly robbers today, and we'll all latch together and sing songs. If he reaches in that coat, doesn't matter, I'm gone.

"No money but the coin of the Lord," Cat says.

The man twists his head around like he's tasted something bad.

"Missionaries. Myself and this, my slave. Can you count the last day you heard the Gospel?"

"Shit," the man says.

Cat looks over and flicks his hand at me like he wants my bag, so I toss it to him and he starts rustling through it. "If you will stay and hear a little of the Word," he says, but the other man's already edging off.

This white man has picked me, all-black, over that white man. May not have been me exactly that he was picking, but he didn't turn me in or shoot me or ride me like a lost horse, not yet, and that is something to remember.

The other man's coattails flap around the bend and he's gone. I laugh and give old Cat a hard whack and say, "Doing the Lord's work!" but his smile is small, like it took all his energy to play that short game. We trudge north again and my heart is a little more steady, for whatever raggedy doomed dream this is, at least I know it'll last a few hours more than I figured.

We've almost run out of good food, and I'm starting to wonder how we'll keep feeding ourselves. I'm not much for catching wild animals. I knew boys who got good at hunting things at night so they wouldn't have to eat only the dull corn and half-rotten meat the master threw at us, but I never fought against what was. If my food was bad, that meant food was bad, and maybe you'd sneak a peach from the basket delivered to the big house, but that was only if no one was around and no one had been around for at least an hour. It took me how many years after my brother took his life before I said enough? I try counting on my fingers. One, two, five, over to the other hand, some more years, seventeen. I've missed my brother for seventeen years.

I smell smoke, and then Cat's stomach comes at me loud as an overseer. I let my nose sniff us toward it until the smoke smell turns salty and warm. I'm feeling new confident after Cat's antics and figure we can take whatever mystery's waiting around that fire. We scramble up through the brush and over the bank and there, sunk in a clearing, is a pigeon roasting on a spit, as haloed as the baby Jesus, and behind the fire is an Indian standing with his bow drawn and his arrow pointed straight at one of our faces, I can't tell which.

I grab Cat's arm. We must look like two statues, just waiting. The Indian waits. It's too early on the trip to perish, so I call halloo. He brings his arms down so the arrow's pointing at our feet, and then I can see his face, which looks like maybe something I've seen before.

"You a trader?" I ask, but too quiet because I'm scared of frighting him, so he doesn't hear. "You trade skins?" I say louder, and he puts down his bow. I heard Indians aren't afraid of anyone but Indians.

We come half-stepping closer, or I do and pull Cat behind me. "I bring rum up to the villages," I say, miming a drink with my hand, *glug glug*. "Tuckabatchee, Tallassee." He blinks a few times, so I go on. "This here's a friend who's awful hungry. Don't want to impose, but smelled the fine cooking and could offer something in exchange." I look back at Cat, whose eyebrows go up. "Or we could just be good company, tell you a tale." I don't know how much of this he's getting, but I'm doing various things with my hands to put him at ease, making peaceable gestures and whatnot.

"Sit down," he says, and then takes his bow and walks off into the woods—as it turns out, to shoot us another couple pigeons.

"Now there's a man for you can hunt animals," I tell Cat.

When we're all cozy with meat in our mouths, he and I talk about the journeys we've made on this one path, back and forth. He does English very well. Some of the Creeks I've met, especially on the road, are remarkable good at this and I only know a few words in their tongue. As our bellies fill up, I say maybe we should be getting along, no point dilly-dallying. But the Indian nods over at Cat, and I'll be damned if that white man isn't fast asleep, cross-legged, his hands folded neat in his lap, his head bobbing along on his chest like a nut in a stream. I come all over with a kind of affection for him, sitting so quiet there though he's with two strangers who carry killing weapons. It's enough to think that he wouldn't mind being killed, and because I myself am nowhere near so much despair, it makes me sad for him. Makes me wonder what all he lost, to have nothing left to hold on to.

So I sit a little longer with the Indian and we get to talking about this and that, whatever subjects we both have words for, and I tell him he looks familiar. He looks at me and nods and then sure enough, I say you're the one I've traded rum for skins with once or twice, and he says you're the one that goes on and on with tales once you get started; you're the one that bargains so hard, I say, and you're the one who rides a horse, he says, like it was a rare pleasure.

Maybe Cat's got me in the mood for getting close to folks, or maybe it's how the hot food steams up my belly, but I drop a hint like I'm looking for another path altogether.

"This isn't your master?" he says. He has scooped together all the leaves close by and stacked them in a pile, neat, with the edges matching.

"Well, no, not when you put it quite so. We're just walking

alongside for a bit. I'm headed up to your people with some letters—that is, I was until old fool here set my horse free—but my plan, roundabout, is to take myself on a longer route. For reasons."

"You're escaped."

"No, no, I'm doing my duty. Just a little extra in mind." His coolness is waking me up fast, and the leaves trouble me. "For my master back home. He's the one wants me to head west, afterward."

I can usually tell an Indian at peace, and this one here has something twitchy going on in his eyes that's not ordinary; he may snatch me up, after all that, with Cat asleep and none the wiser.

"It's not my concern," he says, "what you do."

"I'm not doing but what my master ordered. Straight and narrow."

"I'm escaped too."

We watch each other for a minute or so, him wrought up in the eyes, but not on my account—he doesn't have the least fear of either of us, simpletons that we are, and to any other man watching he'd probably seem mighty easy. But I know what it looks like.

"Who from?" I ask.

He looks straight up, but I don't hear any birds. "Where do you want to go?"

"West," I say. If I only speak in short words, maybe he'll like me more.

"There's a spur trail, just over a day's walk south from here." He shows me with his hands pointed forward, together. "You must have passed it and not seen. It heads west."

"Reckon I better see it this time, then, or I'll walk right into my master's arms again, and I don't think either of us'd be laughing at that. Thank you," I add, going back to short words.

"I can show you. I'm going south too, for hunting. What about the white man?"

I look over and see what he means. Cat seems like no more than a pile of sticks, or fine china all broken up and put back together. I smile and stretch my legs out in front of me, so the fire will warm my feet. The Indian sits so still that if I didn't know he was there, I'd think his shape was just a hunch of rock.

"Why does he follow you?"

"Some folks just have no place to go," I say.

"You're not traveling with him farther?"

"Well," I say. Even an Indian knows better than to fall in with a white man. But he's been useful twice now. "We leave him here and he won't make it much longer than a day, the way I figure. I don't even think he'd eat for himself. Saw a man coming up said they were looking for a fellow who fit that description, wanted for murder." The Indian's eyebrow seems to rise, but that may be just a trick of falling light, so I go on. "So either he's a rascal and we're best shed of him, in which case no worry here, or he's just a poor kind of man who needs a hand up." I stop, because what I'm saying is such foolishness, you don't just pick up men on the road and carry them with you, no matter how bag-of-bones they are. But he's a good listener, I tell the Indian, sharp ears, and if we're spending any more time on the trail, why, it's better to be three men than two.

I don't know if this is true, but I push back from the fire and let my body sprawl out next to Cat, shuffling around a bit to settle myself in place. I made all that fuss to get away from folks, and here I am gathering up whoever I can find. Idiot Bob, that's what they'll call me. I have to close my eyes tight so I don't see the Indian still sitting there, maybe thinking of how he can get rid of the two of us at once. If I were picking a man to sleep next to, I'd pick the maybe-murderer over the Indian any night, and I can't say why except something about him makes me trust. A man that lonely-looking would do anything to be in company again.

SOME BLACK SMELL comes furrowing in and splits my dream in two, and before I even wake, I think, *Damn you, Winna— double damn you*, and I sit up like a dead man with my eyes still closed, flinging one arm out in remembrance of the night bugs, and pray that Primus hasn't set the big house on fire, or maybe that he has. I open one eye, and I am not in my cabin with my brother's shoes lying empty by the door, and I am not in my shack with a woman's arm flopped across my chest. I'm in the woods, and a white man is pivoting a squirrel on the spit, its tail flopping through the fire, flicking around the sparks, and my heart is a little pained from not finding myself home. The Indian stands there watching, not an expression on his face, which leads me to think he must find something funny—or else he's angry, I can't tell which, damn Indians—and Cat's quiet as ever, looking hurt, so I open the other eye and say, "You stop it now. Go on and give that beast a rest."

I stretch up and grab yesterday's shirt and wrap it around the black-burned tail with one hand while I saw it off the ass with the other. "No one teach a man how to cook," I say, shaking my head, and toss the tail as far as it'll go, which is about as far as the Indian, those things being all hair and not carrying much weight. The Indian looks at it and looks at me and sidles a few feet to the left, with that look of disdain, or maybe affection.

When the ground rat finishes cooking, Cat cuts it up in three and eats his share straight off the bone, a pocket of blood oozing out down his chin. He's the savage here, no doubt. If he were a dog, he'd either be the one that's been kicked too much and wants a pat or the one that's about to start foaming. I finish my two bites of rangy squirrel and fiddle around in my sack to check for the lace cookies I nabbed from my master's kitchen. The things are damn tough, but they hold up for days and sit in your stomach like guests waiting for company. I don't plan to share.

The sun's starting to creep its way up the sky. Planting time's already past, and I suck on a bone trying to picture the others bending down, feeling their creaking backs and the sweat coming down their necks. I don't like that we're turning on our heels and heading right back toward those sugar poles. Cat bares his teeth and I flinch, but he's just fiddling out his food again. The Indian folds his sleeping cloth, and when he starts brushing straight the needles beneath the trees, wiping away the mess of us, I remember there'll soon be men on my trail. And the kind of men they are—well, they're the ones who wouldn't blink to kill you, who don't have any sort of poor dreams at night, who look at you and see not a man but a runaway pig. Now that I'm outside the fence I'm in the range of their guns, and everything I left behind suddenly seems like the worst thing a man could ever meet. I don't know why I stayed so long, except leaving has brought me to this: a fearful panic in my bones. I think of myself as a decent man—good to the woman that was given me and good to the little ones too, and I took my whippings lying down—but I start to see how a man could want to kill, how a man might be driven to it, how goodness is measured in all sorts of ways. If I saw a white man with a whip coming through the trees, apologies to Cat, I'd shoot him through the eye without thinking twice.

We finish up making camp look like a regular old dust wallow and move on quiet down the trail, the Indian looking ahead and Cat looking down and me every few steps turning my head around to see who's coming. Cat doesn't ask once why we've turned right around again, and this gives me some comfort, though I'll keep my rope ready for the day I need to tie him up and leave him, another white man to put aside.

What do three mostly-strangers talk about on a long road with nothing to see but sometimes a knocked-down log in the path or a drunken man with one leg shorter than the other or a woodpecker flying over, the size of a child? I talk about all the stories of my life and leave enough spaces in the telling to hear their own, if they ever want to speak on it. I wouldn't want to make Cat say whether or not he murdered a man, but I'd like a little detail, some wife, some child, something of what it was like growing up as a white boy. Sometimes the Indian stops to listen for a far-off noise, and sometimes Cat just stops to think, but we keep catching up to each other. I learn a few small things: the Indian has a name, Ispallina or Istillosha, and when I asked if either of them had a lady at home, their faces both got funny. I learn that wherever the snappy sticks and leaf piles are, my feet find them right away, while Cat and the Indian seem to walk right around them, though they don't appear to be studying the path more than me. And so whenever horse hooves sound from far off, they're the first to clamber off the road, and those are the times when I'm glad they're so quiet and I'm attached to their oddness by some strange accident and not all on my own.

You'd think a day of walking after days of planting cane wouldn't be so wearisome, but I find the slower you go, the more your legs catch on and start to have some contrary thoughts. I miss the horse my master gave me, and wonder what happened to these other men's rides. Maybe they aim to shrink, to show men walking past no more than the smallest sliver of their guilty selves. Now that we're creeping backward, my feet are nervous and I'm holding my breath until we make that western spur.

We're getting closer to Winna now, and her voice comes weaving in again, saying if she were going to run, she'd head south to the free towns and the pockets of Florida maroons, not straight into the belly of the Brits, but I said they aren't Brits anymore and who knows but maybe they'll be confused now about who belongs to who. Lord knows I asked her to come. Leave the children with the granny, that's what she's there for. Winna's a good woman, even if I can't quite remember how her face fits together just now, and I think of how to get her out of there, save her skin. I'd buy her if I had the money, and maybe that'll come once my crops are planted all straight in a row. I don't try to think of how things would be different if Beck had married me—if she'd be here now, or if I'd've been so dulled with love that I'd never have found myself on such a brazen path.

Up ahead, I can hear the Indian asking Cat the same questions I've asked him. Who he is, what he's about, why all the moping around and the following strangers. But more delicate than I did. Like if he turns the right key, all the man's secrets will come tumbling out. I've only known the white man for a day, and I know better than that.

We stop under one of the endless stretching oaks for biscuits. Mother of god, I can hardly keep my knees from bouncing. I'm antsing to get away, to break west, and every little pause sounds like the men with guns are coming, though there's not a soul yet has cause to be suspicious, other than the two men who sit right here. I say how hungry I am in a dozen ways, but no one is listening, not even my own self. I gnaw on a biscuit knowing my lace cookies are still hidden in the bottom of my sack. I'm holding on to them like there'll be a tomorrow when I'll eat them up. Cat is sitting next to me against the trunk, making little patterns in the dirt with his fingernail, and the Indian—Istillicha, he corrected me—is hunched a few paces off, just where the longest branches start to dip down, somehow eating without crumbs. We've only passed a few traders; some we've let walk right past us, I figure because the Indian can smell from a mile off whether they're trouble or not, and the others we've watched from our perch in the shrubs. Whether we're walking or sitting, I can't stop talking, and even though the others seem to need this rest, I ramble on. I don't even care that I'm giving myself away to two strange-eyed men.

"When I get there," I say, "everybody'll know about it. Everybody'll stop and say 'Who, Bob? Never have thought,' and maybe they'll get to thinking of things on their own power, so as I'll see them out there one day, plowing a little field alongside mine, and our donkeys'll greet and we'll set up on the porches and share water." All this, though I can't bear the thought of sharing. The only man I'd welcome on my porch is long since dead.

"And you?" the Indian asks Cat. "What man will you tell these secrets to?" Meaning not just mine but the Indian's, though he certainly hasn't given us much to tell.

"Lay off him," I say.

Cat scrapes up a fingerful of dirt to taste it. "I don't know any men."

"You're sneakier than he is, we want to go talking about sneaks."

"No sneaks," the Indian says. "I want to know the risks. What risk is this man. He has no weapon, but he has a tongue."

"Some fellows are just fellows," I say.

"You are still young."

"No younger than you, the way I see it. Just because I don't tie the man to a tree doesn't mean—" But I don't know what it doesn't mean, because tying Cat to a tree is very much still part of my plan. "I've got it all figured," I say. "So you keep to your own worries."

"And if he is a murderer?"

Poor Cat, watching all this and not blinking. Just sad.

"Then he'd have done us in already," I say, not really knowing.

We finish up our biscuits without talking, our eyes moving from one body to the other and back again.

The farther we walk, the dimmer it gets, not because the clouds are congregating but because the trees start standing in closer together, all in a pile, breaking up the daylight. I've spent too much time plowing that western field in my head, feeding my donkey gold-rimmed hay while I pat its fat belly with my hand spread out wide, and not enough time wondering about why no woman has seen the same, why no woman has believed in that patch of free land that's waiting for the man who'll plant it. Spending a day with two men will make you miss a lady.

Istillicha says there's a creek ahead where we'll stop for water, and I'm wondering if he or Cat's ever had troubles with women. Maybe they too are poor understood and want to rope themselves a mule and come on out, though I'll ask them to sit on their own porches, all three of us of an evening watching the same sun that sets on my captive brothers set over me.

COUPLE HOURS LATER we stop again, and I tire of stopping, but this place is as peaceful as it comes. We're about a half-mile east of the trail down a red dirt path and can't hear any footsteps here, just the gurgle of smooth water as it goes shallow over sand. The bottom's got pebbles and caught leaves and slippery greens, and the water is sometimes fast and sometimes slow, and I wouldn't be paying it much attention if it didn't remind me some of the creek by my old home in Virginia, the one that tickled Primus's toes. On the red banks are bright yellow flowers on leggy stalks that flop toward the water like they're thirsty. Remembering, I can't say there were any flowers by the water when I was young, but that may be because I wasn't looking. Sometimes things go right through you and sometimes you just want to sit and watch for as long as the daylight lasts. A pudgy bird swings blue over the water, flying low to look for fish. The chirpers that sounded like saws on the plantation now come together like chimes. Everything here has a sweet sound, kind of distant.

I try to slap some water into my mouth, but Istillicha stops me and shows me how to cup it, waiting for the tadpoles to swim out. We're all a little calmer here, less like strangers.

"I must've walked past this two dozen times," I say, "same as you, but never knew such a nice place was here." I wipe my hands on my shirt and smile at the way the water still cools my throat. "Where does this go?"

"A few miles down, it falls into the Conecuh."

I try to sound that out, but let the word go. It occurs to me what a handsome man too this Indian is, and how big he must be among his people. Where is he going all by himself, with not even a horse? I know plenty of Creeks, and I've never seen one hang around a black man, showing him the way, passing time. I hope he isn't looking for a fee.

"How much farther?" I ask. I stick my feet in the water, try to rub the sore out of them. Istillicha looks around for Cat, who's squatted by a tree and is gnawing at something. I always know where the white man is. Sometimes he feels like a child of mine, another one I'll have to leave.

"Half a day's walk, maybe less," he says, "before the western spur."

"You can just point me what to look for, you know, and I can manage on my own." I had to say this to see what he'd say, but something went a little funny in me waiting for his answer. I'd hate to give up a man who knows how to shoot things. First time I get to be alone in all my life, and here I am hoping he'll stick with me a few hours more.

He's looking off to the north, still standing, waiting for the sound of something, but after a second or two he looks down and rubs his knuckles in his eyes, digging the tired out. "It's near enough to some border land with good hunting," he says.

"You got a gun?" I ask.

He nods.

"So which one you use?" I point to the bow that curves around his back.

"Whatever is—what do you say, handy? Closest to hand. It depends also who is around to hear."

"And you're doing this all by yourself? Where are the others? Don't the women come sometimes and cook you meals?"

He stops and listens again. I'd get tired of hearing as many things as an Indian does.

"Where exactly you running to?"

He snaps his head back to me like I was a deer crunching through the wood. "I'm merely hunting," he says.

"Doesn't seem to me like you'd get much on your own. Say you nab a deer and then another, how you expect to tote them around? You're strong, I'd bet, but I don't see you dragging a bouquet of carcasses all around. Maybe you're still hammering out your plan, that it? Waiting to see what opportunities walk past? I'll tell you now, I don't have none of my master's money on me. Check my coat." I start tugging it off, but he frowns.

"I have no interest in you."

Cat is looking over at us, a wash of fright on his forehead.

"Unless you know a chief of the Chickasaws or Seminoles."

"What's going on with them?" I wish he'd sit down, because it's giving my neck an ache to be peering up at him. Makes him look even more like a statue.

"Eventually I'll seek an alliance."

"This is some Indian war foolery. That's all right, then."

But he's not done telling. "I had money from the trade and lost it. Should have led my town, but lost that."

"How'd you lose the money?" That being more interesting to me.

"It was taken."

"Stolen? You plan on fetching it back?"

"I need someone to support my cause. And whether that's

another Muskogee town eager for an unseating, or a garrison of Americans, I must buy my way into those talks."

"I told you," I say, laughing, but quieter now, "you can't carry all those skins. Cat'd help you, but he weighs less than a deer."

"It's not skins I'll barter with. Money. It's coins that move nations now."

"And how're you going to get those coins?"

"Ah." He nearly smiles, I swear he does. "Selling skins?"

Cat is lifting up water with his right hand and pouring it over his left, and back again on the other side. He's easier now that the Indian has loosened.

I say maybe he could work his way into the employ of my master, since there's a man who'll be hard up for a trader soon. I've known Indians who got snatched into slavery, though, so he'd need to strike a deal on his tiptoes. He listens and nods, and it's almost a relief to know he's still figuring. Same as me.

"And once you get that money and a bunch of men to get your town back, what're you going to do then? Start yourself a little shop?"

He finally sits down beside me, letting go of whatever the forest was sounding like, and breaks off some tall grass to roll between his fingers. "Become chief," he says.

I nod. *There's a dream*, I think. *Running away, running to—all dreams.*

I pick at him with a few more questions but he won't talk about it anymore. I tell him I'd vote for him for chief. If I look half as handsome and proud in my foolishness as he does, well, it's enough to make you think we'll get wherever it is we're going, nothing to be scared of, no bother that we're fugitives and

penniless. I peek over at Cat to see how he compares and decide
if you gave him a new suit and a haircut and slapped a smile on
his face he'd be no less than a ladies' man, with those big blue
eyes and that moony way. The Lord doesn't make ugly fates for
such good-looking men.

The Indian sees me looking at Cat and asks again if I think
the white man's a killer. I whistle and throw up my hands. Out
of his bag he pulls some bread that's hard as stone and calls Cat
over, showing us how to dip it in water to soften it up, and then it
tastes nice and beany and we thank him for it, or I do and Cat just
gobbles it like a wild person. The sun's getting low, so he starts
back to the road and we fall in line, Cat coming close behind me.
Sometimes he walks near enough that I think he's about to reach
out for my hand. The dirt here is so red that it lights our way.

We crest the bank and climb back down to the road and are
about a mile farther south when Istillicha stops and Cat stops
and even I hear it: *tomp, tomp,* the sound of metal shoes on earth.

A trading party, or travelers, Istillicha says, coming behind
us, down the road we took but faster. I start toward the bank,
but he holds up his hand like this time he wants to see who it is.
We wait.

Four white men in English coats, two brownish men, the
poor kind who carry or haul or dig, and three black like me,
but wearing Indian clothes. They must be Creek slaves coming
along to tell the other men where to step. The white man on
the first bay horse has a heavy, pleased face. He pulls up and
the others stop, the men on horses prancing, the mules behind
shifting around with the heavy weight of loaded bags. Istillicha,
who's standing in front of me, has his head pointed at that first
white man like a bloodhound. He must know him, or think he

knows him. One of the black men says hello to Istillicha, shaking him out of himself, and they talk for a bit in Creek tongue, him pointing south and them nodding.

The white man interrupts. "Can he tell us where to find fresh water? A stream or other clear place."

Later, the Indian will tell me this is Kirkland, a man he'd heard of, who'd passed through his town a few days before, and the young folks with him he figures are his son and nephew, all bound for Pensacola.

The white man shouts like we're all hard of hearing. "We are travelers from Carolina bound for West Florida. These men from Hillaubee, near the Tallapoosa, are guiding us. We have no trade, but only wish to move forward in peace. Do you know where we can find water, sir?"

Istillicha points to the fourth white man, the one who isn't Kirkland or his son or his nephew. He still doesn't say anything, hiding that he speaks English fine, and I shift back and forth on my feet, wondering if this is how wars start, with rude fingers.

Kirkland turns awkwardly in his saddle, looking back at the man in question. "Thomas Colhill," he says, "trader to the Creeks."

Istillicha drops his arm and I'm still standing behind him so I can't see his face, but his knees take a quick dip, less than a bend even, but just like something suddenly went soft beneath him. Who is Thomas Colhill to shake my Indian's knees? Just looks like a regular medium white man, with quick dark eyes. His face is blank, like he's never been guilty of anything. We all wait for Istillicha to say something, to stop standing in the middle of a road like a warrior, stiff, heart-fast. I look at Cat to make sure he doesn't run.

One of the mules hears a rustle in the bush, maybe a fox, and when it skips to one side, its bags go *clink clink*, clear as bells, and the black and brown men look down and off to one side and the white men keep looking at Istillicha like nothing has happened, that sound doesn't sound like anything to them, and as I freeze up, something melts in Istillicha, and somehow without anyone saying a word but that little fox in the woods, the game has changed.

"There is water a mile back," Istillicha says. "The creek flows east of the road. A path in the brush will lead you there."

He points north again, politely now. Kirkland glances at me and Cat skulking in the back. His bay snorts, and Kirkland nods. The men turn their beasts around and with every shuffle and sidestep the bags go *clink clink clink*.

THE SOUND MADE an echo in my head that won't go away. We sit by the side of the road, three in a row, looking straight before us. Cat stands up, spits in his hand, runs it through his hair, but when he sees we're not budging, sits down again.

The Indian isn't saying anything, but he knows and I know what's in those sacks, and it's not cloth and it's not corn cakes, and we both know what a little coin would do in our straits.

I start to say something, but stop. What is a free man except a man with money? I'll lay it down in taverns from here to the Pacific Ocean, and every man among them will take it with a grin. There is no farm that can't be bought with money, black or white.

We whisper, like we think God's watching.

"What do you think?" I say.

"There's nothing to think."

"This is freedom here," I say. "This is what it looks like, those bags."

"It's not ours."

There's a hunger in the Indian and I smell it. "No," I say, "just like your money doesn't belong to you, but to whoever's the man who took it. Just like I don't belong to myself but to my master, or at least Treehorn, who treats my body like his own dog."

He doesn't look at me, is thinking.

"And those fellows weren't even good men, were they? You knew them, didn't you?"

Cat has stood up again and is pacing behind us, shaking his head.

"That Thomas Cowbell—"

"Colhill," he interrupts me.

"He did something bad to you once?"

Half of Istillicha's face twists up, as if he's trying to remember finally the difference between good and bad, if there's one at all. "This is not my plan."

"We do it while they're sleeping," I say. "No harm."

Cat sits down and is frowning now, his arms across his chest, his hands pulled tight into his armpits. I think he says *no* a couple of times, but it's hard to tell. Could just be a cough.

"He's the father of a woman I know," the Indian says.

"He take your money?"

He chews at the inside of his cheek, his eyes wet and dark. "I think *she* did."

There's a deeper story there, and I let him have it, let him flip through it over and over again, because I can see that each time he does, his anger gets hotter. I scratch up a stick from the dirt and roll it between my palms, looking up at the sky to see how the clouds are tumbling together and counting how two sacks split between three men. My mother before she was stolen taught me not to steal, but this is not because she didn't want me to have cake from the kitchen. It's the whip she was saving me from, not my own conscience, not right or wrong. Slavery's all wrong, no matter what went on, and clambering out of it is nothing but right. If she is watching me clamber from up on high, then she is surely nodding her head.

"This is a god-given right," I say, just now getting a sense of what God might be. "This is a right from God himself, who hid me in his folds the night I left and who's shining his light down on an Indian and a murderer—apologies, Cat—and if there were signs in the world then surely this would be one. Out of everything you've ever seen in life, all the animals running across your path and the shooting stars and the women put in front of you, have you ever been a witness to so clear and loud a sign? To finally see the thing you most want in the world, prancing around and chiming like a goddamn bell? You think a god as great as him doesn't know how to send a sign?"

Cat coughs again, *no.*

"And then?" The Indian wants me to tell him it's all right, that's what I hear him asking.

"And then we start great lives," I say. *Free lives.*

My brother Primus is swimming in my mind, swimming in the creek below the rope that hangs loose from the willow, his brown limbs dipping through summer water, his laugh a long string of joy. My mother is bent in a knot in her garden, scrabbling out cabbages, and looks up at me with a smile, her hands packed with green, a chicken pecking at her bare heels. My grandfather Abraham is running fast, is running by a bank of grasses that hides a cool stream, is running without stopping because the crocodiles are asleep, the white men are ghosts, and the big house burned down, burned down at the hands of his grandson, who is not dead and hanging but is swimming in my mind, and all are free.

BY THE TIME the sky has turned from red to black, we've sorted our packs and marked a plan. The white men and their guides and their horses and their laden mules will be laid up snoring for the night and our steady silent hands will sneak into their bags, taking a few guns also for just-in-case, and when they awake with the first birds, they'll find themselves a few pounds the lighter. By then I'll be halfway to the west, Istillicha will have bought himself a chiefdom or a rum empire or whatever it is he wants, and Cat will probably be lying under some tree, still thinking about his wrongs. I imagine quick what that money could do for Winna, how she once said in the fuzzy middle part between loving and sleeping that I better come buy her once I'm a rich man, but she's a good woman and I know she'll find another man to fill the bed, one who isn't already in love. *This is my money, Winna*, I say, as if she'll hear and understand. I'm a bad husband, but I'm a better man.

We turn back north in the dim light of nighttime and retrace the trading path, which is now scuffed with the steps of well-fed men on horseback, and I smooth my shout to a whisper. "You sure we heading the right way? You don't think they can hear us coming? You think they'll be asleep by now? What if—" I think maybe this time Cat will answer. Istillicha grabs my arm and squeezes me silent, and in his grasp I can feel his heartbeat running even faster than my own.

I can't tell why I'm nervous all of a sudden except it's suddenly occurring to me how close everything is to touching and how quick it could be snatched away again, and this here is the lock on the door past which is all I ever wanted, at least as a grown man, for all I wanted when I was young is already dead and can't be had. My chest feels about to shatter.

And then I hear the creek waters running, little bells.

March 10, 1788

Le Clerc

TODAY CONTINUES WARM. One of the Indians has a pretty habit of humming that keeps our search lighthearted, though the slave who is ostensibly guiding us, and who was present during the murders, continues to glower at the back of our train. The tunes are mostly Indian, using a limited range of notes, but occasionally he slips into a European song he must have picked up from a trader's fiddle. I must prevent myself from singing along.

At first light, we passed near the creek where the atrocity took place. The slave asked if I would care to view the site, but I could tell he wasn't eager to see the bodies again, and time compelled me to keep moving. I strained my ear but the water must have been too far distant. When the other slaves had straggled back to camp yesterday with their borrowed horses—none of the blacks having fled, I must compliment the Creeks—they said it sounded as though the killers had headed south. Was it terrible that I chose to leave the dead uncovered so long? As I am not much for Fate, neither do I trust much in God, or at least in the version of him that demands weekly service, honest confession, and prompt burial. I told my men to ride on.

We were well fed and watered last night at one of the public houses along the trail. These taverns are always of great interest, as they gather a wide spectrum of men beneath their roofs and construct a sense of security that permits thieves and gentlemen to lie down in the same bed come nightfall. That the taverns are always chock-full, in spite of the high rates of pickpocketing and brawls, suggests that this security is easily blinked over in favor of more valued offerings—conviviality, perhaps.

The Creeks shared a common room with several other traveling Indians, and I permitted the negro to have a cot in my private quarters so that I might question him further about the events of the preceding night. I could tell that he was either rattled or naturally taciturn, so I began by inquiring about the details of his life, hoping to ease him into conversation.

"And how long have you belonged to the chief Seloatka?"

"I don't belong to him."

"But you have lived in the Creek nation for some time as a slave. Were you born here?"

"No."

I was undressing at this juncture and asked him politely to fold my clothes, which he did with some haste. He was back on the floor beneath his blanket before I was quite in bed, so I had to fetch my own candle and pull down my own sheets. I am fairly self-sufficient in the Indian towns because there is a shortage of domestic help, either feminine or indentured, but being once again in a civilized room with a proper bed and a negro who refused to assist me made me peevish.

"You seem to have quite a bit of freedom," I said, once I was in my sheets and enjoying the softness of the mattress, however lumpy. "I would think many of your black brothers would be envious."

"I have no brothers."

"Well, in a figurative sense, of course. And guiding parties of travelers must give you many opportunities to study your fellow man. I wouldn't be surprised if you were also wiser than the average negro." I laughed softly so he could catch on to my good humor, but he did not respond. "At the very least, you must be observant. Can you not remember any other details about the men you saw that night?"

Was he already asleep?

"I know it must have been a shock to witness the gruesome deaths of four innocent Englishmen and their servants—perhaps you were even pretending to be dead yourself—but surely you must have seen something of their faces."

"It was dark."

"Ah. Were you frightened?" The candle was guttering down—the proprietor in his cheapness had given me only a stub—and I was beginning to question my wisdom in inviting this surly man into my room. "You would not be sorry to see these men brought to justice, would you?"

"I'm showing you the way, aren't I?"

"You are hardly cooperative." The candle went out. I plumped my pillow once more and pulled the quilt to my chin. "It would be reassuring if you were to give some indication that you have the same goals as the rest of this party."

"You're here to catch the men. I want to catch the men. They took eight hundred dollars worth of silver and didn't offer me none."

. . .

I UNDERSTAND FEELING cheated in life.

The death of a mother such as I had was not an occasion for great grief. I inherited the manor in Thin-le-Moutier, still a half-haunted place to me, and promptly sold it to a cousin, taking my fortune with me to Paris and knocking about the city, investigating all the pleasures that a country upbringing denied me. The more I saw, the more I was curious: the depravity, the stench, the sweep of carriages riding high above the muck, the mansard roofs with dormers jutting out like eyes. It was all very ugly and grand, but as a young man privileged with money, I found myself still pacing a narrow path. My driver would not take me to a tavern unless paid extra, and then my attire drew such glances that there was no hope of silent study. I tried to pick up dialects so I could eavesdrop on discontent, but I understood nothing. I wandered the city with a ready system of classification, but few scenes would let me near enough to dissect.

Some called me idle, but I toyed with a genuine sense of purpose. I wanted to prove that there was a sublayer to humanity that was common across the classes, and that no matter the station one was born to, some universal concern made one recognizable as a man as opposed to any other beast. I suppose I believed in this not because I felt pity for the poor but rather pity for myself: I wanted to belong. Oh, to be embraced by those who shunned me, and to prove my mother wrong for keeping me locked up and out of sight of all that was roiling in the world. If I could only find that common marrow—I vacillated between thinking it was grief and thinking it was love—then I could propose a new system of laws, a twist to justice, a revision of education that would lead, one day, to the end of wars. The end of walls.

This was the age when men thought such things.

But being young, I was also easily dissuaded. What little I saw merely confirmed my assumptions about my country; it was old, and nearly rotten. I retreated from my philosophy and allowed myself to be a noble, adopting what might be considered a typical schedule. I invested some of my fortune in schemes, I learned how to shoot pistols, I drank until I was drunk enough to throw scarves from my window at women on the streets, all of which was accompanied by the laughter of a dozen other rakes. And just when I thought I was immune to feeling, I fell into something that resembled love.

She was soft-throated and already engaged to a *boulanger* in the king's service, but she had a pedigree and a lively eye, and had been sent to the city by her kin to find a match. He wasn't her equal, and I told her so. A cousin of hers was a friend of mine, and she still enjoyed dancing, so we would find ourselves often in the same debauched rooms of the wealthy. There are men who love girls solely for their beauty and who think little of the endless days beyond that mask, the days that require conversation and good humor and sympathy, so it is hardly surprising that the state of marriage in France is dismal. Our parents cannot speak to each other and soon we won't be speaking to our wives. But though she was beautiful, I flattered myself that I saw deeper than that, though what I saw was wit, and this has no relation to kindness.

Her betrothed soon learned of my attentions and sent me a neatly written challenge via a *sous chef* in the pastry kitchen. It smelled faintly of anise, and I accepted. In the ensuing duel, his became the first life I took, and far from damning my soul, the act won me her. Small and dark, an eel when she wore my sheets. She ribboned her black hair around her bird-like head, and when I unwound it after the candles were snuffed, it fell flat as bowstrings. We felt no compunction.

The night of our wedding, I wondered what my mother would think of her; I felt unmoored in the happiest sense.

But days turned to months, and life resumed an ordinary course, which is to say we breakfasted late, bought more mirrors than were necessary, and hired carriages to take us a quarter of a mile.

The canker that I began to nurse perhaps first bloomed on the night the peasant woman came to our door. My new wife and I had moved to a small villa beyond the city to bear children and collect servants, to build flower beds for others to tend. The poor, whom I once approached in the dirty inns of Paris, were here quieter and better fed. We saw them through the gaps in the garden, though every season the yew hedges that my wife planted grew taller. The peasant said her husband's leg had been caught beneath the plow and the manager was absent, and though she needed my assistance there was terror on her face: not of her husband's plight, but of me, of my position. I did not take the time to wonder if fear could be the human sublayer. I rushed to the field, summoning a few other men, and while we displaced the plow she stood some meters distant, insistently looking away—at the dark hay fields beyond, at the stars, at her wooden shoes. When her spouse had been rescued and the damage was seen to be minimal, I tried to inquire after her children and the condition of her dwelling. Her immediate need having been met, she refused to speak any more to me. The pair hobbled away, ashamed or proud. I let her go back to her life with her uncounted children, and I saw my home for what it was: still an empty room, boarded-up and bare, nothing to be seen.

That evening I rode to a local public house and drank enough ale to drown a pig and decided that if ever I wanted to be a scientist in the manner of the cartographers I idolized in my youth, if I wanted to advance my own embryonic theories, then I must renounce the self that over the years had become a prison.

We had no child yet, so when I told my wife that I no longer wished to live in France, in any place where man was so impossible to measure, I had little guilt about what I abandoned. I adored her, genuinely, but this was not enough and even this she would not believe. I was bored, I was impatient, I was a shockingly young man who was hungry for any country but his own. I would have followed a river to the sea provided it was untamed.

I AM GAZING off to the east, looking idly for signs of the old burial mounds that rise like cresting whales from the earth and contemplating what manner of precious icons might be found if the graves were uncovered, when the Indian behind me, who has sworn the Creeks are no relation to the mound builders, stops his humming.

A man comes toward us down the trail, dragging behind him a rickety two-wheeled cart that kicks up puffs of red dust. My best guess is that he is a Spaniard, or perhaps English with a small dose of African. His large dark eyes move over us as though we were nothing more than trees, but when my companion calls out to him, he pulls his cart up short.

"Care for the news?" he asks.

"I'll take the news if it concerns the men I'm looking for." My horse is nervous beneath me. I have learned he is quite sensitive to smell, and has a strong preference for well-groomed men.

"Where were they born?"

"That I cannot tell you."

He pulls a folded paper from beneath a rock in his cart, and now I can see that his load is composed entirely of newspapers. He carries no other bag with him, so I cannot think where he keeps his personal effects.

As he opens the paper, it becomes evident that the darkness of his hands is due not to parentage but to smudging. "Well, do you know the times? Were they born in the early morning, or around dusk?"

"My good sir, I have merely their descriptions." I turn around to the slave and nod.

He brings his mule up to the front and says without intonation, "One man Creek, some tattooed; one man white and thin; one man negro like me, but lighter. All dirty. Carrying heavy sacks."

The newspaper man pivots his head back and forth. He is still engaged with the printed word, which at this distance is not distinguishable as one of the common papers of the day.

"Have you seen them or not?" I ask.

He looks up. "This is news from the stars," he says. "Not of men. You'd do well to find out what it says."

"Astrology?"

"I can see the twins here, but they're not ready yet, and they're only two men, not three. No, all that's above you is the crab, and hear me, he's ornery. He was sent to topple Heracles, but Heracles was many-muscled, much too strong, and stomped him once then kicked him to the heavens." He turns his head up to the late morning sky, which is silken blue, empty of both clouds and stars. "Shh, he can hear us now."

"I will be cautious," I say. "But the three men we mentioned?"

"Yes, I did see three, not two, and with heavy sacks. But the news is sixpence."

I shuffle in my pockets for the change and toss it to him.

"I saw them this time yesterday, headed south, as you're headed south, on foot and very dirty." He runs a hand through his hair as if to prove his own superior hygiene, but a moth flies out from one of his curls. "One was born in Carolina. You'll catch up to them soon if they don't head west."

"And why would they head west?"

"Because that is where the heavens go." He picks up his cart and trundles past us, heedless of the stamping horses.

WHO IS SETTING their course? Are they aiming north toward freedom, east toward home, or merely circling around the Indian towns, hoping for asylum? I am keen now to every scuffle in the dust, each branch leaning over the trail that might have caught at a shirtsleeve. We eat while riding and we ride at a modest clip, not only because of the slave's tetchy mule but also because speed inhibits perception. This has been a late lesson of my life, and if I could wind myself back and advance at half the speed, I believe I would derive significantly more pleasure from daily affairs.

The afternoon's conversation centers on the afterlife, and whether the second Creek man will see the first Creek man once they are dead and under.

"If you're satisfied, you'll stay put in your grave and then I don't think you'd see anyone at all. Otherwise, you'd ghost about, scaring children, but not sitting around with any other ghosts. So either way, no, I don't think we'll meet each other."

"But ancestors talk to each other to sort the lives of the living."

"We're not ancestors yet."

"We could be, down the road, unless you marry the Iroquois and then none of your sons and daughters will be Muskogee and we'll be ancestoring in different countries altogether."

"I thought he was too ugly to marry an Iroquois," says the third.

"What if we were buried under the same house?"

"There'd still be dirt between us and our eyes would be closed."

"But we'd know we were side by side."

"Maybe, but no one's going to put us in the same house, and if we can't talk to each other, what's the point?"

"Are you saying you want to talk to me forever?"

"No! You're the one wanted us side by side."

"That was an example. If anyone's dead next to me, it'll be a woman so beautiful she'll be better than life itself."

"Did you kill her?" asks the third.

"You two are pointless. The Iroquois have twice as much sense."

It may be surprising to European readers that the native peoples here, often considered superstitious and spiritually primitive, equal our modern philosophers when it comes to uncertainty about the hereafter. I need to make a note that one aspect of the connective human thread may be faith, or rather the lack thereof.

The light is falling when I see it: a broken trail into the western brush, covered immaculately by an Indian hand and thus perfectly legible to me, his artfully scattered leaves as artificial as footprints. I pull the men up short. I can see fifty yards into the forest before the creeping darkness covers the rest.

"Is this the way we go?" asks the third man.

The slave is several paces behind us, his mule gnawing at a hoof. The poor negro is hunched over in a position of complete reluctance.

I have not been given a particularly promising retinue; the slave's actions suggest he would as soon cower in a cave as confront the bandits, while the Creek men are as noisy a bunch of chatterers as I have seen in the Indian territories. I have tracked villains before, and being black-hearted and craven, they are easily startled. It will be easier if I advance alone. Not only can I come upon them more quietly, but I can take in their character; before I capture or kill them, as the moment requires, I need to learn what drew them together. If this is to be a central case in my proposal to the Royal Society, I must have adequate firsthand evidence. If I were not nearly middle-aged, I would think myself nervous. What will they be like? There must be a strain of cruelty in every breed of man, along with the good in him.

"I shall proceed from here alone," I say.

The slave gives a brief smile.

"Aren't there three men?" the third man asks, looking at the other Creeks, sizing up a three-man force. "How'll you catch them all?"

"I have caught a group of six before. It's a matter of picking them off individually, which is not at all difficult if you retain the element of surprise. An element, I might add, that is dependent on noiselessness."

"We can be quiet."

"In this instance," I say, "you must trust that it will be easier if I am unaccompanied."

"He's right; we'll wait on the trail for you. Stay at a tavern till you bring them back, or need us to come fetch the bodies."

"But what about your horse?" the third man asks. "Isn't he noisy?"

I rest a hand on my horse's mane. She's a fine one, with pale flanks and golden hair, and is patient with the type of saddle I prefer. Uncomplaining, like the best kind of friend. I think of a man to compare her to, but the closest friend I can name is the little cat that spent a summer in my mother's garden. I am not unlikable, nor misanthropic. Why, then, can I not name a soul to whom I would write real letters, or for whom I would lay down my life? The need for companionship must not be the link between all men, because I have lived thirty-six years without it, and I am still healthy.

I scratch behind her ears and pat her twice on the neck.

"You're right. They don't ride horses, and neither shall I."

"Speed is important," says the first Creek.

"We've caught up with them significantly. And without eight hundred dollars on my back, I can walk much faster than they." I dismount and hand the reins to the second Creek, who of all the men seems to have the most sense. "We passed an inn just to the north; one of you wait there while the others return to the creek to carry the bodies back to the hunting grounds. I should return within the week."

They watch me unload my pack, tighten my boots, and strap on my musket. I feel a *frisson* at the image of a man striking off into the deep forest, hunting the human temperament.

Cat

My father was the first woman I knew. His hands split the knots in my hair, folded me on a straw bed, spooned me soup. Belted me, caned me, hided me. He never touched me but to hit me. I was not afraid of him in any way but this. He slept by the day fire and cut sticks at night into beasts. Twisted things, not cows or lambs. Vermin. When he had enough, he'd bury them by the walnut. The dirt around it barren, poisoned by the falling leaves. Bits of his soul, he'd say. The darkness put to rest. With each one, I thought, *Ah, no more pain*. Buried well. Except he never stopped carving. The wood turned into rats eating their own legs, snakes split two-headed, spiders with a dozen arms. After a heavy rain, their spasmed faces peered from the walnut roots. I'd stumble on them playing, hide in the cabin till the wet leaves covered them again. They were never buried deep.

We lived in tree country, had anybody asked. Trees all over. Ice in winter, too hot in summer, bugs. Cracks in the wall so big my finger found the outside. My father sometimes there and sometimes not, though which was worse. He looked like a smudge. Like someone had run a finger down his face while the paint was wet. I only came close when he was sleeping. I'd sit long enough for certain, then crawl into him. Lift his deadweight arm over my little self, my knees tucked in. Just for warmth. A small bear pressed into its mother bear, careful for claws. I knew when he was waking because he did nothing quiet, and I was by the far wall before he could see.

"You always up," he'd say.

I would never sleep if he didn't.

Eating was him finding food, tossing the bones to me. He had a gun, all men had guns, and some days he'd be gone till dark and come back with fat birds and others he'd sit at the fence and blow holes in the post. Our posts so weak with all that wood-peckering they'd come down at the tail-flick of a wild hog. But when he pointed the gun at food, he'd bring it home and pluck it or skin it and roast it and eat it and at the end he'd throw the gristle to the corner where I was always sitting, waiting, never not hungry. I was little, even for a little boy.

I don't know when I knew I was his son, or if he ever knew.

He didn't speak but in growls. The times he wasn't shooting, or drinking, or asleep, he spent remembering. Or that's what I thought. Sitting that long, staring at nothing. That's when he'd dig into the wood with his knife. I didn't know the words to ask him what his mind was on, what kind of blackness led to such blackness. Guilt wasn't something I knew of. The drink loosened him up, caused him to spill himself, but his loudness then, those words, had no sense. There was a *she* and sometimes a *knocked her head*, just in anger and he was sorry, always sorry when he drank. What *she* he killed I didn't care, for he was all the parent to me.

My father sometimes danced. Wild nights, men would gather, men I'd never seen, and my father, who was my mother, would jerk his heels up and slap the floor. His arms flailing above his head, his beard trembling. One man in the corner with a fiddle, the rest with whiskey mouths. The house would shake and I would watch from the walnut, never knowing what a woman was. One night I saw a black man there, elbows bent, feet shaking. I thought he was a warm wonder. There was no violence in that violence. Only noise that washed hard over me, like a belt on my back. If asked what was a woman, I would have said likely just a man I'd never seen.

What did I know that I was waiting for word of them?

There were soft apple spots in my father. He took me once in spring to where the flowers grew. So many trees, it was hard to find the space to bloom. But in the meadow they spread wide. Between eating berries he wove a crown for me, clover knotted in thistle. I wore it and saw my joy in the dirty smudge of his face, and we were boys at play in a field. I pretended to be a bird and swooped, and he pretended to be a mouse and cowered. There was a creek and we fished our toes in it. Clear blue, the sky, the creek, the blue-eyed grass. I reached for his hand, not knowing where I had learned the want, and he was still. A moment, my short fingers tucked in his. And then he was up, shaking off his watered feet, breaking the knots in his hair. Back to the meadow, where we shared a block of cheese he'd bartered. Just cheese, its skin sweaty like ours.

He carried a flask with him, was never flaskless, and he drank himself into a nap, and when I saw him sleeping I slept too, though not too close. I felt the sun suck away the wetness on my creek feet, brown my cheeks. I watched the fireflies inside my eyelids. A spine from a thistle leaf dug into my ear. I wouldn't have taken off my crown that day, not for money. I spreadeagled into the green grass and pulled my body close again, swam out, swam in, fists full of broken leaves, me a happy fish. I didn't dream because I had no memories.

I slept too long. He was already awake. The flask was empty when he threw it at my head. He told me to get up, but he was pulling at my feet, which made it hard. He took my hand—his fingers finding mine!—and dragged me to the creek. I was in the creek, and he was scrubbing at me, angry, yelling about dirt, about how no one looked after me. I saw this was true. Who would have looked after me? He kept scrubbing. "Not mine," he said, though I *was* his, and he left me floating while he went to puke into the bushes, and when he came back, wiping the yellow foam off his mouth, he grabbed the back of my neck and I was under, the whole water was my world. I thought he was cleaning me, setting me to rights, but he wasn't moving. I didn't move. I didn't move until I couldn't breathe, and then my arms and legs flew out, frog-like, kicking, kicking. This made the water dusky so I couldn't see the minnows or the green muck. Just the shadows of my arms. And then the fireflies came back into my eyes, and it was black and gold in flashes. My father's fingers locked into my neck, not moving, still. I breathed again, and it was water this time, and my lungs filled up heavy, sinking me. My skin was dirty, and he wanted to make me clean.

On the bank, I gave it all back, clear creek water. He was slapping me hard, and I felt like an ocean was pulling itself out of me. Like the boy was being pulled out of me. My insides flipped. He hauled me standing and since my legs too were full of water, he lifted me and held me like a baby and like that carried

me home. Made a fire, dried me, gave me his quilt. There was
no food, but if there had been, he would've fed it to me. He sat
with me while I grew sleepy, and when he saw I couldn't sleep
with him sitting there, he patted my head with an open palm and
went out into the new night, and as soon as he was gone I didn't
think at all, not about whether he loved me or wanted me dead,
and I slept, no dreams.

I was happiest with my father then. He beat me frequent for
little things, but I could've been a poor-trained dog and gotten
the same. Only his son would he hold below water with such a
furious hand. Only someone you loved would you want to kill.
If that's what it was. *Not mine.* If I wasn't his, surely I was my
mother's. And who was my mother but my father? He was it,
the all of my world, whether he was good to me or whether his
eyes turned dark and strange. He could drown me and I'd still
be his. As I grew up, grew stronger, I'd be more use. Could help
him with his work.

My father made rye whiskey when he wasn't haunted. The
still was past our clearing and the next, tucked in a blackberry
dip. He drank half and sold half, and sometimes half was stolen.
I once dug the leaves away from the copper pots, dulled with
use, and swallowed some. Burning pepper. Mostly I'd hunch in
a shrub and watch him stir until the stinging smell jellied my
legs. I'd fall asleep. I'd wake in dew and crawl home. Barely tall
enough to reach the latch. My father would be stretched by the
fire, his brown hair lank against his shoulders. His grease shone
in the firelight, his hat still on. He stank. I put my white child's
hand against his cheek and smoothed the dirt. I tried to match
my breaths to his, and when our chests rose and fell and rose,
perfect, I slept.

The men who came to fetch the drink were tall. I was smaller than I should have been, and they seemed giants. The room crowded with them, even when it was just one and my father. Most were dressed well in clean coats with buttons. I hid under blankets, beneath the table, thin by the broom in the corner, outside. Safer outside. No one said much, because the drink was the language. They came with coins, or fresh rye, and walked away with jugs. I wondered what roads they took to bring them here. Roads we never saw. In all those trees, with seldom flowers and one blackberry dip, there were no other homes. Just one man and one boy, who never moved past a mile, who never saw the innards of other people's houses. I guessed these other men lived in cabins of the same size, but they could've lived in trees or underwater or in rooms papered with steel. I didn't know what a family was, and no surprise. If I could have made myself a fly to slip inside the stone bottles and be carried to any elsewhere, I would've, though it made my life but three days long. But I could never get smaller than I was. Never brave enough to wander. The leash that kept me tied to my father was my only belonging. Just one invisible strap between us, keeping me out of some black hole. I stayed quiet and quieter as the men came and took their poison and my father his coins, and when he was hungry he'd shoot something and I'd eat it, chewing softly so as not to bite down on lead, and I never left, not till they took me away.

AT AGE AROUND six, I was in a flooding rain, days of wet. The men stopped coming, their rye fields swamped, and the fire under the still went out. My father took the pieces apart to clean them and saw he needed a new coil, so he walked somewhere—

a town?—and left me with the rain falling. There was a shelf
in the house with apples and oats. If I stood on a stool I could
reach. I sat in the rain until I was wet through, and sat in the
house until I was dry. I watched the beads on my hands shrink
or slip off, my dark pants grow slowly lighter. My hair as it dried
moved on my scalp. No more than a few minutes to get all-the-
way wet, but it was most of a day to dry out. My father wouldn't
let me keep a fire.

He was gone for two days, and I drank out of his mug and
wore his extra coat. I ate all the apples. I coaxed a squirrel in the
house with walnuts and trapped him. He threw himself around
the walls until he knocked his head hard, and then we both slept.
I was close enough to put my finger in his little clawed palm. If I
was still and didn't breathe, I could feel a pulse in his hand like a
whisper, blood from a tiny heart. The fur bristles trembling, his
rubbery pads warm like skin. I squeezed the little paw. When he
woke, he bit me, and then I let him go.

I was asleep under my father's quilt, still in my father's coat,
when he came back. He threw off the covers and found me in
a little puddle. I hadn't made water before bed because it was
raining and my penis was scared of the weather, and because I
was still just a boy it came out on its own, a bitter mess on my
father's quilt. He pulled me up in one hand and the blanket in
the other and took us both outside, where finally some sun was
showing though the rain still fell, and he took off my pants and
threw them over a bush with the blanket and he pulled a switch
off the possumhaw and thrashed my bottom. The more I wailed,
the harder he hit, which was a lesson I never seemed to learn.

The world shrinks when you're getting hit. Most of it fuzzes
away. What I saw was the new coil by the back door, a squashed

copper worm, picking up winks of sun. The rain slow now, like a boy weeping. He threw the switch into the woods.

"Don't piss in the bed."

I wanted to tell him about the squirrel, but I guessed he would be angry. I still wanted to tell him.

He took off my shirt and turned it upside down and put my legs into the armholes, one by one. He tied the wide bottom around my waist into a knot. He patted my head again, once, and then slapped me on the bottom, but I think this was consolation. He took his coil and a jug of whiskey and walked away. The blood came through the shirt in thin streaks.

I didn't see him the rest of the day. I made water before bed and pinched myself halfway through sleep so I could get up and do it again, my urine splashy like the last of the rain, and in the morning the bed was dry. Outside, pointy leaves still held on to water drops. The ground was spongy where I stepped. I thought I was in a new place for how new everything smelled, like clean dirt.

I climbed a hundred-year magnolia. I lay upon its thin top limbs. I rubbed my chin against its liver-spotted bark, gray and ants all over. My skin crawled. I ate a few, just to see. Their legs along my tongue. With my eyes closed, the day was patterned. Golds and greens moving in my eyes, ants walking in my belly. I heard a bird settle near. It sang like a wren and perched on my back. Its tail bobbed against my shoulder. I was its earth. I stopped breathing to hold a stillness, to hold its body. Its toes through the thin cotton clung. It pecked me once, for food. I wished I'd been a worm, to give it that. I stayed still, the earth, not moving. When it flew away, the sun gold in my eyes had grayed. When I went sleepy home, my house was empty, my earth rolled over.

My father wasn't home, but his hat was there. He hadn't gone away. I stood in the door and whistled into the falling light. No sound. I waited for a man to come, one with gold buttons and rye, but no one came, though I waited many minutes. I took a pail with me to gather nuts. If my father was hiding, I'd find the squirrel again and train it and it would be my father in my father's stead and I would be its baby. No sounds on the path to the still, no nuts to be found. It was too dark for seeing. But I was looking for small things, and my father was large. I forgot how large until I saw him.

I found my father by the still. His mouth was full. What smelled of pepper now smelled like something spoiled. I pushed him on his side to let the dribble out, but he was stiff and his hands instead of flopping froze. His eyes were open and were brown and his face was brown and his neck was gray. I called his name and he didn't answer, but he never answered. I tucked his hair behind his ears. I wiped his chin. I crossed his hands upon his chest and stole his shoes.

ASLEEP IN THE house is where they found me. I had been there enough days that I no longer knew how long. One of the men came with rye and asked me questions and I said nothing. Another man, and I said nothing, took a sack of coins from a hole in the fireplace. I didn't know it was there. He left me bread. Then the men in simple clothes with plain hair, three of them, who kneeled to where I lay and touched my forehead with dry palms. They lifted me and I thought it was my father again, but backward, and I fought because I thought they would drown me. Only kin could kill me, I tried to say. They put me in the back of a cart and opened my mouth to spoon honey in. I tried to spit it out but it stuck to my tongue, the backs of my teeth. Sweetness. I licked it off myself and swallowed. They swore they wouldn't harm me.

"Will someone bury my father?" I asked.

I had tried once myself, but he was swaddled in flies. I stood some steps away and told him I was sorry for what I had done to his quilt. I slapped my face to show him he wasn't wrong for hitting me.

They told me he was at peace.

"In the ground?"

We'd had dead men before. Men my father may have shot, though I didn't see. He told me bodies haunt you if they're not put well under. I could hardly lift the shovel, but I helped him. Scrabbled the dirt with my hands, heaping it out, heaping it back. We buried the men like my father buried his twisted sticks. Maybe too the *she* was there, the one that once belonged to us. Things died in the forest, and you had to put them under.

I didn't want my father haunting me.

"In the ground?"

One of the men nodded, though he was looking off, and the other two drove the cart on. Out of the forest, away from the creek and the clearing and the still and the squirrel and the body.

AWAY FROM HOME, nothing looked like home. We were going south. Some trees and fields, but houses too. Long stretches with all-the-same plants. The hills went away. I'd peek sometimes, but mostly I slept and feigned to sleep until Savannah. Easier not to look. We stopped once at an inn for the night, though I was asleep when they carried me in. I didn't get to see the cows I heard lowing. The mattresses were up on stilts. I thought they'd swallow me, so soft. There was even a pot beneath my bed, as if they knew. In the morning, the men gave me tea in a leaf-thin cup. I didn't break a thing.

It was hot afternoon, me still eyes-shut in the back of the cart, when we stopped. The house was long and wood, with a stick stuck in the roof and a smaller stick across it. The road rolled in clods of dirt. I looked ahead and behind and didn't see anything else but that long house, like it had grown up from a seed with no company. They lifted me out again and I tried to ask.

"Where is this?" I said. It had been a long time since I'd spoke.

The man set me on my feet and took my hand. The others went ahead, walked the stone path between the prickly bushes. They looked such a long way away, knocking at the door. Someone came out. Everyone moved their hands. My hand was still in the man's, which was sweaty. It was hot afternoon. Then there was nodding and the man started walking forward. My feet didn't know to follow him. I tripped, and he waited. We stumbled that way to the wide board porch. I stood in front of a door wider than five of me, their hands on my arms now, calling me *orphan*. The one who took me was low and soft in long black robes and had a chest that ballooned toward me. I placed my hands upon it and pushed into its softness and when she chirped, I learned what a woman was.

The three men patted me and shook hands and bowed at the woman, who they named *Christian*, and the woman bowed, and then they turned back down the prickle path. I said, "Wait!"

"Where?" I said.

They turned and nodded, and the one who held my hand just waved. Why did it take three men to carry me here, and one woman to take me? What was in her front to make it so soft? I pushed at it again. She grabbed my wrists in one hand and pulled me inside. It was dark and cool and the shadows moved.

She showed me the rooms where children slept, the room where children ate, and a big room where children put their hands together and thought about goodness. All children, no fathers. As we walked, we saw other women. Swathed in black robes, crows with belly-pale fish in their mouths. I was still six, and deathly scared. They flocked around the beds, in the halls. I saw them kneeling and striding, wings spread, chests bobbing. At night, they hunched over us and cawed in a language that was not our own. Most raised their eyes when walking, so I'd only see their underlashes. They did not smile, though some glowed. Women, if these were they, were not our kind. Women were not to be befriended, touched.

The other children were thin as stirring spoons, all named *orphan* too. Their eyes bulged like fish, caught by crows. My own hands trembled to feel. The husk beds, the white basins, the wavy windowed glass. The first night I curled into a pill-bug on my bed, then saw the boy one over had wool. I peeled back his blanket, scurtled in with him, closed our woolen nest. I wrapped my arms around his middle and slept. Dreamed it was my father let me hold him so. In the morning, the boy kicked me in the stomach and screamed for the women. They bundled me away and plunged me in cold water and combed my hair for nits. They slapped my cheeks and fed me mashed corn and dressed me in shirt and breeches so small my legs could not bend enough to sit, so when I was weary of standing I lay down.

Each day before dawn came, we were forced onto knees, my seams split. The older boys chanted loud, and I mumbled along.

They all were addressing my father. I was some surprised but said, "Yes, Father, I hope you are well in heaven, hollow though you be." We sang songs that sounded like moans. We ate from wooden bowls as the sun woke, then washed our ears and went to field. Cotton grew, and corn. Melon in the summer. No lazing here, no pausing to nap by firesides or gaze antward. I was not a farmer but a boy. I followed the one in front of me, who bent with pudgy hands for weeds. I thought to pull what he pulled, but he pulled them all before me. I walked close behind. Our work was twinned. We did this for not long—there were black men who did the rest. They were older and didn't mind. We did it for our morals, is what I learned. After an hour of morals, we were inside again and at our lessons. I pulled my fingers up to count, but never knew what to call them. One, two, three, and stopped. The books I never figured. The other boys were all kinds of sizes but to the last they knew their letters. One would stand in front and say rhyming things, and another would sit at a desk and spell out loud, and another drew loops of lines on slate. Proud they were, to speak of things that made no sense. I thought them stupid.

"You'll learn," the teacher said.

"Learn what?" I said. I had never seen a man in the world say rhyming things. Not even the men with gold buttons carried slates in their coats. I saw no hope for these boys with their letters. I moved my mouth when we all recited, but nothing came out, and no one minded. No one minded, long as I remembered my father in the evenings.

One night I hated him. Or was afraid. The coldness of his hands returned to me, and I wanted shed of him. I bent down with the other boys and while they praised I cursed. "Damn you, Father, damn you," and when the master heard, my back grew bloody wings, stripes laid all across. Another boy stood and showed me how to speak and for his pains was given figs. I watched the juices in his mouth. I rolled my tongue into a curl. My back burned. His lips dribbled. "He is not my brother," I thought. "He is not my father's son."

So I made no friends. None among the made-up kin would let me hold them.

There were girls too, things as small and straight as we. They rooted in their own rooms, bent above their own chores. Our broken clothes were given to them, sewn to be split again. Negroes shared the field with us, Indians brought meat and hides and went away with bundles. I was the only one who resembled myself. The only one still brought to tears by women's breasts. Who'd never seen a kiss, could not guess the placing of lips to skin was kindness. There may have been others. I never asked. I never spoke. The matron crows would hum in foreign words. The negroes dipped their calls in something brown and wet so I couldn't tell the sounds apart. The Indians barked deep. My father stopped listening. I took my bread as it came. When I was told to ask the Lord to differ us from evil, I asked myself. Myself answered, "Yes."

Two girls were not negro or Indian or orphan. They lived in the attic, closest to heaven, and served our master and the crows. Brought and took dishes, helped with linens, sewed things with their young fingers. A girl with few teeth, who nightmared us all, and a girl with red hair. Children, but with parents somewhere. For a week they'd be gone, and we knew. They came back fatter, like they had slept sound, like someone had kissed their faces before sleep. The one who wasn't ugly was beautiful. She didn't walk but skipped. Everything was dancing, and it was light, nothing like the men in my father's cabin who pounded till the plates fell down. She talked with her hands, and they danced. Little fingers dancing. None of us knew her name.

There was a day when she cupped my chin and said, "Look at that face. Who was your mother, to leave you?"

I whispered. "My mother, I believe, is dead. I believe my father knocked her head." A rhyme, though it was true.

One robed woman felt almost kind, and to her I gave my thoughts and whatever I found, the summer blackberry, the winter nest. She was mostly still, moved only if poked. Dry and old. Her cheeks hung in pockets. The day I brought her a dead mole, its dunness for her boned hand, she asked me what I hoped for, roundabout. "Where are you going after this world?" is what she asked.

"To the next to see my father."

"And where is your father?"

"Asleep."

"In heaven?"

"He didn't say."

"What will you do to get there?"

I hadn't known there was a map. My head I lay on her hard thin legs and clutched her knees. The mole was on the ground. She hadn't touched it. I watched its hand, stiff and scaled, grasping in its last breath, as she told me how to go.

"God loves those who love," she said. She steered me from hitting, biting, from telling lies, from stealing rolls. She never said what love was. I dug my fingers in her leg, my eyes shut tight, till she pried them free.

As she stood to leave, her skirts hushing, I said, "You are who I love."

Her pouched face hardened. "No. God is who you love."

In bed beneath the summer linen, I wondered had I met a man named God. Or didn't he care to meet me. What was love but a touch. My hands around her knees. His belt against my back. Love being warm fingers, hate being cold. God had no hands. When we woke at night, dream-sweated, we were meant to pray to fall asleep. I stopped praying. I wept instead.

ABOVE ALL THE women was a man. Men I knew. He marked our comings and goings in a little gold book. In the belt around his robe lived a leather lash. He was a fancy man, who used his belt not for whippings but to hold a whipper. His nose was so long it almost touched his mouth, though I never saw his tongue come out to lick it. Some days he wasn't there, some days he was. Mornings, he stood over prayer. With all our mouths mumbling, even the crows, he didn't speak. He had wet eyes. I couldn't tell if he was sad. The less I remember him, the more I think he was.

He brought me to his room once. Gave me a cross made out of sticks. I started, for I was no fool and knew about sticks. He smiled and opened up my fist. The sticks were smooth, all the nubbins worn off. When his eyes were closed and he was speeching, I looked about. A small room for a grown man. White walls, no dirt. A bed and a table and a jug. I was thirsty so I stepped over on soft toes. His eyes snapped open when I spit it all over the white wall.

"Stronger than my father's," I said for apology.

He kept staring, there on his knees with his hands together and his nostrils wide. I inched out.

I inched in again. "Thank you," I said, holding up the cross. I ran.

When next I saw the woman my friend, I butted against her. She was washing plates in the yard. All the dirty water smelled of fat. Hungry, I gnawed soft on her arm. She pushed me away. She didn't want my too-big shoes to get wet.

"Where do you make the whiskey?" I asked.

She looked like I had something foul on my face.

"I can help." Though really I knew nothing. I couldn't start a fire. Fires started in spite of me.

"We don't drink whiskey, son," she said. Me and Jesus were sons, and everyone else was a father. I told her about the jug of the long-nose man and she put her hand across my mouth and shook her head.

"We tell our own sins," she said, "not others'."

Sin was not a word I knew.

Some of us were worse than I was. Would go down pond-ways on full moons and swim clothesless, boys and girls. Would drag their shirts back wet to bed. I followed them once, young as I was, and climbed a tree to stare. The red-haired girl was there, laughing. Their forms mirrored out in the night water. They pushed, they ducked, I thought they'd drown. I held to my branch and waited for ants. An owl hooted by and they gasped and dove, all bodies down. Bubbles surfaced and the girls' hair. Wet mats of muddy brown and gold. Then they were serpents, dolphins. In lessons, they told us of the ocean, as if we'd seen it. We smelled it. The creek here ran straight to sea. There were boys who could swim it. But here the cattails shivered round the wallow, and we were in the middle of ourselves. No sea to see, no mountain, not even flatness. Just our bodies in the water, in the arm of the marsh. You could smell brine on the dusk wind. Beyond that edge was nothing human. A mile of swamp, untouched. Unheld. The creeks snaking toward each other and darkness. To the ocean where dolphins flew.

The red-haired girl climbed out first, shook herself, saw me on the branch. "I've never seen a lizard like you," she said, and twisted her hair in loops so the water seeped out. She put a finger to her lips. I nodded, and she laughed again. Danced back up the slope to the house that was not her home. Her head like a flicker of light.

In my watered thoughts, I fell asleep. I could almost hear the creeping of the children, their sloshed footsteps in August dirt. But I could not open my eyes. My branch was my father, my arms held close. In my dreams I was walking hand in hand, him in one, death in the other. I think it was the mole. Its hand was furred. I woke to not a wren but an angry blackbird, her hands clapping in the air beneath me, yelling damnation, cold breakfast. I crawled down and didn't speak. I traced the footprints of the night demons, their toes still spread in the muck. I got no dinner but welts, no supper but a dark small room. I was left to sorrow and to pray. I thought of sins, but they were not my own. I thought mostly of the water, wondering could I swim if taught. I thought it was something like running. Only you must do it faster than the water runs downward, for at the bottom was nothing but more water, and deep. When the other children huddled to bed, I was put to mine and told to pray. The one who once seemed kind said, "And think what could've snatched you in that tree," so I knew she was kind again. I thought about what could have snatched me, hawks and foxes and mice, till I fell asleep, dreamless.

WHEN I WAS ten and older than some, a man came to find me. Men had taken others. We weren't to live there forever, our feet kicking the same waters. They trained us to hire us to discard us. We were not forsaken, we were sold. He was shorter than my father and thicker and his arms bulged. He had a nose red from drinking. Cheeks tight as plums. Dark bristle beard that I touched the first night he fell asleep before me. I stood in the morning room and said I would not go. The bony woman I thought was kind stood behind the master, who shook his head.

"Brother Sterrett is a good man," he said.

I had no brothers. I took off my shoes and held them in my hands. I said I would not go.

"He has a child, a boy your own age. He's a physician and will teach you to be a good assistant."

I thought he looked like a grave robber. "I want for no more teaching," I said and hugged my shoes against my chest. I had been there four years now. Four years more of learning, or not learning. Of counting all the bad I did so I could tell my master in confession. I stood on one side of the wooden closet, and he on the other. I saw his lash when I closed my eyes. This is how I remembered to call him father. *I said God's name out loud.* I'd press my hands together, formal. *I bit my bedmate. I stole Sister's apple. I have wished I were not here.* I said many prayers to wash away the bad. He'd bless me, but he didn't love me. This was his punishment for me, this man.

"I'm sorry," I said. I looked at the master. "I won't do it again."

"This is a blessing," he said. When he tried to smile, his lip caught in a twist. "Brother Sterrett is sent to you from God."

The visitor shifted on his feet and pulled his beard once. This I did not believe. I was not so unlearned. God didn't know who I was. I looked at Brother Sterrett. He looked down. He knew

Master was lying. The red-haired girl opened the door and on seeing us shut it with a laugh. She had come for the breakfast tray. I heard her steps as they changed from wood to earth. If I turned my head, I would see her spinning in the field. My feet were cold. I said again I would not go. The master begged his pardon. Said, "Return tomorrow. He will be ready then." I shook my head and let the crow pull me from the room.

I could not tell if we were damned or saved. They did not make that clear. If what my body did mattered. Forgiveness, though, was like a wheel going round. My body moved out into darkness, my body moved back in. As long as it got on the wheel in time. In time being before my body died.

Every house I went to was worse, and so I would not go to his. At his house I would die, no time to confess, and go to hell, and there I would see my father, and not wanting to see my father yet because of fear, I wanted to live instead. I would not be taken by a false brother. What I had learned in four years of not learning is that there are such things as women, and they are the ones that hold and men are the ones that punish, and if I had to leave a home again, I wouldn't be riding in the cart of another man. I would take my own self. Run away with my own self. Whatever I did to save my body would be all right, just more for the sorry wheel to carry away.

After prayer that night, we rustled into beds. When the candles were guttered, I slipped away, nothing to carry. The long hall was dark. My soft feet noisy down the stairs. I paused to see all the empty space. The morning room, at night, was empty. A light marked the desk where children were entered into books. The master's pen across the page. I crept to the desk to see the candle. If I knew my letters, I would open the book and find my name and cross it out, one thin line. No one would take me but myself, though if only someone would want me. I tried not to cry and my trying-not-to-cry made the master's candle toss. I sucked back in my breath, and the flame went still. This would light my way. My hands took his candle in its silver stand. It felt like a body in my hand, still burning. It would show me where my steps should go. Would light me to a house with a woman inside who would hold me and cover me in blankets.

I heard a step above. The women were walking. A door opened. I started. An upstairs voice. The candle with me, I turned and ran. I followed the afternoon path of the serving girl into the night darkness. Out of the morning room. Down the hall. Across the board porch, and into grass. Grass for miles. I stumbled and was caught by the furrows of a tulip tree. In the darkness I crouched, my arms across my face. My ankle hurt. I wanted to sleep. Maybe I could wait. The brother who was no relation would come and go, and Master would come out and find me here, would speak to Jesus who saw everything, who knew the hearts of every man, right down to the lilies, which are just another kind of man, and Master would bend down to me and his lash would be missing and he'd say, "Son, I would not give you to another. I would not leave you, not even for the shadow of the valley. Not once more will I stroke this lash on your skin," and I would say, "I do not mind the lash, for I am a sinner, like you said."

I dreamed, and my heart slowed, and when my eyes opened, the darkness was alight. The house, my home, the wide wood walls were flaming.

My candle was nowhere. Not in my hand.

It was in the stairs, in the hall, dropped and hungry. The sky was burning. I had not meant to leave it. In the fleeing, I had dropped my fire and the house had caught it. Bodies were running out like ants.

I stood and walked to the marsh pond. I crawled into the water from the dock and hugged the post, my body floating out behind me. Here the water, dark and spangled, matched the night. Only the cattail tips were lit with pink. The smoke still faint. I held and buoyed and might have slept. Sleeping is a comfort. Not just for the tired. The shouts and slosh of buckets were too distant now, nothing to be heard but frog yells and lake water lapping on the bank. There was no sound but nature made. I told my body to still itself, would have let my wicked hands go except they were the only thing holding on. From there, I could not see the house crashing down.

IN THE MORNING they found me cold and white in the pond, a floating fish. My arms had held. I had not drowned. They bundled me back and lay me in the cow barn, where beds of boys spread end to end. The girls slept with the sheep. I listened to their talk of us. I ran when others ran, is what they said, afraid as any other. All redeemed, no harm, except the one.

"What one?" I asked, and someone said a girl, the one who brought us tea and breakfast. Red-haired, who slept in the attic and had so far to come. Down the narrow wooden stairs, down two stone sets more. Farther than the others. Just a serving girl who couldn't save herself. I nodded.

"Where is she?" I asked. They touched my shoulder and said it again.

But, I wanted to know, was she damned or was she saved? If no one blamed me it was not my fault. And no one blamed me.

I waited for her to twirl into the cow barn. I asked the other boys to tell me if they saw her. They laughed. I laughed, getting the joke. But I waited. Hay kicked up by the wind made me flinch. I could not even save myself.

In the afternoon, the brother came and got me and I could not say a word. My shoes were tight and we rode two days into Carolina. We ferried across oceans that were not oceans, that were only sounds, he said. Pelicans crossed our path. When we stopped the horse for water, one dove near. Shot out of the sky, a tangle of bones plummeting. I thought it dead. None had come to our orphaned pond. But in the drowning, it wrestled a fish and rose. We slept beneath the cart. I wrapped my arms around a wheel so as not to clutch my master in my night wanting. It was April and the dark still cool. I briefly wondered at my life.

"Your mother dead?" he asked in the morning.

My mother. I didn't have a mother.

"Father?"

"Sir, he was a drunkard," for that is what the crows had called him.

We rode two miles more. I sat up this time, kept my eyes wide. I was mostly grown, not the worm I was when last I rode in such a cart. Everything I saw could be used for when I next escaped. A creek there, blackberry bushes, a trunk with a hole in it, perfect for hiding. I knew I would never see them again. I was too lonely to go where there were not men. I sat tall next to Brother Sterrett and tried to guess how hard he'd hit.

"Are you much religious?" I asked.

He turned to me, surprised. The reins looked so easy in his hands, I wanted to hold them.

"I am not much," I answered myself, staring straight forward, man-like.

"You haven't seen a lot one way or the other," he said.

He was stupid. "You can't *see* God."

"You'll see plenty before you're done. Squeamish?"

I didn't know the word. Didn't answer.

He patted his belly. "Does your stomach turn easy?"

Whiskey'll do it, I thought. Dead men. Fires. Serving girls. Men with lashes. Urine. Wooden closets. Moles.

"You work hard," he said, "you'll earn your dinner, so no fear I'll starve you. I don't know what the nuns gave you, you're a sack of bones, but any tool needs its oil. This is a job, though, not a home. Just stay on the right side of that."

Not a home. How should I live in a house with a man and his son and eat their corn and sleep with dreams and shit in the same distant hole and not have a home? Where was it? The woman who was my friend before I killed a girl would say all that will come when I am dead. The good comes later, when we claim it from heaven. So long as we keep coming back to our forgiveness wheel. Nothing to do but wait. Nothing for me now. I only worried how long I'd live.

WE WERE BACK in South Carolina, where I may have been from. Near Beaufort, he had a house. Small and wood and washed white. A woman had lived there but was dead or gone. The boy had not my years but fewer. We matched in thinness, in wary stares. The three of us shared a room. A second held the hearth and an old quilt frame, boards across it to make a table. The third was where the bodies came. Broken and bruised. Cracked skulls, festering feet. Spider bites. They'd said he was a doctor, but I never guessed the ailments. How twisted the body could get and stay alive long enough to reach his office. So there were no ladies with sweet coughs, I didn't mind. I was brave enough for worse. And, secret, I wanted to learn how to heal a man who was choked with drink. Who was lying in a puddle of his filth, cramped in a blackberry dip by a copper pot. I wanted to know if that was a man you could save.

The first day I thought I'd learn to heal. I had my hands out straight, strong. I was not to hold the binds or bandages, though, but to empty the basins. Blood, piss, puke. The little one watched me from the corner of the house, squatting. He wore a shirt that touched his knees and nothing else. Sterrett said it was a negro shirt, left over from the man they used to have. The negro had held the binds and bandages until he cut himself on a little knife and his veins boiled open. The boy chewed his hands in sorrow. I was no negro, and they would not care for me. The boy whistled at me as I scrubbed the pot out with elm leaves, rough to catch the clots. I once flung piss at him sideways, but he ducked rabbit-fast behind the house. I thought for days he might be mute.

I had practice in being quiet. I knew to listen. Knew my own voice was weak and not worth hearing. No surprise that another boy knew this too. We were mirrors of each other, broken. But I was holding the offal and he had no duties. Seemed almost wild. I thought, that is because his father is not dead yet. There was no affection between them, no touched hands, and if I could have written a story of fathers and sons, this is what it would have been: he lashed us both when we mischiefed, but hit his son harder. I could've told the boy things but didn't. In the surgery, there was no talk of kinship. Bodies came in, bodies went out. Men tied to nothing, not even their own limbs. Just pieces to be sewn up, skin to be patched. No heart, no thoughts, unless there really was a heart, or a brain split wide. We were not meant to feel.

The first man I saw die on the slab in the surgery had been shot with a musket by his wife. She wanted to give a fright, Sterrett said. Half his chest had torn open, his left arm hung by a cord to his shoulder. His eyes still flickered. His heart, bare, shuddered. Sterrett gave him something, whispered in his ear, pressed his eyes shut, closed his own. I saw him flinch and breathe and then expire. Like nightfall, fast. Sterrett left the room and I stayed quiet. I watched the dead man and waited. I touched him once before he was cold. I slipped my fingers under his thumb and bounced it. It fell heavy each time, turning paler. I backed away. The blood was leaving through the hole Sterrett cut in his back, a thick leak into the white bowl below. When it filled, I could not yet move, and watched from the corner as it flooded over. I rubbed my fingers on the scratch of my pants. I worried the dead would stay on them.

I was not jelly-kneed. I was not a child, or a coward. I had seen dead men, had buried some, had touched one, had killed a girl. But I knew of hauntings. Vapors in a man come out when he has passed, and body or not, they linger. They cling. You can smell them like old eggs. The crows had said this was not true, that the spirit was invisible and anyway was holy, it did no wrong but went up to heaven direct, no dallying, to be with our father. I knew better. What spirit would want to be with its father? I took to washing myself in the marshes. Taking on the swamp smell to drown out the dead. Nor did I go walking at night. The ghosts would not know me to haunt me. They must have draped around Sterrett like ivy. He did not mind when men came in and old flesh went out. When a man walked up with "My chest is sore" and left with pennies on his eyes.

Suppers were silent but not without sound. Sterrett chewed his meat open-mouthed and swallowed loudly. The boy ground his teeth, scraped his spoon across the tin plate, and sucked his food from cheek to mouth and back again, making pulp from solid. I made my mouth work as hushed as I could. I was a deer, safe among the wolves. We ate meat every night, and my belly slowly pouched. Bread, cabbage, and on Sundays, pudding. Neighbor women brought the dish as payment for his presence. My first taste of raisins. They drank a cider that was sweeter than my father's whiskey, and if we were well fuzzled, Sterrett would play his fiddle in the dusk and the boy and I would wrestle or sleep. There was nothing wrong, or lacking. Nothing that hurt. But I was cold every night, on the floor, under wool, in the summer dark.

WHEN THE HOUSE was empty, the father lying half drunk beneath a tree, as fathers do, the son would walk me to the shore and show me bones. Was this the first time I had seen the ocean? I wouldn't know it, for how familiar it was. Like my home creek running clear through the still, like the rotten backwater marshes by the lake where I dipped to hide, like rain coming down, except wide, wide, wide. The boy thought me a fool, but I knew what to do. I ran in up to my knees, then dove. What boys do with water. I remembered every cut I didn't know I had. I couldn't see below, not with my eyes open, so I let him show me. He made the dead horseshoe crabs dance, the empty mussels play. If I laughed, he'd kick me in the calves. If I spoke, he'd run into the sea until his head was under. Some things are so thick with marvel, one person is not enough to see them. I wanted to show someone the ocean. There was no one near. I pointed to the waves, still coming, never not coming, but the boy didn't follow my hand.

When once I slept half in the sand, the boy wrapped a jelly-fish round my head. I woke in screams, thinking my face was being shred. He said it was a man-eating weed, and I spat at him. Sterrett rubbed my face with wet sand and made me wash in vinegar. I cried and said I was not crying. When he was calm, the boy would sit on a dune between the marshes. I would rest stick's-length from him. The sun was hotter than I ever knew it. The cut of wind made us think we could sit endless. He dug holes to piss in, and I broke apart dead crabs and threw their bits at the seagulls. We moved as little as we could, like we were dying.

Such sea days were rare. People hurt themselves more than they did not. My stomach grew harder. Filled from inside, sickened from out. I was not scared long. I sawed bones to fold men in half who would fit in a child's box. I cut fingers and baked them and gave them to lovers who begged. I held a baby, unborn, and washed her and buried her though Sterrett said to throw her out. I saw the insides of negroes, as red and pink and wet as our innards. Or regular innards, I had not seen mine. Little ails too. Splinters, corns, coughs, baldness. A man with a snake still in him, the fangs spread wide, grinning. A fingernail pulled off. A girl with no mother, thinking she was bleeding to death the first time she got her courses. A boy who found a nest, swallowed an egg, hatched a bird inside. People who wanted to smash their heads against rocks. No man is never hurt. I grew precious toward my body. When I cut myself on an urchin, I wrapped my own finger. Swaddled my own blood, kept it for myself.

The only time my sickness overswamped my belly was when they brought the girl. I was thirteen, and she was not much older. A serving girl, or poor. Burned raw. He could do nothing. She looked at him until her eyes stopped looking. Her skin in puddles. I did not ask what fire was set. What crime. It was mine as a boy. Her feet had not been fast enough. High up in the attic, where unwanted things go. Old wicker chair, box of curtains for winter, wooden horse for riding, what is put in attics? Serving girls. Red-haired and slow. I never had to see her body. If she had had a body left. Fingers dancing in the flame. She will keep dying. Here she is again, a ghost of a ghost. She left her skin on the table when they took her body. The rag in my hand would not move. I had lit the pyre. My dinner dribbled up and burning from my mouth. The candle had been in my hand and then not. Sterrett hit me once and took the rag himself. There is no wooden closet here to tell my sins.

ONCE, WITH STERRETT gone, the boy and I brought inside a three-legged toad. We'd found it coming home from the shore. It crossed our path, streaking the blood from its once-leg. The boy patted it dry with a leaf. I rolled it in my shirt. In the surgery, I gave the stump a bandage. The boy sang a frog song to keep it still. Its wet eyes got bigger. In the hearth room a flat ladder grew up to a hole in the ceiling. A narrow space sat empty above us. We crawled up with our patient, made a grass nest in a box of laudanum bottles. Thimble of water. Two worms, cut in half. The boy said they'd grow back their heads and be four.

Sterrett came home, we ate supper, eyed each other with panic and mystery. We twitched in our seats. Every branch against the window was the toad resurrecting.

The next day Sterrett was called out again, and we took a candle up the ladder to the space above. I wouldn't call it an attic. I didn't hold the candle. We peeked into the box. The toad had moved an inch and one half of the halved worms was gone and the others were dead and the bandage was gone and the brown grass was a little blood-rusty. The toad's eyes didn't look so big. I told the boy to touch it and he said no. He grabbed my hand and forced it in the box but I swung out my elbow and jabbed him in the ribs and he put my neck under his arm and I had my knee in his stomach and his hands were grabbing at my hair and my foot kicked him in the crotch. We were too old to bite each other. I thought that was a victory but after he finished clutching himself, he leaped at me again and in the tumble my leg went through the floor. We stopped. I wasn't much hurt. A leak had made a soft patch in the wood. He sat and considered. I hung there, my hands keeping my weight up. The candle had gone out. I wished one of us had touched the toad, to see.

He pulled me out and we climbed down the proper way. We were too clumsy to fix our clumsiness. He swept up the bits of wood from the hearth floor. I said maybe Sterrett never looked up. We waited. At supper again, and he rolled his mouthfuls between his cheeks and swallowed down two mugs of cider and bent his head to scratch at his scalp. The boy and me sweating. We looked down, we pointed out dirt on the floor, we shook our shoes to draw attention to them. The food was gone, and Sterrett tapped his pipe. His yawn was horseapple-sized. Back in his chair he leaned and looked straight up. Like he was moon-gazing.

He made the boy fetch the toad. Sterrett lifted it from the laudanum like a ball and threw it out the open door.

"Which one of you?" he said, pointing up at the hole.

"The toad I found," I said, but he didn't care about vermin. His hand was still pointed firm up. "It was—" and I made a bowl of my hands to show, but the lash cracked against the table and I stopped.

"You fall through my ceiling?"

His eyes said I should not say yes. I did not say yes. He snapped his wrist again and the plates jumped. How was he so quickly armed? His beard twitched on its own. I brought my hand up again and crooked my finger, to show the cripple of the toad whose story I was going to tell, but the boy punched my arm.

"Me," he said, and Sterrett took him outside and beat him. He did it lower than my father, at the knees. This made walking sting. I heard him crying out. I stood where they left me, my finger still in a crook.

Under the blanket, I couldn't sleep. Sterrett was spread out on his stomach, muffling snores into his pillow. On the floor with me, the boy was quiet. I nudged him. Whispers were for nighttime talking.

"Why?" I asked.

He tucked one shoulder in.

I pushed him harder. "You didn't do it," I said.

He flipped around and stared. "So he lashed me. He would've lashed me anyway. Shut your loud damn mouth."

"Do you think the toad was still alive?"

He lay so still, his eyes open, his brows a straight line, that I thought he was asleep again, however strange.

"I hate you," he said.

I did not feel less bad for being spared. I felt I had skipped around God's judgment. I was not afraid of being beaten, except that my leg already hurt from falling through the ceiling, but this was all right, I would've taken it. True, I was not his son. There is something about being a son. He maybe wanted the lash more than I did, it being his father's hand, his father's judgment. It is good to pay for the sins of the son. He would be loved more for it, when all the counting up was done and the world was over. But I was angry that he stole my burden. If boys were going to steal my sins, I must find a way to pay for them myself. I let him hate me, for hate was something I could carry.

I was still young. The worst was not knowing whether the toad was dead. Did he eat his little bandage?

The boy and I tried not to be friends again. He wood-wandered. I scrubbed blood.

AROUND US THE world was fighting too. The bodies that came now were soldiers. I didn't know what it was for, and Sterrett never said. I knew how men jabbed at each other. Each with a sense of what's his own, and the fire to stake his life on it. In a war there are many ways to die. When I was almost sixteen, when the wind and sun were cold, they blew up the fort down the road from the town. Men came to fight us for our homes. What homes? Sterrett went to battle, his knives in a bag. He hid behind a tree behind a hill and they brought him the wounded. The boy took his drums out and tattooed the march. I stayed but heard the cannon. Not many men, a skirmish, but it was our river, our hill, so guns were pointed and popped. A game, if anything, though at least four dozen died. They returned with lit eyes. The boy's arm in a sling. The father proud. The only time I saw him proud. By the morning, the light was gone, and the British.

The next year, the boy left in regimentals. Was blown apart in some larger battle. Sterrett never wept, though I did. It made no sense that those I halfway loved were stolen. I'd go where they went, if only they showed me the way. The two of us remained. He didn't urge me to pick up my gun, so I stayed. Beside each other, we worked through bodies. I came nearer the table. Began to dig bullets from muscle, from pillows of yellow bile. My world was a red world, and green with decay. He was careful to teach me nothing. He never named the parts, never pointed out the cure. This would be my only job, he said. I'd be useless if I left. I nodded and dug my fingers deeper in flesh. My hunger was not for the dead but for the living. I never said.

When the war paused, seemed to have ended, I was older than my indenture. I knew this, I knew my own age. Remembering it was remembering my father. A day came without any sick, and Sterrett told me to follow him to the woods to look for herbs. He knowing them, naming them silently, gauging their powers, and me picking them. I had a pouch and papers and I would lay the weeds between sheets so they would not touch. I saw which ones he pulled powdery from jars to give the fevered, the nauseous. I wasn't wholly blind. But because he would have me so, I let him think it. Would point at a tiny tufted pine and ask if it was dogbane. These trips, we didn't speak much. But it was damp and my clothes were thin.

"I'm plenty old now," I said. "Think I'm free of any papers."

He pointed out some large, flat leaves for me to sever.

"Whatever you signed to take me. I'm older than that now. Can't keep me without pay."

He stopped and dug a hard straw in his teeth. "You got somewhere to get to?"

"A wage is all, not much. I'm a white man, and old enough."

He watched me fold up the leaves and pack them in my pouch. I stayed extra quiet now, to let him think. I pressed the leaves so soft they were like locks of lady hair. I fastened the pouch deliberate. I did not look at him but kept walking. Slow. The holes in my shoes let the chill in. Birds didn't sing much in a drizzle.

He stopped me. Laid the terms. He'd feed me, house me, clothe me, teach me a little more. I told him I wanted paper money. I wanted pounds. He held up his hands—empty, for he carried nothing into the woods—and said that's all he could do. We looked at each other, older and younger. I don't think he either had somewhere to get to. I nodded. It's hard to ask for something the first time.

He held me another year, filling me with meat. Not shouting so much. Offered me pence on Sundays. I kept them in a wooden box that once held barks, slipped beneath my bed. A year, and I started to feel like I might die the same man I started as. Full of holes, empty-handed, no-hearted. On the same wheel, nothing left to forgive. With no sins, how would God remember me? If I didn't move, he'd forget. When we died, he'd forget to call my name. If I had no one to love, I'd have nothing to show for this life. I was a wilty plant, dried up to nothing.

A woman came who'd had a child and could not stop her bleeding, and all were there, the woman, the man, the screaming infant, three other children. All were crying. Sterrett stuck his hands deep within her and blood came flowing down his arms, running along his own raised veins. He turned something or pulled something, and then staunched it and took a needle and thread below and made a fancy stitch, and though she was white as bones she was not dead. The man fell across her chest and held her tight. Kissed her shoulders and neck and breasts because her face was still too white and wide to touch. The children could not stop crying. We sent her home, where she may have died soon after, but in that room there was a family, whole, and I was awed by everything I didn't have.

A whole year passed.

I was twenty-one and a man and not a son. In November the sawgrass glowed. The air was cool salt as it slid in and out of windows. The last of the duck flocks settled. Sterrett was sharpening his knives when a man came. I was in the field coaxing peas. His head was pumpkin-sized. His eyes labored to open. A line of red ran from one ear. A man had struck him in the public house. Words about a woman. We laid him down, me with his hand in mine. Sterrett trepanned him. Cut a burr hole in his head and let his mind swell. I patched him with cloth, stroked his cheek as he slept. Sterrett washed his needle and handed it to me and asked me would I stitch him together.

"I am not a surgeon," I said.

"And when you leave, what will you do? Hold the ill and whisper to them?"

"I will not be a surgeon," I said.

He laid the needle on the man's chest, heaving slow, and dug his fingers in his beard. "And what will you do?"

"Whatever makes a living," I said.

"Am I not a wealthy man?" He left the needle on the chest and walked to the door.

"I know nothing," I said. "I am not your son."

"I do not want a son," he said, and left.

I looked at the man, whose hand I still held, whose head was turning paler. I shaved where Sterrett had cut, stitched his scalp to itself. I washed the wound in water and whiskey. The pepper smell recalled my father. This man was living still. I crossed his hands upon his chest, removed his shoes. Washed the tools and mopped the blood. Set a candle burning for the odors. Sat with him until he woke. In the silence, I thought of the living I had said I'd make. It was arms holding me, and nothing more.

Sterrett came back after dark, after the man with a hole in his head had risen and gone, after I sat moonlit with my peas, watching the shoots tremble. He ate some corn cake from breakfast and slept. I stole my box from beneath my bed. Took the cake's remainder and a knife from the surgery. I had seen him cut bone with it. These wrapped in a sack, I heaved myself through the kitchen window. I could have used the door but wanted to leave another way. Three miles past town I found a hollow. The darkness settled on me. I clutched a rambling root and let myself fall away.

IN THE MORNING I climbed a cart and rode north and east. The man said he wouldn't mind the company. I spoke in bits at first, for payment, but then was silent. I seemed to lose something each time my mouth opened. Saw bits of myself floating off. He took me through sun and night and brought me to Dorchester near the city. So I came close by the cities, to Savannah and now Charleston, but never saw them. When I was sturdier I would go, when I was not so afraid of men. He asked where I was bound, and I pointed, a little farther. But then I saw a church in a field, a house and a tower and a cross, and the field was gold and purpled with flower, and the sun was enough to touch, and so I spoke, and when the cart stopped I fell to the ground again. The church was small and brick and bare, and if anything made by man would not hurt me, that was it. I thanked the driver and said I was a servant of God. Which was a lie, as God knows. He nodded, blessed me, rode on, his bags of rice molded to my sleeping shape.

The doors were open to me, and on the wooden bench I lay, my sack beneath my head. I didn't sleep, but dreamed. The windows gold and green, sun shaking through the glass. I let my legs melt, my arms around myself, my eyes open to the light. No man came to visit, no hazy vision. No lord on a cross dripped blood upon my cheek. Nothing there but light, and I swallowed it and it filled my limbs. I was hungry and forgot my hunger and though I never slept, I never felt so still. The air deepened. I kept swallowing. No one had come to prod me, none to save me. The light inched away. Still dense enough for a child to ride on. It did not take away the hope when it was gone. In the dark, I chewed the edge of my sleeve, sweat-salted, and my tongue whispered me away. I was a well man, wrapped in the windows of God.

That night, long and smooth, was a single faith. In the morning the light, shifting east, had left. The building was brick again. I slept and snored until a man in vestments roused me. It was Sunday, he said, and time for service. Would I stay? I did, sat in the back while the women and their men filed in. They spoke with a familiar strangeness. Strung together words I knew. They kneeled and stood and sang. I saw one weeping.

After, the man asked if I sought relief. I nodded and he set me many labors. I could now do anything without surprise. There was no blood here but wine, no hardship but the heat. This was a man who smiled and softly. Was I too old for it to touch me? I asked where the wooden closet was, but he said here they did not tell each other sins, only God. He showed me a cabin behind his home and gave me a blanket for the cold. Slaves lived there once, he said, so it smells sometimes still of sadness. I helped him dig his fields in trade for the cabin and the blanket. I earned nothing, but I was not a slave. My body had begged for a refuge, had sought out this field. I was being kept from nothing. I soaked up peace like I had never seen it, and maybe I had never seen it.

We put in crops and cut wood and built a wallow for pigs and bought pigs and went to church on Sunday, though sometimes him and not me. We had a little snow, but soon hot and mostly hot. Some folk thought I was mute, and those liked me best. In a year, he gave me part of his land to farm. The yield being mine to eat or sell. When he met a woman who would be his wife, she asked for it back. He said he'd given it in good faith, it was no longer his to claim. I was surprised a churchman could marry, knowing only the master of the crows, who was only and always alone. But he said everyone has a heart for love. I saw he was blind, but I said nothing. In my new field, all my own, I planted corn. He said it was not wet enough for rice. I planted squash because seeds were cheap but would not eat it, the watery slick, so sold what grew. I planted sunflowers and pretended they were sown wild. Weeds, I called them, and watered them at night. I only visited the man now when he asked. There was a woman in the house, so I was careful. I kept to myself. I knew now to keep to myself, that was how it would be.

Though I was alone, I saw what it was to belong. The minister taught me family, the town taught me town. People moving in circles round each other. Peeling open the neighbor's weakness and his joy. I was the only one alone, so I could see. Words and touches like bits of light. A man sees a man in the street, a hand on the shoulder, a cap tipped, spark of light. Women knotting the bonnets of babies, more light. All this giving without asking. Myself on the outside, a dark spot, but calm. This was a good place. I had felt no whips. I had not heard God's rumble. If I stayed here a hundred years, someone would touch my shoulder.

But in between all the goodness, the town was dwindling. I had seen the dying before, but not so many so fast. I stayed on the edges of it. Watched. Tried not to make friends, though most everyone was kind. Fevers here ran swift, and not just among the young. Some left for fear. The fort was falling down that had held the British off, then held the British. A boy threw a crumbled brick through a window of the church. It was left broken. Broomstraw grew where the grains had been, and goat's rue. It was a plague without a name. I didn't know the medicine for this disease. Sterrett had left me nothing. As the souls slipped off, I saw the world was pulling in its edges. Was shrinking around me. That soon it would just be me, and then I too would go, and this was not sad. A crab tucking into its shell for the long evening. I dug graves for the victims, held their coffins going down as I had once held hands with the dying. The forty families winnowed to twelve, and five.

And then she appeared.

New to town, orphaned old, ward of a maiden aunt. She was Dorchester born, had gone to the free school where girls were numbered. Had known the town when it jostled. Left before it decayed. She wore the fabrics of the city, had a hat with paper flowers. I saw her first in church.

No, before that. I was a boy and I was dreaming.

Straw hair and eyes a color I couldn't name. Later she told me blue. She moved in circles in my dream. She had wings. She spoke in words that didn't sound. She looked just like herself. I was a boy, and when I woke, my shirt was wet with sweat. My father still alive, and I had never known a woman. But she knew me. Had found me as a boy, left me in a marsh with crows for mothers, left me with my hands in blood and gore, led me here to a prairie of religion. The church on a hill, my cabin in a field, my crops in a row. The minister had tempered me. I was ready for her.

I saw Anne in her body first in church. The hat, and a blue dress for her eyes. I didn't speak, but looked and looked. Sunday next, I had milkweed in my hand. It was summer and all was blooming. As she left on small shod feet, I dropped them in her path. I shook too much for reaching out, for greeting. She smiled and knelt and before her hand touched the stems I fled. Sunday next, she brought the first of the goldenrods and laid them on the last bench. The bench where I sat unseen, having no holeless shirt, no well-soled shoes. Sunday next, she sat beside me, and when we bent to pray I took her hand. She tried to shake me free. I clung harder. With her other hand she pinched my ribs. I scowled and squeezed again. She laughed. She laughed in the middle of a song, so none heard. She told me I had a fine face.

I knew not what to do, so with my bone knife I cut a stick. Cut it like my father, but in place of vermin carved a bird. Took her past the empty fort to the Ashley River. The water settled me. If something happened, I'd thought since a boy, a river would carry me away. We lay beneath the bell of a willow and mingled hands and from my shirt I brought the bird. A wooden wren, a jenny wren, she called it. She told me wishes. She wished a house and fields and a rose garden like a lady, and I stopped listening to wrap her arms about my neck. I sat there, held, while she dreamed, and the river flowed.

I had believed that love was a difficult road. That the beloved would trick you, would tease, would let you burn. Would shoot a musket at your chest. Love was something got, not given. But here she was who looked at my eyes and let her hands be held. When I was weary she moved her hands upon my arms. When I sorrowed, she dug for the roots of it until I'd told her every past lash, every man I'd known. I gave her buds and bread and stones and she gave me surprise and kisses. She had been loved once, cruelly, and me not being cruel earned me her. This is what she said. But *earn* was not right at all. She came in spite of myself. The iced quick of me was melting. In fall when the birds were on their wings, I asked her would she stay with me forever. She would, she said. I asked her why.

"You're a good man," she said. "With such a heart."

"And we will be like this always."

"Till Jesus takes us," she said and smiled.

I said we would have a child. Two, she said. Four, I said. Till we counted to eleven and thought that sounded right. All would live, and all would prosper. She wanted to call them after flowers. I searched for my father's name, but in my years of remembering, I had lost that. I wanted to name one after my father, I said, and knowing, she never asked what it was. All days were days of sun. My chest was built of bubbles. I kissed her and was nothing but warmth.

I met her aunt when I asked to marry Anne. She seemed not to mind. The aunt was dying slowly. Her eyes were milky and she looked above my shoulder when I spoke. Rubbed my hand and said I had a fate. Fates are almost always good, she said, and smiled toothless. She nodded at my shoulder. She placed Anne's hand in mine. A fate for a fate, she said.

WE MARRIED IN December. It was 1786, the tenth year of the independence, and I was twenty-three.

As the town was dying, we built a home. That is, we took a home. I made a new door and she washed the walls white. She planted a dog rose by the window. I cut a path to my old fields. I could have planted acres, been a man who owned men, but the town was not hungry enough. I bought a horse and a whip and took my crops to Charleston. In the spring evenings, she read to me aloud. The gospels and the psalms. "All your children shall be taught by the Lord," she read, "and great shall be the peace of your children." Great shall be the peace of our children, I said. "The glory of children is their fathers," she read. Yes. I would be the glory of my children. Just as my father. No, not my father. I saw him burying wood rats in the dry dirt. I looked to my whip in the corner of the room. My children would be the glory. I was nothing.

At night, if the candles were out and we were not sleepy, she would talk. "My parents?" she'd say. "They weren't wealthy, of course, but laughed more than anyone I knew. My mother had a little flute that she would take to the poorhouse to play, and my father could jig, so everyone that saw them caught a glow. Faith, to me, was this. Charity was making men smile."

You make me smile.

"You have a smile like my father's. There was plenty to eat, though it was plain, and I had a dozen friends at school who

would come once a week to make paper figures and melt choco-
late if we could get it. There was a washline between our house
and the neighbor's, and the girls and I would send messages out
by clothespin and wait for replies that never came. There was
always an animal at our house being mended by my mother, and
we'd play at doctor, feeding a sparrow or knitting a harness for
a lame dog. It was a loud house, busy with love."

You miss it.

"I do miss it, but if my parents could be revived and I were
sent back to them, I would miss being with you. There are two
sides to life, the noisy and the soft, and you're my soft. But our
children will change all that. You'll have to build a barn for
yourself to hide from all our bustle. This is what love does, it
keeps getting bigger. You know that, of course. Think of those
years when you had none of it. It didn't go away, did it?"

She said this with a smile. I thought briefly that she knew
nothing of sorrow, and briefly I didn't trust her.

Finally by summer she began to grow. I had wondered but
not asked and now she was growing. I held her belly and waited
for the child. Was hungry to begin on another. Love could not
come fast enough. Now that all days were days of sun. When
she was sick, I worried. She'd heave her stomach once, then say
she was well. And she was. I prayed at her. I told the heavens
to cast an eye on her rounding body. What a marvel they had
made. An infant, the fruit of me. He was swathed in his mother.
He was shy. He was a seed invisible. Whatever strange herbs she
ate, midwife-given, I ate too. We bathed in the river together.
When I felt her belly, she felt mine.

"What will we call it?"

"Jesus," I said.

She scrunched her face.

"Hero," I said. "Best Child."

"Protagonist," she said. She brushed her fingers fast across my forehead, rubbing out the serious.

"Protagonist," I said. I didn't know the word.

"What was your mother's name?"

"It will be a boy," I said, though I could not know this, and though I was afraid of men. I felt a boy would be the fate of me. That I deserved one for what I had done, all the evil I caused needing repayment. But this would be a different boy. Blessed and calm. I would be a different father. We had Anne.

At the end of summer, she bent over in the garden. Her hand to one side. Her face a slant. I was building a shelf beside the hearth, could see her through the window. I came outside and asked if she were ill. She shook her head. A little blood, she said. She asked to be let alone. I gave her the house and sat in the bed she'd been furrowing for the squash and listened to her crying through the wall. I stuck my thumbs in the soil and twisted. Waiting. A worm came rudely up. If any animal had no family, worms would be it. I never saw two together. I stroked its side and it lashed around. I wished for a toad to feed it to. It found the dirt again and dove. A little dirt fish. I didn't want to lose anything.

Dark now. She opened the door and said come in. I waved my hand and kept my eyes down. Looked at every brown grass flake, each gnawed stone. She said come in. But she had said a little blood, so I stayed still, my bottom in the dirt. I shooed her. She closed the door. I didn't want to know. I was sitting and then I curled over, my knees to my chest. I fell asleep in the furrows. No dreams, just outside sleeping. Me in a long, long emptiness.

She brought me milk in the morning and put my hand on her stomach.

"We'll try again," she said.

I shook my head.

"Darling," she said, which was my favorite word of hers. It made me feel young and not like a boy but something dear.

Where did he go, our child? I'd done no bad things since I came there. I asked her if I could see him.

"Nothing left to see."

I was angry because she wasn't crying anymore.

She said, "Here. Listen. This is what women do. This is what happens. We will have another. Shh." Her arms were all the way around me now.

I didn't understand. I didn't want her to understand. *What women do.* She knew things she would never tell me. She would never tell me where our baby was. She pulled me up and brushed the dirt from my clothes and kissed my cheek and picked at the dirt beneath my fingernails and kissed my wrist and we kissed and we went inside and lay next to each other, but only softly touching.

ONLY A YEAR, and she was rounding again. This time would be different. I walked behind her. I stooped to pick the weeds so she wouldn't. I held her elbow on the path to church. I nailed the shelf a foot lower so she needn't reach. She got so sweated in the heat that I carried a bucket and cloth with me, to damp her face whenever she sighed. She said she didn't like the fussing, but the baby liked it, for he grew and grew. When her stomach became a pouch, I'd lie in bed beside it, my head by her hips, and the skin would thin away in the dark so I could see the limbs of him. Small foot, small fist. He didn't smile at me, because he didn't know me.

Her aunt was sicker. Anne visited her once a day, but this was a danger. Surely the sickness had fingers and could move from one to another. So many had died. And if the sickness found its way inside my wife, dripped into her belly? I told her she was not to go again. She said this was needless fear, and I said this was a husband telling his wife. Once a midwife came to feel the kicking, but two weeks later she too had caught the sickness and two weeks after that had died. It did not matter that our town had lost its midwife, because I no longer trusted a stranger to touch my wife.

In the fall, a letter said her aunt was at the end. Anne begged to see her. Another letter came when she was dead. They would bury her along the old brick church with its corners in crumbles, another stone among the rows. That day I had to ride to Charleston with the crop and told my wife to be still. Don't go to the church, I said. Your aunt is dead, nothing to see. I told her plague can rise through soil. Standing on top of the newly dead, she'd feel the sickness climb her skirts. She gave me a smile that wasn't strong.

I was gone a night and day and when I opened the door to our house again, my whip in one hand and white asters in the other, I half expected to find her gone, a vapor, just a vision I'd once had. But she was sitting where she should be, in the chair with her cloth and needle by a cold hearth, for I told her not to light it alone. Under the window on the table were goldenrods.

"You went out," I said.

She rose to meet me. It was hard to hold her, the belly between us. I set my poor flowers down beside hers.

"A short walk," she said, fidgeting her fingers along my arm.

"And if you had stumbled?" I tried not to look at her beauty. I loved our family more even than her face.

"Someone would have caught me." Me not looking at her, she looked away. "I went to see her buried. The churchyard is so near."

I said what she said again in my head. Her hand on my wrist burned. She had been with the dead. The plague was on her. The baby. I couldn't see him now, through the layers of skin and skirt. I couldn't see him to hold him. Just wanted to hold. And she. I'd said she couldn't go. If we lost another. She was rubbing my arm, trying to stop my red face before it cried. All the lives I'd seen bleed out. Chances gone wrong. No love, and then this, my new love. If someone should take it from me. If anyone. I shook off her hand, and in the shaking raised the whip and hard lashed her once across the knees. Lower than my father did.

She sucked her breath into a pang. She didn't step back. I didn't move. I dropped the whip. We didn't move.

WHEN I CAME home, I brought her flowers. Anything colored. Blazing star, horse mint, green eyes, dog tongue. Leaves that were gold. I don't know why I always reached for flowers. I had stayed in the woods to hide my shame. *I'm sorry*, I said. *I'm sorry I'm sorry*. She knew. She said she knew. I sat her on the bed and pulled down her stockings and put my face to her knees and kissed the welts. She said I was a good man. It crushed my bones to hear her. She trusted that I wouldn't harm her, not knowing. She was a woman, married, her skin as thin as silk. I hated this for her. I loved her.

I buried the whip in the yard.

"How will you get the horse to trot?" she asked.

I whispered in her ear and kissed her and showed her how.

I held her more than I ever had, I stepped back, I let her bend into the garden, I looped her hair in the morning, we went for walks and when she sat on the old wharf on the river I didn't clutch her hand. Every night I stumbled into new depths of needing. I kissed her face until its paleness pinked. We slept coiled like snakes. Three bodies in a nest. I didn't speak of hurting her, and she said nothing. Oh, what it is to be a woman. To pretend to forget.

We had a snow that winter. What children were left gathered it and ate it with sugar. The fish were drowsy in the Ashley so we caught extra. I found a rabbit-fur muff in the city for her. I told her all the stories I could think of to show her how ready I was for love, the noisy kind. She knew, she knew. When she had pains, I sang to her until she laughed to quiet me. We warmed our toes at the fire, we tried to lace them in each other's like fingers. The fields were sleeping. Our son was growing.

He would farm. He would ride jumping horses. He would box with other boys. He would learn letters and maps. He would eat oats before they had cooled. He would kneel to pray. He would cling to his mother's knees, would always know what a rare and wondrous thing it was to have a mother. I carried ten-pound sacks of rice in my arms, to practice holding him.

Anne walked behind me, said, "Girls weigh just the same."

SHE BEGAN TO scream in March. Before a moonless dawn he came. Blood, and a baby. Blue-faced. A tangle at his neck. I pulled it clear. He wasn't breathing. Anne whacked his back. I blew into his mouth. "Warm him," she said, and I took him to the fire. The sheets around my wife were filling up with color, her face growing white. He coughed once. We stared at each other, wild, mouths open in hope. She pushed the wet hair from her cheeks. On her elbows now, knees up, a crab. "Rub him," she said, and I stroked his back in circles by the fire. He gasped a bubble. His little knotted face. His blue would not warm. He would not move his hands. A chill on his skin.

"Wake up," I said, "wake up." My son that made me a father. "Wake up."

"Darling," she said. I turned. In her hand a twist of sheet. The red was all around her. Her face the missing moon. My wife was bleeding out.

In the terror on her face I saw the woman Sterrett healed. I was the man that should be kissing her shoulders and her neck, except there was no Sterrett and the midwife was dead and I was the only one who knew that by putting my hands inside her and sewing something shut I could save her. But what would I feel for, in that womb? What if I pulled out not the pain but her life and then it was me that killed her? And where, during all this, would I lay my son?

I was on my haunches by the fire, my wife beyond my reach, the baby in my hands. Sometimes breathing, sometimes not. How long now was it since his last? If I put him down, he would die, would forget he had a father. I could not move. My son was in my hands. My wife across the room. Calling me. I could save her if I knew how, if I could put down my son, but I did not know how, and I could not put him down. I was in the lake again, my arms around the post. The house on fire. The girl caught in the flames I dropped. I lost her, and my father.

I could not touch my wife too. Please let God damn me for all I haven't done. She wept like all women. She could have been any woman. The red around my wife. Her face asking. My heart crawled. I could not move. My wife was dying, but my son was in my hands.

March 8, 1788

Cat

A CREEK DOESN'T MAKE a sound but I think of her. Straw hair, blue eyes wide. I fled my house eight days ago on a horse that died. I have been missing from her for eight days. When these two men talk, I hear the hole that is her voice. Eight days since I've heard her words, like bells. The closest sound is the creek water running. Sweet creek, that never knew a wife.

We are here to thieve the strangers. I know what little sense this makes. They rode on horses, asked where water was, stared some, turned back the way they came. And the black man and the Indian were crouched within a minute, their fingers in a twitch. Were they criminals? Or just sinners?

One said, "It'd be nice to have what they have."

And the other said, "I know that man."

"They're rich, is all, and surely more of the same at home."

"It was her father."

"We've just been talking about how to get on with these empty pockets."

"She who never knew her father, and there he was. Sitting there."

"We can guess what use they'll make of it; I'll tell you what. Spend some on liquor and some on whores and some to buy a safe to put the rest in."

"Damn him who made her, and damn her."

"Are you listening? Now's the time, we've got a chance. Been given it."

"Men abandon, and women ruin."

"Stop muttering. Plenty of fine folk in the world, I'm just guessing these aren't them. You had your money stolen, right? Who's to say this isn't it?"

"The world is not so circular."

"Damn wrong it's not circular! Wake up!"

And all I was saying was *no, no*, but silently. I knew the circle of the world, and it had sharp edges.

They made speeches with closed ears. One kept pulling at his pants, fingering at the scruff on his cheek, the other picked at a spot on the earth till it was clean of leaves. They did not know they did this. Our wants were greater than their wants, is what was figured, and our hearts better. Between fiddling and neatening, they judged themselves. But how did they judge the others? Those men who passed never told us who they loved. This is a lie, I said, or did not say. I did not want the money. Nothing left in the world must be given to me.

I am trying to clean myself. I am walking so many days away from the woman and the boy and even the horse that died beneath me so that I will come to a place where I am reminded of nothing. Am empty. The first two days were crying. The third was burning need for her, to touch her again, her face, to bury her. The shame at not having buried her. I turned back. Walked a few miles back. Why didn't I put them in the ground? Because if she is not below ground, she is not fully dead. I could not put dirt on her white body, though it is worse to have left her. I know. Turned around again. On the fourth day I had cried all the water out of me and so the world went hazy. My mouth stayed open, my eyes lost their blink. This was close to empty. Then I thought how good it was that she was gone. Peace now, Anne and boy. I was not meant to be a father. I hurt my wife, I would have hurt my son. Yes, better they are sleeping.

I was not walking for penance until I was. *Forgive me, clean me, save me.* Everything I knew of myself I had to break. Love was all I knew of myself, so I would let this go. What had it brought me? Go away, heart and need, flee. When that was gone, I would be blank, and then—then could I die?

This I kept asking.

But I am poorly trained. The first sleeping man I saw I held to.

I should have let the man with the mule take me. The one who asked if I had killed. *Yes yes yes.* Can no longer count the times. So what if I wasn't the one he was looking for. I too have sins to pay. I sat there in my home, on every chair a flower, and held my son in my hands while my wife lay on her bed, my son blue, my wife red. I could not move, and neither lived.

I am needing to be alone, but wanting these men to never lose me.

After the dark had settled on the path, they nodded. The Indian worn down, or the black man wanting to see his own courage. Decisions made that would've been dust if we'd been fewer than three. We turned to trace their steps, always turning on this path, walked, are walking, and now we crawl up from the trail in silence. The black man stops his chatter. We creep, and I creep because I have given up, would follow anything alive, am waiting to see what God does to me. Have been waiting for eight days.

South from South Carolina, west from West Georgia. I rode with nothing but my fear and ghosts riding behind. I rode the horse until it dropped. Left it by the trail, a dead pile, wishing I could crawl into its deadness. I hid from men until it came to me that I could not kill myself. My hands could not kill one more thing. My arms missed holding. I was weak. I found a black man sleeping, his knife in a sheath, and I took that knife so when I crouched above him to feel his warmth, he would wake to something ordinary. A highway robber, or a man pretending to be. The black man brought me to an Indian, and here we are, after a day, creeping like brothers.

Never had a brother, but a wife. Soft. My loves were lost to me before they even lived. My son in my hands, his own young brother who I never saw. His mother crablike on the bed, red sheets swimming her. I could not leave one for the other. I was alone for all my life and then there was one and then there was two and myself frozen to the floor, my son in my hands, and I hadn't the strength to move. Strength, courage. Courage, muscle. I didn't have muscle to move. I was given too much. Now the world fixes itself.

I don't know where I am, some miles above Florida, but it smells like home. Part salty. Small palms. The air goes on forever. In the dark, the pine spindles under my feet feel like the pine spindles of Carolina. I have lost the best part of me and the earth makes no difference. I want no money. If I do one more wrong thing and God is watching, I will explode into fire.

Have always had men watching me. Been plagued by them.

My father, my priest, Sterrett, the minister. Saying move just so on this narrow path or I will hurt you. Not the minister, but he passed his rod to God, and there was punishment enough. God worst of all. I have found more men to watch me but they are poor at it, for they are drawing me down a bad path, and never having led, I do not know how to save them. I cannot save them, who am so rotten. *Clean me, save me.*

Eight days on the road and I never asked for food. Never looked for water. A woman on a farm saw me and gave me a jug to swallow. A child held out a cake. I shook my head, but the child would not drop its arm. I took the cake and it watched me eat. Eyes like stars. I fell asleep in a horse yard behind an inn and when I woke a carrot had rolled before me, kicked in the night by a mule. I ate it. Tried to throw it up, but it clung inside. When it rained, I opened my mouth. I passed a slave in Georgia without a shirt. He leaned on a fence by the road, his mouth working on some tobacco. He asked me if I knew his master. I shook my head. If I needed work. I shook my head. If I was from these parts. *No.* He laughed and said he'd give me supper if I wanted, but his master was out, wouldn't come back any time soon, maybe wouldn't ever. A line of slaves stood in the trees behind the field. Two of them were dancing. He saw me looking. He had a gun slung on his back. *You hardly a white man*, he said. Pulled an apple from his pocket, rubbed it once along his bare arm, his arm that was too dark to show whether there was blood on it, and passed it over the fence to me. I ate. I could not throw it up. I walked eight days and tried not to live and kept living.

Grief carried me here but now is tired. Is sliding me from its shoulders. I cannot hold on because my hands are broken. I am a spoiled man. I cannot live without someone's warmth against me. Cannot become alone again. After all this, I am my father. My mouth as spiked and sour as his. My want has brought the end of me. These hands have burned a girl alive, left a hundred bodies bleeding on the slab, killed my own and only hope. Now when they grasp a branch to pull my body up the bank, I think the branch will turn to ash.

We are away from the path now, quiet. Our feet like doves in the leaves. The sweat on my lip tastes like her lips.

"Are you sure?" one says.

"This is your plan," the other says.

"We do it together, right?"

"We take the bags, guns if we can, and walk out."

"Horses?"

"Too noisy. Leave them."

"We're doing the right thing?"

"You told me we were."

"What about Cat?"

"Give him my gun."

"So you don't think he'd kill us both?"

"You said—"

"What do I know!"

I linger in their wake. My feet heavy from lifting. My son still blue in my arms. His mouth an open bubble. His eyelashes long against his cheeks. Anne, unreachable. What creeks I would not cross to touch her. To prove that I can move, can hold, can save. I climb back on my grief. I have killed my wife and God will not kill me.

THIS IS HER story. Grew up in Dorchester, went to school, went away. Lived in Charleston, came home. In the big city was a plague, like ours. A pox. She followed a cousin to a house by the shore, her parents coming after. They wrote letters. *Coming soon, putting the shop to rights.* Her childhood was nothing sad, all sun. Her father rich and her mother kind. No brothers and sisters, not even dead ones. Just her in blue dresses. *Hold on, be good.* Believed in God, and won a prize for penmanship. She had dolls with real hair and wood faces. Little doll shoes. Dreamed of being a mother. Her own mother like an angel, putting sugar on Anne's fruit. *Be patient.* She took a doll to the shore, though she was too old. Men eyed her, and one had asked. But she knew that somewhere I was waiting so said no. I said she could not have known. She said she did. The doll sat on the sill, her face out to sea. *On Sunday, we'll be there.* The plague was spreading, though she didn't know. When the rider came to the house he couldn't speak at first. *It's Sunday,* she said, *where are they?* He breathed heavy, having ridden fast. *Today is Sunday. Are they sick?* He shook his head. *They have no fever?* He shook his head. *Did they leave the city?* Yes, yes. *Where is my mother? Where is my father?* Oh, her mother and her father, they climbed in a carriage with their trunks and two wild horses and halfway to the shore, a fox ran out and startled them, and oh, those wild horses broke apart in panic and the carriage shuddered and smashed, and in the broken wood and axles, her mother and her father fell apart, were dragged with the splinters half a mile before the horses calmed and the fox found its den, and then they weren't her mother and father but were bodies, and did not belong to her. *This is not true,* she said, but it was.

The cousin kept her through the sorrow. More men asked for her. She prayed on her knees morning and night until she was thinking not of their twisted legs but of their happy eyes and all they did for her and all their love for her. God told her that love was living yet, and she believed him. And then she tried to be better. (Though she was already so good.) By the time she came home to Dorchester an orphan, like I was an orphan, she was looking for me. Wanting to share her luck at having been adored.

"Do you not still think of their bodies?"

"Their bodies were not what I loved."

"Do you blame yourself?"

"For what?"

"They wouldn't have died had they not been coming for you."

"That isn't how life works."

"It is; they were coming for you, and they died."

"If they hadn't loved me, they may have died long before."

"You don't know."

"But *you* don't know."

"God is supposed to know better."

"He does. I am happy again, and now I have you."

"You could have been happier."

"No, I couldn't."

"Where is the doll?"

"I buried her."

But when the fever came to Dorchester, she did not want to run away, did not want to climb in a carriage with her son in her belly, because an inkling in her said it was worse to sit in a cart than face the plague, that if her mother and her father had not moved they would have lived, and though she swore this wasn't so, I know how the mind cripples and gnarls around loss. We stayed. Slept in our cabin while neighbors died. Waited for her aunt to die. Death and waiting. She wanted myself as a father to be like her father, her like her mother. She told me of their games, I thought of their bones. I wanted to carry that guilt, except she didn't carry it. Thought it was her fault, but *It's not my fault*, she said. And it wasn't.

And it wasn't the plague that took her either.

THEY HAVE TOLD me the plan. The gun looks broken in my hand. I offer it back to them, but Bob presses it to me. He knows my life is just a thin thread, and wants to save me. Why do strangers give me food and guns? It is supposed to be night, and they are supposed to be sleeping, and we will sneak in like weasels and slip things from their bags. Bob will get the guns, the Indian will get the money. Or whoever is closest. I am told to look for food if I want something to look for. I do not. I am told to use the gun to save them if they need saving. *I* need saving. The creek is louder now, my wife. The bank spreads out. The water is between us. They have crossed with their horses and settled on the other side. A sandbar cradles the bodies of the men. If the river had a tide we could sit and watch them wash away. I have sat and watched so many things, my legs are criminals. The white men rest on cots, hands draped over the side, brushing sand. The bags are under the cots, behind the hands. The brown men sleep on cloths beside them. The sky is high here. The black men sprinkled like pepper in the far brush. Near the horses.

We stand next to small trees. Our breath goes in and out. The first time I saw these golden flowers I thought of her. I pick two. Thin trumpets. I wonder why they don't close up at night. Of all the pretty things that go away in darkness, these do not.

All these men in a clearing, waiting, all these flowers. Nothing moves except my hand. I rub the flowers, back and forth. My breath in and out. My wife waiting for me to put down my son and save her. Who will find their bodies? Her aunt is gone to heaven, and her husband here. They slipped away, one by two, and I could not move. Could not hear through the loudness of myself. A night passed, and when the light came I kissed my son by the hearth, once, and kissed my wife on the bed, once, and walked through the door and through the garden and down the road and out of Carolina. I left the door open. We're all bodies waiting.

Bob reaches out. Brushes my arm with two fingers. His head tilts across the creek. Toward the sand, the men in their scatter. I shake my head. He nods. In the dark, he glows like coal. Everything about him warm. He wants me to want to do this. The Indian on his other side is cold. His eyes straight out, not down, not at us. If I made guesses, it would be that he has no family, moves only because he tells himself to. No loyalty. Not like Bob, who once he loves would not leave. I, who have lost wanting, wonder what men want. I shake my head. If my legs were not criminals, I would slide down into a squat, but they are bound to do bad things if left alone, so when the black man and the Indian creep one foot by one foot from the brush into the water, I creep behind them, not liking to creep, not wanting the gun in my hand, not knowing where to put it. It isn't mine, and they would be angry if I lost it. It is a scalpel that my master won't let me touch, that I don't know how to use.

The night bugs are rattling. The air tastes sweet. We time our steps so that the water past our knees sounds like wind. The creek pulls on my legs, begs them to buckle. What fishes are beneath us. To get to land, I think of nothing at all. Empty out. Slow steps. No thought. When we are on sand again, our legs between cots, I clutch at Bob. His skin jumps. I can see stars through his eyelashes. He crouches beside the heavy sleeping man and lifts his gun. As he bends and then rises, my hand on his shoulder goes with him. The Indian stands over the white body of the man with dark eyes, the one who froze him on the path. The one who is some woman's father. He waits for him to answer an unasked question, but the man is asleep. The Indian takes his musket. They slip their hands between the white men's hands, putting gentle fingers on the bags. Listening. One goes *clink*. They both stand straight, nod through darkness. Nodding to say, *We three will be the same person in this instant*. I shake my head. I am not ready to be one with anyone but her. I let Bob go and go slow in backward steps, back to the water. Listening for her voice.

I see them drag out the bags. A rustle on the cot. An arm drawn in. I stop. We hold our breath. A turning.

A slow world turning.

The fat man starts up first. His shout like a muffled dog. The men are awake. God damn it. I had said no.

The sand scrambles. They are up now, sitting, standing, crouched, all the men who are kin to those coins. Arms crooked, knees bent. Moving like someone lifted the rock that was hiding them. The moon floating in the creek lights their jaws.

Somebody shoots. Bob's gun explodes. The horses in the trees kick against bark. The shadows of the black men slip below bushes. What was I to do? Was I meant to use this gun? They are moving fast, and I am slow. I step again backward. My feet are in the creek. I look at Anne, her eyes surprised. Her calling to me from the red sheets. Asking could I save her. Her straw hair wet against her cheek. I'm waist-deep in water now. I must be too thin to see, because everyone is shooting but no one is shooting at me. I still have a gun in my hand. It says nothing. We are quiet. A young man runs toward me, fleeing, but the dark lights up again with powder and he skids, wavers. His body crumples on the sand. His ankles in the water, bobbing. Too late for a boy to finger out that bullet. He would be dead on any slab. There are empty spaces while men reload their muskets. Is this what war was like? Shots, and then noisy grabbing. Their breaths heavy, their hands reaching out to clutch hair, to smash in noses. Cries like birds. They look for their knives. Bob and the Indian shoot again. Now I can't tell man-shout from gunshot. The moon on the creek is red.

For two nights now, I've slept near a body, first one and then two. I fell asleep while they were talking because they were not talking to me. But when it was still and dark I woke and watched them. I crawled to their sides. The black man boneless, loose pile of limbs. Skin dirt-colored. Not any dirt, but what you find when you scuff off the top layer of rot, dark, and dig an inch down to where it's dry, where it's brown and orangey and sheens if you spit on it. I brushed his arm, the skin beneath the arm hairs. His body flopped so open, like it once had a wife and was glad now to be free. I wanted to scoot him back together. Make him make room for somebody. I could not touch the Indian, though I smelled his hair. Watched his tattoo to see if it would move. If a breeze brushed the blanket off, he'd snatch it close again. Hated his skin to be uncovered. These men and I, we had not hurt each other. I smiled and then felt guilty for it. I sat deeper in the trees to wait for a rat or a deer, but nothing warm walked by. The woods were cold. The fire was out. I found my spot again, not too close, and closed my eyes. *Do not let me dream of her*, I begged. I was too afraid to sleep. I took the shoes of the other men, holed brown boots and leather slip shoes, and wet them from my mouth and smoothed them clean with the tail of my shirt. *There.*

I step back through the water, watching the light from guns and the sides of knives, watching the shoes of strangers dance around each other, slide into the sand, kick at other men's legs. The heavy man is on his bottom, the cot pulled against him for a shield. The Indian's arm coddles the neck of the dark-eyed man, like they were brothers, choking. Someone young is slashing at Bob with a knife, and Bob is cringing back. He lifts his gun and beats the other man on the head with the barrel. I am walking away from them, from their heat. I need them to live. The gun in my hand is loaded.

The black men are in the trees. I can see their shiny eyes. They wait to see who will win and claim them. Wait to see if in the loudness of the killing they can step back into the deeper night and take themselves. Someone's bullet passes near my head, a fast exhale, soft, and I sink. I let my body dip down. Chest, neck, chin. Only my eyes above cool water. My shirt is slow and billows out. My pants cling. I ask someone to watch my brothers. I close my eyes and let my knees collapse. My face sinks below. My hair floats away from my face. Sounds like armies marching. Sounds like towns on fire. I hear a high yell that clutches in a gargle. I open my eyes beneath the water.

My father floats past upon his back, feet bare. His mouth trails whiskey. In his hand a wooden gnarl that is my soul. A flock of crow women soar smoothly through the water. Their robes wide as wings, their mouths open like fish. Behind them walk a thousand dead. Heads open, guts untwirled, their blood turning the water dark. I think I must be dying, to see this march. Anne swims before me. Her eyes surprised. She circles her legs slow to stay in place. Her dress rivering around her body, the blood floating up in strands like smoke. I say how perfect her face is, that she is the woman I loved before I knew what a woman was, in all the darkness of my youth, there, do you see my father floating past, how little like a woman he is? All the shapes I hungered for, and none were mine but you. My words come out in bubbles. Her hands on her belly. I say I never touched a piece of earth but I thought of her. All my life. *But listen*, she says. Eyes wide. She cannot hear me. I reach my hand for her. *It is you now*, she says, *not me*. Her mouth opens slow. Her hair floats in fingers toward me. It is always her. What can I do but fail to reach her again, again. There is nothing of me left. I squeeze my eyes shut. My heart is hot as simmering fat.

The first time she came to church. The yellow of her hair, the blue of her dress. She was a summer sky. She would rest the soft of her hand on my cheek. Her murmur. When she was fully mine and I rode home on the horse that now was dead, she'd spot me from the window and whistle like a jenny wren. A bird that flew into my hands. My body could not be loved, I thought. I thought, until she put her arms around my neck. The water comes in at my cracks. Finds my heart and cools it. Water pumping in my heart until the beast of grief I'm riding drowns. Our son was just a shard of her, and I could not put him down. I should have put him down, crawled over to sew up the holes in my wife, saved the holy heart of me. I was mistaken. I was a mistake. She was the one of all.

You cannot cry at the bottom of a creek.

I am almost empty. Am almost stripped to nothing.

I wait below the water until the sounds still. It is too dark for anything worth seeing. None of these men are killing for women. None have killed their wives. Love is not above this water, and there is only sin beneath. Minnows. Some find my legs inside my pants and pick at my hairs. Kiss me. I wish for a fish to swallow me. To hold me in its belly the way she held my child. I want to give up my senses, one by one. To lose the taste of her. Forget the feel of her scalp on my fingers. How long does it take to drown?

I hear a man shout *Cat!*

Cat!

Someone wants me.

I taste the water one more time. Then I let the little current push me up. The dark has settled, the moon white again. The fat man, the young men, the brown men lie in blood. The black men roped to a tree. The horses still tied in the brush, fluttering. The night smells like smoke. Bitter. Bob and the Indian rummage in sacks. They empty out silver. A thousand extra moons. I crawl up wet on the bank, the gun wet in my hand. *I thought he was a killer,* I hear Bob say of me. He groans through his teeth, one arm clutching the other. I lean down to touch the fat man's face. How did they find him behind his cot? His heavy body soft. Rude to treat it so. They slide the money back in bags, shuffle through the other packs for food and bits of scrip. Bob one-handed. Even in no light, moonlight, I can see their hands shaking. This was not the plan.

I sit by the fat man and wait. I can tell by his eyebrows he wasn't cruel. Wasn't a bad father. I put my fingers beneath his.

Lean down to check his breath, but there is none. I am almost sad, but I remember there is no justice. God takes, or man takes, what he wants. Heavy gentlemen, and wives. Girls. Soldiers on both sides. I don't want to see the other bodies. Just this one. The Indian said he was from Carolina, where I'm from. I wonder did he have a father with a still, did he not see the ocean till he was old, did he know a boy who went to war and never came back. Did he love. He is on his back, one hand by his side, the other reaching far out as if to say *Help* or *Stop*. His legs bunched up. Eyes half open and sleepy. I close them so as not to see their blue. I cross his hands on his chest. I stretch out his legs. I take off his shoes. He is not in his nightshirt but all his clothes, for it is March and cool and he was shy among all these men. I unbutton his waistcoat that is squeezing tight, to let him breathe. I pat him now like a pet or a donkey. His coat looks warm. I only have a shirt, which now is soaked with creek and crying, and I am still alive enough to feel the cold. I rub the wool. Slip my fingers wet into his pockets.

Inside his coat is a letter, rimmed in red. I save it from his blooming side and wipe the blood away. An address on the front, four lines in loops. Unsent. He has drawn a tree on the back. A little house beneath. A man and woman scratched in beside it. The man and the woman and the house and the tree. Inked hands touching. I wonder if he had a woman and a house and a tree, like I had a woman and a house and a tree. Now someone will be alone, like I am alone. It is my fault for burying myself in water when I could have stood by his cot and saved him. Saved the woman from having lost a man. Who am I to know why the black man and the Indian did what they did. What they needed. I only sit here holding a man's heart in the night cold. I feel a roll of blood uncurl down my arms. A little aliveness.

They tell me to stand up, come on, their backs heavy with silver. Their hands still shaking. I look up the bank at the black men tied to the tree. They have no faces in the dark. They are not scared, this being the least of what they've seen. Of men not knowing what they do. They wait for the next slow turn. We leave them the horses. Behind me, Bob and the Indian are splashing slow across the creek. The minnows scatter. *Cat!* They want me. Even the Indian waits.

That they call my name, that they have killed these strangers and not myself, that they do not leave me here. What is this country?

There are men killed today, and I am not to blame. The Indian must carry it, who has no town or home. Bob must carry it, who has no wife. Or if he does she is weak or cruel, else he could not have left. This I know about my brothers.

I put the wet red letter in my pocket. I will eat it if I am hungry. If not, and when have I been hungry, I will find a man to carry it. He will bear it to Carolina, where Anne too lies waiting. Her body still on the bed, my hands still red with the blood I didn't touch. Our child, the flower of us, waiting. If God is watching, let him quiet that blood shed with this blood saved and sent.

March 12–17, 1788

Winna

My MASTER'S SPANISH wife is stretched beneath an open bedroom window, her fat feet propped on the sill so when the wind comes it goes straight down her skirts. I wait in the door until she decides to see me. My husband, who was not of my picking, has been gone more than a week. Someone finally thought to fetch me. She raises a hand, fidgets her fingers. I come over, stepping around the noisy spot where the floor is weak, and sit on the stool that puts my head about at a level with her raised ankles. She plops them on my lap.

I'm the good kind of slave, the kind that doesn't talk too much or think. I start digging in, my thumb fiddling against the rough ball of her foot. I pull her skin hard enough so it won't tickle. The bottom of her toes have caps on them, husks or horns that come to a fine edge. When she's off on her topic and not paying attention, I run my fingers along them because she can't feel. This time it's my husband.

"José's already had a letter from the Creeks; not there."

"Mm."

"Out nine hundred dollars, José. He's a strong man, yes? Which one is he?"

I think of some way to describe him. I don't think she'd know what a handsome black man is. "Six foot," I say, "and then some."

"Scars?"

"Not that you'd know to notice."

"It does not matter to me, him missing. But José, of course."

"Me neither."

"He was a fool to lose the horse. Came right back to where it should. So we know, without a horse, either he is dead or run off. The trail is not that dangerous, so my guess is he went *shoo*. He say nothing to his wife?"

"He's not much for talking."

"Of course." She frowns, then giggles and jerks a foot away. I say sorry and lift it up again.

"You ever do this for him?"

I stop, my fingers laced between her toes.

"No, I think not. I wonder why a man run off and leave his lady, and here you go. You don't serve him well."

"I served him two babies." I move up to her ankles, ringed in fine black hair.

"But love, no, that's not in the bed."

I cannot tell a white woman, however swarthy, that I do not love my husband, even if it isn't true. "We get along fine," I say.

"Mm, yes," and she closes her eyes, dropping her fat round head to one shoulder. "You want to ask about José, but you are shy."

I am not shy. I am very practical. I started off in the fields and I worked my way to the kitchen. And then into the house and up the stairs until I got here. The Spanish lady blabbers, but she doesn't whip, not much. I don't mind hearing about another country, or even my own country, because whoever it belongs to now surely won't keep it long. This woman, her head lolling around her neck like an orange about to drop, can name her kings as fast as she can name her husbands. When I'm tired of listening, I just think about other things.

"We talk little," she says, "but when he visits the bed we say very much. He even likes my horny toes. Like you."

I glance up.

"If these lands did not belong to me, I think he would like *mis piernas* less. But who says this is no good? Foolish are the ones who wait, who pine, who say, 'Is this how you feel?' If love is not one way, it's another. *Frente al amor y la muerte no sirve de nada ser fuerte.* Eh?"

"I agree," I say.

"But here you are waiting! You Africans think too serious about everything. Think about you, not him. See what I do. Do I let José show me which way? No, no. I make commands." She draws one of the curls from her head beneath her nose until it is straight, then lets it spring back. "But also do not let them go far, because the rope is shorter than you think and they will be off if you blink too long. Oh, I see. This is your case. Well, it is from being serious. Loving is very push-pull like that."

I pretend not to hear. Her toenails are grown too long.

"You think he comes back?"

I don't say anything, because I'm not a fool. But the truth is I don't know. More importantly, I don't know if I mind one way or the other.

She doesn't like it when I'm quiet. She kicks her feet free and stands up, wrapping her shawl around her. "You do a terrible job. I see you tomorrow."

DELPHY IS PEELING potatoes on the steps. She is nine years old, but looks at me like a grandma would, haughty and suspicious. She hasn't asked about her daddy today, so I'm waiting for it. The baby is taking the fallen peels and pushing them a few inches into the darkness beneath the house. She says cats live there, but she also says there are rabbits in her mattress.

"Up, Polly," I say, and she hoists herself off the dirt, wiping at her knees. She gathers up the naked potatoes at her sister's side and follows me into the cabin, where the fire has almost gone out. I throw some sticks on and poke at it. "Tell Delphy to get the water."

"Let me," she says. Her arms shake under the weight of four potatoes.

"Delphy!"

I hear my older girl put down her knife and set out with the pail, and Polly drops her burden and begins to cry.

We're quiet at dinner. I told them the day he left that family means nothing here. Men move around. They know that. Slave folks are brought together and busted up at the white man's whim; it's not our business. They asked didn't I love them like a real mama would, and I said yes, but different too. I was raised to plant cabin gardens small so the master wouldn't complain, to look down whenever I was looked at, to help folks around me but only so far. We don't mourn Papa's loss, I said, because crying draws attention.

When the plates are clean I wait for it, and it comes.

"You think he made it?"

"He's only a week gone, Delphy, no telling."

"But do you think he'll come back for us?"

"Doesn't help that he lost his damn horse." I throw the plates in what's left of the water in the pail. "Tell me why you want him to so bad. It doesn't hurt your feelings that he left you behind?"

Polly screws up her face again, and her sister finds a roll of fat on the girl's arm and pinches it. Polly takes a gulp of breath. "He's my daddy," she says.

"And I think he wanted to take us and you wouldn't let him," Delphy adds. "I think you were scared."

"Or sensible. You know how many runaways get killed?"

Polly's face falls into a shock. Damn it, what kind of mother has to say things like "killed" at supper? In what kind of life is that so ordinary? I lift her and rock her, and above her bawling head I lock eyes with Delphy, who raises her brows at me as if to say, *What kind of a mother indeed?*

"Your father's fine. He's looking for some free land, and knows enough of roads and Indians to get through."

"Then why can't we be free too?"

Polly sticks her hand in my shirt, looking for comfort, though she hasn't found milk there in months.

"If he can go off on his own so easy, then that's not a family," Delphy says.

When the *señora* first allowed the black preacher to visit the plantation, I thought nothing of it. But then the girls came home with stories that didn't sound much like life. All about daddies looking out for their children, and mamas so sweet they can get a baby without even taking off their clothes. And now our own cabin doesn't look so shiny to the girls.

With her arms crossed on her little flat chest, and her short hair a ragged halo around her head, Delphy asks me if her father is even a father, and why we give him that name.

"Because he loves you," I say. I know she knows about love, because Jesus says it all the time.

Polly squirms to get down and bends over, squeezing her legs together. I send her outside to pee.

"If he loves us—"

"All right, listen." I kneel down in front of her and reach up to her ears. I hold them in my hands like shells. "There is being a father, and there is being a man. And sometimes what makes sense to one isn't right for the other. Sometimes you're my daughter and have to think of me, and whether I'd like you to be getting the potatoes done, and sometimes you're just a girl and you want to go climb the pecan. You hear?"

"So daddy wasn't thinking of us when he left."

"Well." I want to say no, he was being a selfish son of a bitch, but I don't know if that's the whole truth.

Polly creeps back in—she's always pleased with herself after peeing—and lies down on the mattress with a smile. "He plays hide and seek," she says. "We find him."

Delphy leans down to me and whispers. "You don't even care that he's gone."

I have never heard such a cruel voice out of my girl. After all that, and he *was* being a son of a bitch, she's disappointed not in her daddy but in me. How I failed to give them some kind of damn Holy Family. I am too tired to correct her. Tomorrow she'll find another way to ask about him, and I'll try to pretend that it doesn't matter. Slaves don't get families. There's nothing to fight for.

. . .

I SHOULD BE grateful to be out of the fields, away from the kettles, but my mistress is near as dangerous as the boiling sugar.
She doesn't want a foot rub today but a stroll in the garden, me
carrying the wooden buckets sloshing with water to refill her
tiny can. She likes to be the one to water her roses. They don't
do well, maybe because of the salt and sand in the dirt, maybe
because she's a fickle waterer. It comes out in five little streams
from the wide head, sprinkling the limp petals, the curled leaves.
Nowhere near the roots, but I don't say anything.

"They have made nothing at all nice," she says. The English,
now Americans, are a favorite subject. The Spanish have had
Florida again for a half-dozen years, but she can't stop railing.
They are all rural, knock-kneed, buck-toothed. "You go south
more, or west, and see what the Spanish have built. No lazy
farms. And you, you could walk to town in a pretty dress and
no one to say a word. You are black, yes, but not that dark. Here
is boring, all the same, nothing but master and slave." She holds
out her can for me to fill it. "I am sick of here."

She always says she's been here too long. She was born here,
is what she means, though she likes to pretend she is true Spanish and not a colonial. Married off at fifteen to an Englishman
because that's the way the wars seemed to be going. She hates
the blacks with dark skin, the Indians in our fields but not the
princesses that visit with their chiefs, all the English, most of
the French, and the convicts and the runaways and the hungry.
She hates the poor and people who are richer than she is. She
tells me all the time about the free blacks, how they're soldiers
and shopkeepers, all over Florida. She wants me to complain as
much as she does, but I won't out loud.

A wasp hovers down to see what's going on with all this loose water. My mistress lets out a shriek, ducking away, and her short curls bounce. Her stomach leaps along with her. I wave my hand in the air a few times, and the wasp sighs and moves on. I am sick of here too. Maybe always was, but didn't know the words to say it. Is it being a woman? Was I raised to bear things as they came? I take pride in putting up with shit. But I'm afraid to think what it would mean if Bob wasn't a coward taking the easy way out, but a man finding a solution. Maybe being a woman isn't the same as setting your teeth and taking what's coming to you. Though I am a strong believer in that. Not because God tells us to, but because someone's got to take the shit of the world, and I still think it's a sneak who lets someone else carry that burden. But in my strength I seem to be carrying my children down with me. And I am not sure if that is being safe or being wrong.

"Have you ever thought to be prostitute?" She laughs. We have moved on to the yellow rose that she waters twice as much as the others. It was a cutting from her mother's garden, back in Spain. "It is not so bad as you think, and money is good. Being wife is just the same, but no money. Look at these, my lands! What did my husband have? And everything he takes. Your husband just take himself, not so bad."

I heave up one of the buckets to fill her can again. "You'd tell me if they found him?"

She pauses, clutches at the bag that dangles from her elbow. She is looking for her half whip, a lady-sized thing that some man before Josiah had made for her. Is it lambskin, even? I shift a few steps to the side, stare down at the gravel path. She can't find it and moves on to the oleander flopping against the old brick wall. She pulls off a leaf and looks at me. "Poison," she says. I wish she wouldn't laugh so much.

That night in bed while I arrange the cookies on her tray, my mistress says she's written a letter to her cousin in Seville and is done with this petty New World, it is too confusing and she is given no respect.

"Where would you go?"

She considers this as I rub a cream into her plump cheeks, along the lines in her forehead. "To a true city," she says, "or the Indies. Rich, rich."

My back aches from where she whipped me two hours ago. Her little crop was hanging in the pantry, of all places.

"And the plantation?"

"Sold to high bidder!" Her laugh is more like a cackle. "Cane goes away, it doesn't grow good here anyway. Slaves go away. My husband shrivels, comes begging for me. Don't mistake me, I am a woman in love. It is right to make them work hard."

Slaves go away. It's a miracle that after changing hands from Spanish to British to Spanish, my family has not already been broken down, sold in pieces. Though now, of course, I'm not sure about the word *family*. But my children. One more whim, one more shift in hands, and they're gone. Shipped to Louisiana or Virginia, as Bob was once sent from Virginia to Florida, or as I was sent from—I don't even remember where. Family for us is just what we can count today. It's not memory, and it's not future. And this is what I have given my children.

What is there to be practical about?

THE GIRLS ARE in bed when I get home, late, but not asleep. Polly is sticking her finger in and out of her nose, waiting for something to appear. With narrowed eyes, Delphy watches me undress. I crawl in.

She started the field this year and I don't ask how it is because I know. Long and hot and the clenching pain in the back moves to the thighs and the knees and the taste of your own sweat is a sustenance. My mistress said she could find a place in the kitchen, but I thought the men would lash her less. And they do, because they are waiting for her to stop being a girl. When that happens, I have no plan. So they pull her shirt up to beat her every now and then, so they check for breasts. They haven't yet done more.

And Bob *left* us to this?

I don't know if I love him, but he looks like my daughters, and I'll be damned if he gets away while I have to watch my children get churned under whatever wickedness we're given.

Polly is asleep now, her hand still stuck to her face.

"Anyone touch you today?"

Delphy turns to me, reaches her fingers to my back. Rests them like little moths on the welts.

"Delphy?"

"Do you know where she keeps the key to the stables?"

I can't ask her more. I don't want to know how close her life is to mine. I want to give everything to her and then let her decide. "You miss him?" I ask.

"I guess I liked him better than you did."

"That is entirely possible." I untuck the blanket from Polly's neck. She always wraps it around herself so tight that I worry she can't breathe. "So this is what you want."

Delphy's hand is a five-legged animal that canters up and down my arm. A trick her daddy taught her.

Family, is it? That's what's being asked of me? I can't figure how my girls got to thinking they weren't just slaves, weren't just going to settle. There was none of this a week ago, even with the preacher's talk of Moses. We were all the way ordinary. Did the work, fell back to the cabin after dark, squabbled. Woke up and did the work.

What is my life? I'm up before the rooster is, gathering food from the scraps that have been handed out five days before and the meager greens my garden makes. By first light there is a poor breakfast for my girls, and they are out, Polly to the granny and Delphy to the fields, a trowel in her hand that she has promised not to break. Her shadow walking away from me looks like no more than candle smoke. Don't know where in her small body she fits the muscles that will pull up the earth, chop back the cane. I'm in the master's house before anyone stirs, a bowl of warm water ready for my mistress on her stand, her skirts laid out and ironed, lavender rubbed into her underthings to cut the stink of sweat till wash day. She is up and I am kneeling— sponging her, dressing her, brushing out the night-knotted hair, mixing the rouge for her cheeks. She rattles on about her father or her father's father, the glory of Spain with all that citrus, what she would do if her husband woke up dead one day. I'm given a lash once across each palm for pulling at her scalp. She says there are places where I wouldn't be a slave at all, though what use would I be. I top her hair with a lace mantilla and not till she's left the room to start her day do I take up her chamber pot and carry its slopping stench down the back stairs. And all this before the white folks' breakfast.

I turn back to my daughter.

"You want your daddy," I say again.

She smiles, my oldest girl, who hardly ever smiles. The longer she lives, the more things she won't be able to tell me. And then she'll have babies of her own and know what it's like to watch your children hole up their black secrets. Though it is no secret; I too am black. I know.

"And Polly?" I ask.

"Oh, she'll be quiet. We've been practicing being quiet."

WHAT I REMEMBER about meeting Bob is that my master, who was not Josiah but a man named Cunningham, sold me from his farm because I spit in his daughter's pudding. There weren't any witnesses, so I don't know what evidence they had. I was angry and young enough and not especially patient toward men. And what was Bob but a man being thrown at me. They set us up in our own cabin and said, "Have at it," and now that I'm more grown I can recognize that I wasn't entirely kind. I was tired, and I couldn't explain this to him. It's different for a woman. He wanted to flop his arms around me, even when he was mad, and all I saw was another weight. Without saying anything, he begged me to love him and I said no.

I was pleased when he started riding to the Indians because it gave me time alone, but that passed when Delphy came. Though she was not a trouble but an ally. A girl who'd grow up and know what it was like for me when I was ten, and fifteen, and twenty years old. This was selfish, to want that, so I did what I could to turn her path different from mine. I made her daddy hold her. I kept her from the kitchen. I talked to her about her grandmas and great-grandmas, even when I had to make it up. I sewed all the holes in her clothes so nothing could be seen.

As we got older, I didn't mind him so much. He was like a

pup, and harmless. He wanted big things and I wanted to keep us all alive, but he was lovable and I don't lie when I say that it got to where I loved him. If love is relief when they come home in the dark in one piece.

We kept finding each other. Holding on tight. There was a baby that didn't make it past the first day, the baby that died of the cough, and Polly. And the beginning of another one who decided, before she even saw this misery, not to live at all.

If you add it all up, with Bob in there too, it really does have the look of a family. No, I have no memory of my own kin. Unless this is it. What I've been given to defend.

ONLY WHEN MY mistress is in her nap can I sit and not move for a minute. A siesta, she says, for beauty. Each time she wakes up I widen my eyes as if sure enough, she's already looking better. This day is the same as other days except I'm not thinking about what else can be made with a handful of yams and an egg but about what my plan would be if I was going to make one. Stupid that I didn't sit in on Bob's planning. I might've learned a few tips. Maybe I can visit Mingo. They were always whispering.

But this is what a woman can come to on her own:

One, kill myself and my children. This is not a good idea because it doesn't bring them closer to their father (though I don't know, maybe it does) and I'm squeamish. And can't help believing sometimes in God, who maybe is wrathful about such things. Two, kill my owners. Or wait till Josiah—or José, or Master—is visiting some other rum dealer and just kill my mistress, which would be easy with a little oleander tea, she even showed me which it was. Or tying her to her bed while she siestaed and setting the bed on fire. Which might be difficult unless

I stacked the bed with kindling and even then, I'm squeamish. Three, run the hell away. Not on foot because of the girls, but I guess on a horse. Pack some bags with food (yams, an egg) and head out at night when there's some other commotion, like one of the fancy parties they sometimes have for the diplomats and the soldiers, or ex-soldiers, depending on which war. Once you're over the Florida line, the slave patrols stop knowing who you are, especially if you've got papers written in Spanish with words that look like *libre*. And then the only trick is finding where my husband went. Not to the Indians, I know—they checked. It's got to be west, to that made-up farm. Somewhere west. Well, I can follow a sun and ask people politely if they've seen a black man who talks too much, and as long as the horse I pick is the fastest in the stable, we've got a chance for a while. We'll get to the Mississippi, and if we've had no sign of him, maybe we'll think about starting up our own farm. When he hears tell of the rich negress and her wild plow-pushing daughters, he can come find us. If he's listening for us.

My mistress grunts and heaves herself over on the mattress like a grub flopping out of the dirt. She thinks being fat is pretty, and so she is mighty pretty. She once asked me what I dreamed about and when I said I was usually too tired to dream, she scolded me. "I am always tired," she said, "and I have most wondrous dreams! Castles and cold rivers and many, many kittens. People don't dream only because they don't think, they're stupid. I do not say you are stupid, but." I could have told her what I dreamed about, but the shock would've kept her up at night and it was best for me if she slept sound.

I know she wants to leave too. I could write her a note, tell her where the keys to the stable are kept.

That afternoon we feed the birds in the dovecote, which aren't doves at all but blackbirds who are happy to have found a steady supply of crumbs.

In the evening, my back somehow unbroken, I pass Mingo's cabin on the way to my own. He's carving at the posts holding up his roof. I stop, see a man who's a husband too, who talks big but hasn't left, isn't missed. I look hard at him, trying to think of what it is I really miss about Bob. How open the man was. How honest, and needy. If I had clutched him back in those first days, maybe we'd have grown into each other. Put all our griefs in the same basket. Don't know why I never thought how much my own children would love him.

"You need something?"

I shake my head. I don't have many friends on this plantation, but not enemies either. "What kind of foolishness are you doing to that post?"

"Rot," he says. "Digging it out."

"Thought you were making some kind of statue."

"Any word of Bob?"

"No word. And good riddance."

He seems a little more surprised than he should. "They send out the dogs yet?"

"Master's still on his trip. They're waiting till he's back. For all I know, they'll wait even longer. It's planting time, and he'll have visitors that don't like hearing of runaways."

"They won't tell you, but it's harder to find a man once he crosses out of Spanish lands. Never build a farm near a border."

"Never dig good wood out of a bad post."

He throws one of his tools onto the porch. "You ever need

some warming up at night, you know where to come." He does a little swivel with his hip that I believe is supposed to be sexual.

"I'd bed your wife first," I say, and walk off.

After a slim supper I make the girls practice their best quiet faces. I sit them in the middle of the floor while I tinker around, cleaning up the dishes, sweeping the dirt out, mending a torn shirt. Delphy must have promised some treat to Polly, because neither are making a sound. When I'm done with this torture, I kneel down in front of them. Between my daughters and my mistress, my knees are as callused and dry as stumps.

"I think you're right," I say. "About your daddy."

"That we need him," Delphy says.

"That you don't need all of this." I mean yams, dirt, cut skin.

"You find the key?"

"The fastest horse?" Polly says, then puts her hand over her mouth, not sure if she's allowed to be talking yet.

"If we get caught, I don't have to tell you what happens."

"Beaten and sold," Delphy says.

"Or *killed*." She claps her hand up again, this time smiling. Look at this world they're in; listen to their jokes.

WE DON'T HAVE to wait long for the party. Three days later the master's back from a trip and brings with him a half-dozen Spaniards who are new to the New World and who trip over themselves flattering my mistress. She runs her hands across her belly as if to goad them further. We serve food on trays, fill glasses, carry coats and hats from room to room. Even our children are dressed up and paraded; one of them knows French, I can't figure how, and she garbles out a few words so the guests can marvel at the negroes and curse their enemies. After a few hours of this, everyone is very drunk.

The key is kept on a loop by the mirror in my master's room, which is not my mistress's room. The only people upstairs are a Spaniard and a slave, halfway to fornication, though I can see that her hands massaging his backside are actually in his pockets, fumbling for whatever's there, and I keep walking. No one stops me. On my way down the stairs, one man grabs my breast, pressing me hard toward the banister, but I slide limply down onto the step and he assumes I'm as fuddled as he is; unable to reach down for me and still keep his balance, he moves on. The children are in the front room, watching a man snore on the sofa, and I nod at my girls and they follow me out and down the front steps. I stop when I hear her voice from the porch.

"Winna!"

I turn around, my legs prickling.

"Where's my watering can?"

"Ma'am?"

"Just look at all the sad roses!"

She looks like a white toad dressed in black, happy and sad the way toads sometimes seem, both at once.

"I put it in the attic," I call back, and she smiles and nods and teeters back inside.

In an hour, they will fall down in their places and sleep until they don't remember what they swallowed or who they screwed.

"Maybe when you're a hundred you'll forget all of this," I say, but my daughters are too far ahead of me to hear, jogging on their short legs toward home.

I've sewn straps onto sacks so they can carry their bags more easily. I don't know how much food or water we'll need, not knowing how far we're going. I made the bags heavy enough that they'll feel some confidence, like I've provided for them and we're going to be all right. I feel more like a mother these days, even as I'm sending my children into the wilderness, away from shelter, toward bounty hunters and maybe wolves. I don't even know if wolves would eat a girl, but I'm sending us toward them anyway.

There's no way to tell which is the fastest horse in the dark. I let Polly pick her favorite. It's a black one, sturdy enough, who doesn't protest as I lead him out and throw a blanket and saddle over his back and slip a bit through his teeth. I learned all this from Bob, who brought me here to show off what he knew. Everything's heavier and harder than he made it seem. With a little grudge I give him some respect. I pull a stool over to hoist the girls up. Polly is giggling like mad and Delphy's eyes are wide, scared. I crawl up, the horse sidestepping from the weight of me, and fix myself between them, holding Polly in front of me and making Delphy hold me from behind.

"Now we're quiet," I say.

They don't respond.

"Only time you make a noise is if you fall off."

Silence.

I kick the horse a couple of times before it senses what I'm after. In the tarry dark, no sun to follow, I aim it for the north road, away from Pensacola, toward Indian lands, toward paths that go west and somewhere near my daughters' father.

After about a mile the horse figures out how to gallop, and we all make little noises like women and clutch each other hard.

March 11–12, 1788

Le Clerc

I ADMIT TO BEING lonely for my horse. Though she did not speak, she seemed to understand me with her muscles and fur, and now that I'm alone in the woods, peering at the little breakages of sticks that suggest a man's footstep, I think how much better it is to be seen even by a beast than not at all. How lucky these men are that I am hunting them.

I am already disheveled from a night in the open air, though I have a sturdy blanket that wraps beneath and above me, just the size to warm one person. The forest here has been burned by Indians within the past year, so a fine layer of ash still lies under the winter leaves, and my breeches are sooty. I address my hair, but without a glass I cannot confirm its arrangement. The criminals will not care how I look; they'll only see me for a minute at most as free men. Then, depending on their instincts and response, they will either be killed by my own hand or taken back to Hillaubee to be killed by Seloatka, who in these uncertain territories happens to be the chief of all of us. I use a dogwood twig to clean my teeth.

My Indian wife has covered the bottom of my boots with a soft felt, and I walk quickly on the balls of my feet into the dawn. A casual listener might interpret the noises I make as a dry wind, or the distant patter of a riverbed. Birds that avoid me on horseback congregate when I'm on foot, as though I leave uncovered seeds in my wake. You cannot love a bird as you love a horse, perhaps because the eyes have no rest in them, but I assume some tissue connects them just as the species of humans are joined. Do both feel no sorrow? I scare up a barred owl, the only kind I know that can hunt his prey with light, and I pause as it falls from its branch in a heavy swoop, gliding off through the beams of March. It would have been easier to study the animals of the New World than its inhabitants. I would face less resistance, and would by now be already published. It is not wild to imagine that my father, wherever he is, might read my name in a borrowed journal and feel some pride. But I pursue my interests not because of but in spite of my lineage. I am tired of its stale order; surely I am not the first to see that it has no future in a world increasingly scientific and democratic.

And here in these woods, in these endless, wall-less woods, not a soul can say I do not belong.

I play a game with myself: How did a white man meet a black man meet an Indian? The white man is the negro's master, and the Indian a hired guide. The Indian and the white man are trading partners, and they purchased a black man to do the shooting. The black man and the Indian are both slaves, fugitive, and they found some low drunkard in a tavern to join their scheme. They are all sons of the same mother, born of three separate fathers. If this story is ever told, will someone ask what a Frenchman was doing on their trail? Will this become the sort of tale where even the name of my horse is remembered?

I could stay here and never return to any company and become a man entirely attuned to the seasons, who after several years loses the gift of speech, then of empathy; maybe that's what it would take to make me miss my mother's garden.

And then I see them.

The light is still dim, but the figures moving at the farthest edge of the forest are bipedal and slow. They are each earth-colored, as though the dirt has ballooned up into the shapes of men.

I HAVE SPENT my life looking for them.

I said I left my wife because I was bored and unhappy with our privacy, lonely again within our walls, but this was only a partial truth; I made these confessions to her but had no firm thought of escape until she left on a Tuesday and came back on a Thursday and said she had been in another man's bed. What did I expect? I had been the first to profit from her disloyalty, and surely could not assume a complete reform. I asked her to explain her behavior, and she asked me to explain mine. Love is not giving up, she said. I felt, with some righteousness, that she had gone further in the direction of giving up than I, but she believed that mine was the first offense and deserved repayment.

"Do you want me to leave?" I asked her. "Are you unhappy?"

"Ask yourself that," she said.

I wanted to inquire if she loved me but could not bring myself to, not wanting to hear her deny it. I felt newly forsaken.

"You're a decent man," she said, "and moderately clever. You'll sort it all out. You'll see what I mean. Then, if you like, we can try again."

We fought for three days and, despite using all the reason and passion at our disposal, came to no conclusion.

I was brokenhearted, not because I lost her particular love, but because now there was no one to call me theirs.

I packed two sturdy suitcases and threw myself recklessly onto the world, searching for a place free from the strict classifications of France so that I might write about it with the sheen of discovery and rebuild my self-esteem. I was more than just a lover, and grew grateful that she had freed me to become what I considered the apex of modern society: that is to say, a scholar.

Because the earliest ship out of Dunkerque was northern bound, I went first to Norway, where the atlas of my childhood had shown mountains that looked as frothy as waves or piling clouds. I believed the Arctic ice would hold something elemental, but I found a society little different from the one I left, with each man in his house and frightened of what he didn't know. I can't say much of my time there because I was still engaged mostly in my own misery, a condition that is anathema to pure observation. I was cold, and the women reminded me of her, their every glance suggesting infidelity. Tiring of the snow, I boarded a boat for the New World. We were told that the American was calling himself an individual, that there at last was a country free from the fetid strictures of the past. At each juncture I did write a letter to my wife, without return address, to inform her that no matter what she might imagine, I adored her.

The great eastern cities of America were priming for rebellion when I arrived, and this was heady, to watch the lines between men dissolve—or rather, to wait for their dissolution. Despite the rhetoric, I saw few encounters between poor and rich; even at the most impassioned talks on liberty, a slave would circulate with glasses of wine. Nights, I would open the window of my rented rooms and listen to drunkenness on the street, repeating the anger and ardor to myself until I'd found the paper to write it down. One evening men stormed out of a tavern with a large doll and set it alight beneath my window, though the smoke from the burning cloth sent the rioters away coughing. I was left alone to watch the body turn to cinders, and despite it being inanimate, its abandonment pained me. I turned to maps again, saw the borders of the colonies bleed out into forest and field, and so departed the coast for the interior twelve years ago, just as war was breaking out, for it wasn't war I wanted to see, not even if it promised something new; what seemed to set this country apart from its cousins was not its ache for a republic but rather the hearts that held that ache. And in Boston and Philadelphia, even under the sway of drink, few men opened those to me.

I continued to be a young man, full of weary hubris. I was warned that any journey into the interior of this country would bring me to savages, so I nodded and swore to keep to the coasts and then hired a horse and servant to take me into the darkest forests, where I found the Creeks in Hillaubee and now am married and a Great War Chief; though the title is honorary, I believe the wife is genuine. What the Creeks gave me was a respite from the expected, at least while I studied how they were bound to each other and defined their enemies. The wife was simply so I could sink into daily life unremarked; I was not prepared to give my heart to anyone new, if indeed it had ever been given. I once sent my French wife a basket that my Indian wife made. But before long even the novelty of Indians began to follow paths that I knew: a man defended the men who resembled him.

So a week ago, when the chief of my adopted village asked if I'd sit in on a diplomatic meeting that evening with visitors from the Carolinas—the white men's war had come and gone and I had confirmed the Creeks' good opinion—I said yes, of course, but returned to my cabin and opened the wooden trunk I arrived with years ago, to imagine what it might look like if I filled it again. Endless talk of war, even after the fighting had settled, merely reminded me of everything I'd already seen. I wondered if all men lived by the same self-preserving code. If guilt was foregone. If it was no hardship to grow up alone, because all men are fundamentally so.

I CONTINUE AT a generous distance, keeping them in my sight but only just. I am interested in how they walk, the Indian leading mostly but sometimes the black man striding ahead, both of them turning every minute or so to confirm the others' presence. These are not men trying to lose each other. Have they made some pact? Is there a sense that if one escapes, he'll turn the others in? What do they have to hold over each other's heads? Though they are not always silent, they do not converse in an easy enough manner to convince me of a prior relationship. There are no trading partners here, and I doubt even that the slave belongs to one of these men, for they do not make him carry the bags or prepare the food. Of course, it is possible that he is not a slave but a Creek, as they have sometimes been known to adopt negroes into their clans if the circumstances allow. But he does not seem to speak their language beyond a phrase or two. I suspect the white man of leaving the plainest signs on the trail behind him. The leaves are shuffled up in trenches as if he were not fully lifting his feet but rather being pulled by a force mildly stronger than the force bidding him to collapse. Though he may have shot the travelers, he certainly did not plan the attacks, and doesn't appear to have any aim but to watch for flowers and keep close to the others. He is almost a child.

At noon they sit down in the brush and pull food out of their sacks, which is oddly domestic for men on the run. In the noise of chewing I am able to approach closely enough to pick up a little conversation.

"How is it?" the white man asks.

The black man rubs his upper arm and nods.

The Indian passes a cloth bag of parched corn to his left and each man takes a handful.

"What was the best thing you ever ate, Cat?" the black man asks.

The white man's smile is shy. "My wife had a garden," he says.

"She was a fine cook?" The Indian spits out a kernel of corn, which without boiled water must be painfully hard.

"No," the one called Cat says.

"I had a ham once, or part of it at least, that my mother stole from the master's kitchen on Christmas—told him the pig wasn't near as big as he thought it was, which is why there weren't more cuts. It wasn't hot, but lord it was juicy. I wrestled my brother for the last piece and lost, but that taste sat in my mouth for days." He runs his tongue across his upper lip. "There's good moments and bad moments."

"Not good men and bad men," Cat says.

The others seem surprised, as if they were not accustomed to the white man speaking, or at least not speaking philosophically. He reaches out a hand and pats the black man's knee.

"As we get worse, you seem better," the Indian says.

"No. But even the people we love can fail."

"Who's failed? Us two? Or you? Don't start spouting for-giveness like you're some kind of saint, because that bounty hunter'd say otherwise." He turns to the Indian. "I told you, didn't I? Said there was a blue-eyed man wanted for murder, and seemed to think Cat was it."

"Was he?"

"What do you think?"

They look at the white man, who seems unconcerned. He apparently said his piece.

"You're not getting off from this," the black man says. "We all did it."

They halt again at dusk in a broad meadow, congregate around something in the weeds. They stand so close together it almost looks as if their arms are linked, or they are praying. The distant figure of Cat moves behind the black man, whom I now know to be Bob, and after a further pause, all three move back onto the main path, the white man casting a last glance at the spot in the prairie. A half dozen sandhill cranes fly up near the tree line like some ancient species.

WHEN THEY STOP for the night, I stop well behind them. They make a fire to cook something and although the flame is small, I am surprised that the Indian lets his guard down to this extent. I am too far to hear any of their whisperings, but an hour after they settle for the night, I creep closer. The slave's snor-ing bursts through the underbrush. From behind a holly, I look at each in turn. Oh, to always see man when he is unaware of being watched. Their faces give away so much: the black man, though he snores through an open mouth and his arms and legs are flung wide, has a furrow to his brow that interrupts his sleep, causing him occasionally to flip and moan; the Creek's face is stone, is sadness, and he is tucked tight beneath a blanket so that his hands and feet are not exposed; and the white man—he is awake. His eyes are open and flit back and forth, as if watching meteors, but the sky is cloudy and he is heedless of my presence. I could take him now, but that would answer none of my questions. He does not look as ferocious as I'd imagined, but there are bloodstains on his cuffs, so I assume he took the lead in the killings. They are universally unkempt but oddly trusting. What guarantee do these men have that one of them will not steal the money from the others?

I crawl back to my camp and sleep as light as a bee, which is to say in dozes, and hardly at all.

ON THE SECOND day they are beginning to slow; Bob has an injury that is making his steps uneven, and the others attempt to keep pace. If I did not trust in my own stealth, it would be almost unfathomable that they hadn't yet felt my presence. I have moments of wanting to step hard on a branch, or throw a walnut, just to enter into their sanctuary. I should have roped their wrists by now, but they are leading me like a tide, deeper into the west.

Last night I found a blister on my heel that had bloomed into a pink bubble with the same sheen as mother-of-pearl. I pricked it with my knife to let the pus out and made a pancake of wet leaves that I stuck between the skin and my stocking. All these years of walking and I am unaccustomed to blisters. My feet have traditionally been as sturdy as my psyche. I am glad

I stopped the Creeks from walking with me on this spur, for in such moments I have a small fear that something within me unravels. But a blister is a natural growth, an obvious outcome from hard walking in springtime.

When the men turn north at a large dead oak, I pause. I did not expect any movements that would point to a coherent plan. So they are not aimless wanderers; do they head for the camp of some ringleader? Is there an architect of the scheme that will explain the miscellany of these particular individuals? Are they merely men-for-hire, without the free will that would justify my own justice? No, I will catch them regardless. If there is a man orchestrating their actions, he will simply be folded into the guilty. The Indian is leading them now through the tall grass in this unburned territory between rival nations. It's he who knows the way.

Just as I resolve to follow, they stop. The white man and the black man are turned toward each other with some intensity. My body is behind a young sassafras, one of the last bits of cover on the edge of the field, and my eyes peering out are dark enough to look like nothing, though no one glances my way. After a moment of apparent speech, the black man's arm explodes outward, punching Cat in the shoulder, the sound of which reaches me a half second later, and the white man falls back a step, his whole body in a convulsion of surprise.

This is it, the moment when they will fall to pieces, a rotten structure like all the other rotten structures that men have built from Europe to the New World. What misguided faith I had in them, if faith is even an appropriate term to describe my hunger for these men to be unlike others. In any country in the world they could not subsist together, yet here they were, wandering in a polite clump through woods that belonged apparently to no one, ignoring all the reasons to strike out on their own, to take the money and fall back into their segregated homes, for even America has rules. Their initial act of violence, of course, has voided any rational sympathy, so by all rights they should crumble now, should abandon the inexplicable amity of the past few days, should permit me to stop wondering. Let me capture you and put this to rest.

I take my musket off my back.

But when the black man walks on, shaking his arms in frustration, the white man follows him, and then the Indian.

Damn them.

BY NOON THEY come to a house in the woods. I sit at a distance and wait for whatever might happen, and in this moment I am admittedly content. The Indian knocks at the door.

Istillicha

I AND MY MOTHER and her kin belonged to the Wind clan, which is why our people so often led the others. My mother told me this story when I was young and still went to sleep in tears. In the time when everything was born, the Muskogee awoke in a fog cloud. They had been asleep for centuries, buried in mud and mist. In this new world, they reached out with tender fingers, for they could not see their own noses. They clutched at mushrooms growing among damp roots, stroked the flanks of passing deer. Scratched at the ground until squirrels burrowed into their hands, curious for nuts. The people in their blind search lost each other, but calling out only drove the animals away, so they kept silent. After years of grasping in the fog, a strong wind rolled through the forests with the scent of mountains and blew the mist out in wisping bursts. The first people to see each other in the new clarity were my people, and they called themselves the Wind clan. We led the others from the white cloud, and we lead them still. This is your responsibility, my mother would say, kneeling as she kissed my nose and smoothing my damp cheeks with the side of her thumb.

My stars were split in two: one half painted me as a hunter, fighter, chief. The other half was dark.

IN OUR HOUSES off the square, my mother lived and my father before she sent him away and her brother my uncle and their mother who was old and salty and my three older brothers and one younger. Our town was like an eddy in a river. War parties came through, and trading parties, English and French and Spanish, and Muskogee leaving other towns, and Choctaws or Cherokees bound as slaves, to be carried off to another eddy when the moon turned. Some people came like sticks and stuck in our current, cleaving to the water that turned round and round—Natchez, Yuchi, Shawnee, Coosa, all who'd lost their homes because our country was increasingly not our own. I saw men doing great things and what happened to men who were caught. Mostly I saw my mother, who tended us all with squeezes and slaps and knew more about the ways of birds and the passage of clouds than any man I met. We had endless questions, and she faced them all with a story. When we asked why the alligator looked so frightening with his crooked snout, she said he once played in a ball game with the eagle and the crane, four-foots against two-foots, and they hammered him on the nose to make him drop the ball. "Nothing to be afraid of," she said, "just bad at ball." So the world was laid clear to us. Each piece had its place, and what we did shaped those next to us. There was no such thing as independence.

I fetched water, I helped in our vegetable patch, I fed my grandmother hominy. I chased my little brother through the

thickets of river cane, across the fallow fields, and up the ter-
races that climbed away from the broad, clear river. My mother
threw me crabapples in the summer, high enough so their blur-
ring pink spun into patterns of blue. When they reached their
peak, my mind slowed them down and they fell soft as feathers
while my bowstring stretched back. Hit one clean through and
she'd give me breakfast. She kept throwing until I stopped missing. I said hello to my father whenever I saw him, before my
mother set his belongings outside and told him to move on, but
the man I loved most was my uncle, who was chief, who was
golden.

I loved my mother's brother as a boy will love a bear he sees
through spaces in the forest. His shoulders were sharp and narrow and though he was young yet, he had been in enough wars
to lose an eye and wear the *mico*'s feathers. To be chief was to
hold the town in your hands, to soothe it and to battle for it both.
His missing eye was a trouble to me; I wanted my world to be
ordered and clean and here was a hole in the man I most loved.
He moved faster than other men, spoke more gently. He touched
women on the arm like a moth, alighting and then moving on.
He cut my older brothers boy-sized bows and told them stories
of meddling rabbits while I knelt in the shadows and sopped
up his words. I was too young, but when I was older, his gaze
would fall on me, and—I thought—we would rule the town
together. His justice, my heart.

My older brothers were next in line, and they were rough
and cruel and would have battled with a crow if it cawed while
they were sleeping. They pummeled each other on the ball field
and inked their arms with spirals and skulls, signs of the animal
world. We lived in a red town, a war town, and they were built

for their fate. I would follow them to the open council house some summer nights and we would crouch beyond the cast of firelight and listen to the men, smell the smoke of their tobacco. The old men talked about their wives, about the flood twenty years before, about how best to turn antlers into powder. They'd share the priest's new prophecy and some would nod and warn and others would laugh and say the time for prophecy had come and gone. It was a new age, that was what the men were always saying, one that required not courage but cunning. The next man to be *mico* would find himself with strange duties. Listening in the dark, my brothers sucked on fish, and I swept up the bones they tossed aside.

Our uncle the *mico* was always getting older.

IT WAS BECAUSE he promised to watch me that my mother let me hunt with him, my first time. The men were preparing for their months-long winter trip, not for food but for the trade, from which they would return heavy with skins for the women to scrape and cure, so this would be a short journey, just to give the younger boys a taste. I still saw him as mine alone. His one eye, I thought, would follow me as I followed him; the love I had—though it was a more desperate feeling than love—would draw him like a pulling moon. How could he look at me and look away? My heart was loud.

We left in the afternoon, and he was tall and his arms swung an inch farther than any other man's. The stripe of his hair was pulled up tight, and the ring in his nose gleamed silver. His feet in shoes were silent, almost no feet at all. I knew the short paths we took that crossed each other through the village and into the farming land that lay along the river. But when we moved past the cornfields and beyond the burned woods into land that was new to me, I abandoned my human self, my upright legs, and I was a creature. No matter the men I was with. I swam through pine needles. My thoughts floated off from me before they ever made a noise. I was cold at first, for it was the slow drift into winter and the trees that had been golden were now muddy. The wet leaves clung to my heels. But my skin turned into something else, something like a shell or hide. I no longer felt the thorn vines clutching, the buried pointed rocks, the pricks of the pine cones. I had eyes, and fingers enough to hold my bow, and a heart that steadied me onward, the blood pumping in drums through my chest and in my ears, beating the thoughts to fragments. Only the beeches still held their leaves. In the light of afternoon, the forest ahead was fiery brown, the color of a deerskin in sun, the sky beyond cut with winter branches and the russet of the shaking beech leaves. Our sounds were the sounds of the wood. Wet leaves stepping, squirrels flipping acorns, the chatter of the chickadees in the low branches, the wind matching the water. The sun's crispness as it fell, a faint ringing as it marked our path and gave us to the dusk.

We lay down to rest in this new land, taking our women's food from our bags for supper and then lying in a mass under skins for warmth, the damp scrub like a slick beneath us. I swept my spot clean and piled the broken branches at my feet for luck. The night sounds were different here, the owls with a dialect. My hands balled into fists in case the animals were evil or the ghost children found us. I took pleasure in my fear because it gave me yet another thing to conquer and possess. I slept for the first time without my mother, and in the ring of bodies, hunters all, I smelled myself a man, or the beginning of one, and when

I fell asleep at last, I had creature dreams. I was running far and fast, I was climbing and falling, I dove and buried. There was no thought but movement. We were animals in an animal world, and I was the newest of them.

I woke with a low growl in my belly to the grayness before dawn. The men were already rubbing out the leaves where we slept, and I, the last to rise, felt like a child again. Someone had kicked aside my pile of branches, so I bunched them back up. We were moving before I remembered where we were and who my mother was. I was cold, and I no longer felt like an animal, and no one had given me anything for breakfast. There was a thin fog that dampened our clothes and misted my eyelashes. I envied my little brother Oche and his nearness to the women. How much more sense it made to plant seeds and coax their stalks to the sun and pick their fruits to grind into meal than to be a lone boy in the woods, searching for food you cannot see. At home, my mother would have clean blankets.

The legs of my uncle looked like stone, carved in muscle shapes. How had he ever come from a woman's body? He stood up fast, he ate little, he wiped no sleep from his eyes. He was wrapped around this forest like strangler vine, like there was no difference between his breaths and the breathing leaves. I trailed behind him, putting my feet in the prints his feet left. One of the other men was wearing a deerskin on his back, and in one hand he held a head: a dried deer face that he raised and pivoted, becoming a strange two-legged half-dead animal that was meant to seem ordinary to the wild deer watching. My uncle looked more deer than him.

We crossed another creek as the sun spread on the edge of the land, and through the last of the mist—which would live on my clothes all day, the sun never rising high enough to reach its heat—I saw the stand of deer. They hadn't heard us, our wet-leaf footsteps or my belly. In the dawn their skin was as golden as beech leaves, as smooth and unbroken as the bark. Two bucks, four does, and a fawn. A family, like my family, a band of woods warriors, like my woods warriors. A surge of something warm tripped in my throat. I wanted to protect them and seize them in the same childish instant. As we paused to watch them blow through the leaf litter with their muzzles, the fawn reaching back to lick her shoulder, I drew an arrow, fit its notch to my bow, aimed it as I would at a flying crabapple, and loosed it at the baby.

It cut a line through her flank and fell away and the stand of them exploded in a flurry of thin legs so fast the first thing my eyes could settle on was the leaves drifting down from where they'd been kicked. One of the men cuffed me across my face and another took my bow. In the clearing, we found a vein of salt and a spatter of dropped blood from the fawn. I took a leaf that had been curdled red and slipped it in my shirt. This was my blood, blood that I had drawn. The men laughed at me and called me the names of women and one twisted my ear until it rang, but I could not be shamed. My brother, girlish, attached to my mother's leg, had never done what I had done, would never understand the swell of possession.

We found more deer to catch. I stood behind the others without my bow and touched my shirt where the leaf was hidden, and grown men brought down the animals with guns, clean shots to save their skins. We carried the bodies back on sleds. Half-homeward, we stopped to eat and I sat beside my uncle as naturally as if there were no other space in the woods. He didn't look at me or grab my shoulder, but unlooped a pouch from his breeches and opened it on his lap, pulling out his charms.

"A foot," he said, and I looked over, pretending that I hadn't been looking all along. "You take it from the last kill to trick the new deer. They smell it and think their brother is still running."

I rubbed it with a soft finger. It had been cut off at the ankle, was thin-boned and cleft. The hoof was black and milky, like dark water. I touched it quickly to my lips.

"Physic-nut," he said. The yellow fruit rolled around his palm.

"What does it do?"

He shook his head. "Slips in their minds and fuddles them. I don't know. Draws them near." He turned to the three small stones and tumbled them beneath his thumb.

"They trip the deer," I said. "They keep them from running far."

He laughed. "No, these are from my grandmother's grave. Just bits from her grave."

A woman's spirit on a stone didn't sound like a deer charm. There weren't women on the hunt, except to cook for us and strip the bodies we caught; their smells and the red richness of them were too potent to be masked. Even wrapped in skins, they were never less than women, less than intoxicating. I didn't press my uncle further, because I didn't yet want to know their secrets, which I knew he knew.

He let me hold his talismans, and I kept them safe and clammy. He dug his fingers into his scalp, feeling along his neck for ticks. Other men were standing. They wanted to get home that night and give the kill to their wives and sisters for cleaning, for pulling the skin from the flesh and scraping it, smoking it. But my uncle the *mico* sat still against a tree and waited for me to finger his charms and so all the men waited. I saw his power and it was greater than anything in his pouch. I held the pieces as long as I dared and then slid them back. He patted his thigh.

When I returned home, cold with scratches across my legs, I told my mother I was a man. She slipped her fingers in my hair to tug out the tangles and said, "And what good is a man?"

MY SMALLEST BROTHER, Oche, was the one who didn't want the *mico*'s feathers, who kept sick animals in a little bower near the fields, who some said would be a priest. He wouldn't let my mother shave any part of his hair. Some said ghosts followed him, but I never saw them, and he said ghosts followed everyone. Every village holds the spirits of those who pass on, ancestors ready to help, but it's the dead children who move around, who are too restless to lie still and who search for playmates when all the living go to sleep. Oche, who could not concern himself with war, with the ways of life and men, whispered when others shouted; he spoke of things that had happened seasons before, as though his memory was a slow runner.

I loved him because he was there. He was younger than me and earnest, only doing what he liked, and he spent time with me because he loved me back and he saw no gain in denying this. He didn't mind that I liked to line things up and put things in order. But I pretended not to love him because he was a baby and never tried to be better than he was. At night, when men were smoking or watching the women dance with their turtle shell shakers, we would sneak to the chunkey ground and roll the stone. Though young and lanky as a mantis, Oche threw his spear closest to where the round stone came to rest. Mine went too far. I wanted him to see how strong I was, how if there was a Choctaw or an Englishman, my strength would stab his heart before he ever made it to the rolling stone. My brother was not violent, and always won.

Oche had a way of telling truth that I never understood. Time didn't matter so much to him; the world circled around in his knotty head. He could tell myths like they had happened to him. Once on the night-lit ball field, as I stretched my spear back, he said he'd found the dog I had lost years before. I gaped at him.

"Red Dirt?" I asked.

"I gave him food and told him where you were."

"Quick. Was he by the river?" I dropped my spear and let the ball roll into the far ditch.

"He was with the men riding out against the Choctaws. Perhaps he fought with them."

I bent over and placed my fingertips on the grass. "That was two years ago, brother."

"Yes, when you lost your dog."

The others laughed at Oche, the way our mother coddled him, fed him secret foods on moony nights to call the spirits onto him. Our three older brothers, all still learning to hunt, had little faith in priests. They would speak to the animal they killed, or had to kill twice for poor aim, but then would laugh between themselves when the priest riddled the meat with prayer. Oche wasn't hurt by this, couldn't be hurt. He simply liked to be alone. He wandered in the woods searching not for deer or demons but for mushrooms. He told me his dreams, and they were little different from my dreams, except that in his brush-soft voice they sounded like prophecy. I wanted to whisper with him, even as I was chasing after my older brothers to punch and claw them and soak up their valor and learn how to be grown. Being grown meant doing things one was afraid of, meant not being afraid. If I wasn't quaking or sweating or twisting the inside of my cheek between my teeth, then I wasn't yet brave.

During mulberry moon, Oche made *sofkee* as my mother guided his hands. He took the cracked hominy she had already pounded and sifted from the corn hulls, and he stirred it in our iron pot with water and wood-ash lye until it turned to soup. I asked him questions about animals and what they did and who they were friends with until he paused to think and the hominy started to stick and our mother slapped him on the bottom with a broom.

He took me from the men's world to the women's, for he seemed to be neither, something in between. And the women held a world that was still soft with my youth and pungent with something new. In the early spring before the deer were moving, Oche and I would crouch beyond the girdled stumps marking the crop meadow and watch the girls planting. They bent like saplings in a strong wind, their hair floating in wings around their faces. Oche would draw them in mud ink on bark, admire his work, and set it floating on the river, bored. I stared at them. I was a warrior hidden behind shrubs, peering into an enemy camp, finding the gaps in their defenses. Taking in details. Small waists, twisted hair, a hand scratching at an ankle. I asked Oche to pick his favorite, and he pointed to the one farthest away, who was round and faceless. I waited, patient, till he asked me mine, and I showed him Polly, the girl who stood above the others and whose skin looked like something you could eat. Polly I had seen before, had always been half seeing. I didn't tell him how she planted seeds in my head long after the fields were empty. He would not have been interested.

When Oche was old enough, my mother sent him off to learn the priesthood. He went across our river to a far creek with the old priest and a few other boys and stayed for four days, and when he came home, he was greenish and damp and his hair was a knotted mat. He said they drank *mico hoyanidja* from a willow root and threw up their bellies and went without food, and while the priest was whispering the secret formulas and showing them the making of medicine, he only thought how hungry he was and wished for his mother's fry bread. I patted his shoulder as if I had never had the same loneliness. The priest sat them in a steam hut and then made them swim, and one of the boys cried a little. But he was proud too and boasted that he could fix me if I were shot through with arrows from eyes to toes.

"Did you see things?" I asked, meaning monsters or his own future.

"Lots of light," he said, "but I was sick so maybe this was nothing."

I began to worry that what I knew about the world, he knew too. Maybe even knew better.

THE RIVER HELD our secrets, before and after, was the clear thread that tied our town to all the other Muskogee towns, tied us to ourselves. Its wetness swallowed our bare feet, our bitten ankles, and when Oche first dove under, I would pretend he'd rise as a fish. For these visits to the water, I would borrow his imagination.

"Look," he'd say, always *look*, and hold up a crawfish by its tail. He found stone teeth from the ancient animals, fish eggs in strings. "We'll be otters," he said, and I crouched in the fast water with him, the two of us rubbing our paws together, flapping around our tails, ottering. He was the quick minnow and I was the shark, and we chased until the current tired us. We were rabbits hiding from each other in the towering, knocking thickets of cane. We were not boys, but wild.

On the bank, the glory of our abandon seeped away.

"Did Uncle ever play like this?" I asked. "Were even his games better than our games?"

"Would you love Polly so much if she had only one eye?"

Oh, Polly. No, I wouldn't. What were women but their faces?

Oche thought our uncle was just another *mico* and Polly nothing but a girl. He had larger concerns.

"What animal do you think you used to be?" he asked. "And would you change back?"

I was hot now that the water had dried from my skin. I wiped my feet clean and pushed the leaves beside me into a pile. There was little to control besides debris.

"Would you rather be a fish or a bird? What if you could live a thousand years as a turtle or ten years as a boy?"

As I tired, I always tired of him. "A man," I said. "Why would you not want to be a man?" The scales had flaked off me. I left him by the bank.

WAR SWUNG AROUND our town in those years, whirlpooling the familiar. The English were fighting each other now, and some of our towns chose sides and others stuck with older enemies. Our diplomats traveled east to the Carolinas, north to the Great Lakes. What we needed from the English we mostly had, and if we found ourselves wanting for more guns, more rum, the

Spanish lay just below us and the French beyond the Choctaws. We lived in the middle of chaos, and all we had to do was stay right where we were and the storm would blow by. But we were a red town, and the *mico* was a young man, and the trade was growing so hungrily that we couldn't pull back without losing some pride. My brothers, with bows and knives and muskets, took their undirected fury to distant fields, and season by season, fewer returned.

When my first brother died in war, I thought, *No more. I have no interest in this.* I was terrified, my family having lost a limb. A whole man was suddenly absent, and I could not find where he had gone; not even Oche would tell me, though I was certain he saw things in other worlds. We buried him beneath our house. I retreated. And when my second brother died in war, I thought, *I want it. I want to be a* mico. This was how we whipped ourselves into froth. Revenge played in our hearts, weaseled down our arms into our hands, which could not stop clenching. No man could take my brothers and not in turn be taken, or I was not a man. So my mind rolled over, nightly turning redder. I snuck beside the council house and listened for the next plans, the war that would happen the following week, the one that would rage by the summer. In the shadows, I squatted and stood, lifted stones in my hands, punched the tense of my stomach. I willed myself to grow stronger. I no longer found comfort in Oche, who by then was pounding corn with women, tending them in their bleeding huts, abandoning raids for nut harvests. Even through the loss, he could not see what war we were fighting.

But my third brother, the last between the *mico* and me, was hungry for control. I watched him closely, mimicked his long steps. I drew a snake on my ankle, like his, with ink, though it washed off in the next storm. He had the same narrow shoulders as our uncle, that compact strength of a coil, an arrow flying, but had thicker limbs. The elders saw a solid future in my brother, from his fight-broken nose to his legs, which were long enough to cross creeks. Once I heard him whispering with my mother—he was angry and she put her words into questions, and she seemed to be guiding him away from me, pushing his fierceness out of our house, beyond the quiet of the home, away from the children.

THE SUMMERS WERE hot, no wind. The summers, then, were when we fought. My first battle was before Green Corn, when even the nights were no relief and men boiled outside, their bodies too hot to be still. My uncle the *mico* said the nearest Choctaw towns had struck a deal with the Spanish and would soon be raiding our fields, but the town above us refused to fight. The men there were grayer and honored old alliances. Our *mico* was young, and had his name still to forge. We all came to the council houses then, I in the back, behind my mother even, whose seat closer to the fire was meant to remind me how little I knew. The farthest ring was crowded with boys and girls. We sometimes watched the speakers and sometimes stared at the carvings on the posts, animals with their mouths open, claws outstretched. I searched for Polly, just to see the flame reflected on her cheek.

The elders voted to move out first, to cross the river, to goad the enemy. Those who disagreed threw up their hands and called my uncle names. This was democracy. We had been warring with the Choctaws in bursts for as long as there had been Muskogee to gather arms, for our lands overlapped and our deer ran into each other's woods. In the smoky dark as we were leaving, I told my uncle I wanted to hold a gun in this war. If my last brave brother would be there, so would I. He tilted his head and cupped my chin in his hand and shook it till my teeth rattled.

"Eager to die?" he asked.

"I'm ready to defend my people." My voice sounded louder than it should have.

"We're defending nothing, boy. We're killing Choctaws."

"I'm prepared to die," I said.

"And welcome to it. Being prepared is halfway there." He laughed and left me standing clench-fisted.

My mother didn't much like the sound of my bravery when I told her that night I'd be fighting. Oche retreated to the storage house to allow us the space for argument. Her bread was half in her mouth when she pulled it out again. Did she ever wish for daughters? She scooted over to me and placed her hands on my crossed knees and bent her head until it almost touched the dirt floor. For a moment, I thought she might be weeping. I should be ashamed to bring my own mother, the woman who'd taught me to shoot, to such tears, and yet her sorrow seemed a further line between us—if she was not a crying woman, then I was not a brave man. But when she sat up, I saw a strange fire in her face that wasn't anger and wasn't pride either.

"Do you know how many of your brothers have died?"

"Two," I said. I always answered questions.

"What are your reasons?"

"To protect the village and seek justice. The Choctaws are our enemies." The smoke from the cooking meat looped up and through a hole in the ceiling, and the smell of it made my stomach jump. I wanted my dinner. My uncle's rhetoric sounded hollow in my mouth. "They've killed so many of our men,

Mother, what else can we do? Your own sons, and you don't want vengeance?"

"And where do you think your body goes when it is dead?"

"In the ground," I said.

"What do you think I will do when you are dead?" The bread was still in her hand, half gnawed. When she spoke, her hands fluttered with her words and the bread dragged in the dirt. Her hair was untied.

I thought about this. I had seen her grieving my older brothers, elaborate ceremonies but few tears, no loud emotion. But they had been grown, one was married, and were not my mother's pets anymore. My third brother, the one warrior left, wasn't here tonight because he was chasing a woman, playing night ball with his friends, gambling under a tree somewhere. What did it matter if we were dead? She spent more time in the crop fields, in her own garden, shaping square baskets and round pots, than she did tending us, asking about our feelings, sewing up the splits in our leggings. She seemed to me not so much a mother as a farmer. When we were gone, she would keep turning the earth over. The squash would still ramble from the dirt. The corn would still grow high and pale in summer. The hickory trees would still drop the nuts that she would gather and grind for oil. And when the men brought deer home from the forest, she would sit with the other women around a fire and scrape at the skin with knives until the hair and gristle fell away and the hide was water-smooth.

"If I die, you will love Oche more," I said. "And perhaps you will have another child."

She laughed. "Yes, I will love Oche more."

My mother was not a pacifist.

. . .

I RODE OUT with them on a bay pony, her reluctant head pointed west. Her back was sweated thick before too many miles, and by then my bones were scared. The dogs had already turned back toward town. Beneath my blanket the night before, which I hid under hot or cold to stop the ghost children from touching me, I heard my uncle speak to my mother by the fire outside our house. His low voice I could not make out, but hers rose high into the thick night air. "I will not. Do you remember?" she said, and then, "It's your head if he's harmed." She made sounds of protest and then laughter, and in the morning she let her brother take me to war.

We camped partway, and being an older boy now, I didn't cower among the roots or think about my home. I didn't even sleep next to my brother, not giving him the chance to push me away, though I did straighten his arrows when he wasn't watching and clean the dirt off his quiver with spit. I ate the peaches and boiled bean bread with bites large enough for a scalper of men. In the dark I covered my legs with leaves—the ghost children are everywhere—and dreamed of axe-wielding. My dream-hands spun like maple seeds and men fell down before me in baths of blood. My uncle stood to one side, applauding.

The next day, by the time the sun was straight above us, we were in the borderlands, the forests where no one hunted. The growth was thicker here, unburned and wild. There was a beaten path for war and trading, but we stayed to the north of it, weaving our ponies through the brush to mask our coming. Once or twice we passed a little hut where a woman—neither Muskogee nor Choctaw but someone whose tribe had been worn to nothing—sat with a pipe and sold rope and meal and

bullets to the white men who were always moving. They had
their cities and still they yearned for the forests and fields, the
emptiness that we filled, and so they marched back and forth between these places without end, taking what they found, writing
down what they saw when they passed by. We raised our hands
to the women at the posts, and they waved their pipes at us. War
did not touch the traders. All men needed food, needed guns.

At a river, we dismounted, tied our ponies to the basswoods.
We drank and rested and sat still for hours. I crept to my uncle,
whose face was painted red and black, and asked when we were
raiding. He told me to settle myself, to find a tree to fit my back
and practice waiting. I did until I began to doze. The air was so
honeyed with heat that the mosquitoes were drowsing. It was
easy to dream of Polly in this idleness. I let my mind dance away.
Beneath my legs the earth hummed with the tiny movements of
underground animals—worms and grubs and the snakes that
held up the very foundations of the world—all turning over
themselves in brown darkness, the steps of men above them
nothing more than thunder. We didn't mind their wars, and they
cared little for ours, except when we scooped out their heavens
to lay a dead man in their midst. To have the power of a god—to
be anybody's god—and to bend the paths of little beings to your
own vision, this was the peak of all living. No matter that I had
no vision, could bend no paths but that of my pony, who only listened to my heels when she had been well fed. The first step was
to prove my strength. To kill men, to woo a woman, to direct a
town, more towns, a confederacy. To hold dominion.

I wiped the sweat from my forehead and dried it on the bony
ridge of my shins, just fleecing with hair. Dragonflies were
dipping on the river, lined on its bottom with skipping stones

and spikemoss and the whole black leaves of sycamores, rotten but not dissolved. Everything around us made a sound: water, stone, fly, spider on bark, sparrow. What I didn't know was that the river was a border, and that Choctaw men crossed it to hunt when they shouldn't have, and that such crossing justified attack. I thought my kin were lazing, and as I drifted into a heated sleep, I wished I were the child of a braver town. I was certain the Choctaws didn't sit for hours staring at their toes on the warpath. My uncle wouldn't even stripe my cheeks in red.

I woke from sleep when something sharp grazed my ear. The forest was moving, the river swirling up around bodies and motion. Stealth had been abandoned and it was loud, shapes were moving loudly, and I saw they were men, and the sounds were war cries and the stick that scraped my ear was an arrow. My fathers and my cousins were fighting—men were getting struck in the open skin of their chests and thighs—and no one had shaken me awake. I rose raging, the sleep still in my eyes, my bow arm tingling and woozy from a cramp. I yelled out, and in the calling all around me, in the shots that echoed among the twangs of bows, I seemed to make no sound. I had seen Choctaws in our town before, sitting in peace talks, bringing cloth or kettles to trade, and now they were like so many deer for my arrows to find. I had been deemed too young for a gun. I shot three arrows straight and watched them snake between the swarming men. For all I wanted to kill, and with the killing prove myself, I couldn't even hit a body. My ears were full up with blood. The animals had gone, and we were all that was left. I was not afraid. I was not afraid. Some men had knives now and were upon each other. I could see faces. I hid myself behind a pine and pulled my arms in and thought how much I didn't want to die. From close came a choking scream. I peeked out sideways, afraid to miss the gore, and saw a Choctaw drop to his knees and pull one of our feathered arrows from his gut, its bent point trailing his innards like a hook drawing an eel from the stream.

My eyes were fixed, my mouth still parted and tasting of sour brine. I wanted my uncle. I wanted him to come and find me, take me up in a bundle, and tell me this was all a game. Before I could undo myself, could turn back in to safety, I saw a man in our red smudges stand behind the line of fighting, his string drawn taut. I looked to see where he was shooting. If there was a man running at us, I would have climbed the tree, straight up like a bear. There were Choctaws across the river, right and left, a few mired in the banks, pulling at their hatchets. There were none in the clearing before us. So why did the man's arrow point straight? There were no backs to shoot there but Muskogee. I saw his fingers unclench as slow as growing grain.

In the days it took the arrow to fly the string, in the time I took searching for its target, not finding a body where it belonged, I saw a Choctaw scramble the banks and run knifeward to our party, caught in the heavy syrup that held the moment still. My eyes left the creeping arrow. I called out in a broken boy voice, "To the right!" Beside me, the man with the sprung bow turned—Seloatka of the Wolf clan—and took my face in his gaze. I turned from him to watch the arrow coursing. It stayed true. As I stared, Seloatka twisted around, arm raised to meet the coming enemy, and in the gap between their nearing bodies, I saw the arrow's point pierce the back of my uncle's chest and plunge until it crossed his heart. He fell to his knees. Seloatka wrestled with the Choctaw. I turned back to the pine and closed my eyes. *My eyes have seen a murder.*

In the darkness, with the sounds of blood far and faint, I saw again the man, the arrow, my uncle—the man, the arrow, my uncle—and wondered what sort of a life he'd had all those years when I was watching him and wishing to be his mirror. He hadn't lost his life because he was a one-eyed man, or a narrow-shouldered man, or a man whose soft face looked sweet to women. He was lying with an arrow in his back because he told men what to do. He helped sort the grain in the winter, said yes or no to plans of war, got first tasting at Green Corn. He couldn't make us act, but he was wise and strong enough to earn our nods. Would I have killed him for this privilege? Could I kill? Most every night, I felt black boils inside me. I was cowardly and starved and boiling over with unpointed desire. My uncle wasn't dark with evil or white with peace, but red. We lived in a red town. We all wanted to be the *mico*.

I wished a ghost boy had found me and swallowed me. I opened my eyes. I turned from the pine trunk and saw my uncle on the spot where he fell, an arrow in his back, his hand cupped.

I waited until the last brave Choctaw had been killed and the sounds of the cowards' feet faded in the shuffling brush before I pulled the arrow from my uncle's back and snapped it. The men lashed the bodies of our own to our ponies' backs and wept over my uncle, who had simply fallen in war like others had. We rode east in silence, leaving behind the slain that made up for our warriors, raided and surprised two seasons ago. Our blood had been quieted, and none knew that a fresh claim on vengeance was riding slumped across a pony's shoulders. I rode behind, my young blood tingling. The battle we had begun was now my battle. I could hoard my darkness, pet the cowardice in me, become nothing, or I could carry this rare chance to retribution.

Carry it to manhood. This was the moment when fates were turned. But my fingertips were sore from clenching bark, and it hurt to ride, and my cheeks were reddened with my hands' bloodlessness, and I was hungry once again for home. I thought of Oche, tending the fire beneath a summer stew. I closed my eyes to better taste the image, and when I opened them, Seloatka's pony was in step with mine.

He said nothing. I clenched my knees around my pony's chest and bent my head. He rode with me till camp that night. I heard all the threats he never made. *You are a boy who tells lies. My broad hands could break your body in two.* He slept next to me and our breaths sounded like a boy running and a man walking slow behind. In my half-dreams, his hand was around my throat; I kept waking to pull at it. He didn't touch me. I couldn't sleep for pushing his hands away. In the nadir of night when my mind was usually lost in girls, in the curves of Polly, I found myself believing that this life was done. That my boyhood had been a fancy. I was too young to think of killing, could not have killed Seloatka if I wanted to, and I didn't want to: I was not the man who killed, but the other. I wanted to be as good as the *mico*.

Not until we reached home and my mother saw the body dangling and shook herself with wails did I understand that I had lost my uncle, simple, and I fell from my pony and wept, nothing like a man. No sleep could comfort, and the stew that had simmered since dawn went uneaten. My first secret began eating into my heart.

THE MOURNING STRETCHED over days, for a *mico* is greater than a man. I saw him buried below our house, saw the round hole in which they lowered his body. He sat up in his grave, a blanket over his shoulders and a pipe in his hand, because he was a warrior and was always watching, though he'd never have more than one eye. I looked away when they threw dirt around him, my slim brave kin. Where my uncle went, where the spirit of him traveled, I was never certain. Some said he was in the hole, or the house, or was back at battle, ghost-fighting his enemies. Oche said he saw him waiting.

"Waiting for what?" I asked.

He waved his fingers gently above his head, making loose loops.

If we could choose where our spirit goes, mine wouldn't rest. Mine would hunt and battle. Mine would haunt the wicked. I said this in a quiet voice so Seloatka, who was with us filling the grave, wouldn't hear.

"What wicked?" Oche said.

I opened my eyes wide. We could speak at each other silently like this, and neither would understand.

The night before Green Corn, a smaller council gathered in the meeting house and threw conversation about a successor. It was the last day of the year's fire; tomorrow the flame would be doused and all debts and wrongs would be forgiven, though by whom I never knew. The next in line in the Wind clan was the one left of my older brothers, who was panting for the reins. He had ridden with us in the river fight against the Choctaws and had claimed several lives, but he didn't speak to me on that journey, for we were not friends but kin. I could have told him what I saw, but he was older and fiercer and laughed at jokes too coarse for me to understand. When he saw me in the town or practicing with my bow in the fields, he would pelt me with stones and husked-out shells. Had I told him of Seloatka's careful aim and the dreamlike path of the arrow through summer air to deep between our uncle's shoulders, I would have had to tell him of my vantage, my cowardly crouch behind the sap-sticky pine. Being still stuck between boyhood and courage, this I could not reveal. I also worried Seloatka might be a spirit, or at least a man who could read my wishes, so when I found myself thinking of the slow arrow, I pushed my mind to something safer. Girls planting seeds, or fishing. Polly, whose form I always returned to. My mind divided neatly between politics and her, between imagining myself chief and wondering what I would say if I found myself alone with her, our hands nested.

I stood outside the meeting house and listened for my brother's voice. All I heard was Seloatka's, burrowing blunt-headed through the conversations. He didn't question my brother's place, or claim some greater strength. He didn't object to the elders' reasoning. But he made his voice carry low across all debate, so that when the men went home that evening to tell their sisters and wives, all they would remember was Seloatka, Seloatka.

This was not a time when any man could be made *mico*. The British were begging for our allegiance and our sole custom. A white man's war was disordering the deer trade. The skins we got sometimes could not be sold, and if we turned elsewhere—to the French or Spanish—the British withheld their rum. No one knew what games the others were playing. And who we were was quickly changing. Cattle now roamed through our fallow fields, herded by uncertain warriors. Our town became home to two white traders, several men from a Cherokee village that had lost its fields, some Seminole women, and slaves who were Choctaw, Chickasaw, African. To be Muskogee in those years was to hear your name in a half-dozen languages. How could you lead when you didn't know who your people were, much less your enemies? I waited to hear how the elders, who were around when white men were rare, would push us into a future. But all I heard was Seloatka.

My brother walked out of the council house pale and sweating, a cough trembling his chest. He was the tallest of us, broader than the brothers who were already in the ground. His body was one that admitted no suffering. After the council fire was snuffed and the Beloved Men were sleeping next to the Beloved Women and only the possums and ghost children were left on the ball field, my brother, next in line, lay in his bed coughing.

Oche said he tasted evil on it. I was afraid to know what evil was. I said there was no such thing—if there were, surely I'd find it in myself—and that it was nothing more than a summer fever. Whichever it was, Oche didn't mind. He just spoke things aloud and then turned over into sleep. The peace in his heart was bottomless.

And so when I saw my brother growing sicker as the Green Corn days passed, I tried to think of something else, tried not to think the one who should lead our town was wasting. A doctor looked him over, opened his eyelids, kneaded his stomach. He gave him *pasa* and wormseed. The night the council met, my brother could not go. His skin was wet and nearly white. His eyes fluttered about the room but never settled. His limbs began to twitch like a rabbit in a trap. The council determined he would not live. We stayed quiet one more day, and as the women dressed themselves in rattles for the dance and Oche walked with the priests to start the year's new fire, my brother slipped into an unawareness. He would not respond to touch, to pinch, to slap. We sat around his bed and gave pieces of melon to the guests: men who stopped by to see a brother warrior, women who swore they loved him, had almost been his wife. They came through in quiet lines like shadows, their small stories thrown into silhouette by the great fire that was my mother. She didn't move. Her eyes didn't move from his face, which was paling away, one step from ghost. I sat with her not because I loved my brother but because I wanted to see the moment when he passed from man to something else. When my uncle was dying, when the arrow I had not prevented was holing his heart, letting the blood find all the empty spaces of his body, my eyes were closed. Now I kept my hands on the sides of my face, holding my eyes on my brother, imagining what I missed before. He grew smaller and smaller, like a weed without water, crumpling in the faintest ways. I had to blink, and at some instant when I was blinking or not blinking, his spirit walked away.

The doctor came and tasted his blood and told us it was poison.

My mother's tears dried into fury. She said she'd finger every man and woman who had stepped past our door until one confessed and was burned alive. When the doctor was gone and Oche was asleep and my mother was making lists of suspects and rivals and bloody methods of revenge, I stepped outside my body and saw that our family had been hacked at until it was splinters. We were of the Wind clan, and we were lying split in our home, in broken poses: asleep, afraid, raving, dead.

So I told her what I knew. I told her of the singing soft arrow in my uncle's back and Seloatka's pointed menace, and asked her not to tell a soul, especially Oche, who would be afraid. I didn't guess, though, how much fear would be my mother's part. I thought she would burst from the house in a crusade, might even strangle Seloatka with her knuckly hands. But when I finished my story, her eyes went dead. She did not cook for the feast to break the Green Corn fast. She did not speak to me anymore that night and slept silently. In the morning when she roused me, she said, "My son, you have had such a dream. A terrible dream has come to you, but it's all right now. Your mother is here now." We never spoke of it again.

With my uncle shot through and my brother poisoned, I was the next to claim *mico*, but the council agreed I was unfit and green. Seloatka told them he saw me crouched behind a tree during the river fight, my breechcloth soaked with urine. I didn't contradict this version of myself, valuing my life as a boy does, though when Oche asked if I was angry, I said I was ready to crash heads and set fire to the meeting house. In the last seasons of my boyhood, we would battle with wooden axes in the ditches behind the cornfields, one of us the *mico*, the other the usurper. Perhaps all this false anger prepared me for a realer kind.

One of our cousins became chief, the one who was married to Seloatka's sister. Within a year, the elders had stopped bringing us meat to fill the hole of my uncle's loss, and by the time my voice dropped and I was mostly a man, we were pushed to a smaller house on the edge of town farthest from the fields. My grandmother had passed three years before from some kind of pox, and with fewer numbers and less sway, our family handed away our home. Like my brother, we were shrinking. When our cousin the new *mico* died hunting—no one knew how, no one asked—Seloatka seized power. The feather was now in his hands.

The elders painted his face ghost-white and sat him on a white skin and reminded him what white meant, that it was his duty ever to hunt for peace, even in our warring town. He nodded and was grave, but sitting on the back bench of the council house, I could see the firing of his hungry heart, which pumped not white but red. Then he took the white drink, and we all drank with him. He gulped the roasted holly water until he vomited. I could not sleep that night, and though my mother said I was too young for the white drink and now I'd have dreams, I only thought of the man in white with the beating red heart and wondered how to pull that out of him.

AND POLLY WAS his other sister's daughter. Her eyebrows ran straight across her face, above eyes that were black with mischief. She wore a blue bead in her hair. She played with the boys when she was young and no one took notice of her until she stole her slenderness away and stayed in a hut with women and brought back something full. We threw sweetgum balls at her, and she simply stared and walked off. My affection for her, or was it awe, grew with the same breaths that fed my anger at her uncle. There was something in her that I wanted, and though it felt sincere and young, I cannot swear that my love for her wasn't born of a greater hatred.

I began to leave presents by her door—feathers wrapped in a bunch with twine, sweet cakes my mother made—and to watch from behind a shrub as she stepped out into the mist of morning to discover she was admired. Her face melted from the last of sleep into a quiet pleasure. She would put down the water pot to hold the feathers close, bite the cake, and I thought she was pressing me to her, nibbling at my mouth. In the days before she knew it was me, I felt a limitless power over her welfare. Not knowing who I was, she could not refuse me. One day I left her nothing, just to watch her face pinch in disappointment. If I was cruel, I blamed the great loathing that simmered under all my movements.

I went down to the river where the women were fishing, roping in the last of the rockfish and red drum, to ask Oche his wisdom. While he washed out his clothes, he told me that girls are no mystery. They are not spirit people, not ghost children, not creatures to be shot or skinned. He laughed at my gifts and my skulking, and when I told him I didn't know where the love came from, he told me all love was good and pure and I let myself believe him. Oche knew nothing of Seloatka, disliked him because he took more grain than was his chiefly share and fought sometimes for sport rather than revenge, and I could not tell him any different. He asked if I wanted Polly forever.

I did not respond, but watched a young man paddle by in a newly dug canoe, testing it for a summer journey.

"Would you ever tire of her?" He squeezed the water from his shirt and laid it on a rock, smoothing out its folds. "Could you hold her when she's unhappy or when she makes no sense? Would you hold her if she hit you? If you saw another woman that you loved and Polly said no, you could not have her, would you listen? If you lost all your children so there were no more threads between you, would you love her still?"

I had been growing into a panic until he mentioned this last. "I won't have children," I said. I took my feet out of the water and dried them on the grass. "Unless I had a son like you, to do the washing for me."

He looked so slim standing there by the young trees along

the bank. His chest small, his hair long as a girl's. I asked him if he was old enough yet to love, and he smiled and held up his leggings dripping from the river.

The first time I spoke to her, I started coughing so she had to fetch me water, and all I could do was thank her and hurry back to my knife-sharpening, cheeks on fire. The second time, she asked if I was all right, as if I were an old man with little time to live, the light in her eyes gone soft and comforting, and I said I was perfectly fine in a deep voice. My mother had given me honey to smooth my throat, and I glared at Polly and walked on.

The third time, I found her crouched in the notch of a hickory. She said she was hiding from a friend and begged for my silence, so I crawled up and sat beside her. We didn't speak as the blackbirds flocked to a branch above us and settled in a beating of wings. I ventured that she might be too old for hiding and stared anywhere but at her body. Her arm pressed against mine. I closed my mouth until the blackbirds had all flown off, in search of a tree less fraught. A girl appeared from the fields, paused to glance between the rows, and then ran to the river on the tallest pointed feet, as though wanting to be admired. We kept our places, shoulders locked. I asked her in a whisper if she liked the gifts. She looked at me quick and said, "You?" I nodded, feeling like a man again, and she squinted her eyes at the gathering dark.

We stayed in the tree through nightfall and star-rising. We could hear the town's murmur from the council ground, the ball field. I never asked about her uncle, so she told me of her mother and her brothers and the father who was an Englishman she'd never seen.

His name was Thomas Colhill and he had married her mother in a traditional way, which is to say not in the churches that he knew, so when he left a few months later, he thought he took his freedom with him. This was not uncommon, and her mother kept no bitterness. Just an old rifle he had given her as a bride gift, a silver chain that she passed to Polly, rudimentary English, and the use of his name in trade. His use of hers proved more valuable, and with his Muskogee kinship waving like a flag before him, he took his whiskey to the Indians and brought back skins. The fortune he made must have kept his white family in fine clothes. How would it be to travel between nations with nothing to lose? There seemed a certain power in that, and I admired the absent Thomas Colhill for choosing his own life.

"Do you think of him?" I asked.

She paused, as if thinking of what thinking of him would be like.

"Or wonder if he has the same chin?" I looked out into the dark fields so as not to stare at her chin, which fell into a little bowl at the base of her face. Just the size for rubbing a thumb across.

"No," she said. She put her hand to her face, feeling her features. Not as slowly as I would have. "He's just another bastard. White man, Muskogee man, all you want is more than the man next to you has."

"What will you do if he comes back?"

"Kill him."

I laughed, swallowed my laugh into a cough. I was grateful the night hid the sweat on my face. "For leaving you?"

"For not taking me with him."

I didn't know what to say. I understood how someone young

could grow such an old bitterness, but I lost the sense of myself as a rare hero when I heard that anger lie so easily in someone else's mouth.

In the unraveling night, she had already moved on. She wondered about an animal that was gnawing at the squash, a friend who had taken her favorite comb. She taught me some English words, said she'd teach me more. She came to her uncle in her own wanderings. Seloatka took no interest in her, she said, but spent his empty hours with her brothers, teaching them the arts of war. Cruelty, she called it. He was an old-fashioned Muskogee, had no vision, knew nothing of the English like her father. My heart was thumping hard at the image of Seloatka resting his hand on my shoulder. As she worried aloud that her hair would not grow fast enough, I saw the spirit of the man dig his fingers into my arm. I took my knife from its sheath and cut at his chest, gently, as if I were planting seeds in soft dirt.

The owls began calling in whispers while we shivered in the night cold. I was sleepy and could smell the cooking fish from town and began to think Polly was childish for hiding so long. The bark felt dirty to me; I couldn't straighten the sticks up here. The sound of a sliding in the tree made her shiver and grab my hand. I said I thought it was a snake, so she laced her fingers into mine. If only Seloatka found us here, his niece stuck to his enemy like ash on a hoecake. But I could smell her hair in the moonlight and it smelled like the warmth of a deer when it is still alive. She told me she liked an older boy, one who had his first scars already, but I didn't listen, and it must have been just a game because later when she put her mouth on my mouth it felt real and I had no more questions about my love.

The battle had been fought, though at that hour I couldn't

have named the victor. We climbed down, or rather slipped and scrambled, scraping our palms, and at the base of the hickory she took me in her arms and squeezed—the embrace of a comrade, a fellow warrior—and evaporated into the night. I walked home, my arms wrapped around my chest to mimic her warmth, and my mother shook me and fed me cold meat. I slept for the first time without dreaming of Seloatka.

We were lovers in the youngest sense, and I brought her back the hearts of deer from hunting. One summer she spent wooing another boy, and for a few days they escaped into the forest to play a game of togetherness, but she came home bored and swore she still loved me. When I began to look less like a tangle of sticks and more like something that could grip and twist and shoot, I told her I would marry her. She said she was worth a lot, and I would owe her uncle a great sum in gifts, and she wasn't even sure she'd say yes. I said it wasn't a question. I just wanted to warn her. She said she'd be ready, then, and good luck to me. I told my brother and he laughed and said the same. He knew her well from farming with her, pounding grain, the things that Oche does with women. He said she built baskets from piles of wet stripped cane faster than the others. I never knew whether to worry over him or to envy what he had, something like the clarity of a river in spring. He said he saw something in my heart larger than love, and to watch for it. I said he was still a boy.

WHEN MY COURAGE had grown into a full-sized fruit, I asked Seloatka for a favor. The Englishmen's war was over now, and the Muskogee towns, along with the Cherokee towns, were lashing out against the new Americans pouring into the spaces opened by peace. How we traded, how we fought: it all deserved rethinking. We had fresh enemies, found allies in old rivals. Our once-solid world seemed to be rafting out on a black river, but I had forgotten nothing. For years I had watched him, from my boyhood to my manhood, and though he had committed no great treacheries since taking the *mico*'s feathers, none but the minor abuses of all rulers, I hadn't once abandoned my plans. That my village might not believe what I had seen— that Seloatka himself may have long since discounted me—did not concern me. I would unseat him and reclaim what was my family's.

The first step was to move close. Make him believe I had forgotten. It was a night during little spring moon, the warmth just seeping into the air again. He stood outside his house, looking up at the clouds across the stars, his hand against the skin flap. My hands had made that house, I thought. That was my uncle's house, the one in the center of town with its roof higher than the others, beside the chunkey ground and near the council house, where wars were plotted and travelers slept. I had squatted with my mother and buried my hands in pots of daub, spread the coolness over the cane frame, smoothed it between the woven vines, roughed it with grass and my own collected hair. I handed straw bundles to men who were taller to coat the roof in a spiny fur. The man who killed my uncle was living in the house I built.

The words that came from me were small and squeaked. I said I wanted to be a trader.

"You've grown tall," he said. "Your aim is improved." He let down the door flap and moved a few steps past me, farther into darkness. "A trader? You want to get out of this village, you're tired of hunting. I can understand that. You'll need to know their language, of course, and must learn not to steal." He seemed to think this was humorous. I needed him to trust me, so I said nothing. "And Polly?" he asked.

Had I known he was watching? I said I knew some English. Wanted to make a profit. Wanted to move beyond the split hickories hanging by the river.

"Earn a little bride price, perhaps. I see. But you leave her alone for a few weeks here and there, and she may get loose from you. That's my advice. Women, you know. I think your mother was the same." He laughed again.

I remembered her face when I told my mother what he'd done. Seloatka hadn't killed my uncle, she said. She erased that night between us. Had she loved him? Had he broken something of hers? I didn't know what drove a woman to act, what made her shrink. I let my mother go that night. I lived with her still and we spoke of nothing more than detail. I told Seloatka now not to speak of her, though I didn't know what I was defending.

"You have fought, I think," he said.

The burning in my insides seeped to my skin. I told him I had seen men fight.

"And now you want to deal in Englishmen. Seeing how men die is the fastest way to understanding how they live." The stars were now fully beneath their cloud blanket, and I could not see whether his eyes were cold or if he was still laughing at me. "What else do you know? You've lived so many years here, and I hardly remember anything you've done."

I said I would be useful to him, that I was strong and fearless and could learn the paths. Would never steal. Was fearless, I said again. Some pots were strewn by the door, still wet from cooking, and in my anxiety I wanted to pick them up and stack them.

He turned and moved away from the wide night, put his hand against the house I built. "Visit me again in a few days," he said, and went inside.

I came back in the morning, my hands still held before me, and he told me of the man I would follow to learn the paths and of the goods I would earn in exchange for skins.

But I was a young man, and ambitious, and saw a future to which he was blind. "I don't want the goods," I said. Not the powder or hatchets or vermilion or pots. I didn't yet have a wife or a home, and I saw how little the white men valued those saddles, those looking glasses. "I want the coins."

"They're no use here," he said.

"This town is not all there is in the world." Let him think that I would move away, release his conscience, and meanwhile I would stockade a currency that white men, who were taking acres from us faster than we could plant them, would kill for. When Oche told me what the future looked like, I was no longer too afraid to listen.

He raised his hand and let it drift onto my shoulder, resting it like a fly there. My mind swirled with the vision of my hands and the knife and his belly, but through his warmth I felt his common need. We were men of mirrored desperation, though being still young, I couldn't guess at his fear. His power was built on the shaky backs of us all. I wanted him to suffer and perhaps he wanted me to leave, and thus we sealed our bargain.

I told Polly I was collecting her bride price and my mother that I was forging our way back to the center of the town and Oche that I was headed out adventuring. They all, in their way, let me go.

. . .

THE PATHS TO Pensacola—to Panton, Leslie, and Company and the independent traders—wound south through hardwoods, burned clearings, the beginnings of swamp. The Muskogee man that first guided me crouched on his horse like a man at a fire, and I rode my pony behind, leading the pack mule with a rope. We stopped by rivers to drink and rest and soften our ring-shaped bread in water, and he told me short tales of boyhood. There was a woman he had loved, for there are always women. "And what did you do for her?" I asked.

"Do! What did she do for *me*? What a prize I am!" He chuckled as he dug behind his knees for itches. He was old and raisined. "I made her carry water, fry me cakes, sing me ditties—*'Oh handsome man, sun-faced man, dance around the fire on your pigeon legs, pigeon man.'* " I said I didn't believe him, and he rolled up his breeches to twist his calves in the purple dusk. "Don't you let a woman grab you, no, you let them stay in the field and you go prancing woodward and when you come two-by-two in the evening, you tell her what's going, and if she tells *you* what's going, well, then you just let it be, for she's no worse than the mother that bore you. *'Pig legs, pig girl, dance close for a squeeze, snorting girl.'* "

"Where is she now?"

"Dead," he said. "Dead, for I didn't love her." He settled back with a pipe and wouldn't say more.

In Pensacola, we brought our skins to a trader who lived in a wooden house near the Spanish cemetery, where I wandered while the exchange was politely argued over tasting cups of whiskey. Live oaks leaned down on wooden crosses and stone humps. The wind from the gulf sent the fallen leaves scuffling around the markers, some so small they must have been babies, lost to the world before the world turned foul. These were the homes of the ghost children who brushed against my bare legs at night. I sat on one half-sized stone, fresh-faced and free of moss, and tried to remember being so young. When I sought to remember myself, I remembered my uncle. Narrow-shouldered. He had grown inside my heart like a fungus, and even my lover had taken on his hue. When she looked at me through two eyes, I saw his one eye peering.

A woman in red drifted through the graveyard and paused when she saw me. She spoke to me in Spanish. She pointed to the grave I was crouched upon, her eyebrows now furrowed, and as I sensed that I should not be there, her eyes became wet. She covered her face with white-gloved hands, and her hiccups blended with the wind catching in the low branches. I stood and snuck away, ashamed, and when I turned back to look, she had fallen in a heap over the grave, one hand grasping the small stone, quiet now. We are all killed by somebody, and the deaths live forever. But there is something precious in a woman's grief; it's the twin, the remnant, of loyalty. I slipped through the graves to the peddler's cabin, where my pigeon-legged guide had loaded the mule with jugs of whiskey and rum and was holding my pony's reins in one hand, waiting for me. As I mounted, he handed me a few shillings, the first of the coins—English, Spanish, American—I would collect to capture my future. Pennies for my bride, pounds for her uncle. My plan was not that of a wise man: I believed my wealth would bloodlessly unseat him.

A certain kind of face filled the paths snaking between the Muskogee towns and the once-English, now-Spanish settlements. They were hungry men, all hunting something. I saw white men burned so sun-brown they looked little different from the slaves that trailed behind. Scars crossed faces like maps. Bodies smelled of dirt and decaying food caught between teeth. As men passed me, the pines breathed after them, exhaling a sweetness into their wake, washing the path clean of their scent. Gnat clouds hovered at the mountaintops of men's shoulders. On the southern trips with my guide, I couldn't keep my gaze from these walking desperates, curious to spot their own bitterness, but when I began to journey alone, I kept my eyes down and away like the others.

Some of the travelers I came to know by sight. The one with his sleeve pinned to his chest who growled about the heat. The girl who dressed as a boy and bartered her preserves, the trail walkers keeping her pretense. The slave who was the color of creek silt and could not stop his tongue. We all were waiting for the end of our trails, for whatever lay there, and yet we only saw each other in the coming and going, as though we only traveled, never arrived.

The money I kept in a deerskin purse Polly made, with a moon cut into one side—to remind me of her face, she said. She at first was baffled by my plan but came to relish the sight of the shiny coins. They were a path out. In my mother's house beyond the circle of our town, I dug a little hole in the dirt beneath my bed, buried my purse, and marked it with a red stone. This was where I planted my growing fortune. The coins began to sprout when I took on the route alone, Seloatka trusting me, the rum sellers in Pensacola knowing the sound of my step and the quality of our skins. Certain men came to our town to be taken south, with our traders as guides and our slaves—purchased blacks or captured Indians—as guards. They paid well for the privilege, and from the little I was allowed, my purse began to bulge. I needed it to burst before I could claim Polly, could silence the protests of her uncle. After I took her, the steps were few to chiefdom and revenge. I would buy an alliance with poorer neighbors, some Chickasaw or distant Muskogee towns, even American traders, and with the money show them my strength and my intentions. They would back me, would refuse to treat with my wife's uncle, and then my wife and I would rise in his stead and he would like a puffball turn to nothing. Was I naive?

Polly was my accountant, and made me tally my gains after each trip, which she would mark in little lines on a stick she kept by her bed. She said she needed to know when she'd be mine. She'd then toss the stick below her bed and pull me down and I would find all her goodness there, waiting, just as she promised. With my arms beside her, around her, in her hair, she listed what we'd do with our wealth. *Richmond*, she said. She wanted to live in a white man's city. Her father had left her without an image of himself but a silver chain and a sense of something other, and she had not found her right place in this small village, doing what our mothers and uncles did, and their mothers and uncles before them. She said she felt half her limbs were pulled by white strings, and if her bastard father thought they were better than Indian strings, maybe they were. *Richmond*, I said, and didn't tell her my fate was here, where the dead were still unsettled. She too may have picked things not to tell me. *Richmond*, she said, and my arms were vines around her neck, her waist, her legs.

As the trails became worn beneath my feet, the *mico* slept worse at night. I saw little of his suspicion, but Oche told me on my rests from riding that Seloatka kept a band of men tightly circled about his house to keep the ghosts from stealing his skins, though there was little to trade them for besides rum, which ghosts could not swallow. He was saving for something, perhaps for the pleasure alone of saving, which is an early symptom of a greater sickness, but perhaps for some scheme against me. We may have been hoarding in opposite corners of the same town, both to destroy the other. Both waiting for our fortunes to burst and the plans we made to spill into action. I hoped his plot was as little formed as mine.

Oche said he was worried, said that long ago when I was in trouble I had gone to a woman in the country for help, one of the hut women, but farther out, west of the trading path. She used to live in a nearby town, and I remembered her, tiny and dark, without family. But I told him this had never happened, so he gave me directions—*and then turn north at the dead oak*—so I would remember that moment in time, whether it had happened or not. He saw the game we men were playing for what it was.

Just before winter Seloatka hired a Frenchman who had been living among the Muskogee and leading war parties against the colonists, and he paid him to be a double pair of eyes. Le Clerc sat at the *mico*'s table and filled his belly hard with pawpaw and persimmon and found himself a girl to keep, one who was motherless and could not tell the white men she could use from the white men who would use her. His eyes were black, like my lover's, but when I shook his hand, I could not see into them. He never learned my name, for Seloatka kept him among the elites, passing him from cousin to warrior to guard, all trusted men who greased the visitor with rum and showed him how to throw the spear on the chunkey field. Oche and I stood under a walnut shadow and watched his small French body coil itself behind his throwing arm. The spear always went wide.

Le Clerc was not a dangerous man. He seemed to already have whatever it was he wanted. Stories to carry with him when he returned home. Women and whiskey, an adventure. He was too vague to be menacing. Like most white men, he'd pass through. That Seloatka never introduced his trail man to his Frenchman reminded me that though we were connected in business, the *mico* never fit me within his circle. He had not forgotten. He only kept me near so he could watch my movements, could predict when I would finally strike. We both knew that cowards and the quiet were the ones whose hands would eventually turn.

Early mornings, when Oche was in the fields with our mother and I was home and had nothing to do but carve a new bow and wait for Polly to find me, I would see Le Clerc wending through the river trees, one hand out to brush the bark as he passed. He walked slowly, but never aimlessly. Was that what Polly's father looked like? A white man walking through an Indian town, on his way to somewhere else? Except the Frenchman was not impatient. I never saw him hurry, and even when he missed the chunkey stone, over and over, he never angered. And when he was alone and thought no one was watching, he chose to walk among basswood and sycamore at dawn, feeling their skin, occasionally looking up into their branches as if hoping to see someone beloved there. If I were a superstitious man, I'd worry he saw my own past body, crouched there years ago with Polly, or else some future version of myself.

I HAD BEEN on the paths for a year when spring rolled open again with the first wood flowers and airy nights. Polly caught a basket of new dandelion leaves and fed me their crispness on a grass bank by the river, just out of sight of the fields. She watched me sideways as I chewed through the bitter, and when I reached for her hand she tucked hers between her knees. In watching my purse fill, we sometimes forgot how to love each other, or our love was just siphoned into different ruts. There were times when I came back grimed and weary after a week's absence and she flinched at my touch. She said my skin was getting rougher, my skin hurt her skin. I'd step away and sleep that night on the floor beside her bed, reaching out to brush her cheek only after I knew she was asleep. I asked my mother, whose eyes were milking over with age, if this was a normal thing between a man and a woman, and she raised her eyebrows and turned down the corners of her mouth as if to say, *You think I'd remember?* Her heart had fallen out after one, two, three of her children died.

On that new spring night, Polly fed me greens but wouldn't give me her kiss. I don't think it hurt me when she pulled her hand away.

Plucking grasses and skinning the reeds between her long fingers, she told me of her uncle's guests, a fresh party of Englishmen, loyalists they named themselves, heading south for Spanish lands and safety.

"I thought you might guide them," she said. "The man who leads them, Kirkland, has enough money to purchase half of Pensacola."

I lay back and crossed my hands on my stomach. The sky was dying away, purple now and sad. Night too was lovely, but it stole something from the day, and even when this theft was quiet, there was a violence in the act that made dusk a sorrowful thing to watch. A loss.

Polly was describing the quantity of Kirkland's silver.

An owl flew large and thick above us, two beats of the wing before we lost it to the dark again. It had heard the rustle of a shrew, too fine a sound for my ears to catch. My body seemed as fallible lately as my mind.

"He's staking out lands for his family, a wife and daughter he left behind somewhere. In the Carolinas, near Charleston, I think. Maybe as far as Richmond."

"That's not in the Carolinas," I said.

"He's very handsome and fat and dresses neat—you should see him, get a nice waistcoat like that—and has skin like a cloud. Did you hear what I said about his silver?" She waited to see if my eyes would catch the fire in her own, but I was looking up, watching for the owl to fly back with the shrew in its mouth.

"Last night I saw him in the council house. He stayed after the others left and smoked no pipe at all but drew out thin paper and ink in a bottle, and he scrawled along line after line in these tight bunches on the page. If he were staying longer, I'd ask him to teach me to read English, which I'm perfectly good at otherwise. Looks like the marks spiders leave through the dust. What do you think he was writing?"

I felt the reed she flung at me bounce against my neck. She knew I hated things out of place. I half listened, trying to decide if I loved her voice.

"I think it was a message to his family. All white men have families somewhere else." I could have reached out to her then, but didn't. " 'My wife! My children!' he'd write. 'Bounteous English love is yours!' Don't you think that's how they sound? 'I will build a Pensacola paradise, and you will join me in the summer when the red flowers bloom, and you will never again have to plant corn or pound hominy, for we will be choked in riches.' "

I shook my head. "English women don't eat hominy."

"How do you know? Have you met some?" She crawled over to me and hovered her face above mine so her long hair brushed in my eyes. "Who do you see down there when you go? Do you keep an English lady whore? Do you buy her cotton dresses, which is why your purse sometimes seems smaller than it should?"

I sat up, pushing her aside, and decided that I did love her, though no one had told me what love meant, and maybe it wasn't wholly sweet or giving but just the way two people needed each other. I wanted Polly in my life, with all her flits and needling, because without her I'd be even more alone, one step farther away from what it is I wanted. My days were better with her than without her, though my days were never fully good. I assumed she thought the same of me. So I said, "My love," holding her shoulders, "it's just us, no English lady whores. I show you each coin I get. You've seen them. I'll have enough to marry you by the next Green Corn." I held her shoulders until she nodded.

She stood up and danced to the river with small foot-stomps, brushing with the toes, digging in the heels, until she reached the water and let her feet sink in an inch of muck. She looked back across a bare shoulder. "Kirkland is leaving in a few days. You should ask my uncle to join them."

We were both thinking then of money. If an owl had flown by again, I wouldn't have seen it. Polly didn't return to me and I thought she might want to bathe alone or else be silent, so I stood and left her, walked down the river to the set of stones that made a path across the water and stepped from one to the next, pausing in the middle of the stream. It was almost full dark now, and the rocks beneath the water, round and brown when the sun scissored through, were invisible in the wash of black. If I put my foot in, the water would be cool, but there seemed a long distance between my wanting to feel the coolness and the heaviness of my feet, so I stood still, my head dropped to my chest like I had been newly created, no bones yet, and left to dry. I needed to think of my love for a woman, to sort out whether she was as good as my mother, but I only wanted to deal with the world of men, where good and evil were evenly split, red town from white town, boy from ghost, and where destroying the killer of my uncle was so little complicated that it allowed me to stand perfectly still in a river at night, my muscles slumping into peace.

I don't know how long I was gone. I didn't watch the stars to see how they'd moved; I didn't feel a creeping dew on my skin. I came back to my house and my mother and brother were sleeping, so I left again, my feet not done with wandering, this time taking me into the cornfields, picking through the rows of new sprouts. They were tangled in the threads of cowpeas. It took me hours of not-knowing, of looking hard in my heart for feelings I couldn't find, of trying to see a version of myself that had nothing to do with Polly or Seloatka, with my uncle or my purse, before I gave up. My path so far had taken me unharmed and with increasing purpose to this night wandering, and there was no reason to think it wouldn't continue to carry me through. Doubt had little nobility in it. And what felt selfish at times— love, anger—wasn't at all, because I did it in another's name. My life was not my own, but my clan's. After the storms that unsettled my village and my people and after the wars that had taken away the very steadiness of our ground, there was a great void that begged to be filled.

I didn't see anything living that night because I wasn't watching. This blindness returned me to my purpose, which had nothing to do with the ghost children that Oche saw, or the turtle shells we gathered to rattle on our ankles, or the clouds we studied to see whether they'd bring water to our fields.

Not till dawn did I return to my mother's house with fired eyes, to dig under my bed, to gauge my money, and to chart the next step—marriage and then alliances and then Seloatka's seat, my mother in his house, his body bent and wretched in our cabin, pushed to the outside edge of belonging until he slipped off entirely. This all depended on power, which, without violence, only came from wealth. This was the new world we lived in.

I passed Oche at the door, who was taking his hide and needle to a cousin's, still wiping the sleep from his eyes. He stopped with his face open in a question and said, "The *mico* came looking for you last night. Mother was still in the fields. You weren't here."

I was surprised, and asked if he was sure this hadn't happened years ago.

"I told Polly when she came by later, but he was gone and you were gone, and this all seemed to make her pleased, so we shared dinner with her. She borrowed your pony."

Seloatka must have come to beg my help, to place Kirkland and the English in my hands, to crawl on his belly like a night worm. If he was afraid I'd plant that vision-knife in him, he didn't understand. I wanted his dignity, not his life. I wanted the traitor to watch my power spread from field to river to hunting ground, to see an untasted peace settle on the town for a century.

I left my brother and slipped into our house, stooped low by my bed. I needed to count the coins again, count out the distance between now and what was to come. My fingers were in the packed dirt under the red stone, digging. I fished out the purse.

It was empty.

It hung like a spent stomach in my hand.

March 9–13, 1788

Istillicha

WE CROSS BACK over the creek, our shoulders weighted down with new silver, and crash through trees to find the trail again. Our boots are filled with silt. This is not what we intended. Not these lives lost. A deer skitters as we push through the woods, heedless of sound now. The blood on my hands smells like the fawn, like something young and newly broken. Bob and I keep pace, hurrying, our breath heavy. I turn my head once to make sure Cat is keeping up. Why, I'm not sure—because he belongs to Bob, because he is a witness. Is this how my brothers felt when they brought down men in war? No, because that was just, and this is not, this is merely bandits stealing. I am not a thief. I was convinced that this had some nobler purpose, and I can admit that I was easy to convince, thinking of myself, as I did, as noble. This theft is not for me, but for my people, for whoever I decide are my people. They deserve a good man for a *mico*. If I am still a good man.

We climb the bank again, skid down onto the trading path.

It's empty of life. Cat comes behind us with his mouth open, his eyes numb. I am sweating in the cool night, my thoughts splintering on what little I saw as I hurt men in the dark, taking their money while saving my life. Self-defense. I try to settle on some image of peace. Forgetting my suspicions, I think first of Polly, of her father's-daughter face, but on her slim body perches the fat head of Kirkland, the ruddy-cheeked man, her laughter melting to a scream. He sounded like a calf dying. I shake my head to blur the image. In all that fury, I saw my uncle. The bodies of everyone I've known are becoming the bodies of everyone else I've known.

When I first saw Thomas Colhill on the road, saw how his dark eyes danced like Polly's and then heard his name, I thought, *Here is the man who fathered my girl and then abandoned her, she who is not sweet but who in all likelihood stole my purse from me, here is the man who left a rotten woman for me.* I cannot believe that she admired him, or his white blood, beneath her hatred. And yet she talked of Richmond. No one wronged her family, so what is she hunting for? It is no use trying to fathom her, because she is a liar and a thief.

I am a young man, but not a stupid one. In the panic after finding the empty hole beneath my bed, I remembered my brother's words: that Seloatka, and then she, had come to see me. What had been my plan in packing a bag and marching through the dawn, horseless, blood behind my eyes? I feared if I stayed in the village I would kill him. I would kill him that day. So I would leave and on my own find a path to wealth and with that wealth come back, in two years or five years or ten, and topple his kingdom. Bloodlessly. I'm a good shot and I know English and many of the white traders, and I could be-

come a middleman, earning a wage for my services in negoti-
ating trades, guiding travelers, evaluating goods, before using
that money to build alliances; I know there are Muskogee chiefs
who want to extend their reach, and Chickasaws who could use
assurances. The revenge I wanted was a clean one, a triumph
not of strength but of power. He had taken my uncle, he had
taken my money, my means to marry, and now I would take his
chiefdom, my birthright.

Except that as I walked, as I waited for deer, as I met these
men who would pull me down their own uncertain paths, it
seemed less and less true that Seloatka had taken my money. He,
after all, was the one who had given it to me. I was his servant
on the trails, he paid my wage without complaint, all because he
wanted me close, wanted to have his hands on my strings. Could
I imagine him bent and scrabbling in a hole beneath my bed?
The *mico* dirtying his fingers for a purse? He didn't even know
where I kept it. No, he didn't need my money. I lost track of the
features of the trail—the tall sweetgum that marked the path
to the watering hole, the signs men carved for each other—
because I was circling through every word she ever said to me.

She told me about Kirkland, knew about his fortune, knew
about my purse, counted the coins I brought her, wanted more.
As we grew older, everything Polly knew was what we didn't
yet have. I couldn't see this, didn't mind this, because I was the
same.

I can picture her with them, with Kirkland and his kin, flirt-
ing with her shoulders in the dark near the council house, the
fire lighting the gleams of her teeth as she asks them what ten
pounds can buy in the city. Whether she can pass for a white
woman. She must have already fled, not knowing that her theft

would scatter me too. So the pony she took from me was as borrowed as the purse. What is the first thing she will spend my coins on? A mirror?

Not until I saw the trading party and stood before Kirkland, who was as white and fat as she promised, and met her father, who must have walked through our town without even remembering he had a child, not until I heard the mule's *clink* did the full weight of my loss fall on me, and my shock at what she'd done turned to anger, the kind that flurries your head and makes you follow a black man into the night. If I'd had a horse, I would not have met these men I'm walking with. And if I hadn't met these men?

We stop in the middle of the road, not knowing whether to turn north or south. We didn't take the horses because we didn't think, because they were noisy, would be easier to track. We haven't thought. I drop the bag from my back just to breathe, to try to settle my sense of wrongdoing. I was not the one to shoot Thomas Colhill to his knees, but I saw it and felt the split of love and rage burn me. Will she blame me for this? She called him bastard.

Bob claws at his shoulder, asks, "Where are we going? How do we hide? Should we split the money now, huh?" as if all his shame was turned to words, but I can see the darkness on his shirt. We don't answer him, and Cat moves to pull the man's hand away from his shoulder. Beneath is the blood that comes from a hole in his arm.

"It's nothing," Bob says. "We've got to move, come on now."

Cat looks at me. The nighthawks bleat. The trees drooping over the road are black and shapeless, the night sky beyond still purpling, the trail empty in its starred and violet stare. It has an ugliness that I never saw before. Bob shifts his load to his other shoulder and heads south again. There isn't time. We follow.

I am marking all the future steps in my head, deciding what will happen based on what I choose to do. What I want now, if not her. If she were here, I don't know that I could keep my hands from her body. If she betrayed me, took my money, loved my money more than me, drove me in mindlessness and desperation to send a trading party off to the dark world, all to replace the coins she stole, is it possible to still want her?

We pause at dawn. I steer them behind a grove of oaks hanging on with root fingers to the clay bluffs. A mosquito has been following Bob and the smell of his blood. He itches at his neck with his good arm, swats at himself because it is something to do with shaky hands. These men crouch among thorns and stare at me for answers. I ache to wash the red off me; it's all disorder.

I tell them what I guess: the *mico* Seloatka, who sent those white men down from our nation with his blessing and protection, will learn of this by tomorrow and will hunt us, within reason, until we are dead and scalped. I don't tell them that I would be an easy man for him to kill, that my torture would not disturb his sleep. But we have torn a hole in a flimsy fabric, and the death of named men in West Georgia must be addressed, will be addressed, or else strangers will take arms again. I have created mischief, chaos, where I meant to solve it. Bob's hand is passing over the back of his head in waves, smoothing, worrying.

Cat asks, "What do we do?"

His first words since before the creek. There is a brightness to him now that is either hope or mania.

"What do we do?"

Bob and I look at him, a man asking for comfort, and say

nothing. I should be least worried about him, a white fugitive surely hardened to violence, but I am somehow not surprised to see his panic. He has in his eyes a stretching, beaten-down need. He must have loved, and been punished, a hundred times. I try to tell the truth. How a man will come for us, the chief's Frenchman, a hungry-eyed tracker, wiry. The Clerk, they call him. How some say he has no mercy, has never held a baby, but I soothe them. He is smart and sure, but he doesn't strike me as a killing man, and anyway he moves so turtle-slow that if we walk quickly and rest little, even horseless, he cannot find us. He is a white man, after all, and these are not his woods. Bob looks at me with such worry, as though I were holding his fate like a whip, and Cat murmurs to himself, pats his shirt pocket. He is afraid of something, but I don't believe it's death.

The first light is rain-shower gray. Cat crawls to Bob and presses his hand against the other man's chest until Bob stretches back, lies flat on the red earth. Cat touches his forehead to feel for fever. He takes off his own shirt, twists it, squeezes the creek water out, drapes it across Bob's eyes. When the slave is masked and Cat's fingers have been washed with his own spit, he tears the sleeve from Bob's arm, rubs away the blood and dirt with a slow palm, and then snakes his finger into the shoulder's wet wound. I turn away at Bob's scream. Surely a doctor would have put the rag in his mouth instead. When I turn back, Cat is holding the bullet in his hand, shifting it like a pearl to catch the light.

"That's all?" I ask.

Bob's breaths now come out loud, each a huff. Even I can see that the bullet is the least of it.

"I can't clean it," Cat says. He wraps Bob's sleeve around the injury and ties it tight, but the cloth is thick with dirt.

"So we get him a doctor."

Cat looks up at me with surprise. Nods.

"You want to leave me, that's fine," Bob calls out from under the mask. "No reason to take me on in this state, I'd just be a weight. If you leave me—" His voice is getting higher, so he stops, breathes deep. "If you leave me—"

Cat wipes the damp shirt in circles on Bob's face, cleaning the emotion, and then draws it off, puts it back on his pale chest. Bob opens one eye. Cat offers a hand to pull him up and then we are all three standing again. The white man holds the bullet out on his palm, but Bob shakes his head, so he throws it into the woods, where some creature will come hours later to smell the human on it.

"We need to find someone," I say.

"I can't hide." Bob wraps one hand around his chest, trying to clutch out the pain. "I'm a free man. I'm a free man." He looks behind him as if this were being contested. The dawn birds are twittering, a high wet sound, and we are all listening for the heavier sounds of feet.

"We need to get off the trail—either you die of that hole, or the tracker finds us."

"That's what I'm saying, go west. I have it all figured. Plenty of land out there. My brother, the one I told you about, told me."

"And your arm?"

I glance at Cat, who looks puzzled. Or content. He's like water the way his face holds moods.

"We should do something," Cat says. In his voice is not our present predicament but a longer vision of events. He is like Oche, for whom time was nothing but a small mat to set your shoes on. The whole world lay beyond it.

Bob scratches at his knee.

I know what we need to do: split the silver, shake hands, share a drink for luck, and leave. There is no reason to go on together. I have nothing to do with these men. I met them two nights ago, and I'm not even sure that the white man's name is his name. But my skin flinches at the thought of parting, as though they're the blanket between my body and the ghosts. They're the sticks that need arranging. Does violence rope the wicked together? If I leave them, who else will understand me? And where will they go without me? The black man will die, and the white man will be scooped up in a day by Le Clerc. None of that is deserved. I have been a coward already too many times.

"There's a woman, an old trader who knows some medicine and keeps a house off the western spur. You want to head west, I'll take you as far as that. And there are some paths branching off that Le Clerc won't know. Give us time to plan, to fix you up."

"You're coming with me?" Bob says.

"Look at you." I can't describe how scared I am of what has happened. "We can't scatter like mice. We've done this, and if we mean what we've done, we need to finish it." I watch him move his tongue inside his mouth, puffing out his cheeks, thinking about what the *it* is.

"You can come," he says, looking at the ring of us. "Get your own land out there."

"We head west, we stop at the woman's house, we decide from there. But we move now. Le Clerc isn't the only one trailing us."

Bob looks at Cat, at the man who maybe already murdered, and I look at Bob, who stole his own body away from slavery.

Who knows what bounty hunters and slave patrols are already sniffing out our scent. We are a circle of glances. What we have for each another is not trust, but need, and there is no future to it.

I grab my bag, heavy with everything I can't put down, and start walking fast. South. I don't look back, but soon hear their footsteps behind me, one half jogging and one in a shuffle as rhythmed as my mother's voice, my mother who has already lost so many sons. We kick up the dust of mingled day and night.

THE TRAIL IS empty this morning, but just as I am beginning to consider it good luck, a man comes over a hill before us. He has a tangle of woolly hair and is dragging a cart with two wheels behind him. Inside are stacks of newspapers weighted down with rocks. I have seen a few in Pensacola, and traders on occasion bring a paper to Hillaubee, but they are usually several months old and say little that we have not already heard. He draws the cart to a stop when he sees us. The handle of the conveyance is attached to his wrist by a long red ribbon. I keep walking, head down, hoping the men behind me will follow my lead without speaking, but the stranger holds out a hand as we approach. I stop. I can see a pistol stuck in the waist of his trousers.

"Care for the news?" he says.

I shake my head politely. I could pretend not to speak his language, but strangers can be quick to act out against Indians who appear stupid. There is no reason to take chances.

"You heard it already?" He sets down his cart and takes a step closer.

"What city is it from?" Bob asks.

I turn around with a stern face, but my companions, even with heavy bags on their shoulders and a feral mix of dirt and blood on their skin, look surprisingly innocent. It is not unlikely, in fact, that this newspaper man has done even worse things.

"No city," he says. "This is the news from the stars."

Bob, pulled briefly from his fear, now begins to trudge on.

"Wait, boy, you'll want to hear it."

"What stars?" Cat asks.

"We must keep walking," I say. "We're expected in town."

"Those that point your fates. Wouldn't you like to know if you travel the wrong way?" With the ribbon still attached, he walks to the back of his cart and lifts up a rock, pulling out a paper with one hand and unfolding it. He turns through it as if inside its corn husk there is meat. "Where were you born?"

"The Carolinas," Cat says.

"What day?"

Cat shakes his head. The man keeps turning the pages.

"Your mother's name? No? What about yours?"

"Prudence," Bob says.

"Lovely. Here it is, then." The man's eyebrows crunch together. "No, no, this isn't the right path for you at all."

"What's it say?"

"Shh. The twins are meant to guide you, but this time of year finds them in another part of heaven altogether."

"Twins?"

"Come," I say, trying to walk on.

"Hold on, now, which way am I supposed to go?"

The man closes the paper and fans his own face. "Only a sixpence, boy."

Bob opens his mouth as if to say, *We have sixpence and more!*, but Cat grabs his arm and pulls him forward, and we walk quickly on while the woolly paper man clucks his tongue loudly.

"I just wanted to know," Bob says.

WE MAKE THE western spur by afternoon. There have been recent burns; the sun cuts through the canopy and the collapsed underbrush and into our eyes. Young palmettos stretch out from the soot. We are obvious here, three fast walkers with loud bags amid a low charred scrub. Bob shouts out whenever a muscle twinges in his arm. According to Oche, the woman's house is two days on, and another few miles on a northern branch. She lived in a village next to ours for many years, but was not born Muskogee, may not have had any Indian blood. She was dark and small-nosed and always had white hair, though she never seemed to age. In that village, she sat in council meetings near the front like a man, and captives would be brought to her to learn their fate. This one she'd lightly touch and send off to the Bird clan, a daughter to make up for the son lost at war; this one she'd grip by the shoulders and send off to be killed; this one she'd hold in her lap and tie strands of rope around his wrists and pat his bottom when he walked away, sent off to be sold into slavery. When she tired of her role, she took herself and her pots and a bag of seeds into the woods to start a lonelier life. There were stories of a brave past, some kind of warrioring, but I never knew where she came from. Perhaps she was a captive girl from another tribe, or a Spanish servant, or a colonist's daughter. As children, we knew somehow that she, a village away and not quite of our world, floated above the prejudices of our own kin. We saw her during Green Corn, at ball play between towns. Oche said if I ever needed saving, I should find her. I am finding her.

The land is still charred where we bed down for the night, so I build a small fire; its smell is no different from the earth-smell here. We cook a rabbit and I find some roots beneath the ash that are still whole and good. Cat finds a spot beside Bob, his body a cocoon, his head near Bob's knee as if that were the real fire. Bob is hungry for the meat, but shakes his head when I offer him cooked roots. He gives his share to Cat. When Bob belches, he excuses himself. Our bags sit just beyond the circle of firelight. My muscles still tremble with the rush of blood, and I can see the jerks of the others' limbs; we haven't calmed yet. There hasn't been time to think.

"What'll you do with yours?" Bob asks. "You have plans for the money? You're already free, right, you're not bound up in any way? Don't need to buy yourself?"

"You don't need to buy yourself either."

"No, that's right, I took what was mine. This is for the next part of life, the setting up of a house and taking care of a big piece of land with some crops on it—corn, probably, no sugar. I hear it's too dry out there for rice or much." He pauses. "You think I still deserve it?"

I can't respond.

"Have you done it before, what we did? Is it easy to forget? Or maybe you just put it away like all the other things you have to put away."

What I have tried to put away are other men's deeds. Years spent seething against men I considered evil. What is the worst thing *I* have ever done?

"Did you leave anyone behind?" I ask. My family. "Someone to purchase?"

He shifts his legs as if to unfold them and stretch them out, but sees that Cat is there and settles back into place. He seems to know his knee is comfort. He raises his bandaged arm instead, twisting his hand at the sky, one way and then the other. "What about you, is that woman you mentioned some kind of family?"

"I have a mother and a brother," I say, "and cousins. A father too, but he's not the same to us as he is to your people."

"No, not my people either."

We look at Cat.

"I'm sorry I made you do it," Bob says. "If I made you do it, go after that money."

I shake my head.

"I wanted it so bad," he says, "something got in my eyes that I couldn't blink back. And there we were, all three of us wanting things, and the men—well, you seemed to know them and knew they weren't worth being friendly with, the way you froze up, it was like a sign, and then the way we'd all been *wanting* things."

I nod. Wanting too much.

"Are you sorry?" he asks.

I roll out the skin on which I sleep. Lie down so the last sparks from the fire fly up before Bob's face, and Cat disappears altogether, just a pile of clothes hazy through the smoke. Pull up my blanket.

"I'm not sorry I did it," he says, "because we were just saving ourselves, first with the money and then when they woke, they would've killed us if we hadn't killed them. We didn't kill anyone who wasn't trying to kill us. You know that? Look here, they shot me in the arm and probably wished it was the heart. I tell you, you just think of all my people, all your people, who've been cut down for nothing, not even so men can be better but so they can be richer, and richness just twists their hearts so after all that, they're worse men than they were. And what about us? Now we can make better people of ourselves, and we will, and isn't that something to justify—to justify— We've done everything right for so long, and we've—well, maybe not you, but me—I've lost most everything good and never done a thing bad. *Never.* And what have I lost? Isn't this a sign that we deserve it? That God is watching and doesn't mind?"

I can't see his mouth moving for the sparks. Cat stands up, moves away from the fire, stutters into the darkness. His arms are wrapped around his stomach. I can't think of what to say to Bob or how to read signs that are not from the natural world. I don't know what deserving means. I wait until Cat is finished heaving up whatever little he ate and crawls back to his patch of dirt. I don't sit up; if I see these men in any sort of clarity, I fear I'll turn on myself for everything I've failed to do correctly. As it is, I don't know how to distinguish us, and in the haze of smoke, with the burned smell muffling everything we say, we are a strange and indestructible creature. Many-headed, various, the good in our hearts—put together—weakly outweighing the bad.

"It's a stone past," I say. "It's over."

Bob doesn't believe this, I don't believe this, but there's nothing else to say. "So tomorrow we'll try not to shoot anyone, that's what you're saying?"

"Go to sleep."

"You might want to get your gun back from Cat here. To my mind, I'm thinking now he's the only one of us hasn't killed yet, and him being the murderer all along. You still got that gun, Cat?"

He doesn't answer. I turn onto my stomach, dig my feet into the soft ash of the ground, hide my hands in the late winter leaves. I am no longer afraid of Seloatka now that we both are villains, I am not afraid of losing Polly or loving Polly, I do not fear the tracker who's now already on our trails, who soon will spot our six-footed steps, but I am afraid of the ghost children. Those haunted little souls who come soft out of the night and brush the skin, breathe through the tiny hairs. I'm not afraid of death but of the dead.

IN THE MORNING, Bob is silent. We eat in silence, he goes into the woods to do his business and returns in silence, and when I point us onward, he says nothing, just follows. Cat now leads him on the trail, and the white man's face has changed from sorrowful to troubled. Ashamed of his own cowardice at the creek, perhaps. I know what it is to be a coward, and I fear it's nobler than shooting a gun. Sleep has changed us, a day too late.

For those two days on the western trail, am I hoping someone finds us? I am missing my mother again, and wanting to erase what I've done, and feeling the press of the coins on my back like something sacred and good. I'll be using this to do something right. But I also want someone to stop us, to take us in, to unclench the choices from our hands so we don't have to make them. I don't say anything, because Bob and Cat say nothing, and we march on together because in this moment that's the simplest decision.

Once I ask if his shoulder is hurting worse.

"It's a bad shoulder," he says. "We've done bad."

I don't know whether we should walk quickly or take the time to clear our tracks, to brush branches in animal patterns where our feet have gone. We cross a few hills but mostly flat-land, and the burned stretch grows green again farther west. The dogwoods curve over the hummocks, white-saucered, and the redbuds are just lighting their winter branches with pink. The land smells like it's been reborn. I look for the signs to the woman's house that Oche made me remember. Signs again.

That first day I left my home, my town, I walked straight south, past Seloatka's house and the council house and the ball field, not looking at the women on their way to the fields or the men smoking pipes in the square, my one thought to control the anger on my face. Of course it wasn't anger at all, which is the only emotion young men claim, but despair, embarrassment. I wished Polly hadn't taken my horse, but if I had been on a horse someone would have asked where I was going. In marching away from my family, I thought of money first: the deer I would kill, the skins I would take to Pensacola on my own back, the purse I would make from a wild boar's belly to hold the coins, the chiefs I would sway to my side, the bloodless war we'd fight. All I needed was money.

Now the money is on my back, my sweat and its sweat min-gling. I was going to wed, become the married nephew of the sonless chief of the town, the next in line. But that plan rested on Polly, who stole it from me. I am not concerned. The ground is shifting as if the snakes holding us up were shedding their skins. Powerful men live in this country who have no Musk-ogee mother, thin ties to clan. It is not so hard to imagine a day soon when my money will be worth more than my name, and I can buy relationships with traders, travelers, the government of whatever white country folds around our thousand-year hunt-ing ground. All this story asks of me is patience. To forget the rage of what I've seen and the shame of what I've done. To stop loving Polly. Polly with her beautiful skin. It was wrong of me to love a dead man more than her.

In the walking, without the low music of Bob observing the ironies of his past, I find I can hold on to a calm, the same stillness I felt on the first hunt when my body grew a creature's quiet. This is my body moving, I say, these are my feet walking away from my village, toward my village, away from Polly who broke my trust, toward Polly who is limb-lovely and no different from me, both thieves.

I sometimes turn to make sure they too are calm, are not liable to dash off screaming to left or right. These men, they are as strangely faced as two lost fawns. One, honeyed brown, with hair bunched and clinging to the dry scraps of broken leaves, his shoulder turning yellow. The other with eyes washed the color of the sky when its blue is paddled out by the heat of late summer. If they were not here and I was not guiding them away from their fates, I might have crawled into a hollow and wept for myself. When will our hunters find us?

Day turns into night turns into day. I keep counting them in my head: Kirkland, his son, his nephew, Colhill, two servants. Six men, surely some with wives. Some with powerful bodies, powerful kin. It will warn a man against walking richly into the wild.

When I first understood Thomas Colhill's face, the Polly in it, there was a space in which I spoke nothing and no other sounds were made, and I was already wondering where the grackles went that moments ago were flocked and chattering in the oak. He met my stare unflinching but mild. This was a ball I didn't know how to throw. He was Polly and a traitor. He was the echo of my love that was not love and my wrath that could not find its home. I didn't know if she cared for him or wished him dead. Who will tell her? And what will she think?

Bob calls out at dusk. I first think it's his shoulder, but he is pointing into the prairie, where a form has pressed a gap into the grasses. Our minds are worn, eager to see something simple. I say it's an old deer bed, or a hawk's dust wallow. Cat is already upon it, looking down with his new puzzlement, as if the whole world was wearing a new dress. A deer, its body splayed over the sharpness of the broken bluestem and broomsedge. Cat moves to stand near Bob, who bends down to brush its fur. The eye is open and empty, and the throat has a tear in it. A blur of flies circles its back half, which has been shorn of skin and meat, opening a window onto a white ribcage, the curve of a pelvic bone, a filmy sack of innards.

"Nothing to eat there, huh?" Bob asks.

I look at its front legs, still whole, stretched in a gallop.

Cat moves, red-eyed, behind Bob. A firefly begins beaming in the twilight, and then two. I could get a scrap of skin from this body, maybe a quarter, and though it couldn't be sold, I could make it into a belt or a sheath for one of these men. I've watched Oche cleaning skins with women enough to know what steps to take to prevent rot and maggots. It's as if I want them to remember me, though why would I? We're together only as long as it takes to erase the scent, to plot our safety, to save the black man's arm before it falls off, and then we'll spin away, each of us carrying our own guilt.

I thought Cat had tried to drown himself that night, that he had slipped into the creek to slip away, and I didn't blame him. Even as I was using my knife on human bodies, fighting to keep their knives away, fighting for these bags that are little more than signposts to a future, I thought, *Yes, let him slip away; there is nothing of life that is good, and maybe we should follow.* But when the night was quiet again, the bodies still, the slaves in the trees silent and awed, we called for him and he bobbed up from the water like a bubble of hope.

"A wolf, probably," I say, turning from the carcass.

"And just eaten the back half?" Bob hops over the high grasses after me. His flailing startles a flock of sandhill cranes, who beat up into the sky with an angry rattle, their red caps catching the last light. The brass of their voice is louder even than our bags. Bob's tongue is awake again. "Maybe it wasn't hungry, or was a young one with a little stomach. Somehow it doesn't seem so bad if it's a young one. Makes me think of how hard it is to feed a litter of little ones, especially when the food goes rotten so fast or they don't give you much of it. I've a daughter who's so greedy she'll eat green fruit off any bush she finds, and then keeps Winna up all night with her aching."

His voice gets swallowed by the swish of our legs through grass. I hang back to let him walk ahead, and I match paces with Cat. I put my hand on his shoulder so he turns his face to me. The blue of his eyes burns through the wet of tears.

"Just a deer," I say.

He pulls his eyebrows down and nods: yes, of course he understands.

"You did nothing wrong."

I SIT THE night watch and watch the night turn. The pig sounds of my sleeping companions braid into the echoes of the love-sick barred owl and the twangs and thrums of the earliest tree frogs, men calling out for women. The cookfire is still churning through the piled ash; smoke coils at eye level and vanishes. I should be more careful, but I know already we have not moved fast enough. I have a creeping sense that the man who was sent to find us is following us, is on this western spur. But I have learned to think the worst. I spread water on the ash.

I lean my head against the sapping bark and, my eyes open, imagine Polly in her calico dress, her phantom coming to me across the distance.

It's ten days ago, and she's asking if I love her. "Am I not beautiful?" she says, stepping back from the shaded under-belly of a magnolia into the slant sun. Her black eyes have gold thrown in them. I have known that body since it was shapeless as a sapling. I slide the back of my hand down the smooth of her arm. When she dances, her toes dig into the earth. There are times she doesn't want me to touch her, but now I can. I used to think that love was need, but now that she's sunk out of my plan, I find I want her. I want to tell her how well I'm doing in spite of her, how I've made my money back in a night. But this is ten days ago, and she dances close and kisses a line across my forehead, down to one ear, and I think I've always wanted her.

The empty purse still lies beside the pit beneath my bed, and Oche must know, my mother must know. My uncle, turning in the sky, his back still holed, is waiting. It's too late to undo crimes; the criminals must keep adjusting. I've now killed a man, but I've shot no one in the back. The path must stay the same: justice, de-spite the mistakes I have made. I will start this journey a hundred times before I allow myself to fail. Power is an ugly thing—to be conquered, not deserved. Yes, it is like a woman.

In the woods now with hope, it is not Seloatka's twisted face that fills the space before me, not my uncle's one-eyed wink, but Polly, whose love was always part of something darker. She lies down and snakes her long body around my back and rests her head on my knee, her eyes gazing at my eyes. I stroke her hair, which knots around my fingers, and she sings a song. She puts me to sleep in these last moments before the sun returns, and I curse her name.

WE'RE CLOSE. BOB complains of hunger, though he has eaten twice what the white man has. He isn't walking as fast as he was, and sometimes when he speaks his eyes can't seem to find us. I can't tell what is the pain and what is his mind, reacting against the creek. We turn north at the dead white oak towering over the spread of open grass, its empty limbs reaching out, wanting always to be a sign for someone. Their feet drag behind me. The silver sometimes seems not worth bearing, but if we didn't have it we wouldn't be running, and if we weren't running, where would we be going?

Cat asks, "Have you been here before?"

"No," I say, surprised, thinking again of Oche.

He takes in the oak and the field and Bob, coming slowly behind us. "I thought I saw her."

"Who?"

"My wife. I thought maybe they came here."

"Women?"

He shakes his head. "Ghosts."

Bob catches up, asks what we're saying. I think Cat will fall back into silence, but he looks at the other man with more concern than I've seen him show.

"Are you ready not to see her again?"

We've all stopped now, and the question Cat's asked hangs between them. Bob can't make it out. If I knew our theft would turn us mad, I would not have done it.

"Your wife," Cat says.

And before I understand what's happening, Bob's fist has shot out and slammed Cat in the shoulder, the same one that holds an injury on Bob, and though Cat shudders back and opens his mouth once, he doesn't cry out. There is a recognition between them that something has broken, a politeness, on the other side of which might lie a deeper attachment. Bob walks on without apologizing, his face still twisted, and Cat holds his shoulder and follows him.

It isn't a woman I see the ghost of in this field but Le Clerc, who is slow and measured but who, I now feel, hasn't stopped following.

HER HOUSE COMES like a pond out of nowhere. A low wood cabin under shingles and a trough to the side with a roof over it. This is a house a white man built and she curled into like a snail. Bob is nervous, asking if she'll turn him in, want to keep him for her own, asking could he stay outside. I knock. No answer. We wait, Cat drifting to a peach tree fat with buds. Both men now touch their shoulders from time to time. I start around back and the others follow, but when we see her crouched in the garden, shrouded in a billow of dress and apron, her white hair hidden beneath a dun-colored cap, I hear Cat suck his breath and turn away. Bob stops in a half panic, not knowing where the white man's going, and then I'm alone in the garden with her and her face turns to me like a dark bowl, rimmed in cap.

"Son," she says, speaking English. In her hand is a white carrot no larger than a thumb.

"I've come from the Muskogee towns. We've a man with us who's been shot. He needs something for the wound. Tell me if you want us to move on."

"Psh. Come help me up. Look at you, standing on ceremony." She puts the carrot half in her mouth and raises her bony hand. A dark bird resting atop a shrunken pile of linen.

Inside, she puts a pot on the hearth for coffee and makes me sit in her one cane chair while she snatches up the odds and ends of living alone, making the room orderly. Stockings off her bed and shoved under, a spiderweb brushed from the window ledge, a crust of bread on the table tossed through the back window. She pours me a bitter cup and then raps twice on the front window.

"You!" she shouts, presumably at my companions. "Get in here!" Her hand jerks violently toward her as if to manually pull them in.

The door creaks open, and Bob pokes his head an inch inside.

"It's all right," I say, but she is already at the door, yanking it open, Bob tumbling through.

"Sit, sit, sit. You and the scaredy one." She sticks her head outside and yells again.

When Cat comes in, I can see an awe in his eyes that restores some of the handsomeness his face must have had. Something in this woman is recognizable to him. His breathing is deep now.

The three of us sit on the floor so she can have the chair but she folds her legs and floats down to us, ballooning, her head a small darting brilliance on the sack of her body.

"Tell me." She pats her knees once. She looks from my face to his face to his face, hoping to see the story there.

. . .

AFTER SHE WASHES out Bob's wound with water and whiskey and swaddles it in a green plaster, we spend the afternoon in her garden pulling weeds, and in the meadow around the house clearing limbs downed by the last thunderstorm, and in the woods calling *sooee* to her hogs, some of which return. Bob fills the trough with water and brushes the leaves from their bristle-black backs. She sidles up behind us to see how we're getting on, making the other men jump. The clouds jostle each other and tumble down low. I told her we should stay in the house, that there were men behind us, that I could sometimes smell Le Clerc, but she took one look down the trail we'd come from and said, "They'll keep," and then handed me a hoe. "And anyway, we've got guns."

Cat comes up from the back slope of the meadow to show a bone he found.

"Used to keep chickens," she says, turning it over in her hands, tapping it along her forearm. "Till the hogs ate 'em. There might be one left around here somewhere."

Cat snakes back through the high grasses with it.

I help Bob roll a nurse log back into the woods, its fungus and grubs clinging on to the wet bark. When it's well off her field, Bob sits on the trunk, wipes his face.

"You know I didn't mean it with Cat," he says. He picks off a raft of lichen growing by his hip and flicks his fingernail in it.

"You couldn't have made the journey with a woman." I don't believe that Cat's marriage was with a real woman, a woman who complained and changed her mind and had her own will. His frailness could not have withstood her. Whatever wife he's carrying with him in his mind is no match for a walking wife.

What would Bob's woman have done on this trail? She would have told us to go this way and not the other, would have raised her eyebrows at how I cooked the rabbit, would have stopped us from thieving. Or after we thieved, would have stolen our bags. No, I cannot blame Bob for not bringing his wife.

"I think I like her more now," he says. He sounds sorry for this. "She wasn't the one I'd've chosen, but she was the best for me and let me run off after all. I wouldn't have gone if I thought she couldn't manage for herself, but she's as tough as they come and made friends with the missus. Could be I wasn't the family she wanted either." He tosses the lichen and scratches off another piece. "I don't want to think about the other stuff. Damn it." The silver is still in its bags. Our women are still somewhere else. He looks up. "What about your girl?"

I wait as a sound in the forest becomes not a man but a squirrel. "We should get back."

At night I dream up scenes between us. She drops to her knees and cries and I comfort her; she asks me to come east with her and I do; she tells me to let Seloatka go and I consider it until I'm asleep, and when I wake up I say no, no. Could she have killed a man, or would she have saved me?

We walk back just as the clouds begin to empty. Cat has found a flower and is waving it at us. A signal.

The rain washes over us in long, light sweeps. We finish our stacking and sorting and harvesting and come inside wet, our road-sweated clothes rich with the earthiness of rain. We drop our handfuls of onions on her wooden table, the carrots, two heads of lettuce, all rolling around in search of the edge. One onion drops off and bounces beneath the woman's bed, and she tells us to leave it, it's good luck.

"We've been bothered by crows," she says. The carrots fall apart into coins under her knife. Bob stands at the window, watching for men, and Cat and I sit on her bed. "They get worse in the summer, but now's the time when they're going around with their babies and teaching them what's food and what's not."

She throws the vegetables into the kettle with salt and fat, and I miss my mother's corn.

"We have an old woman," I say, "who sits in our field and keeps the crows away." I'm surprised to see her in the clothes of white people, leading such an alone life. But she may have been Spanish before she was Indian, or black.

"I've too much to do to sit around all day, and anyway, I'm not hardly old yet." She snaps her head around, eyes wide, so we can see the youth still in her face. She gives a final hard stir to the stew and then puts down her spoon and lifts the musket from the back of her door. "Excuse me, sons."

Bob moves to the back window and watches her walk into the garden. We hear a blast, a pause, and then another blast, and I am stuck to my seat, knowing it is just the woman with her gun, catching a rabbit or a dove for dinner, but thinking still of Le Clerc and his nearness. A warbler flashed through the woods while I was gathering kindling, and I thought it was the gleam on his rifle. She comes back inside, wet again, with two dead crows dripping from her hands.

She clears the table of the tin plates and flour sacks and tufted carrot tops and replaces them with a large wooden bowl. She hums as she gathers ingredients from her shelves. I stand beside her while she rolls them into a paste.

"That's not for bread," I say.

"One ounce asafoetida, four ounce flour brimstone, four ounce gunpowder, two ounce hog's lard."

We all three watch her arm turn in circles, knowing that this is witchiness but unable to leave this house. Even with the dampness of our bodies, it holds an uncommon warmth.

"My grandmother's recipe," she says.

"Who was she?" I ask.

She rolls the paste into balls, walnut-sized, and stuffs them down the throats of the crows. Their beaks spread wide for her dark hands. "There now," she says, cradling their bodies and sliding them under the bed beside the truant onion. She tosses the remaining paste in the trash heap outside and pours a ladle of water over her hands to clean them.

Bob and Cat look at each other like children, afraid and also wanting to smile.

We eat what she serves us, uncertain now what's in it, but swallowing because it's warm and not burned and tastes like lives we had before.

"I haven't gotten enough from *you*," she says, pointing a delicate claw at Cat. "Let's say this tracker falls off the scent, doesn't find you bunch of misfits. You're free and clear, and this one, if his arm don't fall off, is going west, he won't stop talking about it, and that one's circling back to his village one day, though, darling," turning to me, "I think you'd best wait a year or so to build a name for yourself, take over some of the trade from the upper towns before you approach the Chickasaws. That way you'll have more pull going in. But *you*. Where are you headed?"

We all wait. We're sitting on the floor again, and he puts down his plate and rubs his fingers across his lips as if trying to feel for the taste that was just there.

"Carolina," he says. His voice cracks, and he swallows. "My wife was there." He digs a hand into his pocket and pulls out a brownish letter. The woman takes it, looks at the address and the scribbles on the back, but when she raises her eyebrows at him and fingers the seal, he takes it back. "Where is it going?" he asks.

She points to the writing on the front. "Camden," she says. "That's closer to the upcountry. What's that river it's right along?" She's taking her time, fiddling in her cap, to give him room to find his courage. "Wateree. We had some people from there in the lower towns," she adds, looking at me.

She finishes her stew and pushes the plate away. Her fingers work at the knot beneath her cap and she pulls it off, stretches her legs out straight, tries to grab her toes. Bob is unusually quiet again, giving Cat space.

"I want to deliver the letter. This." He shakes the envelope once.

"If you want to take it yourself, you're heading the wrong way, son. You need to be going east."

He smiles, the first smile I've seen that seems at ease, that comes from some emotion I might find familiar. "I'm afraid," he says, turning his hands palm up.

She returns his smile and mimics his gesture. I am reminded of a game Oche and I would play after our mother fell asleep. My brother, who today is probably weaving baskets and seeing spirits, all very gently. This quiet exchange is making me sleepy, and I reach for one of the quilts in the pile on the woman's bed and fold it beneath my head. A black feather floats along the floor next to me. I brush it aside. Bob leans back against the bedpost, and though we are inching away from their intimacy, we're listening. This silent man that we have protected, dragged along, refused to abandon, is speaking.

He reaches out for her open hand and holds it in the space between them. He smooths the pink palm with his thumb and then leans close to inspect the lines and scars there. She lets him, as one would humor a child.

"Your hands are even smaller than hers," he says.

She turns hers over and enfolds his, giving it a squeeze. "Let's see if I have something here," she says, hoisting herself up, showing beneath her extravagant skirts that she is shoeless. She bustles into a corner of the kitchen where a stack of rolled and folded papers seems to slide with every loud sound. After shuffling through them, she pulls out a long white scroll and brings it back to Cat, pinning down its corners with a few stones from her windowsill.

"There we are. Now this is us here," she points, "and this is the trail you fellows came down, and fast, I'm betting. Now," and she snakes her finger up and to the right like it was traveling in a boat on a river, "way up here is the Carolinas, north and south, and there's Camden somewhere in this woody part. That's where you want to go." She looks up at his face to see if he's understanding the distance.

He slows his fingers across the map, feeling for mountains.

"Where are your parents, son?"

"Her parents are dead."

She pulls his hand away from the map. "No, yours."

"Hers died in a cart on the way to see her. Said it wasn't her fault."

"Was she driving the cart?"

"No."

"Well, there you have it."

He leaned into a whisper. "But she was bleeding out. I might have stitched her up."

"That's maybe a half fault at best, certainly not a whole one. And what can you do now?"

"Suffer."

"No, no, what can you *really* do? Bring her back? Throw yourself off a tall tree? Crawl into her grave? Think for a minute, son."

He waits, his hand still draped on her knee where she left it, the map between them. Beside me, Bob has drifted into a doze on the floor. Her voice alone makes us feel blameless. I am proud that I know what can and cannot be done. Though the creek muddled me briefly, and though Polly still has no solution, I need only keep on the same path I've been walking; my plans make sense. There is a difference between killers and leaders, though both may take men's lives. I am neither yet, but I must tell myself there's a difference so that I can keep following the good path, in hopes of ending up at a good end. Life keeps going, and no man is lost until the end. I must remember to tell Cat this. He is not yet lost.

"Who is still living?" she asks him.

Bob snores lightly with a smile. Cat looks around the room, taking us in. The woman, the once-slave, myself.

"Wash yourself of that," she says. "Give yourself a good washing. Do only what can be done." She stands up, pulls him up beside her, takes him to the basin in the corner of the room. She tilts his head above the bowl and pours a jug over his hair, and then digs her fingers into his scalp, pulling out the wet tangles. I expect him to protest, but he stands limply. She is not gentle with him. "Guilt is a dead weight," she says. "Get it on out. Hup, hup." His head jerks with each rough motion of her hands. He murmurs something that sounds like a white man's prayer. *Our father.*

When she is done, he stands up straight, his hair smooth and plastered against his skull. She holds her tiny face in her hands with pride.

"Feel nicer?"

Bob has woken up with all the splashing. "What's he getting the fine treatment for?" he asks me. "I wouldn't mind a scrub."

Cat, with wide-open hoping eyes, formally kneels on the ground. "I don't want to have done what I did," he says.

Bob snorts and shakes his head. "All you did was go swimming."

"I don't want to have done it." Cat is still gazing up at the woman.

"We've got a half dozen bodies on our souls," Bob says, "and you just went paddling around that creek like it was a summertime swim hole." He pulls his knees up, looks at the woman to convince her. "We're the ones who killed them all, who got shot for it. He didn't touch them. He who's probably the murderer they're looking for, who knows how to murder, and him even carrying the gun. Just went swimming!" His laugh is uneasy.

I am seeing all this sideways, my head down on the quilt, and I see how much Cat's jawline is like Bob's, how their elbows both jut. Their waists meet their hips in a skinny bend. Everyone's shoes are collapsing.

The woman folds herself down on the floor and pulls Cat's head into her lap, fidgeting her fingers through the last knots in his hair, and he lets her do this and closes his eyes as he collapses into the puddle of her skirts, beneath which is just a pile of thin bones.

"I let people die," he says.

"Shh," she says. "I know."

Bob sighs and settles down again.

We fall asleep in crooked shapes on the floor.

IN THE MORNING, the woman—wearing the same dress, un-wrinkled, but capless—pulls the crows from beneath the bed and sets their ruffled bodies on the table and with the strength of someone younger, she tears the birds to pieces. She pulls their wings until they pop darkly and rip free; she twists their heads off, the brimstone paste sending a foul burned smell through their open throats; she yanks at their feet until they come off like fleshy twigs in her hands. Then with grace she gathers the broken pieces and takes them into the garden, where she ties them to sticks with twine and plants them around her fresh stalks of young corn.

She washes her hands from the barrel of rainwater and makes us a pan of fried potatoes for breakfast. The salt smells like everything is all right in the world, or at least in this embrace of a house. When she changes Bob's bandage, we see that the hole in his skin is starting to scab. Cat touches it.

"What's it to be, my bandits?"

We are lazily sprawled around the house, waiting for the next task she assigns us. I blink at her slowly, thinking I will offer to find us fresh meat for dinner tonight, something wilder than her hogs.

"I can't keep you forever. A bunch of highwaymen and a spinster like me, how do you think the neighbors would gossip?

No, sons, I've my own business to be about." She digs in her shelves now, pulling down new powders and ground roots.

Bob is the first to sit up. "I don't mind," he says. "It's time enough for us to be heading on." He looks at Cat. "Time for me, that is. Right? My shoulder's fixed, or will be, so— This is how we said it would be." He stands up and starts sorting his belongings, scooping out a small hand of silver for the woman pounding a poultice in her bowl. "I thank you much for what you've done."

"So you're just splitting up like strangers?"

"That's what we are," I say.

Bob turns to me, determined. "If you go back and take over your town or whatever it is you hope to do, and if you find yourself trading down Pensacola way and you see my woman on my master's land, tell her that I'm free now, that I know what it is now, that if it means death, I'll pay. And tell her I'll come for her." He looks at Cat again. "And you. There is no crime so black that God don't see the goodness in us, though it be deep and buried."

Cat rises and takes Bob's wrist in his hand and then drops it. He says something so quiet we make him say it again. "I'm not ready."

"You've got the map, don't you? Aren't you going to give that letter to the captain's lady and woo her, or serve her, or bed her, or whatever the plan is?"

"I want to do that after."

"After what?" I ask.

"Bob," he says. "Probably can't buy a farm without a white man's X. I can do that."

"You want to come west with me?" After their arguments,

I would've thought Bob would be happy to let Cat go, but we have let too many people go. Bob's face and Cat's face match, both open. None of us have the language for saying what we need.

We're all standing now, the woman slowly stirring and smashing, and the safe, sleepy air is being pulled like smoke out the windows.

"If you were to ask me," she says, pulling her hands from the bowl, wiping them on her apron and rumpling them through her woolly white hair, "and some men don't, I'd say this is no time yet to be carving yourselves into bits, especially with one of you still healing." She looks particularly hard at Cat. "Carry on west, I say, keep putting miles between you and the men out there, and when you've gone as far as you can without squabbling, without one man saying, 'I've got to be heading the other way entirely!' then you fall into your separate selves. But you ask me, I'd say you're still all mushed together." She funnels the powder into a small glass jar and then brushes her hands over the braided rug, the anonymous dust drifting in a faint cloud to the ground. Would mice later find it and turn to stone?

I falter on the edge of something. After all I've done, wanting now to do better.

"At the very least," she adds, "someone needs to change Bob's plaster."

We look at each other, and maybe it's the sureness of the woman's voice, how strong it comes out of her small body. Maybe there's a new weakness in us, or a resistance to do more wrong. We sort our bags, pack them, feel their heaviness on our shoulders again. Cat gives me back the gun.

He folds himself onto the woman, stoops down, small as he

is, to wrap her frailness in his arms, and she laughs and pats his back. Her dark face, pocked and pitted, sits like a bird in the crook of his neck. Bob pulls him away.

We have left her with a supply of wood and a basket of dug vegetables, and her garden now is orderly, except for the bits of stinking crow strapped to poles and flapping in the breeze.

Our shadows slide west between the white oaks and hickories as the light catches in the brambles. All that's left after the shepherding of these men is to rule my people, and it is the greatest thing I will ever want, and it is the only act that can redeem the blood I've spilled and the blood I've witnessed, and though I wait for months or years, I will come to it and become a white, white sun for my nation. History is like a map for where to go.

March 13–19, 1788

Le Clerc

AFTER THE MEN'S steps have faded into the general rustling of the woods, I comb my hair back into a decent ribbon, brush the burrs from my stockings, and knock on the door of the lady's cottage. I briefly consider putting down my gun and sack but would rather appear intimidating than unarmed. I follow not their bodies now but the trail of their intention: I have to speak to the woman myself, in the hopes that she can tell me what my own senses cannot. I have hidden in the brush for most of a day and a night, orbiting this extraordinary household, comprehending nothing. Because I cannot piece together the details I've witnessed, it is time to insert myself into the narrative.

The woman who answers is shrunken and balloonish, a lively mix of dark and light. I bow and ask if she can spare water in which to wash my hands.

She blinks once, and just once. "I'd be honored," she says, sweeping back the door to allow my passage. The ceiling is low, but a fire in the hearth keeps the room warm and snug. Quilts of all colors pile on the bed. On the shelves along the wall sit an array of vials and sacks, each appearing to contain no more than a few ounces of herb. I place my hand on the back of the chair, my eyebrows raised, and she nods an assent. I sit while she fills a bowl with water from a ewer and carves a sliver of soap for me. After my ablutions, I pick up the black feather on her table and twirl it, first forward then back, between my fingers.

"This is a handsome cottage. You live here alone?"

"Oh," she says, reaching to relieve me of my bag and gun, placing them against the back wall when I acknowledge that this is acceptable, "it's a pleasure to have guests. Sometimes I think it's the only thing keeps me from dying." She takes the bowl, opens the window into the garden, and throws the dirty water out in a loud splash. She touches a thin necklace that falls into the top of her dress as if to confirm it hasn't sailed out too.

I rise from the chair, noticing that she has nowhere to sit.

"No, no," she says, "this is me right here," and she perches on the edge of her bed, taking a corner of the quilt to play with in her hand.

"You must have seen a wealth of men pass through these woods. What a remarkable vantage for a woman to possess."

She looks around as if to verify this, and then agrees. "There's more to be seen than what they tell me, that's for certain. Men, you know, don't tend to chat much about their hearts."

"Well, it's a delicate organ."

Her fingers are strumming in the quilt as if she were writing down the words I spoke, but I come to understand that she is picking out the threads of the joining squares, plucking them free with her fingernails and then suggesting her thin finger beneath the loops to finish the job of pulling. She does this remarkably fast; after just a short monologue of mine on the weather, two squares have already become detached from the scheme. She never looks at what she does, but sits there quite calmly, her feet dangling youthfully from the edge of the bed, kicking into the covers, while this lovely construction comes apart under the idle spell of our conversation. Will she stitch it back together after I've gone? If I stay long enough, will she disassemble the remaining pieces of her house? Unpeg her meager furniture, unleaven her bread?

Below her dress, her toes spread so wide, each wandering off in its own particular direction, that I have to assume she's never worn shoes.

I point to a calumet she has above her hearth, an object I've not seen before in the house of a woman, and displayed so idly. "Were you long with the Creeks?"

She leans onto her knees, which are hardly discernible under the delta of her skirts. "I'd guess you had a very proper mother."

I sift through my stories of her, hoping to land upon a kind one, but all I can recall is the sound of the closing door and the hard beat of her shoes as she walked away, leaving me to confront myself. I smile. "We lived in the Ardennes, and I'm afraid were rather distant."

"Sons," she says, and shakes her head. "There was a man just here who never had a mother."

I sit up. "I imagine men here don't even need mothers, nor any other prop."

"Here?" she says. "Where's here? What gave you to think that?"

"Did the man say where he was bound?"

"Where are men bound who have no mothers?"

"I meant that there is such infinite space in this country. It would seem that only someone free from encumbrances could properly claim it, someone free of family, or class. I've traveled extensively and—"

"Is that a riddle? I'm a woman who likes sense."

"I'd merely suggest that—"

"Are you a sheriff?"

I laugh. "No, madame."

"Are you afraid of justice?"

I cannot prevent my brow from furrowing. "Not of a certain variety, no."

When the squares of the quilt are entirely unattached, she stacks them in a short tower on her lap and then fans herself with them.

The afternoon sun that falls though the open doors and windows like a drunken guest begins dropping, the shadows stretching longer and the early gnats and mosquitoes hovering drowsily with the motes, coming periodically to examine our ears. I offer to prepare a light supper for us both, and she rises from the bed to give me a tour of her kitchen implements and to advise on the quality of the kindling, which this time of year burns slow on account of the damp. Her shelves of herbs intrigue me, but I restrict myself to what I know. In a flat iron pan I craft a simple omelette, the eggs from a lone chicken that she says has survived the rampaging of her hogs. I whip in sliced onions and a dash of pepper, coarser ground than I'm accustomed to, and in a separate pot beside the fire I roast some of the carrots and parsnips the lady has recently dug from her garden, or that the men dug for her. For the omelette, she offers some dried mushrooms from a jar, which politeness demands I add, and I stir a sauce of ground garlic and nuts for the vegetables that adopts a flavor almost of cream. She lights the candles in the dark corners of the house and pushes the table up to the bed so we can dine at the same height. When we sit down with our tin plates, quilt squares for napkins across our laps, I can see I've sparked a dignity in her. She eats with punctilious grace, dabbing her mouth occasionally, her back straight, her elbows light, as though she were sitting before a sheet of music. We do not speak while we eat; food here, as in France, has a sacrosanct quality to it. In the moment of consumption, we are connected through all the layers of linen and leather, of wood and iron, right down to the soil beneath us and the bounty it produces from the muck of decay.

After, as she boils water for coffee and fiddles in her shelves, I lean back in my chair and stroke my fingers across my whiskers to clean them. Where did she come from, this raisin-faced lady with her rural grammar and indeterminate skin? Sometimes I feel my life is carrying me from refinement, with its handmaidens of hypocrisy and loneliness, deeper and deeper into a purity of both landscape and temperament. From my mother's fastidious gardens I have traveled first to Norway and then to America, to the riotous Boston and the southern colonies and then the southern wilds, where Indians control both war and trade, and I have landed on the western edge of all my travels, here, in a house in a meadow with a lady mystic. I am charmed. I am arriving at the heart of something.

"I must thank you for this hospitality," I say, setting down my empty mug. The coffee tasted richer than any I've had, almost as though a fine loam had been stirred in.

"And you for the victuals," she says. "I should kill that chicken, for every other egg'd be a disappointment."

"The man you mentioned—you never saw him before?"

"I only see the men you see," she says, and her face becomes momentarily dim, so that I can't quite recall if she's wearing a wild white cap or if that is just her hair. "Is it better to have a man visit, knowing he'll pick up and leave and not come back, or not to have a man at all?"

I tilt my head to one side, feeling uncertain in my stomach. Vases that I thought held flowers are actually stuffed with palm spines.

She throws the dishes out the window where the water went before, and climbs into her disordered, dequilted bed, voluminous skirts and all. She pulls her necklace free from the folds of her dress, and I can see the two rings there, knocking against each other as she settles herself. One a heavy band, and one thin with a green stone. When I thought of the empty room in the manor house, did this creature creep into the memory and watch? I cannot ask how she came by my mother's rings. She pulls an old wool blanket beneath her chin. "Would you rather die, mister, or not have been born?"

I stand and push my chair beneath the table.

"Are you looking for something, or are you running from something?"

I pull on my coat and find my gun and sack by the door.

"Do you judge another by how he looks, or what he does, or what he means?"

I snap my feet together and, despite some unsteadiness, give the lady a gracious bow.

"What kind of knowing could get you to what a man means?"

Her eyes are closed now, though she continues to pose questions to herself. I blow out the candles but leave the embers warm in the hearth.

"All of us broken before our mothers bore us, crows and men alike. Sticks in search of grace."

I kiss her forehead, which smells of cedar, and depart.

IT IS NOT difficult to find the men's trail again, though I am temporarily disordered by the lady's vegetable garden, which smells strongly of gunpowder and has what appears to be shreds of flesh lashed to poles in between the lettuces. Though I am a generation removed from jumping to conclusions of sorcery, I cannot help wondering what mischief this woman gets up to in such a lonely place, surrounded by herbs and potions and carnivorous hogs. My forehead is touched with a faint sweat.

In the darkness, I regret leaving my horse on the main trail with the other men in my party. It is a wonder the outlaws came so far without steeds, and foolish, but I follow in their lead. I will be curious to see, when I return to the trailside tavern with my victims, if my Creek companions are still where I left them, or if they have tired of the Frenchman's idiosyncrasies. Without the ability to watch their faces at close range, how would I have understood what these men were after, or known what course to take? I certainly don't dispense justice blindly. But my feet are not so sure as a horse's, and in crossing the meadow toward the woods, I fall once, my foot caught briefly in a dip of earth. I reassure myself that the woman is securely in her bed and the men I'm after are a few miles on; the only witness to my tumble is the vulture that's circling the garden.

They still head west. Which one of them has no mother? The deeper I follow them, the wilder the woods become, the undergrowth craning up into thickets where the Indians have not burned in years. In March, everything is made new again. The structure of the trees fills out greenly once more, and the beasts that hid in the winter come forth to show their young the tricks for finding nourishment. The old and the innocent, all bound in the same wheel of time that rolls over man and creature alike. What dies becomes born again; what we kill will feed the fungus. Any act, however cruel, will fold around until it buoys some other scheme.

There is something of America in all this. I know decrepit monarchy and how intoxicating the rot can be, but the ancient ties keep all men bound in an unassailable web of relation. My father was a minor noble because his father was, and back; I doubt there was a peasant among us. But we have duties to those peasants, and they to us, and so we are all mired in a hierarchy that, if not flexible, is at the very least explicable. We do not worry so much about who we are. There is a desperation about these men that suggests they do not reside on the rung of the criminal but, like all men here, are pursuing what might be called advancement, or hope. Their success or failure will, I can't help but believe, be a reflection on the project of this country. And yet I am the only man on their trail, the only man who may behold their fates. This strikes me as peculiarly lonely.

I have a notebook and pencil with which I record such thoughts, but for these observations to rise to the level of argument, to become a treatise fit for a scientific journal, I must explain the why behind these men. And that I cannot yet do. My hypotheses are useless without more data.

A few hours before daylight, I find the smell of burned wood. Sweat mixed with sadness, and the musk of the unwashed. There they are, in a ring between a stand of trees, their bodies spreading out from the dead fire like spokes. The black man starfished, the white man inches away from the other's warmth, and the Indian, who has pulled a cage of branches over his blanketed body to defend himself from some invisible hand. Such various sheep from God's flock, gone astray. I ache to see them still together.

My head is still mothy from the woman's drink, and the bushes look bigger than they should, so I find a hollow not too distant and curl up for an hour or two, my body knowing how to never fully sleep.

THE FIRST DAY after the cottage, the men are oddly quiet, as though they are embarrassed still to be walking the same path and yet too relieved to speak of it. The black man generally leads the party now, though it's evident he has no sense of direction, for every few minutes when he cannot decide how to proceed he stops to let the Indian overtake him. I'm fortunate that the leaves along the ground are soft and damp with spring, so that the other men's steps mask my own.

I learn little when they do not speak, so my mind drifts instead to my future: I return to Paris with my article on the foundation of man's common nature, his natural and God-given equality, and am trumpeted by the king as a beacon of reform, *merci*, after which I ride to my villa to present my wife with gifts from the Indians, and we embrace and move to a house in the city where we can see all the people at once, nobles and poor, and can observe as they blend together over the years like a fine, shaken sediment, and I will cease being lonely in all that human array. And we shall have a cat. If it takes these criminals to get me there, so be it, and though I will look for kinship among them, I will not become attached. In the short term, they are merely a job I have been given by my employer.

Late in the morning, I hear the stranger's approach before they do; another Indian appears through the trees and my party halts, the black man taking long steps backward so he will no longer appear to be in charge.

The two Indians stumble for a bit to find a common lexicon, and after some gesturing and nods, the foreign man gives a short, hard laugh and walks on, looking back once with amusement. I hold my breath against a tree and am pale enough in the paleness of the woods to go unnoticed.

"He knows something," Bob says, flicking his head over his shoulder to make sure the distance between the parties grows. "You tell him who I was?"

"Yes, that you were a slave, and that your master here had lost the way."

The other man appeared to be Shawnee; they are lucky not to have encountered an enemy. Though what is an enemy if a man will turn on his own people? I am also waiting for more word of this. That an Indian was of this raiding party was particularly galling to Seloatka and his men, who assumed he was Choctaw until the witness slave said, "No, Creek; certain." One of their number had vanished several days prior to the incident at the stream, and though the man's mother had reported his absence, the chieftain of the village had not chosen to pursue this information. I asked what sort of punishment he required, and Seloatka said that the man wasn't of much value, that whether I killed him on the road or brought him back made little difference.

"And the silver?" I asked.

Get it if I could, he said, but it was a white man's conceit, and for them to lose something precious in Creek territory was not the worst outcome, as long as we made plausible efforts. I did not tell him that if the traitor was hoarding coins, he had a better sense of the southern territories' trajectory than the chief did.

It is difficult to conceive why a man would desert and betray men of his own stripe and band instead with foreigners. Though of course here *I* am.

Now that the Shawnee is out of sight, the black man is louder. "Where did you tell him we were going?"

"As far as we could before you ran out of coin to pay me."

"Ah, yes, yes," he says, "make him laugh, take our money. Indian jokes. But you didn't tell him about the Mississippi?"

I can't guess what that river held for them.

"I believe he knows of it," the Creek man says.

"But what's *beyond*. Tell me, did you tell him where to find us? What all we're going to set up? You told him what I've done."

"I said nothing. What's there is yours."

This seems to calm Bob, and they walk a while longer in silence, sometimes shifting the weight of the silver from one shoulder to the other.

"That man know who you were?"

"No," the Indian says. "I gave another name."

"Would they kill you if you went home? That's where those men were from, huh?"

"They might."

Cat comes close then, as if to hear what horrors the Indian will face when forced to account for his sins.

"We did a wrong thing maybe by trying to take that money, but wasn't any wrong in saving our own lives by taking theirs, because their guns were up and they'd have killed us, you saw them." He shifts his bag emphatically. "And wasn't much a wrong taking this money, because you know what they'd have done with it, just add it in a pile to what they already had, and look at what we're doing instead."

In days prior, the Indian scoffed at this same language, attempting to distance himself from the act by the creek, but increasingly he seems to give in to this reasoning—if not to implicate himself, at least to excuse the other men. They are, by some inscrutable means, sliding into a version of his kin, though I know how strict the Creeks draw their clans, how any family sets itself apart from strangers. He now touches the black man on the shoulder.

"We need to change your dressing soon."

The white man smiles.

We walk into the afternoon, and still they talk of the homes they left, of what they'll do tomorrow and a month hence. Where the Indian will store his coins and skins while he rallies neighboring towns. If there is room between the Spanish and the Comanche for a black man's farm. How Cat will look upon a donkey. They grow louder as they seem to put distance between themselves and consequence. Even the Shawnee let them pass. Their bodies move more easily, and the white man begins spilling a few words, which the others eagerly pick up. When they change the black man's bandages even I can see that he is mostly healed. I trail them, every hour less like a pursuer and more like a pilgrim. I can no longer justify my delay in seizing them unless I admit to myself that here before me is everything I once believed to be a dream. Three men, none alike, asking to see each other, to be seen. Each pursuing a wild fancy that only this country, with all its contradictions, can permit.

IN THE DARK of the night, Bob's voice hovers above the resting men like a moth.

"How will I know where to go after you split off?"

"I'll draw you a map."

"You sure you're not coming?"

They are camped on one side of a field, forcing me to stop on the periphery, though their voices carry in the dry air. I climb up a tall pecan, making no more noise than a squirrel, and affix myself in the crook of a limb to wait for morning. The clouds that have drawn over the sky are splitting up, and stars break through. My eyes move idly from those constellations to the one below me and back. Even Canis Major, the bounding dog, looks no different than he did in France.

"So you're really going back to the cheats that kicked you out?" Bob is easily vexed, I have learned, by abuses of authority, but this is an easy mask for his developing guilt; he has taken to rubbing at the skin on his face and keeps his eyes on the ground when he is walking, when I can tell this is not ordinarily in his nature. If he is not aware of these changes, I am.

"They didn't kick me out."

"Or took your money or whatever it was. Doesn't sound like folks I'd want to live around. But you'll fix them, I know. Throw the old man out of town. See if the hussy's already gone. What I wouldn't give to walk back onto that plantation and beat my master's back." When the Indian doesn't immediately respond, he adds quickly, "Though I wouldn't, of course."

"This is all far down the road."

"He has to gather friends first," Cat says, in a thin voice.

"Allies," the Indian corrects. "It may be five years before I have the forces to return." He sounds as confident as any French courtier.

"And Polly?"

"He'll have nothing to do with her, that's what," Bob says.

The Indian shakes out his blanket before arranging it studiously around his limbs. "It's not easy to forget someone."

"But a thief?"

"We're thieves," Cat says.

They are quiet for long enough that I think they've closed their eyes, but then Bob says, "Here," turning onto his side to dig in his knapsack. He brings out something small and hands it over. "There's a cook I knew made the best cookies, just as good a week later. Go on, it's all right. There. You like it?"

I can't hear how the Indian replies, but it makes the black man laugh. The cookie is passed to the white man, and Bob knots his bag again and pulls his coat in closer.

"Funny how you don't really look at the sky till you're on your back. I bet your people got all kinds of stories for what's going on up there. Women chasing men, a bunch of snakes. See over there? Kind of looks like a wolf on his hind legs."

Bob's arm rises, pointing up, a dark shadow in the darkness. A brief flag.

The Indian turns toward him, away from me, and recounts a legend I can't hear, perhaps about how the stars crawled into the sky from some primordial swamp and arranged themselves in stories so that centuries later men would find reason to speak even after it was dark.

I pick my way half down the pecan before I know what I am doing. The ground below me is now close enough to fall upon without sound. I stretch one leg out, just to feel it, and wonder what such a leg might do independent of my better judgment. Might it hop down from this tree and creep over to the fire to warm its foot? Sneak between the men's bodies to claim its spot in the circle, near enough now not only to hear every swallowed word but to offer its own modicum of worldly perspective? It too has dreams; it too has a past that has shaped it like a slow drip of water in a lime cave, and which it too wishes to slough off. Across the proscenium of my mind trots an idea so swiftly that I almost miss it: to once more abandon my previous existence and join these bandits as a brother-in-arms, though perhaps their days of being armed are mostly done.

What stops me? My other leg, the one still notched in the lowest branch, protests. I am weak enough to yearn for fame, the variety that's enshrined in learned texts and passed down as wisdom so that bolder men might adjust their empires. I am brave, but I am not bold; I am curious, but my curiosity needs a purpose. And though I can confess to wanting these men to see me as kin, foolishly, I am still unconvinced that the human family is really so broad. This is the irony of the scholar; though I intend to convince the world of a universal truth, my own heart lags behind. I climb back up the tree silently, and with a certain diminishment of pride.

The black man flops over, letting out a breath loud enough to scare the foxes.

"I'm going to need some new clothes. No one'll think I'm free looking like this. Can't be free until folk believe it. Cat asleep?"

They wait.

"Who's going to take him, you or me?"

THE BLACK MAN and the white man and the Indian man are asleep under the blanket of dawn. Their chests rise and fall, a little organ in the woods.

In my notebook I mark the habits that have grown familiar. The way the black man begins his sleep with all his limbs out, then turns from his back to his stomach, then over again, each shift accompanied by loud snorts and then pleasant sighs. How the Indian man must cover himself with something, like a child afraid to let his hand slip from the quilt, and the white man is generally awake through the night. Yes, he's awake now too. His eyes are closed, but his hands are at work, idly braiding strands of grass. Their campfire is black and cold, for it was small and didn't keep. They needn't have bothered hiding it.

Here I am, a man in a pecan, poised to strip these men of their liberty, all because I believe strongly in the principle of justice, which suggests that men come alike before the law and are punished alike. This fact seems to me a very leveling one and, executed properly, could serve as a primary route to dismantling the outdated oligarchy so rooted in European soil. Whatever I write, of course, will refrain from a political tone. But I remind myself that any nascent feeling of brotherhood I may have in this tree is but a blink compared to the enduring good of impartiality. These men have already negated their freedom through an act of violence, and empathy is nowhere in fashion.

Cat sits up, tossing his braided grass into the embers of the fire. On his hands and knees, he picks past his comrades and crawls into the ring of woods surrounding the clearing. I hear the stream of his urine and then his scuttling deeper in the pines, in search of food, perhaps. From my perch in the lower branches, I cannot be discerned but by the doves roosting above me. The black man and the Indian are still asleep; the Indian's gun is resting between them, as if either could claim it. I wish they were awake and speaking. The hour is coming when this hunt will be done, and I—the arbiter of their fates if Fate is to be believed in—am already sorry.

I once might have watched the white man's absence more closely, but now I know he will never leave, that he is built like a barnacle. Yesterday morning, the others took a bow and a net into the forest to scare up breakfast, and Cat, left to guard the bags of silver, became nearly despondent as the minutes passed and brought no sign of their return. I was unconcerned—the Indian would not get lost and neither man would abandon the plunder—but the white one began gulping, and if I had not known it was fear from the raw smell of him, I would have thought the man was choking on a bone. By the time they returned, he was weeping.

He comes back now, still crawling, with a cluster of leaves in his shirt pocket. He squats by the fire, rolls a few of them into a thin tube, and lights the end of it in the embers. I have heard the other men discuss, in Cat's absence, a bounty hunter that may have been after the white man for murder, even before the events at the creek. But crouched here—damp, lonely, and pipeless—he looks incapable of force. Just because he weeps doesn't mean he is worth pity.

The scent of the smoke first wakes the Indian, who stands and stretches while glancing into the gaps in the surrounding trees, his lean arms still tense after a night of unrest. He kicks the black man, who begins mumbling loudly, complaining of his bandaged shoulder. The Indian takes a stick and digs in the embers. He tosses the wood to one side and nimbly scrabbles in the hot dirt with his fingers until he finds the cache of squirrel meat he had wrapped in leaves and buried the night before, roasted now. He pulls it into pieces for his companions. None speak until the meat is gone.

It is the slave who fully wakes to his surroundings last, and I say slave because I have learned that he fled a plantation in Florida, leaving behind wife and children. So he found the road more appealing than his bride—this is neither new nor criminal. His folly lies in lingering. If he were caught on the road they might bring him safe home, but now with the bags of silver to his name, he's not worth keeping alive. After he finishes his roasted breakfast, he is reluctant to stand and looks confused until he rubs the sleep from his eyes and lets his memory settle around the past few days. Upon remembering, he softly shakes his head.

The black man brings his knees to his chest, dropping his hands down to his feet so he can pick in his toes. They haven't eaten much in their travels; I expect the Indian to fell a deer soon. From my branch, I stretch one leg to shake out the numbness.

"How soon's the Mississippi?" The black man's whisper is remarkably loud.

The Indian bends to speak to him so I cannot hear. The white man is not paying attention, but has untied one of the sacks and removed a coin.

"And after we cross, then we cut loose?"

The Indian nods, pouring water from his jug onto the remnants of the fire and covering it with leaves and dirt. He makes a comment I cannot hear and the black man throws a stick at him, not without affection, then buttons his ragged coat with dignity and takes himself into the woods for a private toilet. The Indian kneels by the white man. His voice is soft, but I cup my ear and catch it.

"If I survive whatever comes," he says, pausing, dipping his head to meet the white man's oblique gaze, "then one day I'll go back. I could protect you there." His hand is on the other's shoulder.

I slowly remove the strap of the gun from my shoulder, bring it into my crooked lap.

The white man makes a sound like a startled horse, which may be a laugh. He pats the Indian's shoulder, and the Indian, to my surprise, pats back.

"Don't think too much of this," Cat says, gesturing toward the bags. "You'll go mad."

I had struggled to understand how criminals could find comfort in one another, how men in America could bear to be tied up in this dependence, but perhaps this was always only temporary. This brief camaraderie must merely be the odd knot in the loom—soon, their paths will be fanning out again. Except, of course, that this knot is the end, for I am here.

I shift in the tree, and a twig falls. The Indian does not hear.

There is a pleasure in watching men who believe themselves unwatched—to see the frustration on the Indian's face when he turns away from the black man, or to hear the lullabies the white man half murmurs when the others are asleep—but it is the pleasure of the voyeur, not the participant. And even after what I've seen, I am convinced that in the moment of crisis, these men must dissolve. That the connective thread I've been looking for must inevitably fray. The whole idea of mine was childish.

After the men finish their breakfast, the Indian shows the white man how to hold a bow.

"Your hands just here," he says.

Bob, who is laughing, nocks the arrow in. "Don't point that at me. You get my other arm, you'll have to carry the sack yourself."

The white man's hands are clenched so tight the bow shivers when he breathes.

The Indian points at a tree trunk across the clearing, where a lizard pumps his chest. Their bags and gun are scattered by the fire. The Indian kicks Cat's leg to draw him out into a proper stance.

I wait, but the white man cannot release the bowstring. The lizard skits away.

Bob touches him once on the back, says, "It's not a man."

He drops the bow to his side and the others turn away.

I do not believe in innocence. I have watched men for years, both out of curiosity and for pay, and each one of them wants something so profoundly that he would abandon his own con-structed sense of righteousness to pursue it. Desire breeds guilt.

I silently draw up the musket from my lap and point it not at the men, whose flesh is vulnerable through the tatters in their clothes, but straight ahead, at the middle branches of a chestnut across the clearing where a woodpecker is inching up the bark, pausing to flash its head left and right, the red blaze along its crown like a signal to fire.

I fire.

BELOW, THEY FALL to the earth, scrabbling, hands in dirt, hands seeking blind for bags, feet kicking at the dust beneath them, insects in a shadowbox. The Indian runs toward tree cover, his eyes hunting flicker-fast above him, searching for the shot's origin, but the black man is already rampaging into a thorn thicket, heedless, shouting.

"Get! Get!" he says. "Cat!"

The white man has dropped the bow and is standing by the

dead fire looking at his hand, which he flexes out and in as if looking for the bullet hole. The Indian has his gun pointed up now, but he's found nothing.

"Cat," the black man whispers now. "Please, please, please, we have to get."

The white man turns his head up slowly and in the arm of the pecan finds me, or what pieces he can see behind the network of new greenery. He watches me, my gun. His eyes, pale blue, search me for some answer. I am trying to measure his culpability, and he is trying to determine if his life merits saving.

I should climb down from the tree, should shoot at least one of them before the silver disappears, but they are the most vital things in this vast forest, and I cannot.

"Come on," he says, "come on, Cat, we got you, over here, please, Cat."

The white man shakes his head, his eyes still on me.

I am witness to the threads between them snapping. In the gaps my gun has opened there is pain. When I hear the sounds of the Indian giving up, slipping away with small crashes through the young trees, I feel a warmth in the back of my jaw like my own mother has turned her back on me.

"I'm ready," the white man says to the black man, who still clings to a thorn bush. "Mine are the sins."

"You didn't lift a finger," Bob says. "Come on, come on, you've got no sins."

"You're just as good," Cat says. "I'll stay."

The bags of silver are gone, clutched up in their frantic scrambling, none left for the white man. Though if he moved now, if he went to his companion by the shrub, I am certain they would share the plunder evenly, no matter their disparity in strength, in worth. He looks smaller in the emptiness around the remnant fire. He was always a small man.

With my gun held shoulder-high, I climb down from my perch, sloth slow, and watch as the black man sees a stranger, white, and trades his devotion for terror. He is gone, and Cat is alone.

I stand opposite him in the clearing and he looks at me with blank eyes. I am not human to him, but spirit. I begin reconstructing my composure. This is what I was sent to do; I will write this all down. What I have witnessed will be duly recorded and these men will endure in the annals of humanistic scholarship, and so it is all right that I have botched the assignment from my employer because justice will still claim her quarry. I am sorry that this experiment of mine lost me the other two men and the silver, the worth of which Seloatka couldn't guess, but this one after all had the bloodstains on his cuffs; his was the guilt that was most palpable. I wish he had not forfeited himself.

After putting down my gun, I pull a rope from my bag and hold it out to show him. He stands, folds his wrists together. I tie it in several knots around the bumps of his bones. I look in the bags left behind for anything of value but find only a dirty cloth and a handful of biscuits cut in lace-like patterns. I offer one to Cat, but he shakes his head.

We turn east now. The low sun is in our eyes.

THE FIRST THING I ask is where he comes from. When he doesn't respond I offer that I was raised in a small town in France, and when he remains mute I take it as a sign that he would rather spend these hours contemplating his soul, or evaluating some of the inexplicable choices he's made over the last few days or weeks or whenever this brotherhood began. I can no more worm into his thoughts than I can require him to speak, but I have not already shot him because I am patient, and can wait for explanations. It's fortunate I can easily follow the trail I myself have left, for the white man seems insensible to his surroundings. I suppose I can no longer call him the white man, there being none others now to distinguish him.

When we bed down for the night I tie his ropes to a tree.

"I won't run," he says.

I tell him I believe this, though how can I? Anyone would attempt escape. When society is stripped away, when we are adrift in the ungovernable forest, man is alone, and intent on survival.

Though if there were a criminal less interested in survival, perhaps this is he. I could swear that Cat was growing lighter over the hours I spent with them, that a burden was being gradually laid down while he nurtured a small contentment, but my appearance has oppressed him again. The sins he has claimed are creeping back.

I tie the rope in a sailor's knot.

"Did you shoot the men?" I ask.

He is quiet, so I pull out my blanket and smooth a patch of dirt for myself. It is hard to find a space in this forest that isn't interrupted by a surfacing root or a patch of fungus that must be kicked aside, and though I prefer to leave little trace, I must also secure some comfort. Sleeping on puffballs won't do. By a spitting fire I read back through my notebook and find nothing intelligible. *Is awake when others sleep. Gnaws at the fingernail. Enjoys the black man's humor. Is alert when others speak of women.*

"Did you shoot the men?" I ask again.

He is wedged into the base of the tree, his tied hands up by his shoulders in a limp prayer.

"Are you the one who has no mother?"

When I lie down, I turn my back to him, knowing that he will be up for most of the night with nothing much to look at but my own form, and though I have been watching him without compunction for two days, the reverse causes me some unease.

THE MEADOW WHERE the woman lives is quiet. The bits of flesh have been pulled from the poles, no doubt causing mischief to the carrion eaters who found them. But with the dead beasts have gone the living, and even the usual snuffle of hogs in the surrounding woods has been stilled. We do not knock at the door but walk on, and if she is at her window I will never know.

I wonder if she was a dream, if she was equally a dream to these men, if somehow we're embroiled in the same illusion that necessarily exists when men step beyond the bounds of their countries. I could visit her again and ask directly those questions that would prove whether she's a soothsayer or a prophet, demand that she reveal the truths I've been tracking since I first left Paris, ask what in God's name is liberty if we are all bound to step only where our ancestors have, but she would merely crawl beneath that fragmented quilt and jangle rings at me that probably every man thinks are his mother's.

Cat never asks me what our destination is or why we're retracing their steps, nor does he pick up his legs and flee in a mad dash to north or south, deep into the woods and beyond my reach; I don't know that I could catch him if he did, being a decade older and not as desperate. Occasionally he hums—or murmurs, although it sounds musical. Where am I taking him? Back to Seloatka? I'm merely taking him with me, as the black man and the Indian did. There is value in a quiet companion; he makes one consider anew one's own monologue.

That night, when I ask what role he played in the murders and he greets my inquiry with further silence, I tell him that I too have killed a man. (Many, actually, on behalf of my employers, but only one on my own account, and I consider there to be a difference.)

"He cooked bread for the king, and we loved the same woman. I assume you understand how that is; that love prompts one to act in unusual ways. No? Well, I had not received a great deal of affection in my life and saw this woman as perhaps a unique opportunity to rectify that. Duels are a matter of honor, and so my actions were justified. I felt slightly queasy when I saw the man's body, for there was some blood, but it was instantaneous and no one blamed me. I recovered. But death is not the most satisfactory solution to a problem. I understand that you may be feeling some guilt at what you've done, and this is to be expected. Even when we believe we're in the right, we have a voice within that knows better; some call it God. Are you religious?"

"Where is she?" He does not look at me, but bends his head down to his wrists, where he sucks the sweat from the rope. "Your wife."

I feel a shiver of fear, unaccountably. If I believed he was a murderer, shouldn't I always have been afraid?

"France. I was tired of home life, and she was unfaithful."

"Will you go back?"

I picture the door opening, her slim figure poised between two steps, her black hair mid-swing. With her husband gone, she must rarely put up her hair, or wear all her petticoats, or powder her face till it's white. What is her expression upon seeing me? Does it approach gratitude? My bags make a dark sound when they fall to the marble floor. Nothing belongs.

"I have not decided," I say. I remember my notes. *Is alert when others speak of women.* "Can I assume, being a man, that you were also wronged by a lady?"

He lifts his head, almost in accusation. To be perfectly frank, I cannot imagine a woman loving him, though his features are regular and he has a trusting, open demeanor. There is simply no fire in him, and if men do not present a little danger in the dance between the sexes, then what's the good of them? The craftier I've been, the more girls have offered their favors; they, like us, merely request some adventure in their lives. Cat, for all his murdering, exhibits a meekness that only a sainted woman could endure. But he did several nights ago mention a wife. Perhaps he once had some wealth and she married him out of greed and pity, and the moment a soldier rode through town, she hopped his horse and bade farewell.

"Bless them all," he says and, closing his eyes emphatically, turns away.

I try not to record speculations in my notebook—only observations and fact—but I hope one day some other man will tell the stories.

I have tethered him close tonight, calculating the distance between a fully stretched rope and my own blanket so that they are separated by no more than two feet. This is a trial to determine whether, given the opportunity, the white man will gravitate toward any other sleeping body, even that of his captor. As I prepare for sleep, Cat at a distance by his anchoring shrub, I crowd my mind with questions and concerns so as to ensure a shallow rest. I think of the citations I will need to prop up my writing, of the overdue missive to my wife and what this one should say, of curiosity itself and whether it is fundamentally noble, representing as it does man's taste for knowledge beyond his sphere, or whether it undermines the simplicity of daily life and breeds displeasure. With these clunky gears in motion, my mind is too unsettled to fully abandon me, and every half hour or so my eyes flick open to gauge the placement of my prisoner. Mostly he is awake, of course, lying on his back and scanning the heavens, but close to dawn I feel a new warmth, and there he is, finally asleep, coiled like a crawfish at the farthest stretch of his rope, two feet from me. The poor fellow is an unwitting magnet. At this proximity I feel new concern for his comfort—is he warm enough without a heavier coat? Are those lice causing the scabs around his hairline? So this is what the black man must have felt, this dependency that turns the heart. But any repeatable experiment only verifies a biological trend; there is nothing personal or mystic about a man's desire for closeness.

WALKING FOR SUCH distances invariably leads to intimacy; if I had not already known it from watching the three men I was following, these days with Cat have proven it. In the mornings he asks to be given some privacy, so I walk him on his lead to a thicket, tie his rope anew, and then allow him fifty paces of distance for his evacuations. He calls me after he has covered his shit with leaves, and we proceed. When the sun has warmed the afternoons, we share the same canteen of water, and any belch or flatulence on the part of one man is heard, without comment, by the other. We stride across land that belongs to neither of us and in this vacuum of possession blooms some primitive fellow feeling. If a panther were to leap from a high branch and tussle my prisoner, I suspect that I would rush to find a heavy stick and beat the creature ruthlessly and when the white man was free, I would attempt to address his wounds. And to all this effort I would go though my intent, unchanging, is eventually to kill the man. I cannot explain this logic, though I make a note of it.

"Tomorrow we'll find the road again," I say, over a measly supper of dried ham and meal. I did not pack sufficiently; or rather, I failed to have a sufficient sense of my own susceptibility. But every time I start to squirm at the indulgence of trailing these men so long, I merely glance at my fattening notebook and swallow my half share of salt pork without complaint.

"Are you prepared for your fate?" I ask. "I expect we'll take you back to Hillaubee for the execution."

He does not respond, so I pick up some of the food he's left uneaten.

"It would be helpful to me if you'd speak a little of your history. Did you know the black man and the Indian for very long? You see, I'm writing an account of your adventure to be shared with men on the other side of the ocean, men who are interested in unusual things. If you'll share your story, I promise to convey it with accuracy."

"There's no story."

"That's hardly true, since my guess is that you were born without having murdered anyone, and now here you are with at least several souls on your account. Unless I've got it wrong?" I offer him the canteen.

"Do you have any whiskey?"

"Pardon?" As it happens, I've saved a small flask in my sack for occasions of great need, and I tippled from it once or twice before I found the men, but about half remains. After a moment of consideration, I dig it out and hand it over.

He has to reach up with both hands to take it. Only one sip, and his face tightens into a grimace. His eyes squeeze shut and open wide again, and after this contortion a little peace comes. "Tastes like my father."

I acknowledge this with a nod. "I did not have a father."

"They are remarkable unkind."

"I hear that sometimes is the case." I stretch out a hand for the flask.

"I have to piss, is why I remembered."

My face must be blank with question.

"You had a son?" he says. "Who pissed the bed?"

"No, no children." Not for lack of trying, certainly. There are men who would be concerned about impotence, but I am grateful for the domestic limitation.

"It's right a father should be mad. Better I had no son."

I offer him the spirits again, but he declines. "I must say, family is given more credit than I believe it's worth. The blood relation seems to give folk a license for cruelty."

"But worse to be lonely." He lies back now, stares up at the sinking sky. The dusk birds are coming out of their holes and hollows, lithe black shapes against the twilight. We must walk a little more before we settle for the night.

"Is it worse, indeed? I have built a life mostly for myself these past two decades, though I have certainly had wives and once a mother, and there is a freedom to it I find very pleasant."

"Free from what?"

"Well, one needn't grieve so much at the inevitable losses, for instance, or get one's heart knotted up in someone who will abandon you or punish you, or someone who will simply not love you the same."

"You haven't been in love."

"Certainly I have." I flicker back through all the early moments of my Parisian wife: the dancing, the long kisses beneath the stairs, my hands wrapping her limbs around me, the fresh bread shared in the morning. Lust, lust.

"And you haven't done anything to be sorry for?"

I stand up, stretch my neck from side to side, brush the debris of wilderness from my pants. "We've another hour before we can rest. Come."

He is always obedient. We turn east again, my men now less than a day off, undoubtedly wondering what's taking so long. A bat tosses between the trees as if in a high wind. The sky is soon asleep, and I can see nothing but the sound of Cat's footsteps shuffling behind me. After several minutes of silence, he pauses, speaks up.

"I don't think being free means being alone."

IN THE MORNING, we slide down the banks to the main trail and turn toward the tavern, where we rejoin my men, who have drunken themselves into a sorry state in the time I've been absent. They raise their eyebrows to see me with a single hostage, but I tell them this is the killer, that this weak and woebegone man is the one whose punishment will redeem the murders. It is no use whether I believe it, for he won't say otherwise.

That night, Cat sleeps on the floor of my room, his leg tied to the foot of the bed. He watches as I remove my shoes and stockings, and when I wince pulling the leaves off my blister, he asks if he can help.

"I used to know some medicine."

"Just too much walking," I say, though I am convinced

the canker has some other cause than mere walking. "If you lot had wandered less, it would have been a welcome preventative."

"If you had not pursued us, we might not have wandered."

What the devil? I lean over to see if this is humor or philosophy, but his eyes reveal nothing. I fear this statement will keep me awake.

We both smell of days without so much as a rinsed face. But my sheet is clean and he has none, and perhaps if either of the other criminals had been on my floor I would not have minded, but this man begs tenderness. Is it his whiteness that is easier to feel sorry for? There, but for the grace of God, goes Louis Le Clerc? No, because I have known plenty of Creeks who share more with me in temperament and ideology than this man. He is just a subject of study grown too dear. I throw him a pillow and blow out the candles, so that when I ask him where the other men are bound, I don't have to see his face.

"I don't know," he says.

In fact, we both know quite well; the black man has shared a detailed scheme for his western farm, and the Indian has explained that the long journey to seizing his village and wreaking dignified vengeance—on his betrothed, on his chief, on any man who allowed his ostracism—that his journey begins with politics. Using coins to build alliances out of modern-minded Indians who will support his claim on his town and will carry him on a red wave back to Hillaubee, may Seloatka beware.

"Then what did the silver mean to you?" I ask. That is what I haven't heard.

"I was already dead. I had no need."

"But you took it."

"Life is for those still alive."

"I'm afraid I don't understand. You took it so that the black man and the Indian would have a healthy start in their pursuits? You'd kill six men to assist two strangers?"

"Whatever is wrong has already happened. I can blame them only once for what they did. You heard; she said to do only what can be done."

"Are you saying the others participated in the murders?"

"I'm saying they're still alive."

I am losing patience. If this man were a butterfly, I would not have toyed with him for so many days, and to such vague purpose; my duty as a scientist is merely to pin him, and let others marvel.

"Tell me, for pity's sake, what possessed the three of you to fall into a common story and hold to it past all reason. I have been in this country for twelve years, and from every angle I can only see that Americans have made a religion of the individual—it's seeping already into the discontent slaves and the Indian factions, you must see it too—but if all humans have a common element, a sublayer I call it, it cannot be fear or faith or even charity because none of these explain why your intentions overlapped into violence and out of it again intact."

I wait for him to speak, but he is like a mirror, only reflecting or failing to reflect what I most wish to see. I wonder what the Creeks are up to in their room, whether they are torturing the negro with Indian jokes.

"I can't tell any story but my own," he finally says.

"That's all I ask."

Finding a place to begin takes him several moments. "My

wife was this beautiful," he says, as if I can see what gesture he is making, if there is even a gesture for beauty. "We had a son. Sons, I think."

I have no children, not even a faithful wife. The room is airless, and the ceiling above me has a spreading stain.

"My memory won't go away. I remember all the bodies that passed before me. My father, and every other one until my wife. My life was mostly losing people."

I pull the quilt close around me, though it is not cold, and find myself hoping he falls quiet again. I remember too how I used to wait by the door of that empty room in Thin-le-Moutier, praying that my mother would kneel on the other side and speak to me, soothe me, tell me she was sorry.

"I am guilty," he says, "of everything man is guilty of. You won't believe me. All I wanted were her arms around my neck."

Downstairs a brawl breaks out. Someone throws a mug against a wall.

"She said it wasn't her fault, the way her parents went, and I believed her. That death born of love is a small death. But I could not believe her. When she was gone, and the baby was gone, I went where my feet went and they followed those men, who did not know my wife, who did not look like my father either but like men I might have been. They still wanted things. And then I began again to want."

He stops, and in the space I can hear myself waiting.

"Here is a letter," he shows me, though of course I can see nothing from my bed, "that a man wrote to his wife. A wife like a woman, like the woman I had. And now he is gone, and I am here. What do you think?"

I can't comprehend all this webbing, why men keep reaching

out for others. "I think perhaps you're sorry you killed him, and now you want me to save your life."

"No, you haven't understood at all."

"Do you want to live?"

"I want whatever is worst."

"But your companions, who I'm prone to believe share some of this guilt, they deserve no punishment?"

"I am here because they are good in the marrow and I forgive them."

I wait for him to explain, but he is silent. Who are all the bodies he mentions? In what life is a man not his own protagonist? I am tired of the mystery, am simply tired. Want to know the answers, but no one will tell me. Those brigands who are no less men than me. *Sticks in search of grace.* I wait until I can no longer keep my eyes open, and then I ask, in the quietest voice of a French man in a foreign country, merely because it is still the task before me, "So how did you meet them?"

He is already asleep.

When I wake in the morning he is sitting against the wall, and my shoes that have tramped through wet leaves and red dirt for the past ten days have been polished to a shine and sit next to each other by the door like new friends.

AFTER WE BREAKFAST and the Creeks assure me that the bodies have been returned to Hillaubee and the horses and mules reclaimed, leaving the creek a blank slate, we mount up in the stables. Cat climbs on one of the mules that carried the missing coins; I wonder if the beast can tell one cargo from another. We wait beyond the open gate while the negro is sent with our debt to the proprietor, and after I have finished securing the white man's ropes to the mule's reins, which I intend to hold myself, I turn back to the tavern to see what is keeping the slave.

He is standing in front of the low door, looking up at a horse that has crept so quietly from the south that I heard no approaching sound. Cat turns in his seat to watch. On the horse sit three women, or girls, or two women and one girl—it is hard to be certain—all dusky dark. These Yazoo lands are distinctive in offering a range of opportunity for individuals who, in the American states, would be tied firmly to a single patch of land. This must factor into my analysis of recent events, though I sense that the time when a black woman can speak to a black man in a public place without causing some outrage is finite. The negro glances at me as if for confirmation, but when I shout at him to hurry along, he speaks quickly to the women or the girls, bundled tight together on that poor horse's back, and they turn their heads south in unison like three owls after a mouse.

"What directions were you giving?" I ask the man when he has mounted the other mule.

He is watching the overburdened horse trot off in the direction from whence we came and does not offer an immediate reply.

"Oh," he says, turning the mule north and setting the pace for our company. We are heading home to face judgment, unless I decide to let the axe fall sooner. Justice, though collective, is still personal, and part of me would rather end this hunt before Seloatka has a chance to touch the fraying thread of the white man's life. "Mm," he says, drawing it out. He turns once in his seat to confirm that the women are out of sight. "A lady looking for her man, is all."

Cat gives a kick to his mule and draws up on my left side, now between me and the negro.

"A philandering husband, I suppose, gone all night and not come home?"

"Mm. Could be."

"But you knew where to find him?"

"I had a guess."

"There's no point in circumlocuting. We have an empty road before us and could use an amorous tale." I have to lean around the white man to convey my impatience.

"Just a particular negro she was after."

"What were the details?"

He pulls a pine needle from the litter in his saddle and jabs one point between his bottom teeth. "One that talked a lot."

"Well, that certainly doesn't describe you."

"Was he honey-colored?"

It's the first Cat has spoken since his narrative of the previous night.

The slave gently rocks his head from one shoulder to the other, considering. Timing his response. "May have been."

"Did she give her name?" Cat asks.

"You know a black lady?"

"Lord, oh lord." The white man rises up in his seat with a straight back, his face straight out and open as I have never seen it.

"Traveled some piece, she said. Looking out her man."

"Their children."

"As I reckon."

"You don't mean to suggest," I interrupt, "that those women had anything to do with the fugitive we have been hunting for over a week."

"*You* been hunting."

"My good man, you said yourself you felt some injury from these criminals, that they offered you none of the profits; you seemed equally intent on a reckoning."

"You didn't catch him. Seems fair to give the lady a try."

"And should we let her on her merry way? Has she not escaped from some plantation to which we ought to return her?"

"No," Cat says, and offers the first piece of biographical information on his coconspirators since I began pestering him four days ago. "They were free blacks."

I cannot explain the frustration that arises from having every man surrounding you become suddenly a liar. So Bob has a wife and children chasing after him. So my negro told them which path to follow. What possible hope do they have of finding a man in the western woods, and one especially who has no interest in being found, perhaps particularly not by his own family, whom he with clear sight chose to abandon? The only reason they have not already been detained is that they're crossing borders. The American slave patrols rarely communicate with their Spanish neighbors, and it would take an acute interest in a particular fugitive to coordinate her capture. In this wilderness, the assumption is that a slave's fate will be punishment enough. I am not swayed; I cannot believe that after such behavior a woman would chase her husband. Disloyalty is death to marriage, and in this regard the sable race is in no way more enlightened than the French. Perhaps she does it for the daughters' sake, but regardless, she will not find him. He will be halfway to his farm by now with a sack of silver to buy a new self. I know his hunger. Nothing shackles an independent man.

"Lord, oh lord," Cat says, and he is smiling.

. . .

MY FIRST WIFE did not die, as I have told the Christians in this country. Nor did I stop loving her, despite those days she was absent from the marriage. I left because adoring her was not profession enough, and her betrayal seemed to justify my release. I announced I was leaving to pursue a vague idea of scholarship, she threw herself into another man's bed in retribution, and, doubly childish, I thanked her for making my decision so effortless. I had thought these wounds were not mortal. I wrote letters from every town I visited, unanswered except in my thoughts, and with some swallowing of pride I reassured her that Fate, which I do not believe in, would somehow knit us together again after this adventuring had run its course. There would be forgiveness. But it is not my task alone to mend our fractures, and seeing an enslaved woman break from every bondage and risk the welfare of her children to pursue her husband—whether out of love or duty, I cannot be certain, but I am not convinced it matters—this sight has shown me what little I have left.

No woman will have me and keep me; no men will welcome me into their fold, awkward and suspicious as I am, raised as I have been on thin milk from a cold mother. Nor can I return to my country to scrub down the failures of the last thirty years, for it is crumbling into war. The irony of this is not lost on me; dissatisfied with the old order, I sought out the new, the republican, the individual, and while I circle around ciphers in a forest that is almost primeval, my countrymen are clamoring against both oligarchy and the tyranny of debt. I cannot go home, and I cannot stay another year with the Creeks. If I am honest with myself, I have failed in my errand. I was sent to catch and kill three men who attacked a trading party unprovoked, and I have used them for my own ends. Justice became secondary to wisdom, and what have I really learned? I am caught in the open, a man in a clearing but with no one calling to him.

Growing up in my mother's garden, walls around her plotted and knotted beds, the yew hedges cutting off sight of the wild fields beyond, I imagined that the creatures around me, the kitten and the damselflies, went off and saw such marvelous sights that they must have pitied me, shut up as I was in a rimmed paradise. I had no playmates, no other children to show me what it was that children were like. And so when I was grown and had done the things that young men do—had scuffled and gambled and seized a wife—I was left with the individual print of myself, which I did not recognize, or could not conceive of how to cultivate. How was I different than any other man? Now those differences confound me. I may take a dozen more wives before I find my way home.

I will take my lead from the black man, head west. Purchase another notebook. I hear there are men exploring the islands of the Pacific.

The man on the mule with bound hands doesn't ask where we're going or what will be done with him. The glow on his face has not subsided since we heard of the black man's wife. Was this what he looked like when he still believed in love? If so, I can sympathize with his wife; he is a handsome fellow, with kind eyes. Does he believe that though a man may leave his woman, or wrong her treacherously, she will love him past any bounds, past life? That a man may always be salvaged?

Why don't I ask him these questions?

I tell my men that we'll turn east at the path to the creek, finish the business where it started, wash our hands in that water, and return to the Indian towns without the weight of doubt on our shoulders.

"NEXT MAYBE THE Iroquois girl will turn up."

"You joke, but no one would come for you."

"Settle down. It's a good thing, have something to hope for."

"And what's yours? Say you weren't born Muskogee at all, but a man with no allegiance."

"Or an animal," says the third.

"All right then. What would you make of all this? What would you want?"

"You mean would I be the first bird to make a stone pot, or a flint tip? An inventor bird?"

"I'm not asking so you can mock me."

"No such thing! I only ask what you mean."

"I know what he means," says the third.

"If you had no uncle to please, no mother to bring game for, no pretty cousin to court, no Choctaws to fight, no friend to make jokes of all day long, what would you do?"

"Mm. Yes." He slows his horse down so he is well behind us all, puffs of red dust floating up from the animal's hooves; when I look back, his head is leaned back as far as it will go, so far that his mouth of necessity hangs a little open. With each step of the horse, his chin bobs. Oh, for the luxury of imagination.

"I'd catch frogs," the third says. "Stockpile them, and sell them to the other birds."

"And then you'd starve, idiot."

"Here it is," and he rides up to match his pace with ours again. "I'd make other people out of clay, all different kinds, and give them fingers and toes—maybe gills for underwater, we're lacking that—and I'd breathe life into them and set them loose in the woods around me, though they'd be smaller so that I need only take a few steps to see everything they did."

"You'd be a god, then."

"Would I?"

"All the world before you with not a single duty to man or woman, and you'd make a set of men and women to play with?"

"Not to play with; no, just to watch. They'd be free to do as they like."

"Well, it sounds tiresome."

"No, you see, they're much smaller."

"Smaller than frogs?" asks the third, already calculating how his own dream will intertwine with another's.

WE CROSS THE creek on our horses and dismount where the corpses of Kirkland and his relations and Thomas Colhill and their servants have been removed. There are still smudges in the sand, between the clumps of grass and the young sycamores sprouting, wide dips that once held weight. I untie Cat from the saddle of his mule and pull him down. His knees buckle on the sand and he looks about him with concern, as if expecting to see ghosts. The lingering smile is gone. He doesn't move as we tie the horses up and my men search for a sturdy tree.

I fix a pipe with a little tobacco that has stayed dry in my bag. The smoke in my mouth soothes me. I offer it to Cat, but he shakes his head. He doesn't know what we are doing here. A dozen yards downstream from where we crossed, a fallen limb thick with new shoots creates a washboard eddy in the stream. The water, which here is mirror-still, breaks over the branch in rippling whitecaps.

The rhododendrons tumble over the red bluffs like brush fires. Cat rubs the pocket of his shirt, where through the thinness of the fabric I can see paper, a small envelope.

When the men are ready and have strung the noose, I turn to Cat, close enough for him to reach for my throat, and tell him of what crimes he's been accused.

"The murder of six men, and the seizing of private property, to wit, two large bags of silver worth eight hundred pounds, and the wanton flight from justice resulting in your capture. I am aware that this act of violence was abetted by two other men who have thus far eluded arrest. Did they take any lives by their own hands?"

He shakes his head.

"You are solely responsible for the death of six men?"

"I," he says, but his throat is dry and his voice catches on itself like cloth on a nail. He could not have killed six men alone, but I allow this.

"What is your defense?"

"None," he says. His eyes move around—from creek to flowers to the negro standing at a quiet distance—as if to seek some explanation for his recent swing from guilt to hope and now abruptly to confession. "Though I am sorry."

"Through the authority of Seloatka, *mico* of Hillaubee, I redeem the blood of his guests with the blood of their assailant."

I can afford no deliberation.

I tie his hands tight with rope again, this time behind his back, and lead him to the noose, which hangs from a thick blackgum branch over an empty spot of sand where a wading bird left diamond-shaped tracks. I take the man's chin in my hand, look into his watery blue eyes.

There is nothing there but depth and endless sorrow, pain like threads of silk drowned in the depths of that sorrow. And floating above, a flicker of desire.

I move him by gentle pushes to stand before the noose. His breath quickens. At the base of the blackgum, where its roots run into sand, a dark stain spreads over the wood. His cracked lips move.

It is the closing of the afternoon and the sun warms the bank; some of my men remove their coats.

He opens his mouth again, and I cock my head. A jenny wren sings in the branches of the blackgum.

I watch his lips but they make no sense. His face, recently washed with optimism, pinches again at its removal—has he not already endured this blow a hundred times? Is it not already familiar? The criminal in him has evaporated, leaving behind a mist. This is what I will describe to the chairbound scholars: a murderer, faced with judgment and the final breath of a meager life, cruel and wrecked as it is, yearns for more. The spirit, however malformed, is hungry for itself, will always fight for its own defense. He doesn't want justice, or the appropriate meting out of the world's endowment; he doesn't want to face his wrongs but to evade them, to cower away from civilization so that he may live unreckoned. For all he followed in the others' company like a loyal dog, he was born alone and lived a lonely life and will perish as an individual—as an American.

After all that I have recently seen of brotherhood, or thought I saw, I am returned to my original impression: that men are selfish, that they fight only for themselves, that this country is their birthright and their promise. I who watch everything, who know men's hearts because they are too busy to watch themselves, can find a partial mirror of myself here—admittedly—but this loneness is no more than a fraction. I have my freedom, employment, the trust of nations, a keen and investigative mind that outstrips a merely empathetic one. I am not beholden to the whims or burdens of familial ties, whether natural or constructed. I cannot be undone at the sight of a wife searching for her husband. If this is what allows me to produce dispassionate scholarship, this too will allow me to take another's life with tranquil conscience.

Justice is not flawed, though its handmaidens may be.

The noose snugs around his neck and he is heaved up, his shoes kicking above the sand. He is gasping for speech, sucking at the air, his blue eyes watering. A man drinking the last of his life.

But five feet in the air his neck bulges and by some final miracle of the dying form, the muscles in his throat press out against the rope and he is breathing still, swallowing the words he is now frantic to speak.

His body is in a twist, legs quivering. In his choking throat is stuck some sentence of explanation, all I've ever wanted to hear, withheld from me.

I signal to one of the Indians, who hands me a pistol. I raise it, point it at the hanging man's chest. In his kicking, one of his shoes has fallen off.

I think not of the murders or the stolen silver or the trail he cut into the wilderness with such sorry steps, but of the men he'll leave behind. Where will we go?

I hear the jenny wren's wings as she flies off her branch, startled.

Epilogue

March 23, 1788

THE MISSISSIPPI IS wide, blue-brown, and has a deep hush
for a current. Compared to the clear rivers and singing creeks of
home, it is like a bear, sleeping and solemn. Men in long canoes
row near the banks where the current is slower. Their paddle
songs carry like a drumbeat above the water. The birds have
fine fishing here; gulls and ibises and big-bellied pelicans wheel
around in jagged patterns. Near the bluff, a dead tree juts out
of the river, and on one of its crooked arms sits a cormorant, its
black wings spread wide to catch the sun. The spring that was
warm is growing hot. Even with the breeze off the water, I feel
sated and lizard-like. It will be good to wash the clothes that
are now thick with dust and sweat. The sun is at my back, and
though I look north and south, the river is all one unending net
of light. I am not used to seeing so far.

Our camps have grown more disheveled since Bob convinced
me that no one else is on our trail. We holed up in a Choctaw

town for three days, waiting for the inevitable army, but no one came, no Creeks or bounty hunters, not Le Clerc. Even with what we've done, there are always worse men to be chasing. The Choctaws, though ready to defend us, had no intention of adopting us, so with a mixture of relief and disappointment we moved on. They were a small village, cut off from the politicking of the larger towns, and forgave us our heritage. Praise to the villages who know no better. Now our cookfires are large and we don't bury our dung. If we tire after a noon meal, we nap a little. I believe this loosening is a part of our molt; we slough off our earlier selves, those that became vile. A bathe in the Mississippi, and perhaps we will be ready to forgive ourselves.

When we reached the river yesterday, I shot a deer, and we spent the evening butchering it, roasting every cut, gorging ourselves. After repeating one of Oche's prayers, I rolled the extra meat in the skin and held it closed with a stone. The deer's head, its eyes still wet, we perched in the crook of a tree to watch for enemies. The river's loud mouth put us to sleep like infants. No ghost children came to take my hand, and in my dreams only fresh things.

We walked to Natchez this morning to purchase two horses with a share of our money, now that our coins are far enough from their source. Both are chestnut but one has a bald face and a blue, Cat-colored eye. On our way back to camp, we passed a man on the trace who had stained his face black. He rode bareback with a white woman perched behind him, and the air around them smelled of berries. Bob, on his own new horse, called after him, "If I paint myself white, can I catch a black woman?" Bob said the day we bought horses we'd be leaving something behind, and though I am not sentimental, this was true.

Curious how a man could live so long without his liberty, I asked one afternoon why it took him nearly three decades to free himself.

"And why didn't you just kill the chief?" he said. He had found a stick along the trail long enough for a cane, and sometimes he leaned on it as he walked and other times he used it to knock against the trunks of trees, which was a pointless and irritating habit. I could hear the birds startling off a hundred yards ahead of us. "When you're in a life, all you do is live it," he said. "You don't make decisions every damn day."

"But then one day you did."

"I can talk about it till summer comes, you still won't follow. Look out at this forest; all the trees look the same to you, right?"

In fact, they didn't. It was a mixed woods, with new saplings and shrubs crowding in beneath the canopy of longleaf and turkey oak, the palmettos clapping in the wind like children.

"But if this was a white man's land, there'd be the trees that get cut down because they're in the field and the trees that stay because they shade the big house. Trees don't get a say in which is which—they just are. One or the other. That's what white folks do, say, 'You are like this, for as long as God sees fit to shine a light on us, and you are something else.' They give you a name that's not your own and convince you it's the only one you've ever had. And if you're a tree in the field, well—" He gave a passing pine a hard whack with his stick.

"But to leave, you had to leave them too."

He didn't respond.

"And now?" I should not have kept asking, but there was little else to speak of on the trail and we had lost the need for quiet.

"You'll continue to plant crops and harvest them, and struggle to feed yourself."

"Yes, but that's *me* struggling to feed *my*self."

"And when you die, who will bury you?"

He was silent for a moment, and then he slowed his pace. I slowed mine to match. When my uncle was buried sitting up in the hole beneath our cabin, I didn't cry because he wasn't fully gone. He would be always within our walls, below that room. Oche said he was waiting, and so we waited with him. Only when Seloatka took our home after he took the council house did I feel all the force of my uncle's death, for now I had lost his body. A man broken from his kin is the only thing I can call unfree. Give me my mother and brother again, but give me too my clan, and my uncle's buried bones, and Hillaubee.

"Maybe some of us aren't good enough for all that," he said.

"WHAT WILL YOU name it?" he asks. "Do Indians give horses names?"

I am stacking the burned firewood beneath a holly bush, though we may well use it again tonight. If not today, then surely tomorrow will be our last, and if I can teach him a little cleanliness before we part—though he does not call it cleanliness, but superstition. Whatever farm he finds will look like a hovel within a week. We rode our new mounts the few miles back to camp instead of staying in town; our presence caused some whispering, as if they knew of someone looking for us. I asked for the names of Houma and Chitimacha men who might be interested in new unions, but people only looked at Bob and asked where he was from.

"What about Cat?" he says.

I drop the last piece of kindling and look over at him. He's running a set of pine needles through the scruff of hair clustered on his chin. We haven't mentioned the white man, though in some sense we know he was just a spirit—not a real white man at all—trailing us like a mute or a saint, sent to save us.

"There's nothing we could have done."

"I mean as a name for a horse," he says.

Our meals have improved since we stayed with the Choctaw— after filling us with sweet potatoes, they gave us field peas wrapped in husks for the road. We stuff ourselves and speak of crops and tilling, and I lie down beneath a tree while he wanders to the Mississippi to gaze out at the western edge of land and build houses in his head. Perhaps I can catch us a turtle for supper.

He is throwing rocks into the river, digging out the biggest he can find and heaving them over the bluff, when I hear the horse behind us, coming north on the road from Natchez. I have my hand on the knife before I turn; Bob of course is deaf to any noise he doesn't make himself. It is a man and two children, not white, and the girls' mouths are open in fear or hunger. They cling to each other on the horse's back, arms locked around waists. Their clothes have no color, but are gray and brown with dust and rain, so that they resemble a wash of dark cloud above the mirror-black horse. Because the man carries no gun, I look at him directly. Certain lines of the face, a softness around the thin cheeks, suggest that he is, of all things, a woman.

I lift my hand from my knife and raise it in greeting. The money has made us cautious of strangers, but if she doesn't have a weapon aimed at us, she's not yet an enemy. We can offer them meat and they'll move on. Bob is sitting on his heels now, lost in some soundless thought.

The girls are crawling down from the back of the horse, falling like limp sacks, and the woman dressed as a man lets them go without calling out. Either they are not her children or she too knows what danger is and has seen enough to know that this is not it. Their horse folds down its neck and starts in on the grass, glad for the pause. The younger girl stumbles past me. Perhaps they are mad, or the road has made them wild. Under her hat, the woman's face is drawn and stark, and she licks her lips once. She has a fresh cut stretching from her cheek to her chin that is too precise and deep to have come from a passing branch. Her eyes narrow on the man at the river, and in her gaze is determination, not anything as weak as hope.

The girl is at his back now and not even having seen his face, her arms clutch at his neck. He jumps up and she dangles down and he turns, half guessing what's about him in spite of the impossibility of it, and her voice cries out so he can hear it, and the man who has so long protested against the chains of his own family circles himself on the bluff, trying to grasp at the daughter on his back, and takes in his wife and children with wet eyes. It is the surprise of them, I think.

When he has captured the crab of his daughter, the other comes shyly forward and he kneels and she bends to his ear to chastise him. The woman drops off the horse and walks past me with no acknowledgment. He holds out his arms to her, and their embrace suggests that the meaning of it is still to be made.

She turns back to me and says, "Sir, this is my husband."

September 19, 1788

YOU CANNOT TELL a man's origin in New Orleans. Each messy street unfolds a different scene: men of all shades bartering in English or Spanish or French, around a corner a darker woman slipping her hand into a white man's pocket while he holds her bottom, two blocks away a swarthy man offering a tray of sweets to a fair-haired girl, and in the center of the town, an oiled black man standing on a block while men call out prices and women, from milk-colored to midnight, parade the lace shawls that someone has bought them. Everything turns on money. Desire is stronger here than pedigree.

With the coins that I have, it is easy to call myself the rightful chief of a small Muskogee town. I gave every detail of Seloatka's perfidy to the Tunica, for whom I'm serving as an interpreter and middleman, but over the months the intricacies of the story have boiled away, and when I come to the city to sell the Tunica's salt, I only tell men what I myself want to hear. I have two suits of clothing now, one my own and one with buttons and ties, tight in the armpits and with hard buckled shoes, and that's the suit I wear to call upon the Spanish traders. They're interested in Muskogee deerskins and don't mind stealing a little of the trade from their cousins in Pensacola. They ask how I and my town propose transporting goods across the hostile territories of the Choctaw, and I say, "I'm here, am I not?"

For my ability to pick up languages easily, I must thank the woman I loved and the English words that looked so full in her mouth. For the ease with which I forget the atrocities I've committed, I thank Bob. When we parted at the Mississippi in a thin mist of rain, we did little more than shake hands. He took one of his daughters on his new chestnut horse and his wife took the smaller one on hers, and they rode off toward the ferry with nearly four hundred pieces of silver between them. The little one looked back at me and wiped the warm rain from her face with a smile; she needed nothing but what she had in this moment. Her name too was Polly.

In March, while we were parting, this city burned to the ground. Through the makeshift houses and storefronts and the bustling of merchants and wives and the calling out of all these busy tongues in the heavy heat of summer's end, the wind still carries the scent of cinders. I take my letter of agreement from the Spaniard's hand and fold it in my bag with a half dozen others. These say men are interested in my commerce and political goodwill, whenever I should return to my town and see fit to send skins their way. Each letter costs no more than a conversation and a few coins, and turns strangers into brothers in trade.

After I have finished the Tunica's business I find a room for the night in an inn where a woman always knocks on the door after dark. I have never opened it before, but tonight I am heady from the day's work. She has large black eyes and wild curls tied in many knots on her head and her long neck is the color of wet sand by a creek. The creek where I played as an otter, or the creek where I saw my lover's father crumple to his knees. He was white, was only white and nothing else, and in this country that was his ruin. The girl at the door holds out her hand, and I put one of her fingers in my mouth to taste if there is any of my Polly in her, and then I give her a piece of eight and send her back into the night.

June 8, 1789

I AM WOKEN BY a child, a young boy who's been sent to see if I'm still alive after last night's dancing. When I roll over, he tugs on my feet.

"Chief, it's morning time! There are birds awake!"

Summer in Iroquois country is like spring at home. I pull the blanket tighter around me. At home I cannot say how I'm remembered; I am a runaway, a traitor, or entirely forgotten. Here, in this dry cool, I am the chief of Hillaubee.

The feast was in my honor, for I arrived not only with my bald-faced horse and my belongings but with a reputation. From the Tunica I had traveled north to the Shawnee towns and then east to the old center of power among the Iroquois. In a pillowcase given to me by a girl in a prairie fort, I had letters and promises neatly stacked from the Spanish, French, Americans, and a dozen tribes from the Caddo to the Miami. My coins were dwindling, so it was the pillowcase that I kept now beneath my bed at night. If I could ally myself with the nations of the Iroquois, dissolving though they were, or this Oneida village alone, I could not be turned away from my home. This was the last stitch needed in my suit of war, if I chose to wear it.

The boy has found one of my shoes—not the kind with buckles—and is trying to drag it onto my foot, though the leather keeps catching on my toe. There is something about children and shoes. Was Cat anything like this as a boy? Or would he have been, if he were born into a family?

I follow him down to a bright river, where he watches me wash. My legs are sore from dancing and my belly is still telling me about supper. Downstream, a black man scrubs a pair of breeches.

"Is he a slave?" I ask.

"Just Old Henry," the boy says, "Ojistah's granddaddy. He has terrible farts."

The war suit I envision has no relation to the world I'm actually in. Clashes still light up the country like fireflies, but the enemy is no longer a stranger. There are outsiders, but there are no more foreigners. Now in every battle you must confront someone whose face you've seen before. You can hold on to your land, fight for sovereignty, but in the morning you will still wash your feet in a river with a black man who is the ancestor of an Oneida.

The new Americans don't understand the nature of the country they've claimed; they have turned the Oneida into Christians and then turned them from their lands. They want to see a mirror of themselves wherever they look, but though they make claims for the rights of the individual, there are no individuals here, only kin. And kin is not a mirror at all, but a mixed woods, where nothing is alike.

In the afternoon I send a messenger with a packet of letters intended for the chiefs of the Muskogee towns surrounding Hillaubee. It is already 1789; most of the villages will have a man who can read a page of English.

The boy takes me to a nearby hill overlooking a lake long and blue, on which the wind makes quick cuts.

"Beyond that is land they'll take from us," he says, and flops to the ground, worn out from the climb.

I sit beside him and wave a mosquito from his face.

"When I'm grown I figure I'll take it right back."

Above us a tulip tree grows so high that its canopy is hidden by the crowns of all the smaller trees. Something moves in those upper branches; clusters of leaves float down to us. We can hear wing beats fluttering from a nest to an insect and back. On the ground, a mink shoots between the curls of bark fallen from the birches and stops, sits up, watches us. All this life I didn't observe when I was a boy of ten. I only wanted to know what my uncle was doing. Beneath the breeze comes the faint sound of pounding meal and men laughing, and those human sounds are the ones my young guide is listening for.

I am old enough now to offer advice, to tell the boy that thirsting after fairness only leads to a parched life, but I am also old enough to deserve this quiet. When I close my eyes, there is nothing behind my lids to see, just a spray of light retold on my own skin. All this hill knows is my body as it exists today; we both stay quiet and smell the mink and the season and the boy's recent snack of onion. The hill and I are not waiting. I surely have not spent my whole life waiting, first to punish and then to be forgiven. That would be the way a life gets lost.

"Do you have ghost children here?" I ask.

"What are those?"

"Spirits that linger after a body's dead. They play games, tickle your skin when you're sleeping."

"Sounds nice."

"No, they're worse than that," I say, uncertain how to describe the precise discomfort. "They're like memories."

He picks himself up, finds a stone to hurl over the edge of the hill like a man of any time, of any color, and after listening to it ricochet against the trunks he turns back toward his village again. "I guess we haven't got them."

February 15, 1790

IT WAS TWO weeks ago, when I came to the American capital in New York to meet with representatives who took an interest in the Indian territories, that I first wondered: Was I seeking

vengeance, or was I running away? That day when I walked out
of the village in anger and with a convoluted scheme of retribution, was I just terribly afraid? Have I spent the last two years
elaborating on my cowardice?

The room I'm sitting in is marble and stone, with four tall
windows that let in the low winter light. The long table is surrounded by upholstered chairs, all of which are empty except
for one at the end, where a round man in a hat dozes, and mine.
Soon the rest will be filled, and men will ask my opinion of the
frontier violence and whether certain tribes must be paid in
cash, or whether calico will do. But now there is time to read
again the letter I found in my rooms this morning.

It did not take long to discover there had been another Muskogee in this city. Mrs. P., a woman who enjoys hosting Indians in her afternoon salons, told one of my companions, and he
came to me with the news. She had forgotten the young lady's
name, but she had returned to the southern territories directly
after the Christmas season. Had left behind nothing but a few
letters to be sent by post. Mrs. P. had distributed them all except
one, which had no address, and sent it along by my companion,
hopeful that I would know the whereabouts of this correspon-
dent, all Indians being surely familiar with each other. My companion said nothing to Mrs. P., but he saw that it was my name.

I sent him to the stables to brush down our horses while I sat
at the desk by the narrow boarding-house window and broke
the dribbled wax of the seal. It was dated November 15, 1788,
too long ago.

It is autumn in Virginia, in Richmond, I made it as far
as I said. You see, I have learned to write. A gentleman is

giving me lessons. And dresses, and whatever I desire, but
you should know I do not always accept. I want to write
because it burns my heart that you must think I took the
money. (Though I did.) But it is not what a man should
think of a woman. I am doing my hair in the new style, and
that also hurts. The ladies like to guess what will surprise
me. They thought I would gasp at their houses. I told them
we have houses too. They thought I would devour their food,
but it is overboiled and bland. I enjoy the clothes but only
because people look at me more kindly. Stockings are an
unusual feeling. I could not see the purpose of your money.
You wanted to buy me, but you wanted to make me happy,
and I would have been happier with the money than with a
husband. So what was I to do? I saw my father, the white
one, before I left. You must not have known. He did not
know me, I think. I painted my face for him and asked could
I go visit an English town and he said yes. He gave me the
name of a man he knew in Richmond and said he would stop
to see me next time he went through. I showed him my pretty
eyes so that he would not forget, but I planned to tell him who
I was next time I saw him. I would not have let it go too far.
But they say he is dead, killed by robbers. I heard this from
an Indian who was not Muskogee so I am not sure I believe
it, though I do not mind if he is. He is a bastard, I told you.
I wondered what the life was like, the one he left me for. I
wanted to know what was better than Hillaubee. I think with
women we are asked to be beloved, and nothing more. Give
babies, and food, and shelter, and not take anything. I know
this, I am used to this. I use it. But I was bad at planting
corn. Oche will tell you. Though good at baskets. I have

sold many here. A white woman sets me up with cane and I do it in a room for all to see. I want to wear a silk dress but she puts me in skins. I make money this way, to add to your money—I am sorry—and now I have two silk dresses I can wear when I am not an Indian on display. I took the coins and the pony, I felt bad about that, to Okfuskee. A group of men were riding for Columbia and I used some money to pay my way with them. They were meeting with the whites to talk about land. In that city, there was a servant who wiped the seats after we stood. I found a woman to make me a plain dress, not from Indian cloth, and I rode the carriage up in stages to Virginia. I should have bought a bonnet. I was stared at. Sometimes I enjoyed it and sometimes I did not. I just wanted to see other places. I was in Williamsburg for a time and though it was big it felt too small, so I used more coins to get to Richmond. I know you laughed at this plan of mine, but here I am and I do not think you are chief yet. So. I stay with the sister of the man I mentioned, who was not the friend of my father's but someone else down a line of friends. The family is good to me and gives me a room for my baskets, but I will not stay much longer. The children make hollering noises when they see me and one called me ugly, which I am not. I thought I would have some mark on my face for being a white man's daughter, but no one seems to recognize it. This should be as much my town as any other. I am not always happy, but I am happier than I was. I will not say yes to the man who keeps asking to marry me. That is in no ways what I want. You won't believe it but I love you. Or else you will believe it because you also love me, and you would not if you thought I did not. Because you are as selfish as me. I will not come back, and I do not expect you will come to Richmond. You thought our town was all there was, and worth saving. I want to repay you for what I took. I have been putting a little aside from my baskets. I call it lover money, and kissed each coin at night until that made me laugh and I stopped. But it is here for you when you would like. I want to see you again. You liked me even when I was rotten, but I was young. I cannot ask for forgiveness too many times or I will seem not worth forgiving. I have dreams that we are lying by the river and the magnolia leaves are dropping on us. We are pretending that we are not in love but we are. It was you I wanted, not Thomas Colhill. In the spring I think I will go to New York where the American government is, because they say those men enjoy seeing Indians.

When the men arrive I tell them what they want to hear, that with the right sort of bribe the Indians can be convinced to stop killing the frontiersmen and their wives. We shake hands after I have their word that in all of this hunger for land, the Musk-ogee will not be touched. I know we both are lying. The room is too cold, and I want to be elsewhere. None of these men were born in this city, but then neither was I. My bones only begin to warm when I am outside, by the wide river, looking north to the meadows and swamps the Americans have not yet turned to stone.

Where did she walk in this city? By then, did she have her bonnet? I see her in all the corners here, as I saw her on the red bluffs and in a glance of sun on the Mississippi. She is not mine, she stole what was mine, and the sentence I return to is not her apology but *a gentleman is giving me lessons*. Damn her gentleman.

I am not, in fact, a coward. I was a coward when my uncle died, and when my brothers died, and when my mother lost her home I ran, and when I saw no way out I robbed a man, and when he raised a gun at me I shot him through, and when the white man and the black man left me, I floated across this country like a feather. But it was not cowardice, that search, because the others too were searching. What we did wrong was not from fear.

A sandpiper in the marshes calls out for its mate. There is no one in this city I know except myself.

I walk back through the winter streets toward the boarding-house, where my horses wait to be saddled again with bags. This, for the time being, is the nation's capital—a nation that, to judge by the nations that came before it, will rise and subside in due time, to be sold or conquered or lost. I have no business here. The letter is in my pocket, where letters belong.

At home, my mother is mending the baskets for the spring seeds, and my brother is in the house of a sick man, brushing his forehead with oil and breathing warmth along his limbs. Polly is showing off the fabrics she was given by men from the eastern coast. No; she is down by the river, her toes in the cold water, the water that runs beneath the corn and the council fire and the trading path and the miles of land I have crossed, alone, not alone, alone again. The first bloodroot unfurls from the leaves and is white, as every flower of its kind has ever been. Someone there will bury me.

Author's Note

MURDER CREEK RUNS through Conecuh and Escambia counties in southern Alabama, and is named for the men who died on its banks in the spring of 1788. It is also, for the most part, just right for paddling. My father did it expertly; I was tipped over by a sunken branch. If anyone downstream finds a green towel, it's the author's.

That afternoon, dried off, I met with friends and scholars in the Poarch Band of Creek Indians, who generously opened their doors and shared their collective memory. I owe a great debt to the knowledge and kindness of Karla Martin, Robert Thrower, and Deidra Dees, and to Marcus Briggs-Cloud, who told me that Istillicha could mean "Man-slayer," but could also mean "one who lays people to rest." *Mvto*.

And on the same day I saw where Cat died, my own cat died, Eudora, a reminder that there is no line between the present and the past.

About the Author

KATY SIMPSON SMITH was born and raised in Jackson, Mississippi. She attended Mount Holyoke College and received a PhD in history from the University of North Carolina at Chapel Hill and an MFA from the Bennington Writing Seminars. She has published a study of early American motherhood, *We Have Raised All of You: Motherhood in the South, 1750–1835*, and a novel, *The Story of Land and Sea*. She lives in New Orleans.